The Perfect Prosecutor

AN IKE THOMPSON LEGAL THRILLER

Gregg Bell

5225

THE PERFECT PROSECUTOR

Chapter One

The silence in the office was deafening, a stark reminder of how quickly fortunes could change in the legal world. Now something had to happen soon. Attorney Icarus "Ike" Thompson and his associate Abby Blum's last big case was a noble cause, a knightly endeavor, a pro bono effort to do good with no expectation of reward. They'd won the case but what had it gotten them? Blackballed—no one wanted to hire a law firm that defended an alleged baby killer. No one except drug dealers, pedophiles, and other guilty-as-sin defendants, that is. Sure, Ike and Abby had helped their client in the case—a young mother unjustly accused of setting an arson that killed her three small children—avoid a terrible injustice, and there was great satisfaction in that, but now they needed business.

As a sole proprietor, the burden fell especially heavy on Ike. He had salaries, rent, taxes, and malpractice insurance to pay. A host of bills arrived in his mailbox every day without fail. He and Abby knew it might take a while for old clients to come around, but they'd *been* waiting. They'd been waiting too long. They'd kept the firm afloat with a few real estate closings that had been on the books before the arson case, but even those were drying up.

Besides the lack of business, Ike had other problems. He was pushing forty and separated from his wife, who'd been a thorn in his side lately, especially since he and Abby had started seeing each other. He didn't know exactly what clock was ticking, but his mounting blood pressure told him undoubtedly one was. Oh, to be sure, there were plenty of good things in his life. He had a devoted secretary, Val, who'd worked for him for years, and he'd come to rely on Abby, both legally and emotionally. But neither of those things were paying the bills. He pushed a button on the intercom phone on his desk. "Abby, can you come in here? We really need to get things moving."

His associate entered the office, tucked her skirt under her thighs, and sat in one of the leather ergonomic chairs across the desk from him. She took off her glasses and rubbed her eyes. "I know. It's like a morgue in here lately. No phones ringing. No walk-ins. Nothing."

"Well, grab your laptop, come back, and let's see if we can turn something up."

She slipped out, and he flipped through a well-worn Rolodex on his desk. Years ago, he'd abandoned his downtown, high-profile criminal defense practice after a bitter defeat to prosecutor Ursula Rush, who'd since become the Cook County, Illinois, State's Attorney. Shaken but not broken, he'd retreated to White Pines, a sleepy Chicago suburb, where he gradually built up a practice with small-time legal work. The change of pace suited him, and he'd found contentment in the steady flow of modest cases. Then came the arson trial.

Ike thought self-employed lawyers weren't much different from professional golfers. They had to score or they went home empty-handed. Pinching the Rolodex open at "G," he picked up the phone and dialed. "Maria, hi, Ike Thompson, is Gino in? ... Great, put me through if you would. ... Hey, Gino, Ike Thompson, how are you, buddy? ... Excellent. How are Lucy and the kids? ... Hey, that's great. Listen, buddy, business still hasn't picked up here after the arson case." He laughed mirthlessly. "I got my fifteen minutes of fame all right, but the phones still aren't ringing. Got any overflow, anything at all, you can send me? ... Okay, sure, Gino, things are off by you too. ... I understand. Take care." He set the phone down.

Abby returned, sat, and balanced her laptop on her thighs. "I'm actually kind of new at the marketing angle, Ike, but hopefully I've inherited a bit of something from my father, who can sell just about anything to anybody."

He gave her a thumbs-up. "Well, let's give it a shot. Let's start with looking online."

"Sure."

"And really we should look anywhere we can."

She typed on the laptop. "I've heard LawCrossing.com and LawJobs.com are good."

After hours of searching and coming up blank, they looked at each other.

"Well." Ike tossed a pen onto the desk. "Not all that easy, is it?"

"No. And I know that from personal experience. I had a really hard time trying to get a job before I came here."

Ike smiled, recalling when she'd first come looking for employment, a pretty brunette clad in a tan business suit with her large black glasses giving her a scholarly air. "I remember."

She went back to searching, then abruptly stopped. Her eyes went wide. "Hey." She angled the laptop toward him. "Did you see this?"

"See what?"

"It's a news article." She turned the laptop back and read aloud. *"An incident took place at the headquarters of pharmaceutical giant Pharamundo International today in downtown Chicago. A woman Eyewitness News has identified as Bree Wilson, a 35-year-old single mother from suburban Tin-*

ley Park, attacked the company's CEO, Thomas Acosta. Witnesses reported that the woman shouted at him and grabbed his arm as he tried to walk away. A private security guard unsuccessfully attempted to subdue the woman. Finally, a Chicago Police officer arrived and arrested her, and the woman was charged with assault and battery. CEO Acosta refused medical attention at the scene and later issued a statement through a spokesperson saying that he was shaken by the incident but otherwise unharmed. It appears that the woman was mentally unstable and had no prior connection with the CEO, hence it is believed that the attack was entirely random."

"Where is that from?"

"HuffPost."

Ike laughed.

"Why is that funny?" She gazed at him over the top of the laptop.

"I'm sorry. Just because you called something from HuffPost a news article."

"But what do you think of it?" She shut the laptop. "I mean, I know you're questioning HuffPost's reliability, but let's say, for argument's sake, the story is true."

"I'm not saying it's not true." He returned to flipping through the Rolodex. "I'm just saying it's probably just one more crazy person loose in downtown Chicago. One more reason why we work in White Pines."

She put her hands behind her head and leaned back. "But don't you wonder about it? Even if the woman is mentally ill, she just randomly assaulted the CEO of one of the biggest pharmaceutical companies in the world? I mean, okay, that's *possible*, but how likely is it?"

"I'll grant you, not very." He wedged his thumb into the Rolodex. "But even if we were to chase that down, mentally ill clients tend to have great difficulty paying even the scantest of legal fees."

"I'm not saying it would pay the bills—"

"Then it's something we don't need to think about at this point, right?"

She raised an eyebrow. "Well, I was just saying that I thought it was weird, that's all."

* * *

The next morning, Abby hesitated outside Ike's office, perspiration from the sweltering Chicago weather beading up on her face, as he was reading something at his desk. She dabbed her cheeks with a facial tissue and waited for him to look up.

"Oh, what is it, Abby?"

Her brow furrowed as she absently tugged at a strand of hair. "I don't know. I didn't know if I should even say anything about it. Actually…" She smiled sadly. "…I was thinking maybe I was being a baby."

"That needs amplification, Counselor. Say anything about what?"

"Oh, it's just that I'm getting more and more of those telephone hang-ups in the middle of the night. I know I should be used to them by now but…" She sighed. "…I'm not."

He nodded to one of the chairs across from his desk. "Can't you block the number?"

She sat. "I do. But whoever's doing it then just calls from different numbers. It's frustrating because I like to leave my phone on for my mother, and even my father has been calling me lately."

Ike thought of all the harassment she'd been through in the Hendrickson arson case. Add to that all the threats from DeCarlo, a lowlife Mafia boss, from whom Abby had been trying to collect a debt for a client. Ike wished he could make it right for her but knew that sometimes intimidation went with the territory of being a criminal defense attorney. "I hear you."

"It's just starting to get to me." She removed her glasses and wiped her eyes. "Lately, when I leave my apartment, I feel like I've got a target on my back. Like DeCarlo, or somebody like him, is watching me, trailing me. Ah, I'm probably just being paranoid."

An eighteen-wheeler approached on the street out front and stopped next to the office, its engine rumbling. Construction in downtown White Pines was taking off. The town's Metra train station, providing easy access to downtown Chicago, created an ideal real estate growth scenario. This caught the eye of the new mayor, who had a reputation for facilitating snapping up old businesses, demolishing them, and constructing luxury condo buildings in their place. The downside of all the construction, besides the disruption and incessant noise, was the dust that covered everything, including their cars behind the building in the parking lot. So far, the end of spring had been unseasonably hot and because of the construction, dirty. Ike waited for the truck and its noise to move on and gave Abby a smile.

She returned it but only halfheartedly.

"Don't get me wrong, Abby. Sometimes doing criminal litigation is risky. However, the threat is more often than not overstated, and the fear exaggerated. Yes, clients may get angry at our representation if they lose, but honestly, most attorneys are more likely to die from heart attacks caused by drinking, overeating, or working too much. And yeah, DeCarlo may be the one making the calls, but intimidation usually comes not from clients but from their friends and relatives. And it could be coming from someone entirely different as well. For instance, Nick Hendrickson, Mia Hendrickson's husband in the arson murder trial."

Abby shook her head slowly. "I don't know if the idea of Nick Hendrickson still roaming around out there makes me feel any better."

"According to what my libertarian lawyer-friend in the prosecutor's office, Josh Chin, tells me, Prosecutor Ursula Rush is close to charging Nick with the children's murders."

She folded her hands on her lap. "Well, it will certainly be a major relief to get that creep off the streets. For Mia and me too."

"No kidding. I've been on the verge of getting a restraining order against him to stay away from her."

"Before it's too late, right?"

Chapter Two

At lunchtime, Ike hopped in his Lexus and headed downtown. It was high time he confronted the mobster DeCarlo's dirtball attorney, Frank Griswold, about harassing Abby or, at the very least, about condoning DeCarlo's harassment of her. Ike had done his due diligence. He'd dug up what he could on the attorney. But the result of that research was pretty much what he already knew. Griswold was an expert at keeping his career-criminal clients out of jail, adept at exploiting legal loopholes, and unafraid, when it suited his purposes, to use intimidation.

The underground parking garage in Griswold's building was air-conditioned. Ike got out and shut the car door, feeling the chill. He walked to the security door and entered the code Griswold had given him when he'd called to make the appointment. He made his way through a little vestibule and pushed a button for the elevator. When the doors opened, he got in and pressed "P" for the penthouse. He was used to dealing with the likes of Griswold, at least he was back in the day.

The elevator arrived and opened to another vestibule, and he walked to a maroon door with Griswold's name on a brass nameplate. He pressed an intercom button, its tiny camera lens glinting in the light, and a buzzer sounded.

Ike pushed the door open and felt like he was in a hunting lodge. Animal heads were mounted on the walls: deer, antelope, gazelle, and an immense moose. He wondered how the moose head, which looked to weigh several hundred pounds, could be supported on the wall. Maroon leather chairs on rollers surrounded a marble cocktail table in the center of the room. Beyond that, floor-to-ceiling windows offered a dazzling view of Lake Michigan. Griswold sat reading at a desk alongside the windows.

Ike was already steaming at how the attorney and DeCarlo had treated Abby. But that treatment was going to stop and stop now. "In case you hadn't noticed, Griswold, I'm standing here." A slow tilt of Griswold's shaved head was the only indication he'd heard.

"Right. What can I do for you, uh…" He finally looked up. "Mr.…uh…"

"Thompson. Ike Thompson."

Griswold leaned back in his chair. Wearing tinted glasses, he looked comfortable in a blue pinstripe suit, white shirt, and champagne-colored tie. "Of course, how could I forget? Ike Thompson, the fabled perfect lawyer. Courthouse chatter has it that you're back in the big time, Perfect Lawyer. Well, what can I do for you?"

"We have a piece of business together."

Griswold scratched his ear. "Oh, we do, do we?"

In the distance, a windsurfer shot across foamy white caps on the lake, sail flapping in the wind as he leaned close to the water's surface, his wake leaving an ephemeral silver trail.

Might as well get right to the point. "Griswold, our client is Mike Goodwin and yours is DeCarlo."

"Oh, yes, I seem to remember something about that. So this is about that silly girl pretending to be a defense attorney? What was her name? Allison…Anna…" He crossed his arms over his chest. "I feel for you, Thompson. It's so hard getting good help these days."

Ike ground his teeth and told himself to count to ten. He made it to three… "My associate's name is Abby Blum."

"Sure it is, Thompson. Tell me, is she putting out for you at least?"

…four…five…"Yeah, wonderful, Griswold. Look, try to be an adult for a minute, will you? Your client owes our client forty thousand dollars."

Griswold smirked.

Ike was done counting. "Forty grand, Griswold. I'll expect it in two weeks' time. If your client doesn't pay up, we're filing a civil suit. A civil suit, where lots of questions will be asked of DeCarlo—and of you. A civil suit where I have a feeling that words like fraud, intimidation, and larceny may arise."

The attorney stared at Ike. "Excuse me. Are you threatening me and my client?"

"He owes the money."

Griswold laughed and went back to reading. "Yeah, okay, fine, Perfect Lawyer. I'll be sure to let him know."

"You do that." Ike's right eye twitched. "Just one more thing, Griswold. If you or DeCarlo ever harass my associate again, I'll be back, and you'll find yourself wearing that," he pointed at the moose head, "on your head."

* * *

Back at the office, Ike, still keyed up from his encounter with Griswold, checked with his secretary, Val. "Anything come in?"

The big blonde tilted her head. "One. He made an appointment for later this afternoon."

Ike's eyes brightened. "Well, that's good news. What time?"

"He said five o'clock."

"This guy's decent? I told you I'm not talking to any more drug dealers or lowlifes."

She leaned on an elbow. "That's interesting actually because in a way he wouldn't say. He just said he was a doctor and looking for representation. Dr. Ernesto Morales. That name sounds familiar, but I couldn't find him in our database."

"Well, we'll see what happens." Despite the appointment, Ike could see the concern on his secretary's face. She had two teenage boys in school, one at Princeton, and that couldn't be cheap. Ike had enough in the bank to keep things going for the time being but carrying two mortgages and paying his estranged wife's apartment rent, it was clear he wouldn't be able to for much longer.

He smiled, headed for Abby's office, knocked on the open doorframe, and caught her eye. "Got a minute?"

She laughed and pointed to one of the chairs across from her desk. "I suppose I can spare one."

Ike sat and filled her in on what had gone down with Griswold.

Abby started swiveling in her chair. "Well, I guess you had to tell him all that. But you don't think the tough talk will come back to haunt us? I think of the priest in Mia Hendrickson's trial, Father K., dying in the hospital under suspicious circumstances. The world is getting scarier every day."

"It certainly seems that way, doesn't it? Thing is, though, if you show fear, if you let them get into your head, like the dogs that they are, the Griswolds and DeCarlos of the world will smell it, and they'll devour you."

Abby stopped swiveling. "Okay. Well, that said, where does that leave me?"

"Well, you've got the Ruger I gave you and a concealed carry license. Maybe it's time you started packing." Ike had insisted that she and—before he'd become estranged from her—his wife, Mallory, both own a gun and know how to use it. He'd even taken the two to the target range. Separately of course.

"Packing, Ike? You make it sound like the Wild West."

"Just for now, Abby. Just for now. Things will settle down soon."

"Okay, but for some reason, unlike me, you seem to thrive on the drama." She picked up a paper clip and placed it in a holder on her desk. "The Hendrickson win put you back in the big time."

He raised his hands. "I don't thrive on the drama, Abby. I'm just more used to it than you are. No, the slower pace here in White Pines suits me just fine. Sure, being back in the limelight during the arson trial was a thrill, but more importantly, when it was over, I felt different inside. I've defended so many lowlifes that to help a genuinely nice, and innocent, person like Mia Hendrickson, well, that changed something inside me. Maybe taking her case was my atonement for all the dirtbags I've gotten off. But for whatever reason, I can't handle representing those types anymore."

Abby smiled. She took off her glasses and set them on the desk. "I know what you're saying. Cases like Mia's may not fill your financial bank account, but they'll fill your soul."

He loved that she had such a kind heart. He blew out a long, slow breath. "Yeah, I suppose that's it. And sure, we'll do more pro bono cases someday, but *now* we have to find paying clients."

"I know. I know."

He stood. "In the meantime, I've got some things I need to take care of before Dr. Morales, a potential paying client, gets here. Why don't you meet him with me?"

"Sure."

"All right." He stepped toward the door but could feel her eyes on him. He turned. "What?"

"Can you talk? I mean, shifting gears, more personally. Just for a minute?"

He sat back down.

"Do you remember me telling you that my father, who lives in New York City, and I were estranged? That I have a rock-solid relationship with my mom back in Denver but a problematic one with my father?"

"I remember."

She bit her lip. "Well, my father's coming to White Pines."

He waited.

"To live."

"Well…okay."

"With me."

"Um." He leaned to the side. "That will be different. And…I'm assuming you're okay with it?"

"Not really, but I hardly feel like I have a choice in the matter." She slipped her glasses back on. "Ike…"

There was no mistaking the distress in her voice. He looked at her.

Her chin lowered to her chest. "I never told you the whole story. I mean, yes, he's my father, and yes, we're estranged, and he *is* in New York City." Her face flushed. "But he was in prison."

"Okay."

She blinked a few times. "He'd been working as a real estate developer. He said the charges were trumped-up. That some board member or zoning commissioner had it in for him and set him up. He was just being efficient, he said, streamlining costs to survive in a tough market." She gazed at him. "He *is* a wiz with numbers, Ike. But they convicted him for failing to report income, overstating deductions, and claiming false credits. Like Al Capone, they got him for tax evasion."

Ike rubbed his chin.

She breathed in deeply. "Now he says he needs to get out of the rat race that is the New York City real estate business. He says he has nowhere to go and thinks the Midwest will be a healthy environment for him to make a fresh start. I…I…I just couldn't say no to him."

"You don't have to justify your decision, Abby. It's a good thing that you're doing."

"He's not evil, Ike. Oh, he's impulsive and he's made mistakes, but he's not a criminal. Honestly, I think he has good intentions. It's true he's made a lot of money, before the IRS took almost all of it away, that is, but before they did, he gave a lot to charity, especially to helping developmentally disabled kids."

Ike scratched his ear. "So he's made mistakes and paid for them. That would make him a man who deserves to live like anybody else, right?"

Abby offered up a timid smile. "Oh, I just wish it was that simple."

THE PERFECT PROSECUTOR

* * *

The appointment with Ernesto Morales came around quickly. "Okay," Ike said. He and Abby were setting up the office's conference room, leather-bound law books lining the walls, leather-bound law books collecting dust as all the latest legal information was online. "Val said he's a doctor. I'm assuming he's a medical doctor and not a PhD, but we'll soon find out."

Abby tapped her fingers on the smooth, long, glass-covered table. "Did he say why he wanted representation?"

"All I know is what Val told me and she said he wouldn't say."

"Really?"

He checked his watch. "That's what she said, yeah."

The front door chime rang.

Val came into the conference room leading a man in a perfectly tailored beige sport coat, open-collar shirt, and leather loafers with brass buckles. Hair slicked back neatly, he wore a thick gold Cuban chain around his neck. His demeanor exuded a casual confidence, the kind that comes from knowing you can buy your way out of most problems.

"Thank you, Val," Ike said, and the secretary left.

"Ernesto Morales." The man stepped to Ike and put out his hand. With what seemed to be a noticeable effort, he smiled.

"Ike Thompson." Ike shook the man's hand, then pulled out a chair for him, all the while wondering why the man didn't introduce himself as a doctor. "And this is my associate, Abby Blum. Please have a seat."

Morales took them in with an unhurried gaze before sitting. With a little bow to Abby, he said, "A pleasure."

Ike nodded. This guy was more than likely rich, but there was no way he was a medical doctor. "What brings you in today, sir?"

The man drilled Ike with a look. "Simply put—your reputation."

Ike smiled. *My reputation for getting a young mother wrongfully accused of arson off, or, my reputation for getting guilty-as-sin drug dealers off?* "Please continue."

Morales took a shiny black leather wallet from his sport coat and set it on the table. "I'll level with you. I spent seven years in Stateville on a trumped-up charge of distribution of methamphetamines. My lawyer bragged about his high ethical standards and then did a worthless job of defending me, and I ended up doing time for a crime I didn't commit. I won't make the same mistake twice. Now they're trying to set me up again. This time for trafficking fentanyl.

"Mr. Thompson, I've heard of what you've done defending clients, and I have a cashier's check made out to you in the amount of fifty thousand dollars." He slipped the check from the wallet and slid it across the table. The check veered toward Abby, who straightened it and set it before Ike. "*That is a bonus. I will of course cover all your fees.*" He produced another check. "Here's your retainer." He slid it and this time it went straight to Ike. The check was made out in the amount of two hundred and fifty thousand dollars.

Ike angled the check toward Abby, who glanced at it and then looked at Morales.

The money. Ike stared at the checks. Where was he going to come across money like this if he didn't defend lowlifes? It was an instant solution. He hadn't prayed, but this guy felt like an answer to prayer. Now all he had to do was accept it.

THE PERFECT PROSECUTOR

Abby pushed back from the table. "That's certainly very generous, Mr. Morales."

Ike exhaled deeply. A glimmer of the satisfaction he'd felt after Mia Hendrickson's not-guilty verdict in the arson trial came to mind—a fleeting reminder of why he'd become an attorney in the first place. The memory began to unfurl in his mind, the weight of that triumph growing heavier, stirring something deep within him. "Very generous," he seconded, though his voice lacked enthusiasm. He stood, and Abby followed suit. "But I'm afraid we're not going to be able to accept it."

Morales leaned his forearms heavily onto the table. "If the money is insufficient—"

Ike gathered up the checks and set them before the man. "The money is more than sufficient, much more. And I appreciate you offering it, but it's clear to me that we wouldn't be able to provide you with the representation that you deserve. We wouldn't be able to be objective in your case, and I don't want to jeopardize your chances of getting a fair trial. Best of luck finding an attorney who can represent you effectively."

"Really?" Morales looked off into the distance. "You're sure about this? If you'd take me on, I'd consider it a personal favor."

"Quite sure." Ike crossed his arms.

Morales finally stood and with a blistering look at Ike left.

Abby waited for the door chime to sound. "Oh my God. Was he threatening you?"

Ike shrugged.

Val joined them. "Hey, you guys, that was one scary dude. I rarely feel this way—I like to give people a chance—but from the moment he walked in, I felt I was in danger."

Abby sighed. "Yes. Agree, Val."

Ike closed his eyes, conflicting emotions whirling. They needed the money. They *needed* the money. Finally, he looked at his secretary. "So, what, Val? How did this guy get through to make an appointment?"

Her face fell. "I'm sorry, Ike. I think what I paid the most attention to was that he said he was a doctor, and I didn't call him on it."

Abby sat back down. "Yeah, Dr. Death."

"No big deal, Val." Ike settled into the chair next to Abby. "All I know is we have to get clients. Decent clients. Paying clients." He rolled his neck. "But God, that was a lot of money."

Val drifted off.

Abby slid her hand up and down his arm. "There's always that Bree Wilson. You know, the woman who confronted the CEO of the Big Pharma company."

"Paying clients, Abby. We have to get paying clients."

Chapter Three

The next morning, as Ike was driving with Abby to her apartment she adjusted the air conditioner vent and said, "I feel guilty roping you in to help with this." They were on their way to meet her father to help unload his U-Haul. "But I do very much appreciate it," she added.

The weather was ideal for a move, but a bank of cumulus clouds massed over Lake Michigan to the east. Ike knew more clouds were likely on the way, as the predicted high was in the 80s, and the afternoons lately had come with a risk of thunderstorms. He wore his yard-work pants, with a grass stain on the right knee, and a Chicago Cubs T-shirt. He brought along leather work gloves because his hands weren't used to rough work—and he hadn't been playing enough golf lately to develop calluses. "I'm happy to help."

"I don't think he'll have that much stuff. He put everything he owned into one of those storage places before he went to prison. I did give him a key to my apartment in case he wanted to get started without us." She fell silent for a moment, and Ike sensed a shift in her mood. "He has a weak heart, you know, or at least he thinks he does, so I hope he doesn't overdo it."

"It's nice that you're letting him move in."

"*Temporarily* letting him, Ike. I stressed that to him. Besides..." She playfully jabbed him in the arm. "...I'm counting on coming over more to hang with you and Leaner."

Ike knew she'd grown fond of his half-lab, half-pit bull with the unusual name. "Well, Leaner will be happy about that."

She tsked. "And you?"

"I guess I'll have to tolerate it somehow." Stopped at a light, he leaned over and kissed her.

"That's better."

He turned the corner. He didn't know exactly what he'd been expecting, but it wasn't a huge U-Haul *truck*. Maybe he expected a trailer or a van even but not this huge thing, its rear door open, teenage kids zipping up and down the ramp, their arms loaded with clothes, plants, and electronic gear. Meanwhile, a portly man in a Hawaiian shirt, his blue eyes bubbly, stood alongside the ramp, calling out instructions. "Is that him?"

Abby smiled. "The one and only Herschel Blum."

Ike pulled to the curb.

Her father's eyes lit up when he saw his daughter. He jogged to the car, but with guarded stiffness, like the senior citizen he was. "Princess!"

Abby glanced at Ike and cringed a little. "He can be a tad demonstrative."

Her father opened her door, practically yanked her from the car, and engulfed her in a hug. "Oh, Princess, it's so good to see you."

Ike climbed out.

Her father rounded the front of the Lexus. It was a vibe thing maybe, but Ike liked the guy right off the bat.

"Herschel Blum. It's an honor to meet you, Mr. Thompson."

The men shook.

"Ike, please, it's Ike. Nice to meet you as well, sir."

"And no 'sir' for me, young man," he said with a little bow. " 'Herschel' will do just fine. Herschel, yes."

THE PERFECT PROSECUTOR

Abby joined them, and her father put his arm around her. "It's a dream being here in the Midwest, Princess, the heartland, where people are the salt of the earth." He smooched her cheek.

"Don't overdo it, Daddy. And how did you get all these kids to help?"

"They offered. Like I said, the people here are the salt of the earth."

She put a hand over her eyes and peered at the truck. "But it looks like you're all moved in already."

The truck was nearly empty, the last kid carrying a palm tree in a clay pot.

"Careful with that, Jeremy!" Herschel called. He turned to Ike and Abby. "It's a Pygmy Date Palm. I bought it just before I left New York. I figured it couldn't hurt to have a few organic things around. Whiskers is already in the apartment."

"Oh, Herschel." Abby crossed her arms. "You brought the hamster?"

"I had to. Whiskers and I are a team." He laughed.

She groaned.

Kids came traipsing down the stairs of the apartment building.

Abby's father waved to them. "That'll be all, boys. Thanks for your help. You're the salt of the earth."

One of the older kids, a White Sox cap on backwards, laughed. "Thanks for the money, Mr. B. If you need any more help, let us know."

* * *

Not having to help with the move, and with the extension deadline looming for filing his taxes, Ike spent the rest of the morning holed up at home doing them. It was mind-numbing work, for sure, but it had to be done. By the time he signed and filed his return electronically, it was late afternoon and his brain felt gutted. He felt like he did after he was done taking the bar exam. Moreover, after devoting so much time and so many resources to the pro bono arson trial last year, his income had been reduced to a mere pittance of what it had been. It brought up what he considered to be one of life's great paradoxes—getting set back for doing the right thing. Ah, but what can you do? He placed the tax documents in a manila envelope, printed the year on it, and stored it in a locked file cabinet in his den.

He took Leaner—the dog, despite its somewhat thick fur, didn't seem to mind the heat and humidity—for a quick walk before heading into work. Spending time outdoors with Leaner always lifted his spirits, and as he drove to the office, he could hardly wait to check with Val to see if any business had come in.

He picked up the mail and came in the front door. Val was on the phone. He took that as a good sign. He caught her eye and waved, then he heard laughter coming from Abby's office. He smiled, but then a flicker of unease caught him off guard, and he wondered why she was laughing. Who she was with. What she was doing. What *they* were doing. As he walked toward her office, he heard a man's voice that sounded familiar, but he couldn't quite place it. Whoever it was, he was making Abby happy. Very happy. Her door was open, and he stopped just short of entering.

Ike's private investigator, Johnny Lagattuta, and Abby sat shoulder to shoulder. Johnny had his feet up on her desk, and she was leaning over him in an attempt to see what he was doing with a deck of cards.

She grabbed at his hands. "It's on the bottom. Let me see! Let me see!" She tried to snatch the cards from him, both of them laughing and tussling back and forth.

Ike cleared his throat emphatically.

The laughter ground to a halt. Johnny jerked his feet off the desk.

"Ike." Abby leaned away from the private investigator. "How long have you been standing there? You're like a ghost."

Not exactly what he wanted to hear. He didn't know what he wanted to hear. And he didn't know what to say. All he had were questions, as he certainly wasn't happy that his girlfriend was having such a good time with Johnny. Then he took a breath and realized it could all be just what it seemed —innocent fun. No need to jump to conclusions. But it was hard not to. "I'm half brain-dead from doing my taxes and, sorry, I didn't think to knock."

"Well, okay." She straightened up. "It was good you got them done. You did get them done, didn't you?"

"Sure."

Now, she suddenly seemed chatty. "Johnny stopped by to tell us about the corruption happening in White Pines real estate development. Then he took a break to show me a magic trick. Well, what he *said* was a magic trick." She gave the private investigator a sidelong glance and a smile. "But I knew he was cheating and had the ace of spades on the bottom of the deck."

Johnny held the deck out of Abby's line of sight and twisted it for Ike to see. The private investigator's eyes were a little bloodshot, his voice husky, and Ike wouldn't be surprised if he'd had a few drinks already. The card on the bottom was indeed the ace of spades. Finally, Johnny turned the deck toward Abby.

"Oh, you are *so* bad!"

Johnny stashed the cards into his back pocket. "Anyway, Ike, back to business. I'm hearing rumblings from some of the guys I'm still in touch with on the police department that a lot of the development in downtown White Pines is suspect. Misrepresenting property values, bribery to obtain building permits, and hiring illegal immigrants to do the construction sort of stuff."

A former cop, Johnny had been Ike's private investigator for years. Ike liked him. He trusted him. But the guy was also a ladykiller. Ike felt like asking him how the topic of real estate corruption had morphed into doing card tricks. "Well, that's definitely something to keep an eye out for."

"You know I'm Italian, Ike, and I'm not about to call out my brethren, but a lot of these Italians out here in the western suburbs have old country roots, and a few of them feel America's rules don't apply to them. But you know what's ironic? When it comes to White Pines real estate development, the guy to really keep a close eye on isn't Italian. His name is Hank Norton. He's an old-school farmer who owns a huge tract of land in unincorporated White Pines that the mayor and the developers are drooling over getting their hands on. And from what I hear, Norton plays the rube, but he's as savvy as they come."

Abby seemed to have regained a serious frame of mind. "On the positive side of all that, though, Johnny also said a lot of real estate sales will be forthcoming, especially from the new condominium buildings they're planning on building, and I was thinking that might be good for us if we can get the closings."

Ike was settling down, too, wondering where that little flame of jealousy had sparked from. "Yeah, well, we'll have to keep an eye on that too."

* * *

The next morning, Ike stood on a stepladder in his office, hanging a framed poster of Tiger Woods with the caption: THE HARDER YOU WORK, THE LUCKIER YOU GET. His golf buddy Howie had given it to him years ago, but Ike's estranged wife, Mallory, had insisted it wasn't appropriate for a law office, and the poster had gathered dust in a closet. Now Ike didn't care what she thought. And the inspiration to hustle up some business couldn't hurt, especially since he'd been berating himself for turning down Ernesto Morales' money.

He was even considering doing lawyer-temp jobs, but those were hard to get. There were paralegal openings, but he couldn't see applying for them because considering his qualifications, lawyers would feel too guilty to hire him for the wages they'd pay. Retail sales jobs were obtainable, and some paid well, but that was how he'd worked his way through law school, and retail sales meant nights and weekends. Retail hell, they call it, and if at all possible, he'd like to stay in the legal field. He sighed—he couldn't get the poster to hang straight.

Abby hadn't been in all morning, and the office seemed lonely without her. Since Ike and Mallory had separated, he found that loneliness hit him fast and hard. He went to the front to talk to Val just to be in the presence of another human being for a while.

Finally, back in his office, just as he decided to give straightening the poster another shot, the front door sensor chimed. Abby, a stack of papers under her arm practically bounded into his office.

She was all lit up. "Ike, you're not going to believe what I learned. I just got back from interviewing Bree Wilson. You know, the woman accused of attacking the Big Pharma CEO? She's out on bail and—"

"Wait just a second, would you?" He steadied himself on the stepladder. "Is this poster tilted to the left? I thought it was but just couldn't tell."

"Yeah, yeah, push it just a smidgen to the right…there, you got it."

"Okay, thanks. That was bugging me. Now, what were you saying? You what?" He climbed down and sat in his office chair. "You visited the lunatic who attacked the CEO? Why?"

She looked away before looking back at him. "Well, yes, I visited her, but she's not a lunatic, and there's a lot more to the story than was in the news." She set the papers in front of him on the desk. "These are just a handful of photocopies from Bree Wilson's research. Look at this one for starters." She singled out a copy of a newspaper article.

"So a reporter got fired from his job."

She tapped her forefinger on the article. "Read here. It says he was fired for posting a story online about Pharamundo International without clearing it with his publisher first."

"So?"

"Well, Pharamundo's CEO was the one Bree Wilson confronted." She tapped again. "Keep reading. The reporter's article that got him fired speculated that Pharamundo had developed a drug to cure ALLD."

"ALLD? That gross disease more and more people are getting?"

"Exactly. Acute Lung Liquefaction Disease. It's fatal, Ike, and Bree's eight-year-old son, her only child, is dying from it. Pharamundo has a drug out to *manage* ALLD, but Bree thinks, because of the reporter's article, it may also have a drug to *cure* it as well, but they're not releasing it."

He shrugged. "And what does Ms. Wilson's dilemma have to do with us?"

"Ike, she doesn't just think the drug may exist. She's almost positive."

"Abby." He checked his watch.

She snatched up the papers. "Can't you see that the media's reporting on what happened with her supposedly attacking the CEO was a ruse, a diversion? It wasn't a random attack by a crazy person. She was confronting the man about not releasing the curative drug."

He widened his eyes at her. "The drug that doesn't exist, at least according to the pharmaceutical company."

"Ike, she says the reporter uncovered information that it does."

He half-smiled. "But he got fired for not clearing his article with the publisher before posting it."

"But that's not the real reason." Her voice grew more urgent. "Bree says the truth is much darker. Again, the reporter was fired because he uncovered evidence suggesting that Pharamundo already *has* the curative drug for ALLD, but they're suppressing it. Why? Because they're making billions from their drug that only manages the disease's symptoms. Releasing the curative drug would destroy that drug's profits. The reporter was on the verge of exposing this, and that's why they had the story pulled and had him fired."

Ike rubbed his chin. "And the mainstream media is backing up this ruse of her randomly attacking him?"

"Well." Abby's shoulders drooped. "Unlikely as that might seem, yeah, the few that reported on it are."

Ike massaged his temples. "I don't know, Abby. It sounds to me like it's more like she's a desperate woman doing some desperate wishful thinking. Her kid's dying—she's grasping at straws."

Abby turned away.

He ran his hand through his hair and frowned. "Hey, I know you care about the woman, and that's lovely, it really is, but even if we're going to do more pro bono work, we've got to stay in business, and to stay in business, we've got to make money." Again, he thought of Morales' offer and it rankled. "And taking on Ms. Wilson's *situation*—it's not even a case at this point—isn't going to accomplish that."

The light went out in her eyes. "Well, okay, what can I say? I had to check it out for myself because I had a strong suspicion something was off about it."

"Okay, sure, Abby, I agree wholeheartedly. Sometimes you have to follow your gut. And there will be times we will, but for now, we need to keep our feet on the ground." He hated to see her unhappy, but what could he do? "For now, we have to keep our focus on what our money-making options are.

"It's a stretch, but what I've even been thinking about lately is applying for one of these jobs." He maximized his laptop screen and tilted it toward her. It was a listing of lawyer-temp jobs. He slowly scrolled. *Legal On-Site Services $18 an hour. Legal Assistant $28.50. Legal Operations Manager $33. Hospitality Associate $17.*

Abby pointed. "I could do that last one."

"Funny," he said, but he sighed heavily.

"Oh, come on, Ike, lighten up." She set her papers back on the desk and sat. "Things will break open soon. And in the meantime, I can't see why we can't at least find out more about Bree Wilson's situation. I mean, come on, her son is dying."

He nodded. "Sure, okay, we can do that but *after* we line up some paying clients."

Her eyes jumped to his. "Do you mean it?"

Did he? "Well, sure. Now enough of this talk." He turned to the poster. "What do you think of this as our new company slogan?"

"The harder you work, the luckier you get. Tiger Woods. He's a golfer?"

"You're kidding."

"Yes." She smiled. "We'll find the business, Ike."

She was right after all. They'd been through lean times before and had always managed to get by. Yeah, he needed to lighten up. "You're right." He took a deep breath, exhaled it slowly, and returned her smile. "Okay then, let's move on to something else. Tell me what's going on with you?"

"Seriously?"

"Yes."

She fell back in the chair. "My father is driving me crazy already."

Chapter Four

The next day, the office phone didn't ring once all morning, and Val offered to take a leave of absence. But Ike and her had been through so much together there was no way he was taking her up on it.

"Great of you to offer, Val, but that's not happening, and it's not necessary either." He wagged a finger at her.

The big blonde secretary leaned back in her chair, crossing her arms. "But there's no business. There's nothing for me to do."

"Yes…there is. Work on drumming up business. Go through old files and send emails asking if anybody needs trusts or wills or what have you. Get creative. We'll get this thing going again, you'll see." He leveled a look at her. "But trust me, no matter what happens, one thing is for sure—I'm not losing you."

"Okay, Ike." She caught his eye. "And thanks."

He was a little choked up at the prospect of losing his longtime secretary, who was like a sister to him. Losing her he'd lose a part of his life. So now he determined to triple his efforts to turn up new business. And forget Ernesto Morales and his drug money anyway. He was better than that. The days of defending the likes of him were over.

The light was on in Abby's office, but motivated by his pep talk to Val, he went straight to his office and started going through his Rolodex again, calling all over, hounding for business. After a couple of hours of coming up blank, he decided to stretch his legs. He was barely out of the office when his estranged wife, Mallory, burst through the front door.

She blew past Val. She'd lost the few extra pounds she'd gained, and Ike hated himself for still feeling so physically attracted to her. She wore bright orange short-shorts and a navy mesh halter top. But there was no hiding her black eye, or perhaps she'd meant to accentuate it. She threw up her hands, letting them slap against her shapely thighs. Then she opened her arms wide in expectation of a hug, but Ike folded his arms across his chest.

"What do you want?" She always wanted something. He laughed. What a joke. She was wearing her wedding ring again after cheating on him for months.

"Come on, Ike." She glanced back at Val. "Look at my face. I need your help. Jimmy hit me."

Ike pointed to the door. "Out."

"Come on. I'm through with that louse. Look at what he did to me!" She offered up her face to him.

He grabbed her arm. "Get out, Mallory. I mean it."

"Baby—"

"Out!"

Whimpering, she ran from the office.

Val gave him a knowing look and resumed typing.

An hour later, in the lunchroom, Abby joined him at the blond wood table there. Ike sliced his peanut butter and jelly sandwich in two and offered her half. He figured she'd overheard everything that happened with Mallory, and he wasn't looking forward to what she had to say.

"No thanks." She went to the little fridge and removed a carton of yogurt and a can of sparkling water. She sat across from him. "You're still sticking with your vegetarian diet, I see. I admire your dedication."

"Yeah, thanks."

She removed the carton's lid and stuck a clear plastic spoon into it. "I...I heard you and Mallory earlier." She caught his eye. "I wasn't eavesdropping," she added hurriedly. "It was just hard not to."

He tore a chunk off the sandwich. "I figured as much."

She searched his eyes. "You don't think we should back off seeing each other for a while?"

"Abby."

"I don't mean long-term." She leaned toward him and spoke softly. "I didn't mean that at all. But just until you figure out what—"

"Absolutely not. I know what I want. I want you. I told you I was done with her and I am."

She stared down at the yogurt. "But the fact of the matter is you're still married."

"Not for long." He set the sandwich on the table. But he *had been* putting off filing for divorce despite having no valid reason for doing so. At some level anyway, he must be hesitant to cut the bond with his wife. And it was taking its toll on Abby.

Val walked in carrying a newspaper. "I thought you'd want to see this. Toward the bottom." She held the paper out between them like a waitress holds up a check to see who wants it more.

Ike took it. "Thanks." He unfolded the paper, read, then said, "Nick Hendrickson was arrested yesterday for the Hendrickson arson."

"Huh." Abby pursed her lips. "So all our hard work pointing the jury at him as the arsonist finally paid off. Maybe there is justice in the world after all."

Ike returned the paper to the secretary. "I tell you what, my respect for prosecutor Rush—"

THE PERFECT PROSECUTOR

"Uh." Val held up a forefinger. "It's State's Attorney Rush now."

Right. Ursula Rush had been elected as the top prosecutor in Cook County and now held the rather incongruous title of State's Attorney. The title came from the 1830s when under the Illinois Constitution, Cook County was considered to be a "state" with its own government. The chief prosecutor of this "state" was called the State's Attorney, and the title stuck even after Cook County became a "county" within the state of Illinois. "Of course, and my respect for her is returning with that move to arrest Hendrickson."

Val drifted off.

Ike looked back at Abby. "I guess Ursula has a conscience after all." Not wanting to talk about Mallory, he excused himself, took his sandwich, and returned to his office, where he thought about all the changes that had been going down in his life lately. Val offering to take a leave of absence. Mallory storming in with her black eye. Nick Hendrickson arrested. But still, the one pressing constant was that they had no business.

He shut down his computer, closed his office door, and eased into the recliner in the corner. He told himself to relax. Was it possible, just barely possible, that life, even with all its setbacks and complications, was still good? For the most part, he had his health. He had Val. He had Leaner. And above all, he had Abby. Yes, the more he thought about it, life was still good. Very good. After ten minutes of such musing, he headed up front to check with Val to see if any business had come in, but before he could even get the words out, she was shaking her head slowly.

"What is it, Val?"

The secretary blanched. She turned her laptop toward him. An email was open.

You think you're so smart, Thompson. You're the Perfect Lawyer after all. But you messed up this time, buddy. You messed up big-time. I've got you on video cracking my client's head open with a pool cue in the parking lot of his print shop. Now he's got traumatic brain injury and you've got a big problem. Yeah, tough guy, thanks to you the guy's a vegetable. The remedy? $100,000 in non-sequential bills, none bigger than fifty, dropped in a barrel at the top of the main slide of the abandoned Jolly Rogers Splash Hideaway water park in the southwest suburbs. You've got one week to come up with the cash. I have the park under surveillance 24/7 so I'll know if you've been there—or if you haven't. And if you haven't, the video goes to the media, and your life goes bye-bye.

* * *

As he stepped into the office the following morning, Ike put on a brave face. As usual, he'd parked at the rear of the building, and once inside, he made a beeline for Val's desk. When he arrived there, he heard the back door opening—must be Abby. He forced a smile at his secretary. "Hey, Val, good morning. Anything come in?"

"Morning, Ike. No, nothing. Only thing is, Johnny Lagattuta called and said he's going to drop by."

"Okay," Ike said, looking off toward the back. On the way to his office, he thought about his private investigator. More specifically about him and Abby having such a good time together lately. Sure, Johnny was twenty years older than her, but he still had a young man's magic to charm the ladies. Especially with the blackmail email weighing on his mind, Ike wasn't looking forward to seeing them together again. It wasn't that he thought Abby was unfaithful, only that she was human. Susceptible to Johnny's immense charm. Or then again, it could just be that he was worrying for no reason. He stopped by Abby's office, offered up a brief "good morning," and then holed up in his office.

He needed to think. And it would've helped to have someone to talk to about the blackmail email too. Sure, Val knew, but did he want anyone else brought into this? As it was, if the video existed, he could be facing an attempted murder charge. As far as he was concerned, the scumbag he'd cracked with the pool cue deserved it, pretending to be a fourteen-year-old girl in an online chat room and encouraging Ike's young niece to commit suicide. There'd been no laws to stop the guy, either, so Ike had done what he'd had to do. But the bottom line? Pressure was mounting.

And anyway, it was possible that Johnny's stopping by would put a dent in the stress. The gregarious private investigator *was* fun. But what if he was just coming to see Abby? All Val said was that he was dropping by.

As it turned out, Ike's concerns were unfounded. Johnny said brief hellos to Val and Abby, then insisted on talking to Ike in his office behind closed doors. Ike smelled a hint of whiskey on the private investigator's breath as he shut the door, and the two men settled in across the desk from each other.

Ike had to shift from thinking about the blackmail email. "So what's up?"

Johnny cracked his neck. "I'm sure you heard about Nick Hendrickson getting busted."

"Uh-huh, so Ursula finally did the right thing."

"For sure." Johnny nodded. "And that priest, Father K., who died in the buildup to the arson verdict—I heard the medical examiner is *not* doing an autopsy."

"What's he calling the death?"

"Heart attack."

"Unbelievable." But the priest's death seemed like old news. That's not what Johnny came to talk about.

The private investigator stared over Ike's head at the poster on the wall. "The harder you work, the luckier you get. You going into the personal coaching business?"

Ike laughed. And it had been a long time since he had. "Just trying to fire up a little motivation around here, buddy."

Johnny stroked his two-day beard growth. "Abby told me business has been way off."

Another little surge of jealousy leaked to the surface. Abby was talking to him again. What else had she told him? What was he telling her? But what could he say? *Stay away from my girlfriend.* That would come off as paranoid. That would come off as not trusting Abby. That would not come off. "It's definitely been slow since the arson trial, yes."

Johnny slapped his hands on the armrests. "Actually, Ike, the real reason I'm here is to talk about Abby."

Okay, here we go. Ike let out an exasperated little sigh he wished he hadn't. What was Johnny going to tell him? Was he going to ask for permission to date Abby? Permission to sleep with her? Or was he going to *tell him* that they were already sleeping together? Another sigh escaped. "Well, talk."

"Actually, it's not about Abby per se. It's more bad news about her father. Ike, word on the street is he's been associating with not the most savory company, including hanging with Hank Norton."

THE PERFECT PROSECUTOR

Thompson, you're so paranoid. Ike blinked rapidly, his brow furrowing as he processed the information. "Well, that's not good."

"Abby told me about her father's wheeler-dealer ways and resulting prison stint. Ike, hanging with Hank Norton is a catastrophe waiting to happen."

"Agreed."

Johnny stroked his chin again. "I didn't want to tell you with her here because, you know, she's super sensitive, and despite her struggles with her father, she really loves him. Also, I'm not sure she appreciates the seriousness of him associating with somebody like Norton."

Ike wasn't thrilled to be hearing about Abby's inner feelings from Johnny, but the heads-up about her father was information he needed to know. "I'll talk to her about it, Johnny. I will."

The private detective gave him a thumbs-up. "Yeah, good. Because her old man going back to the joint would wreck her."

* * *

Great. Suddenly Johnny is so interested in Abby's welfare. But Ike told himself he had bigger problems to deal with. Nevertheless, another twinge of jealousy twisted in his gut as he called Abby into his office.

She sat across the desk from him.

He told himself to be nice. "You know Johnny was just here."

"Yeah, I saw him leave. So what was so important that I had to be cut out of the loop?"

"Well…" He frowned as she was obviously feeling hurt again. "…Johnny said the buzz on the street is that your father is hanging with some unsavory characters involved in the downtown construction development here in White Pines."

She closed her eyes. "Johnny'd told me about the funny business going on with it. Well, you heard that too. But not that my father was part of it."

"Now, he said as far as he knows your father hasn't done anything wrong. Not yet anyway. But he said the appearances are really bad."

She opened her eyes. "Oh God. And there's no chance Johnny is mistaken?"

"I'm afraid not."

She bit her lip. "Ike, I don't know what I would do if he had to go back to prison."

"Well, Johnny said it's not at that stage yet, but of course we'll need to keep an eye on things." He tapped the desk. "I'm sure your father will probably be okay."

She looked out the open office door. "That doesn't feel all that encouraging, Ike."

He nodded. "I'm sorry, Abby. I've just got a lot on my mind. We'll stay on top of your father's situation. He's nowhere near going back to prison, and we'll make sure he gets even further away."

"Thanks." She tilted her head at him, a smile flickering across her face. "And so, you've got a lot on your mind? Are you still stressing about the business?"

He pointed to his empty in-basket. "Nothing's coming in."

"You keep saying that…" She shrugged. "…but hey, what about Bree Wilson?"

"Oh, that's not the answer, Abby."

"It's something anyway."

Yeah, another pro bono potential quagmire. But it wasn't just paying the bills that was tearing him up inside. The blackmail email was hanging over his head like a guillotine blade. He trusted Abby and had come to rely on her advice and support. It was time to spill before he went crazy. He told her. He told her everything.

She crossed her arms, eyes frozen, for the longest time, then finally said, "Well, I'm sorry that happened."

"Thanks." That was it? "Anything else?"

"Hold on, I'm thinking."

He cracked his knuckles, one at a time. The more he thought about the blackmailer, the more his fears were transforming into rage. He wasn't backing down from the scumbag. And the fact that a lawyer might be assisting the guy was pushing him over the edge. "So?"

"I think the whole thing is sketchy." She raised a forefinger. "First, they didn't include a copy of the alleged video."

"Exactly."

Up went a second finger. "It's highly suspect that the print shop owner would hire an attorney to help with blackmail. And as to the attorney's involvement—as if he would risk losing his law license and face prison time just to help some lowlife. And lastly, if the print shop owner did actually hire an attorney, why doesn't the attorney file a civil lawsuit for medical expenses and pain and suffering instead?"

"And how do we know he's even using a real lawyer, with all the artificial intelligence chatbots out there."

"Right."

He was feeling better already. She had that effect on him. "It's a bluff, Abby. I'm even thinking of paying the print shop owner another visit to call it."

She shifted in her chair. "I'm not so sure *that's* a good idea."

"Well, we'll see." He stood. "For now anyway, I'm going to the county law library for the rest of the day to see if I can dig up some business leads."

"Just…" She motioned him back down. "…before you go. I've got some news of my own."

He sat.

She rolled her eyes. "It's more about my father."

"Okay, sure."

She hesitated. "I kicked him out of my apartment."

"Already?"

"It was either that or kill him." A hollow laugh escaped her lips. "He was treating me like I was five again and like we were in our family home. I couldn't handle it. It was just madness."

"So where is he living now?"

"That's the thing; I don't know. He rented another truck, got the kids to load it up, and took off."

Chapter Five

Ike took Leaner for a long walk in the morning before the oppressive heat of the day set in. Spending time with his dog was a stress reliever, and it was as if Leaner could sense his mood—Ike felt he could see compassion in the dog's eyes. Some people say dogs have no souls, but knowing Leaner, Ike knew better. When they returned home, he set out fresh bowls of water and nuggets and headed to the office.

As he drove along in his Lexus, thinking about his problems returned. He slid in a CD, but even Chopin's delicate melodies couldn't calm his troubled mind. Abby's father was on the brink of a catastrophe. Ike was on the same brink with the blackmail threat. He and Abby were on the brink of who knew what? And all of them were on the brink of going out of business.

He parked behind the office alongside Abby's Prius and let himself in the back. The air conditioning was running hard, so he stopped at the thermostat and turned the temperature up a few degrees. Might as well save where they could. He tapped on Abby's open door. "Morning."

"Wait!" She smiled brightly, which threw him, considering how coolish things had been going between them lately. "Oh…" Her eyes flitted toward the front of the office. "…I'll let Val tell you."

Let Val tell me what? Whatever. He went to the front, where his secretary was all smiles as well. What the hell? "What's going on?"

Val stood, walked past him to the fax machine, removed several faxes, and returned. "You know that new condo building they're putting up on County Farm Road in Carol Stream?"

Ike sensed Abby easing up behind him. "Yeah, that building is huge. They had a hard time getting it through the zoning commission."

Val handed over the faxes. "All I can say is, it pays to have friends."

Abby leaned into his back. He could feel her warm energy. Her love. He read the faxes, then stared at Val. "Am I dreaming?"

The secretary laughed. "Nope. Jerzy Filipowski purchased two hundred units in the building, and he's giving us the closings for every one of them."

Ike sat on the edge of her desk. "I'm speechless."

Abby hugged his shoulder. "How about, the crops are saved!"

He took another look at the faxes. "Well, now we actually have work to do."

Ike nearly floated to his office. The closings would be a cash cow, and what was even better, they'd be a steady stream of income as the condos would sell only gradually. Jerzy Filipowski was an old friend that Ike had gotten out of some nasty scrapes with the law. Now Jerzy had returned the favor. Ike settled back comfortably into his office chair, grabbed the phone, and dialed.

"Jerzy, my man!"

"Ike, how are you, my friend?"

Ike cradled the phone against his shoulder and folded his hands over his stomach. "Are you kidding? Ever since we got your faxes, I've been floating amongst the clouds. Thank you. Thank you. Thank you."

THE PERFECT PROSECUTOR

"Well, it was touch-and-go buying in…" Jerzy's Polish accent was nearly all gone. "…but I eventually got my piece of the pie, and I'm happy to give you the closings."

Ike sat up abruptly, snatching the phone from his shoulder. "All I can tell you, Jerzy, is that I'll do a great job for you. The best. I'll make sure all these units get closed properly and all the owners are happy."

"I know you will, Ike. That's why I'm giving them to you."

"Hey, buddy, I know we've looked out for each other through some tough times. But what I want to know now is, when am I treating you to eighteen holes of golf?"

"Soon, my friend. Soon. I'll call you."

"I'll be waiting." Ike hung up. "Oh." He slapped his thigh. Finally, something had gone their way.

Abby knocked on his door. "Got a minute?"

He did, but he wondered about the troubled look on her face. "Sure, have a seat."

She did. "Ike, I know that Jerzy's deal is a windfall for us, but at the same time, I haven't been able to stop thinking about that blackmail email you got from the attorney."

"Okay." Where was this headed?

She fidgeted with her bracelet, her eyes not quite meeting his. "Well, you were talking before about paying the print shop owner another visit."

"Uh-huh."

She looked at him. "Well, I just don't want you doing anything rash."

Okay. He got it. When backed into a corner he could do impulsive, dangerous things. Fly too high before crashing and burning. Maybe it was his destiny with his parents naming him Icarus. Whatever it was, Abby was really getting to know him well and looking out for him. But even so, he wasn't being intimidated by a two-bit blackmailer. "It's a bluff, Abby. The guy is bluffing."

She crossed her arms. "So then you're not going to see him?"

"I didn't say that."

"Oh, Ike."

"Abby, they're counting on scaring me enough to pay them." He ground his teeth. "You yourself said if they had the video, they would've included it with the email. And yeah, what attorney is going to risk disbarment and prison for some scumbag?"

She took off her glasses and gazed at him earnestly. "Okay, so, like you say, it's a bluff. There's nothing to it. Then why get any more involved with these guys? What's the upside?"

He sighed. She was right of course, but there was the satisfaction of setting the guy straight, unleashing his rage, getting the chip off his shoulder. "Look, I hear you, but I can't just sit back and let this punk think he can push me around. Okay, maybe it's stupid, but I want to look the guy in the eye and let him know that he picked the wrong lawyer to mess with."

"And it's okay if in the process you ruin your life—and mine." Tears glistened in her eyes. Her chest heaved with a deep breath. "It took me too long to find you, Ike Thompson. I don't want to lose you now."

He bowed his head, went around the desk, sat next to her, and put his arm around her. "Abby, I appreciate your concern; I really do, but you have to take risks in the legal business. Especially in criminal law. Sure, you have to weigh the risks, but if you back down every time you're threatened, if you flinch, you won't be able to sleep at night. They'll drive you right out of the business. Now, I've weighed the risks in this instance, and, believe me, it's going to be all right." He leaned in, his lips touching hers in a soft kiss that went unanswered.

She turned away. "Well, one thing is sure, isn't it? It always has to be your way. Oh, yes, you have a smooth explanation for everything, but it always has to be your way." She turned back to him. "How often do I ask you for something, Ike? Tell me. How often?"

He stood and walked to the window. He stared at his reflection frowning back at him. He loosened his tie, bit his lip, and went to her. "You don't want me to visit him?"

Her eyes searched his before she nodded.

"Then I won't."

She sat up. "Really? You promise?"

"Promise."

"Thank you."

"Now come on." He offered his hand. "We can get started doing some preliminary work on Jerzy's deal."

"Right." She put on her glasses, took his hand, and left him with a loving glance.

Ike did a preliminary property search on Jerzy's condo building and everything checked out. It felt so good to be working on something that was going to bring in funds. True, it might take a while for the closings to roll in, but just knowing they would was enough. It was more than enough. The phone rang, and he answered without checking the caller ID. "This is Ike Thompson."

"Frank Griswold, Thompson. It's your lucky day—Mr. DeCarlo is willing to settle out of court by paying $20,000 of the $40,000 he allegedly owes Mike Goodwin. I highly recommend that you accept this offer before my client decides to resolve this matter in his own way, and trust me, you wouldn't want that. My paralegal will send an email draft of the settlement agreement." *click*

Ike snorted out a laugh. Another good thing happening. A 30% contingency fee of twenty grand would put six grand in the coffers just like that. Sweet! Could things really be turning their way? He definitely hadn't seen this one coming. Usually when a mobster stiffs somebody, he stiffs them for the full amount. It was only Abby's guts in pursuing the money that had DeCarlo wanting to get her off his back. "Abby!"

She ran in. "What? Why are you yelling?"

"Griswold called with a settlement offer for DeCarlo."

"Are you serious?"

"Totally serious. He's offering twenty grand."

Her face fell. "But that's only half of what Goodwin is owed."

"True, but in a situation like this, it's a *very* good deal."

"Fifty cents on the dollar is a good deal?"

Ike chuckled. She sounded like her father. "With a mobster, yeah, it is. Let's call Goodwin. You want to tell him or should I?"

"You. I'll sound too disappointed." She handed over her phone. "I've got him on speed dial under G."

Ike pressed the button. "This is attorney Ike Thompson. I'm looking for Mike Goodwin. … Mike, hi, I'm calling for Abby Blum and myself to inform you that DeCarlo has made a settlement offer. … Yeah, finally. The offer is for twenty thousand dollars. … I understand your disappointment, Mike. We too were looking to get the full amount, especially after all this time. Now, we could counteroffer or take him to court, but from my experience dealing with his likes and the likes of his lowlife attorney, this is the best we're going to get. My advice is to accept the offer. ... Of course, you can think it over, but the offer can be withdrawn with no notice." As he listened, Ike widened his eyes at Abby. "That's a wise decision, Mike."

Chapter Six

Just before dawn the next day, the house hushed, Ike sleeping like a stone, his phone rang, shattering the calm. He grabbed the phone like it was a snake coiled and ready to strike. "Yeah?"

"Ike, they just shot out my apartment's living room window."

He bolted upright. "Who, Abby?"

"I don't know! I was just lying in bed and heard the crash."

He clicked on the nightstand lamp. "You've got the Ruger?"

"I have it in my hand."

"Good. Keep it there. I'll be right over."

"Okay."

He rolled out of bed. Leaner yawned and looked at him funny.

"Yeah, I know, it's early, buddy, but I've got another fire to put out." He threw on some clothes, grabbed one of his Glocks, and was out the door. Driving over, he thought things *had been* looking up anyway. But then he thought maybe that was how life worked. Whenever anything good happened, life knocked you upside the head to make you pay for it. An oncoming car flashed their brights. He turned on his headlights. And he realized he didn't have his driver's or concealed carry license. He felt the Glock snug in his waistband. Wonderful.

THE PERFECT PROSECUTOR

He pulled up in front of Abby's apartment building and ran up to the second floor. She was waiting at the open door and led him away from the front room.

"Thanks for coming."

She was trembling, and he laid his hand on her shoulder. "So, what happened?"

Her hand reached up to her throat. "Honestly, there's not much to tell. I was sleeping, then I heard the crash of glass."

"How did you know it was a gunshot?"

"Uh." She hugged herself. "I guess I don't know. I just assumed it was."

He stroked her arms. "Well, did you hear the sound of the shot before the crash?"

"I don't know, Ike," she snapped. "I was sleeping and it all happened so fast."

"I'm going to take a look."

She grabbed him. "Don't go out there! They could be waiting for somebody to examine the damage."

He brushed the hair off her forehead. He could see the child in her, especially without her glasses. "It'll be okay."

In the living room, he skimmed his hand along the wall searching for the light switch. When the light came on, it exposed a smattering of glass shards, the heaviest concentration near the window, lying strewn across the carpeting. As he approached, his feet crunched on the fragments. There. He discerned a small metal object nestled among the shards. He plucked it and carried it back to Abby.

"It wasn't a bullet." He held the slug up. "It was a pellet from a pellet gun."

She took it from him. "That's it? This little thing?"

"It's little, yeah, but pellet guns can be powerful. Some can even be used to hunt small game."

She handed it back. "So we should call the police."

He wasn't sure if she was telling or asking, and since the blackmail email was still fresh in his mind, along with the shady real estate deals he'd rescued Jerzy Filipowski from (Jerzy was hardly the most law-abiding developer), and he'd forgotten his driver's and concealed carry licenses, the last thing he wanted to do was involve the police. "Abby, they'll only complicate things."

"But DeCarlo—"

"DeCarlo didn't shoot out your window. After agreeing to settle with Goodwin, he'd have no reason to."

"Then…who?"

Ike breathed in deep, then exhaled. "It's hard to say, but my best guess, and it is a guess, is it was someone from the Hendrickson arson case. Maybe the cop you ripped apart on the witness stand with your cross-examination. But just maybe because I don't know."

"I think we should call the police."

He took her hands in his. "Abby, I want you to come stay with me."

She pulled free. "Oh God, I don't know, Ike. I really think we should at least make a police report."

"The police are not going to find out who shot out your window." He caught her eye. "Come stay with me."

Her gaze lowered. "Oh, I just got things straightened out here after my father moved out."

"Just for a while. Just till things settle down."

"Honestly…" Her voice broke and the tears fell. "…I don't know if I can keep doing criminal law. All the threats. The violence. Maybe I'm just a coward, but with all the hang-ups and now this, my nerves are just about fried."

THE PERFECT PROSECUTOR

He touched her chin, gently guiding her head to look at him. "Hey, you're no coward. What just happened is a big emotional hit. *Anybody* would be rattled. You just need a couple of days to get over it, that's all."

She wiped her eyes. "I mean, it's pretty clear there are people out there that want to hurt me, maybe even kill me."

"They want to intimidate you is what they want to do. And knowing you, you're not going to let that happen."

She shrugged. "So, what are we supposed to do? No police? Nothing?"

He was glad to hear her say *we*. He really wanted them to be a team. In law and in life. "Exactly. *We* are going to keep living our lives as if nothing happened. Abby, intimidation loses its power when you refuse to let it scare you."

A little head shake. "I don't know if I'm strong enough."

"I think you are."

She smiled but it was short-lived. "I'm glad *you* think so."

"Come on." He kissed her cheek. "Gather up some things. I promise to keep you distracted, and Leaner will love you staying with us."

"What am I letting you talk me into?" She sighed.

They drove in two cars to his home. Leaner was thrilled to see Abby and even happier that she'd brought a suitcase and some boxes along. Ike felt good about it too. She was still relatively new to the rough-and-tumble world of criminal law. Staying at his place for a few days would be a safe haven, a chance to catch her breath. Besides, he loved her and wanted to spend the rest of his life with her. But for now—he set down a cardboard box filled with her things on the kitchen table—his job was to protect her.

He went out to the garage for another box, and when he returned, Abby was on her phone, Leaner leaning against her leg. "I know it's early, Mom, but honestly, I'm fine. I just wanted to hear your voice. I love you. Now I gotta go." She hung up.

She'd been rocked for sure, but when she smiled at Leaner, Ike knew she'd be able to turn the corner. She petted the dog and then looked up. "I don't know what it is about this dog of yours, but he makes me feel good."

"That works both ways, Abby."

She pressed her lips together. "I'm settling down a little, Ike. I think I'm going to be okay."

"I *know* you are." He set the box down and took her in his arms. "But for now, I'm going back to fix your window before a thunderstorm pops up and soaks your place. You've got the Ruger. You've got Leaner. You'll be okay."

She nodded into his chest.

He grabbed his wallet and made sure he had his concealed carry license too.

* * *

Driving to Abby's, Ike thought it was unfair how life was throwing one challenge after another at her, but maybe that was life—picking on you when you were most vulnerable. Like the lions on the Serengeti plain, pouncing on the young, the old, or the sick. If you wanted to stay alive, you had to run. He got stuck behind a pickup truck whose driver must've been daydreaming because it didn't move after the light turned green. He tapped his horn, a polite little toot, but the truck didn't move. He tooted again. The truck still didn't move. Maybe it stalled? Mechanical problems? Nope, the driver rolled down their window and flipped him the bird. Unbelievable. Then the door opened. Two hairy legs felt for the ground before settling. In the old days this sort of situation would've been scary but would've led to nothing worse than a fistfight. Today, lives could be on the line. Today, lives could be lost. Ike slipped the safety off his Glock and gripped the pistol. Illinois had no "stand your ground" statute, but the Illinois Supreme Court ruled that there is no duty to retreat before using force, including deadly force if justified.

Ike lowered his window. He took some deep breaths as a hulking figure emerged from the pickup. The man, several days of beard growth, maybe in his fifties but mostly gray, wearing a dirty red sweatshirt, baggy blue gym shorts, and holding a pistol, barrel to the ground, started for the Lexus. Ike felt a pain in his chest as he slipped the Glock from his waistband. He wasn't one to pray but found himself doing just that. *Oh God, make this guy stop before I do.*

After three or four steps the man halted. "Come on!" He gestured with his free arm. "Come on! Or is all you got is horn?"

Ike sat stock-still, avoiding eye contact. Only his heart was moving. Moving fast. He knew the slightest movement—a nod, biting his lip, a grin—could be seen as a provocation. Now it was up to the man. *Please don't make me do this, buddy.* Ike firmed up his grip on the pistol.

The man kept shouting the same refrain. "Come on! Or is all you got is horn?" Cars pulled behind Ike, and eventually it seemed to register with the guy that what he was doing was insane. He spat, trudged back to his truck and screeched off, offering up one last middle-finger salute.

Ike flicked the safety back on the Glock and took his foot off the brake pedal. He could feel himself trembling as he drove off. Like Abby, he knew in time he'd calm down, but he also knew how close he'd been to taking a life or losing his. His only other thought was, what's next?

His phone rang. On the other end was his libertarian prosecutor friend, Josh Chin. Nick Hendrickson, the defendant's husband in the arson trial, who Ike and Abby had pointed to as the arsonist, had just hung himself in Cook County jail while awaiting trial.

* * *

Ike boarded up Abby's window and drove back to his house. He entered on tiptoes in case Abby happened to be napping. He laughed when he saw her and Leaner sitting together on the living room sofa, her arm around the dog. "Just remember, Abby, he's my dog."

"Well…" She hugged Leaner. "You know what they say, Counselor—possession is nine-tenths of the law."

"Ha ha."

She released the dog. "Go to your master."

Leaner bounded to Ike, who petted the dog and wondered if he should kill the pleasant vibe by dropping news of the road rage incident and Nick Hendrickson's suicide? Well, he had to tell her sometime, and maybe sooner was better than later. He piled onto the sofa next to her and related everything.

She snuggled into his side. "I'm sure Nick Hendrickson's death is a huge relief for Mia. Still, he was her husband—sometimes those marriage bonds go deeper than you'd think. And you and the road rage…" She pulled away to look at him before snuggling back. "…what would you have done if that guy kept coming?"

THE PERFECT PROSECUTOR

He stroked her hair, but what she said also had him thinking of Mallory. "You know, I don't really know. It's like the old notion of, what would you do if a baby fell into a well? The only way to know for sure is if it happened. I certainly wouldn't want taking the life of another human being on my conscience. God only knows there's too much on there already. But I believe had he pointed the gun at me, I would have shot him."

She snuggled even closer.

With no pressing concerns at the office, they spent what was left of the day together getting Abby settled in. After a TV dinner, Ike brought up sleeping arrangements for the night. Despite all the drama and nervous energy expenditure of the day, he still felt so attracted to her. And yet, her emotional well-being came first. When she proposed sleeping on the sleeper sofa in the living room, he was disappointed but readily agreed. After a quick hug and kiss—Leaner confused as to who to follow—they said good night and went their separate ways.

As he lay in bed, Ike's mind raced between fits of conscious worry and chaotic dreams. For what seemed like hours, he lay there under the intense mental and emotional strain. He didn't know what time it was. He barely knew who he was. But when Abby slipped into bed alongside him, he woke. Again, his desire arose, but more than anything, as their breathing gradually fell in sync, he felt a deep and abiding love for her.

Chapter Seven

In the morning, before the heavy humidity hit, Ike and Abby took Leaner for a long walk, with Ike keeping his mouth shut about his plans for the day—it was time to put the blackmailing matter to rest. Okay, as promised, he wouldn't visit the printing shop guy, but he wasn't done with these scumbags either. No way was he paying them a cent. Instead, he'd give them a carry-on case with an embedded GPS tracker and follow their every move. Who knew where that would lead, but he was fed up with their impudence and even more fed up with being intimidated. Going out to the site of the drop-off would turn things one way or another. Abby, meanwhile, kept bringing up the situation with Bree Wilson and the CEO of the Big Pharma company. When they returned to the house, Ike let Leaner off the leash, and Abby, reminding him of the safety net of the Jerzy Filipowski real estate deal, asked if he would speak with Bree Wilson.

Ike wasn't up for it, especially since even if he could help the woman, it would almost certainly be another pro bono quagmire, so he said he'd think about it. He told her he had to visit an elderly client to have her sign a last will and testament. Instead, when Abby was in the shower, he grabbed the carry-on case and a Glock and headed for the blackmail drop-off spot—Jolly Rogers Splash Hideaway.

Ike had actually taken his brother Evan's kids to the water park years ago before it became abandoned, and he hadn't realized it had closed. One thing was abundantly clear when he arrived though—he was overdressed and never should've worn shoes with leather soles, as the place was run-down, which was apparent even before he arrived at the deserted, broken-down parking lot. A rusted sign with faint traces of a skull and crossbones beneath the park's name hung precariously on a cracked concrete pillar at the entrance. The only legible word was "Jolly." In fact, though, there was nothing jolly about the place. Ike drove into the lot, dodging potholes, looking for a good vantage point to see the main water slide, which sat on a man-made mountain. He parked, shed his suit coat and tie, threw the carry-on over his shoulder, and started walking. His first obstacle—a rickety chain-link fence. He tossed the carry-on over, then took on the fence, the toes of his shoes slipping as he tried to dig them into the fence's diamond openings. Finally, he used his arms to pull himself up, but his pants split as he jumped and landed hard on his heels, sending jolts of electric pain up his legs.

    Five faded blue slides, the center one dwarfing the others, crawled up the mountainside. Dilapidated wooden stairs, their steps broken and decayed, ran alongside the middle slide. Leaves, branches, and stones littered the fiberglass. Ike climbed onto the middle slide, and his feet slipped even on the slight incline. He started up in earnest, and roughly at the halfway point, something scampered through the brush to the right. He stood up straight, steadied himself, and felt for the Glock in his waistband. His breathing quickened. Maybe it was best to turn around? But his anger at the blackmailers answered that question and he resumed his climb. Several careful steps further along, he heard growling. *Whoa.* He crab-like scrambled to the center of the slide. Through a twisted, withered bush he saw it—a coyote baring its teeth, back hunched, fur bristling, fierce amber eyes burning into him. There was movement behind the animal as well, other coyotes, a pack, slinking through the brush. For now, they seemed headed beneath the slide, but their lack of fear of him was unmistakable. And they sounded hungry.

Maybe a gunshot would scatter them? Maybe a gunshot would draw the police, which he didn't want. Ah, to hell with it—he struggled upward, slipping and swearing and keeping an eye out for the animals. He stopped to catch his breath and peered down the slide. The eerie chorus of growling grew louder. But he was too close to the top to give up now. He kept on but fell hard on his hip and slid a ways down. Cursing his fear, he started back up, even crawling at times.

Finally, he dragged himself onto the landing at the top. He spun around to look for the coyotes. They wouldn't be able to make it up the steep incline—but he needed to go back down. Finally, his mind returned to the task at hand. He looked around, but the promised barrel wasn't there. Could he be in the wrong place? Did the print shop owner or his attorney get cold feet? Was the whole thing a bluff? Oh hell, what was he doing there anyway? He draped the carry-on over a rusty gate. No, he shouldn't have come. He should've listened to Abby and let go of it. Once again, his anger had gotten the best of him and sent him on a fool's errand. Now, he'd be lucky to get out of there alive.

To get down from the top, he'd have to slide. And when he did, he'd run into gravel and sticks and lose track of the coyotes. The only saving grace was that he had no choice. Standing at the very edge of the landing felt not unlike standing at the top of a high dive, staring at the water seemingly miles below. The only difference now was if he lost his nerve, he couldn't climb back down. What would be would be. He sat on his rear end and pushed off. He slid faster than he would have thought, picking up speed and going further than he'd anticipated, ripping across gravel, sticks, and stones. As he slid, he heard nothing, but in his mind's eye, the coyotes growled and bared their teeth, salivating. They'd swarm him, rip at his flesh, and drag him to the ground, like a pack of hyenas tearing apart a zebra. The debris finally slowed him to a stop. He lurched to his hands and knees and yanked the Glock from his waistband. Two coyotes, now three, stood on the bottom of the slide, growling, snarling—and waiting for him.

He didn't want to shoot them. Well, he *did* want to shoot them. He'd been intimidated by the blackmailer and now by them, and he'd absolutely had it. But there were three of them, and who knew how many more beneath the slide? So he jammed the pistol back into his waistband, grabbed the sturdiest branch he could find, snapped off the twigs, and fashioned a makeshift cudgel. Then it hit him—better than the cudgel were the stones on the slide. He picked up a handful and started whipping them at the coyotes, who backed off a few paces but weren't leaving. Then he stomped on the slide and yelled, but the animals stood their ground. It was clear—if he wanted out, he'd have to go through them.

So, sucking in a deep breath, windmilling the cudgel, and yelling at the top of his lungs, he started toward them but after a few feet stopped. One of the coyotes fell, slid down a ways, then leaped into the brush, but the other two weren't budging.

A Mexican standoff. Ike could hear his heartbeat. His legs wobbled and he lost his balance and slid toward the coyotes. The sudden, aggressive movement sent the animals scurrying and diving into the brush. His slide came to a halt, and he hurried to the end of the slide and hopped off. Then he ran as fast as he could—just waiting to feel the coyotes' teeth tearing into his legs—for the rickety fence and somehow tumbled over.

* * *

Busy lawyers typically have two types of offices. One type appears to be in utter disarray, with files piled atop desks, storage shelves, even on the floor. The other has not a piece of paper in sight. Josh Chin's office, Ike's libertarian prosecutor pal in the Cook County State's Attorney Office, was the latter. Ike was there the next day to talk about Bree Wilson. He was there to talk about all kinds of things.

Besides being spotless, Josh's office was simple, with beige walls and only a few strategically placed diplomas and awards. Behind the desk on a credenza, a bronze statue of a blindfolded Lady Justice stood in silent vigilance, while Josh, in a dark gray suit and a yellow bow tie, looked small in an oversized gray leather chair.

"Thanks for making time to see me, Josh."

"Of course." The prosecutor pointed to a chair across the desk from him.

Ike sat. "How are the kids?"

Josh laughed. "They're good. The only thing is they're hardly kids anymore. How's Mallory?"

Ike scratched the back of his neck. "Uh, Mallory and I are…done, Josh. She found somebody new."

"Sorry to hear that."

"Yeah, me too. Thanks." Ike knew his time with the busy man was limited. "Josh, I got a huge retainer offer to take on a client, but the guy's yet another drug dealer."

"And?"

"And well, I'm low on funds too."

THE PERFECT PROSECUTOR

"And?"

Ike pursed his lips. "I don't know. I think something got into me defending Mia Hendrickson in the arson case. That case was a grind, but I hadn't felt that good in years. More alive. I didn't make a dime, Josh, but I wouldn't have missed that experience for anything."

The prosecutor shrugged and flicked his beringed hand. "So what are you saying, Ike?"

"Well, as you know, I've defended plenty of drug dealers, but these days, I apparently don't have the heart for it. I'm more interested in defending people who've suffered an injustice. Thing is, those people usually can't pay my fees."

The prosecutor rested his elbows on the chair's armrests and steepled his hands. "So defend a drug dealer every once in a while to pay the bills. There's nothing unethical about it. In fact, our justice system demands it. Where would we be if all lawyers refused to defend guilty people? Yes, defend the drug dealer, *then* do your pro bono work."

Of course, that made sense, but going back to defending lowlifes seemed beyond him. And now that he had Mike Goodwin's fee and Jerzy's real estate deal, he could breathe a little easier anyway. He could maybe even… He got up and started pacing. He could maybe even see if they could help Bree Wilson. For sure, that would make Abby happy. He stopped and held the back of the chair. "Josh, a couple of weeks ago, did you hear anything about a woman attacking Pharamundo International's CEO?"

"I heard a little bit. The woman was mentally unstable. The attack random."

"That's what the media is pushing, yeah." Ike told him what Abby had uncovered about the media's misrepresentation of what happened.

Josh touched his ear. "I did not know that."

"And Abby feels like there's even more to it." He explained that Bree's son was suffering from ALLD and was near death, with the pharmaceutical company allegedly withholding the curative drug for financial gain.

"Well, with no priors, the woman will almost certainly get probation for confronting the CEO." Josh tilted his head. "But you're not thinking about going up against Pharamundo for the drug issue, are you?"

No, he wasn't…or was he? But if he wasn't, why was he there? He sat back down.

"Because you've heard of the dream team of attorneys that defended O.J. Simpson when he was accused of murdering his wife and her friend? Well, Pharamundo has a dream *army* of superstar attorneys."

"I'm sure."

"And endlessly deep pockets—the company practically prints money—*and* the ability to play the waiting game."

"Yeah, it would be foolhardy to think we could beat them. But then again…" He caught his friend's eye. "…there's the idea of justice prevailing."

Josh rolled back in his chair. "Sure, Ike. Despite the odds, a few such suits have been successful. But it's rare. It's very rare."

Ike left Josh's office, his brain rumbling with ideas, and he couldn't wait to tell Abby what the prosecutor had said. He found a bench in the hallway of the courthouse, slipped out his phone, and dialed.

A man answered.

"Oh, I'm sorry. I dialed the wrong number." Ike was rapidly processing the voice. He laughed. He'd dialed Johnny

Lagattuta by mistake. "Oh, Johnny. Sorry, I dialed you by accident."

"No, no, you got Abby's phone. Hold on, I'll get her."

Ike stared down at the phone. The LED read *Abby's Cell*. He hit the End button.

Chapter Eight

Ike didn't know what to think as he drove home from Josh's office. He didn't know if he *could* think. His thoughts were a maelstrom swirling around his brain. Johnny Lagattuta was after Abby. It couldn't be any more apparent. Okay, Johnny was a womanizer, but Ike had hoped that Abby was resisting him.

And yes, things hadn't been so great between him and Abby, but he didn't think they were this bad. Johnny Lagattuta. Twenty years Abby's senior and still able to knock her off her feet. Ike bit his lip. What had he done wrong? Well, maybe it was obvious—he'd hesitated to divorce Mallory for so long Abby had finally lost patience. And she was probably happier with Johnny. Johnny didn't come with all the baggage: economic pressure, anger management issues, and a wife. With Johnny, what you saw was what you got. Sexy, easygoing, and fun. Ike figured if he were a woman, he'd rather be with Johnny too.

His phone rang. He checked the dash. Abby. He sent the call to voicemail and set the phone to vibrate. He didn't want to hear what he didn't want to hear over the phone. He drove by the office to see if her Prius was in the lot. It wasn't. She was probably out with Johnny. As he drove, his phone kept vibrating, so he powered it off. Maybe before heading home, he'd stop at a bar for a few belts, vent with the bartender a bit. Instead, he drove to a park and pulled under a red maple tree. The weather was too steamy to open the windows, but with the air conditioner running and his palms facing up on his thighs, he closed his eyes and tried to meditate. At first it was hopeless, jealous thoughts crashing through, but eventually his breathing deepened, and his thinking began to clear. He didn't *know* that Abby had a thing for Johnny. He didn't know much of anything. He took one last deep breath and decided what he needed to do was find out what was what.

When he turned onto his street, Abby's car was in the driveway. He pulled in alongside and pressed the garage door clicker. Before he even took his foot off the brake, Abby, trailed by Leaner, ducked under the ascending garage door. He rolled his window down.

"Ike, my God, are you all right?" Her voice quavered. "Johnny said you called, but when he gave me the phone it was dead. I've been calling and calling since."

"I'm fine. Do me a favor, grab Leaner and go back in. We'll talk inside." She seemed sincere. He pulled into the garage and hurried in.

He joined her on the living room sofa, and she took his hands.

"Is everything okay? I was so worried."

"Yeah, everything's fine." The words felt hollow even as he said them.

She squeezed his hands. "Well, what happened? Where did you go after Johnny answered?"

He was already feeling guilty and more than a little foolish. Still… "How was it that Johnny answered your phone?" The question came out sounding like an accusation.

She held on to his hands but pulled back. "You're not thinking…"

"Well, why would he answer it?"

She peered at him, her eyes narrowing. "He answered because I left my phone on my desk, and Val had asked if I could come up for a minute."

"Then what was he doing in your office?"

Her face scrunched up. "He had more news about my father's missteps."

Ike waited. He had the distinct impression he was making a fool of himself, but he couldn't seem to stop himself.

"When my father moved out of my place, he moved into one of Hank Norton's buildings." She widened her eyes at him. "Are you done? Is the interrogation over?"

Now he felt the complete fool, his gaze averted. "Well, I…"

She shook his hands. "Oh my God, Ike. Nothing is going on between Johnny and me."

"Well…"

"Nothing."

He ventured a look at her. "All right. I guess I jumped to conclusions."

She let go of his hands, slipped a hand behind his neck, and pulled him close. "Hey, you goof, I love you."

Emotion raced through him like a wildfire. He loved her too. He did. He felt as if he poured his whole soul into her as they kissed. "I'm sorry, Abby. I love you too. I love you so much." There, he'd finally said it.

* * *

Peace. Optimism. Until last night, those two things had been missing from Ike and Abby's lives for quite a while now. In the morning, they woke up in each other's arms—there'd been no question of where they would sleep last night. Before they'd gone to bed, Ike shared that Josh had told him that a battle against Pharamundo would be difficult but not impossible to win. And Ike committed to interviewing Bree

Wilson. Just interviewing her, nothing more, but yes, he'd committed to at least that much. So they'd gone to bed happy, and now they were enjoying a leisurely breakfast in the kitchen.

Then Leaner, who'd been happily lying at their feet, started growling.

Ike sat up. "What is it, boy?"

Abby leaned away from the dog. "Why is he doing that?"

Leaner barked and Abby jumped. The dog took off for the front door.

Ike heard the door's deadbolt turning and rolled his eyes. "Oh God."

"What, Ike? What is it?"

"I forgot she still has a key."

Leaner's growling intensified. The door shut and they heard a voice. "Oh, shut up, you stupid dog!"

Mallory strode into the kitchen. Her eyes flicked from Ike to Abby, then back to Ike. "What's going on? What's *she* doing here?"

Ike pointed. "Mallory, you need to leave. You need to leave right now."

"No, Ike, I don't." She pointed back. "This is *my house*, and she's the one who needs to leave. *Right now.*" She walked toward Abby. "Get out!"

Ike stepped between them. "She's not going anywhere, Mallory. You're the one who's leaving."

Abby sighed. "I really should go."

Mallory, glaring over Ike's shoulder, looked ready to hit her. "Yes, you should. Now get out."

Ike slapped the kitchen table. "Mallory, this isn't your house anymore and *you* need to leave."

His estranged wife's tone softened. "But, Ike, you're my husband; I'm your wife."

Ike rolled his eyes. "Unbelievable."

"See this." Mallory flashed her wedding ring. "This means till death do us part."

He laughed. "Not anymore it doesn't."

Abby started out of the room. "I'll see you later, Ike."

"You'll see him never, you whore!" Mallory raised her fist and walked after Abby, but before she reached her, Leaner jumped up and snapped at her. "Oh!"

"Abby, stay!" Ike grabbed Mallory by the arm and dragged her toward the front door.

"Ike, no, don't. This is my house. Where I belong. Where we belong. I'm sorry I hurt you. I know I made a mistake, a big mistake, and I'm sorry. So sorry. And I promise I'll never do it again. Didn't you ever make a mistake? Please, baby, give me one more chance."

He pushed her out the door, then hustled back to the kitchen. Abby was putting their breakfast dishes into the sink. He held her from behind. "I am so sorry this happened."

"It's all right." She rinsed a coffee cup. "It's just that I shouldn't be here until you two get your situation straightened out."

"Abby."

She spun around. "She's still your wife, Ike, and I don't relish playing the role of a homewrecker."

He held her elbows. "The divorce is already happening. I've arranged for an attorney to represent me, and I was only hesitating by considering having him file a praecipe—a document that would accelerate the process—rather than a petition. The praecipe would've given me more flexibility, but

I'm telling him to file the petition today, and you'll see, things will happen so fast."

"So you haven't even filed yet?"

"Yes, well, no, not technically."

She pulled free. "This is just too messed up of a situation for me. God only knows that with my father and everything else going on, I don't need any more drama."

"Abby, I promise…"

She walked away. "Your promise doesn't change the situation."

He followed her and touched her shoulder, but she shook him off.

He let her go. He had no choice. And it especially bothered him because he didn't want her back in her apartment so soon. Who knew what the person who fired the pellet through her window might do next? And he didn't want her to leave—he didn't want her to leave because he loved her.

He let Leaner out in the backyard and sat in one of the deck chairs on the patio. Leaner took off for the elm tree in the corner of the yard to warn any squirrels in it that they weren't welcome. The sun was just barely above the fence surrounding the yard, the heat of the day yet to begin its assault. Ike closed his eyes. Why did life have to be so complicated? But certainly, Abby wasn't to blame for the complication. She'd done all the right things in their relationship. She'd even refused to date him for the longest time. And now Mallory was blowing the whole thing up. And the worst part was that it was all his fault. His phone rang. Abby.

"Ike, I can't stay there anymore." She hung up.

He put the phone back in his pocket and called for Leaner, but before the dog reached him, the phone rang again. Hoping Abby had reconsidered, he greedily checked the caller ID. He looked up at the sky and then back at the phone. He tapped Answer. "For God's sake, what do you want, Mallory?"

"I'll tell you what I want. I want every damn photograph of us in that house. I don't want your little whore looking at them. And I'm not kidding, Ike. Every single one and I want them now!"

He fought off the urge to yell back. "Believe me, you'll get them, as God only knows I don't want them."

"Now, Ike!"

"Fine!" He had nothing scheduled. He'd call the attorney he wanted to handle his divorce and ask him if there was any way he could file the petition today. Then he'd pack up the damn photos and drop them off at her place. "Are you at your apartment now?"

"Yes."

"I'll be there within the hour." He hung up.

Driving over to Mallory's—he was late, having talked to the divorce attorney longer than anticipated—he wondered if it had been wise to acquiesce to her demand for the photos so readily. But in fact, he was happy to get rid of as many reminders of her as he could. The air conditioner in the Lexus was running on high, the heat taking over the day as he pulled into one of the visitor spaces at her apartment complex. Lugging the cardboard box loaded with framed photographs through the parking lot, he was thinking, if she got so crazy about the photos, how was she going to react when he stopped paying her rent? But he didn't care. Let her abusive boyfriend pay it. Let her move into a homeless shelter.

He rang the buzzer in the vestibule at the base of the stairs. He rang it again. He glanced behind him. He didn't remember seeing her car in its assigned space in the lot. Okay, he was late, but he wasn't coming back. He had the key, so up the stairs he trudged. He opened her door. He'd plop the box in the middle of the studio apartment, where she couldn't miss it.

Then he saw it. On the cocktail table. A pistol.

At first glance, he didn't know if it was a real gun—he knew she had a Glock because back in the day he'd bought it for her—but it sure looked like a real gun. He set the box down and picked up the pistol. Oh man. It was a pellet gun. He pushed down on the end of the barrel to open the chamber and popped the pellet there into his hand. It was the same size as the one that shattered Abby's apartment window.

Chapter Nine

Yesterday Ike's day started with peace and optimism. Today began with anxiety and pessimism. He'd received a text from Val—Jerzy Filipowski's real estate deal fell through. He called her. Jerzy was accused of coercive negotiating tactics and creating an environment of distrust that ultimately killed the deal. Ike could barely listen. After that, Abby called and asked if he'd accompany her to talk to her father about his associating with real estate lowlifes, namely, Hank Norton. It seemed her father was determined to play with fire. Ike readily agreed, as he was grateful she was even talking to him after the fiasco with Mallory yesterday. And he was hoping she'd forgotten that he'd said he'd talk to Bree Wilson, but she hadn't, so he set an appointment to talk to the woman in the afternoon. But first things first; he drove out to meet Abby and her father at a Denny's restaurant.

Herschel Blum was already there with his daughter, the two of them sitting in a circular booth big enough for eight. Ike couldn't help but chuckle, as the man certainly wasn't shy. Ike sat next to Abby, and she rather formally kissed him on the cheek. She was sitting just about as far away from her father as possible.

Herschel slid a menu across the table to Ike. "I love this place, Ike. I tell you what, you get one of their grand slam breakfasts and you don't have to eat for the rest of the week. Not only that, you talk about doing big deals; I've done more big deals at the Denny's in Brooklyn than I have at Grand Central Oyster Bar. Anyway, kids, thanks for coming. Just so it's understood, I get the check."

Abby rolled her eyes. But the man had charisma. Ike could see him closing big deals, and yes, even at Denny's. "Have you settled in at your new apartment, Herschel?"

"Oh, yeah, yeah. It's downright cozy already. Whiskers and the palm plant really help. I'm feeling more and more..." His eyes twinkled. "...like a Midwesterner with each passing hour."

Ike chuckled. At this point, he could use any sort of levity. "I can hear your New York accent fading even as you speak."

"Ah, thank you. Pretty soon I'll sound just like you and the other people from Chiiiicaaaaago," he said, stretching the word out in an attempt to mimic the Chicago accent. "Everybody says New York, Boston, and the deep South have the big accents, but you guys have a heck of one too." He laughed. "Da Bears."

A curvy waitress, curly blonde hair tucked into a tight bun, approached, and they ordered, Ike feeling compelled to get a lumberjack slam at Herschel's enthusiastic recommendation. He'd resume his vegetarian diet tomorrow.

Abby sat up. "Daddy, we're here to enjoy breakfast with you, but we also need to talk about some serious things."

Her father raised both palms. "Please, Princess, not now. Don't spoil our family outing."

Ike stifled a laugh. Family outing?

But Abby wasn't laughing. "We just don't want you getting into any more trouble."

Herschel held up his palms again and this time wiggled them, Ike wondering if he was going to break into the Macarena. "Princess, I told you before—those days are over. Now here comes the waitress..." He peered at her name tag.

"...with our food, and the only trouble anything's getting into are our arteries."

"Daddy."

Herschel winked at the waitress. "Dana, how does a tiny thing like you carry such a heavy platter?"

The waitress beamed as she parceled out the plates loaded with eggs, potatoes, bacon, pancakes, and syrup. She surveyed her handiwork. "Okay, now, is that everything? Did I forget anything?"

Herschel gave her a thumbs-up. "You nailed it, Dana."

The waitress left, and Abby dropped a napkin on her lap. "Daddy."

"Princess." He scooted over and squeezed her shoulder. "I came out here to make a fresh start, okay? I came out here to make you proud of me. Now, please, stop worrying."

She pushed his hand off. "But you've been seen hanging around Hank Norton, and everybody says he's shady."

Her father laughed. "Princess, all successful real estate developers are shady. Only the shady ones get deals done."

"Oh, Daddy, be serious."

"I am." He nodded, his voice dropping to a whisper. "Believe me, I'm watching my steps. The government stole four years of my life. I'm not giving them any more."

"But you broke the law."

"That's debatable."

"For God's sake..." She threw her hands up. "...you're living in Hank Norton's apartment building."

He looked away, bit his lip, and then back at her. "It was the cheapest place around. Princess, if you noticed, the IRS not only threw me in jail, but they also took all of my hard-earned money, and now I'm hardly rolling in it."

Abby's mouth tightened. "Can't you just get a job like a normal person?"

"What, me normal?" He winked at her. "Now come on. Let's work on the slams before they get cold."

* * *

After breakfast, Ike headed out to Tinley Park, Illinois, to talk to Bree Wilson. Despite the fact that nothing would come of it, he'd promised Abby he'd talk to her, and a promise was a promise. Oh, he supposed that at least hearing the woman out was a good thing. She definitely had a heavy load to bear with her kid slowly wasting away. But hearing her out would be enough. His good deed for the day. Abby had a heart for the underdogs of the world. And while it was true that he, too, had been edified by getting Mia Hendrickson off on the arson rap, what they needed now were paying clients, and Bree Wilson almost certainly wasn't one. Hopefully, his meeting with her would end Abby's infatuation with the woman's unfortunate situation. After this, he had an appointment to meet a locksmith at his house to change the locks. That, and his divorce attorney texted that he'd sent a Dear John letter to Mallory, formally informing her that Ike had begun divorce proceedings. So things were moving forward in that regard. Talking to Ms. Wilson would be a formality before he got on with the rest of his life.

Online directions led him to her place. Not a bad drive. Mostly highway. He called her from out front, and she told him to come up. He figured he'd give her fifteen minutes then head back to meet the locksmith. He took his briefcase for appearance's sake and headed into the two-story apartment building. Ms. Wilson met him at her door on the second floor.

He was surprised by how small she was. Only five-one maybe, shoulder-length reddish hair pulled off her freckled face. A slight person, and yet her blue eyes beamed intensely. She wore jeans, a tan blouse, no makeup.

"Thank you so much for coming, Mr. Thompson."

"Of course."

The room was cluttered with medical equipment, including a nebulizer, an oxygen tank, and two wheelchairs. One of the wheelchairs was manual, the other battery-operated, complete with a control panel on the armrest. It wasn't quite a hospital room smell, but it was faintly medicinal. Maybe it was the nebulizer. Ike figured he should've expected this sort of setting, but preoccupied with his problems, he hadn't.

"Excuse the disarray. These things tend to accumulate on their own." She smiled as she led him across the room. "We'll be best off talking in the kitchen."

Ike glanced down the hall—there wasn't much to see—before they turned into the small kitchen. The table there was loaded with documents. Mostly medical bills it seemed, but he noticed stacks of health insurance forms as well. Scores of colorful sticky notes covered the wall adjacent to the table.

She pulled out one of the wrought-iron chairs for him and then sat herself. She slid a stack of papers to the side so she could see him.

Ike sensed his mood shifting, a solemnity coming over him. And this woman was lit up. An energy, a determination, radiated from her. "I can see that this has been a lot of work," he said.

"This is just the most current stuff. There are quite a few boxes stacked in the spare bedroom."

"Sure." Already he could feel himself on the edge of getting sucked into her dilemma. He told himself to toughen up and get this over with. Fast. He needed to meet the guy changing the locks. "Ms. Wilson, I have somewhat of a tight schedule today, so if we could get started. Abby gave me a thumbnail sketch of your situation, but I'd still like to hear from you."

"Of course." She stood. "But can I get you something first? I know it's scorching out there. I have some bottled water in the fridge or iced tea if you'd prefer."

Ike wasn't dehydrated from the heat, but his mouth suddenly felt dry. "The iced tea would be good. Thanks." Why did he say that?

She was back with a pitcher and glasses.

Ike took a notepad and pen from the briefcase. He sipped his drink. "Start by telling me about your son's medical condition."

Bree sat up soldier-straight. A woman on a mission. Ike wondered if she had a hard time relaxing or sleeping.

"Mr. Thompson, my son is dying."

A wave of emotion passed through him. Her emotion. He had to fight to think clearly. "Abby said as much. I'm very sorry."

"But it's not as if I've given up on him. I truly believe there's hope."

Okay, his emotions were settling down. "Abby filled me in on the fact that he has…" He checked the notepad. "…Acute Lung Liquification Disease. She said it's getting more prevalent in the country. She said most people just call it ALLD."

"It's actually Acute Lung *Liquefaction* Disease, but yes, more and more people are suffering, and dying, from it, and most people do call it ALLD."

"What are the disease's symptoms?"

"Well, I'm no doctor…" She nodded. "…but ALLD is a relatively new disease, and by that, I mean within the last seven or eight years, but thousands have it, and many that do are in the early stages of the disease and more than likely mistaking their symptoms for other ailments. ALLD is an autoimmune disease in which, for some reason that they don't really know, the immune system attacks itself. What they speculate happens is a genetic abnormality causes the body to think that there is a severe allergen present in the lungs, and the immune system reacts to it as a foreign substance, a threat, and begins attacking it. And in the process of attacking it, it begins to fill the lungs with a thick, gooey fluid. As the disease progresses, a fever develops, along with pain in the lungs and shortness of breath. The lungs continue to fill with the fluid and ultimately the patient drowns in their own bodily fluids."

Ike set his pen down. She didn't seem like a doctor, but she sure sounded like one with all she knew about her son's disease. He sipped his drink to deal with his dry mouth that was rapidly getting drier. What a horror story. What a burden for the poor woman to bear. Heaviness descended on his spirit, and he longed for relief. "But Abby said it's treatable."

"Treatable, but not curable. Pharamundo has a drug on the market to treat the disease, but the drug cannot stop the disease from progressing. Even with treatment, every single person with ALLD will eventually die."

He nodded to the stacks of medical bills and insurance forms. "Do you have anyone to help? A husband?"

THE PERFECT PROSECUTOR

"My husband couldn't stand to see my son's suffering anymore."

He fidgeted with his glass. "Friends, family, to help?"

"A priest stops by every now and then to anoint Oliver with oil and pray over him."

Ike folded his hands on the table. "Abby said you think Pharamundo International might have a drug to *cure* ALLD?"

"I think they do, yes."

He raised his eyebrows. "But if they have it, why not release it?"

"Well, it goes back to what I was saying before about them having a drug to treat but not cure the disease. If they release the drug to cure ALLD, it makes their drug that treats it—which earns the company billions of dollars year in and year out—obsolete."

"But the new drug will sell."

"Yes…" She raised a hand. "…but only until ALLD is eliminated. Whereas its drug to treat the disease is a perennial moneymaker."

Ike settled back in the chair, which was hardly comfortable, but neither was what he was hearing.

"It's what Big Pharma does, Mr. Thompson—profits over people."

He frowned. "And in the meantime, people are needlessly dying."

"Thousands."

"And you feel the curative drug exists because…"

She leaned forward, her jaw set. "Because a reporter, Lakota, was helping me. He even published a story, watered down by his editors, about the existence of the drug, but then his newspaper promptly pulled the story and fired him. I truly believe Pharamundo International forced the paper to fire him. And in that firing was a threat to anyone else in the media tempted to follow up on his lead."

"Lakota?"

"Lakota Holt, I'm sorry. He's an investigative journalist." Bree bit her lip. "And after his story was pulled, he disappeared. Mr. Thompson, I believe he disappeared because he feared for his life."

Ike rubbed the back of his neck. He sat silently for a while. The emotion in the room was so heavy. The situation so confusing. Because he knew that even if Pharamundo had the curative drug, they had no legal obligation to release it. Even if people were dying. So there was no legal remedy, no effective way to help even if he wanted to. "Well." He clicked his pen. "You've certainly given me a lot of information to process." He stood, opened his briefcase, and stashed the pad and pen.

Bree remained seated.

Was she looking for a commitment from him? Did *he* want to commit to this mess? Could he help even if he wanted to? Josh Chin said Pharamundo had an army of dream team lawyers. "Ms. Wilson, I understand that you're in a very difficult situation and I feel for you, but all I can tell you at this time is that I'll look into this further to see if there's anything I can do to help, but I can't promise anything."

She remained seated.

"Ms. Wilson?"

"Do you want to see Oliver?"

No. He didn't. His life was complicated enough as it was. But could he really say no to this heartsick woman? He swallowed. "Of course."

THE PERFECT PROSECUTOR

Bree rose and led him down the hallway. "He's probably sleeping. He wakes up only erratically, but not for long. We'll see."

His evidence-gathering an unshakable habit, Ike asked, "Is it all right if I video?"

"Please do."

A bright blue Chicago Cubs welcome mat sat outside the boy's door. As Ike entered the room, his eyes were drawn to a host of sports memorabilia. Posters of Chicago Cubs and Chicago White Sox baseball players and a framed Chicago Bears football jersey decorated the walls. A baseball glove balanced on the handle of a bat leaned in a corner. A hockey stick was in another corner, and a junior set of golf clubs in another. All looking new. Never used. Untouched.

The beeping of monitors filled the room, in the middle of which sat a hospital bed. Next to the bed were two green tanks, an IV stand, and on a card table, a collection of neatly arranged medicine bottles—presumably an ensemble of modern-day elixirs to hopefully keep the youngster alive one more day. Oliver was tiny for his age. Collapsed in the fetal position as he was, he could've been a toddler. Abby said he was eight, but he looked four or five. Bree said he was sleeping but he looked to be out cold, comatose. Ike hated himself for thinking it, but the boy actually looked dead. Thin strands of blond hair, crisscrossing with snaking blue veins, lay sparse on his pallid scalp. Tubes jutted up his nose. IVs pierced the paper-thin skin on his arms. Ike wondered when was the last time the boy had used the grab bar hanging above the bed. He wondered if he'd ever used it. The kid was shrunken, vanishing, not long for the earth.

Ike stopped filming, and when he looked over and saw how lovingly Bree gazed at her son, he felt ashamed.

Ashamed for his good health. Ashamed for his selfishness. Ashamed for living in a world where, if Bree was right about the existence of the curative drug, such an incomprehensible injustice was possible. "Thank you for showing me, Bree."

When they got to the apartment door, he met her eyes without flinching. "I'll do what I can to help you and your son."

Chapter Ten

The next morning, Ike sat at his desk in the office doing everything in his power to find the reporter Bree Wilson had talked about, Lakota Holt, when Val buzzed his phone to say that Herschel Blum was there to see him. Ike wondered what was up, especially since Abby wasn't in the office yet. He was surprised, too, because he'd told Abby yesterday that he'd help Bree Wilson and expected her to be there bright and early to discuss the matter further. In the interim, he'd forgotten about the problem with her father. He told Val to send him back.

Herschel wore a light tan sport coat, blue slacks, and a burgundy shirt. All smiles, as was his way, he put his hand out.

Ike stood and shook his hand. "Well, Mr. Blum—"

"Please, I told you it's Herschel. Mr. Blum makes me feel ancient. Besides, I already feel like we're family."

Ike laughed. The family thing again. But he felt the man was sincere. "Sure, Herschel, what brings you my way this morning?"

"Can we sit?"

"Of course."

"Yeah, okay." The older man sat and took several deep breaths. "I have to admit it wasn't easy for me to come here today. In fact, I asked Abby to stay away from the office until I texted her so that we could talk in private."

"Okay. What's going on?"

Herschel put his hands on the desk, his eyes earnest and pleading. "It's Abby, Ike. She's being so unreasonable. She's on my back constantly, texting me ten times a day. It's like she wants me to abandon my real estate profession and all the hard work I've put into it to get a job flipping burgers at McDonald's. Flipping burgers, Ike."

Ike rolled a pen between his hands. "She just cares about you."

"Ike." He leaned across the desk. "I've secured financing and investors and put together over a hundred properties. I've received developer of the year awards and been featured in magazines like *Commercial Connections, Real Estate Forum*, and *National Real Estate Investor.* Now, I know Abby cares about me, but can you please talk to her and tell her that I can't give up my career to calm her irrational fears? Her..." His fingers sprouted bunny ears. "...*help* has been killing me."

"I hear you, but at the same time, I think her concern is valid. Herschel, trust me, Hank Norton may seem like a country bumpkin, but he is no one you want to be associated with."

"Associated with?" Herschel fell back and slapped his forehead. "I live in the guy's apartment building, that's it. So do a hundred other people."

"I've heard you're more involved with him than that."

The older man straightened his shoulders. "Okay, yes, I've had some contact with Norton. And I've had contact with him because he is one of the key players in this town. I'm still learning the ropes of how things work around here, but one of the first things I've learned is that if you want to be a player in White Pines real estate development, you better have Hank Norton's seal of approval."

"Hank Norton was tried twice for wire fraud."

"And twice acquitted."

THE PERFECT PROSECUTOR

"His reputation is worthless."

Herschel shrugged. "The banks don't think so. Look, Ike, you and I both know real estate development is a cut-throat business, but me probably even more so than you. Think of it this way—everybody involved in the big-time real estate business is a Hank Norton."

Ike looked him in the eye. "You as well?"

"Oh, okay, okay, I get it." Herschel pushed himself up by the armrests and stood. "I hear the same from Abby." He headed for the door but then stopped. "Will you talk to her?"

Ike scratched his ear. Finally, he said, "I will."

Herschel left and ten minutes later, Abby came into Ike's office. She'd been sweating, the moisture beading up on her cheeks. She leaned on the door jamb. "So, what was that all about? Why the need to cut me out again?"

Ike put his hand to his chin. "Abby, he just needs you to back off a little."

"Needs me to back off, Ike? And you're agreeing with him? If he stays on the road he's on much longer, he's going back to prison." She tilted her head at him. "Oh, I can see that he's already got you under his spell. Like he does with everybody."

Ike hunched his shoulders. "I'm not under any spell, but at the same time, realistically, there's only so much we can do to protect him."

"Oh God, you're buying his shtick."

"I'm not."

Her face fell.

"Come on, Abby." *Be kind, Ike. She's hurting.*

She sighed out a breath. "You don't know him like I do. He's devious. Oh, maybe that's not the right word, but he's forever shooting angles and taking shortcuts."

Ike motioned for her to sit. "Okay, so we'll watch him closer. We will, okay? Now, come on, have a seat, and let's talk about seeing if we can help Bree Wilson."

She hesitated, then sat. "If?"

"*How* we can help her. I called everywhere I could think of trying to run down the reporter, Lakota Holt, and although some people seemed to know him, nobody would say a word. It's beginning to look like people are afraid to even talk about him."

"But is that surprising with how summarily he was fired and how threatened he felt? They just don't want the same thing to happen to them."

"Yeah, maybe so." He bit the inside of his cheek. "Anyway, I did manage to get through to one reporter. He wouldn't give his name, but he said he believed Lakota was probably living off the grid. He said Lakota had done reporting to help Native Americans in their land disputes with the government out west, and he wouldn't be surprised if he was there now. Then he hung up."

Abby wrung her hands. "Off the grid. Somewhere out west. So how in the world are we going to find him with that scant information?"

"I don't know."

"Maybe Johnny Lagattuta can help?"

Johnny again. "If he's sober."

"Oh, Johnny's sober all right, Ike. Sure, he's going to have his five o'clock happy hour or whatever, but yeah, he's sober."

Seriously? Why did she know so much about Johnny all of a sudden—and why did Johnny know so much about her? He told himself to stop it. *Grow up, Thompson.* "Yeah, we should definitely get him involved."

THE PERFECT PROSECUTOR

Abby brightened a little. "Didn't one of Val's boys help you find the print shop owner harassing your niece? Maybe he could help us find Lakota?"

Ike raised a forefinger. "Ah."

She looked at him, narrowing one eye. "And speaking of the print shop owner, I'm trusting you on your promise to not visit him."

Was that a statement or a question? But he was done with all that for real this time. Like she said, there was nothing to it. Yeah, he should've listened to her in the first place. "Absolutely, Abby."

* * *

It took three days, but Val's son Tommy eventually tracked down Lakota Holt online. If the teenager's information was accurate, Lakota was living on an Indian reservation in Oklahoma. He was an activist working behind the scenes in a land dispute to preserve tribal grave sites for the Cheyenne-Arapho tribe. Tommy said it was likely that Lakota was Native American himself. Tommy even had a phone number he thought might work. Ike and Abby told Bree Wilson, and she drove in from Tinley Park to join in the call. Ike told Val not to disturb them. He, Abby, and Bree huddled in his office, Ike's desktop phone on speaker. He looked back and forth between the two women, held up crossed fingers, and hit the Call button.

The phone rang four times, then someone answered without speaking. Ike pointed to Bree.

"Lakota, is that you? It's Bree Wilson."

Silence. Then, "Bree…how did you get this number?"

Bree looked at Ike and he nodded.

"Lakota, two attorneys are helping me."

Lakota laughed joylessly. "Well, now that I think about it, I'm not surprised that *you* found me." The phone went silent again. "Listen, Bree, I'm sorry I bailed on you, but I had no choice."

She leaned toward the phone. "No, God no, Lakota. No apologies are needed."

"Still."

"Lakota, let me introduce the good people helping me. Or better yet, I'll let them introduce themselves." She looked at Ike and Abby.

Abby pointed at Ike.

"Ike Thompson, Lakota. Good to meet you."

"And I'm Abby Blum, Lakota. Bree's told us wonderful things about you."

"Lakota." Bree backed away from the phone. "Did you hear about what I did in Chicago, confronting Thomas Acosta, Pharamundo's CEO?"

"I heard rumors and that was it. I'm sure Pharamundo did everything in its power to kill the story."

"I don't know what I expected to come from confronting Acosta. I think my frustration got the best of me. When it was over, yes, the mainstream media didn't give it hardly any attention, and what they did report was mostly wrong—they portrayed it as a random attack carried out by a crazy lady."

"Did you get any closer to finding out about the drug?"

Her eyes dropped. "No, my friend, you're the closest anyone has ever come."

"And that's exactly why I need to stay away, Bree. I've heard they put a price on my head. You know, Pharamundo is a Mexican company with ties to the drug cartels, and they don't hesitate using those ties to remove any obstacles to their money-making."

Bree jotted on a piece of paper and slid it across the desk. *Can I tell him what you said earlier?*

Ike gave her a thumbs-up.

"Lakota, Ike and Abby would like you to come to Chicago to investigate this further. You'll have a motel room on the outskirts of the city, a credit card, burner phones—whatever you'll need. They have committed—"

"Let me stop you right there. Me coming is an impossibility."

Bree searched Ike and Abby's eyes.

Abby jotted down a note and pushed it to her. *Tell him you understand.*

"I understand, Lakota."

"Bree, if there was any way…"

A tear slid down Bree's cheek. She waited. Finally, again she said, "I understand, I do. It was selfish of me to even ask you. Please forgive me. But just one more thing, Lakota, and I swear you'll never hear from me again." She inhaled sharply. "Oliver, he finally finished the bead necklace he's been making for you. He was so excited. Can I send it to you somehow? I know it would mean the world to him."

The phone went silent again and this time stayed silent. Ike and Abby looked at each other.

A heavy sigh on the other end. "Bree." More silence. Then, "Oh God, I wouldn't be able to stay long."

Bree closed her eyes, tears slipping out freely now. "Whatever you could give us."

"And I would have to have complete anonymity. I'm telling you, everything is ratcheted up now. Word gets out I'm there; I'm a dead man."

"Complete anonymity, Lakota." Bree's voice dropped to a whisper. "You have my word."

"And I give no guarantees that I can find out anything at all, mind you, none."

"Understood."

"And flying there is out. It's impossible to stay anonymous flying."

Ike jumped in. "Lakota, I'll get someone down there, and he'll drive you here."

Another heavy sigh. "Oh, good Lord."

They all waited.

"Okay, I'll do it."

Chapter Eleven

Two days later, Johnny Lagattuta was back. He was sitting alongside Abby, and they were across from Ike at his desk. Johnny had flown to Oklahoma City, rented a car, picked up Lakota Holt, and driven him back to Illinois. Ike and Abby weren't surprised Lakota wasn't with him.

The private investigator seemed worn out from the trip. He'd driven eleven hours straight. "I gotta tell you, it was a pretty weird trip. The whole time the guy said nothing. And you know me, I can chat anybody up. But yeah, he just slept under a blanket in the backseat the whole way."

Abby frowned. "That *is* weird."

Johnny slumped a little. "Like you guys told me, when we got here, I got him a rental in my name, and he was off—without saying a word."

Ike gave the private investigator a thumbs-up. "Nice, Johnny. What did you get him?"

"A Toyota Corolla."

"Okay."

Johnny shook his head. "I'm telling you, the guy was like a ghost."

Abby turned to him. "I would think he's just laying low."

"Well." Johnny sat up, bumping elbows with her. "Well, he couldn't have lain any lower."

Ike swiveled in his chair. "It's hard to blame him. He lost his job and now he's worried about losing his life. Needless to say, we've got to do everything we can to protect him. I've set up encrypted texting and calling, but we'll have to expect that the communication will pretty much be one-way, from him to us. We can't press him."

"I feel for the guy," Johnny said. "Especially considering what I've been hearing from some of my detective buddies in CPD. They've been telling me some pretty nasty things about Thomas Acosta."

"Yeah, Johnny, Abby and I have been hearing stories about Acosta too, especially about his connection to the cartels."

"The cartels and more." The private investigator adjusted the belt holster on his hip. "Then you've probably heard that he's a killer too. At least that's what they were saying."

Abby put a hand to her mouth. "*That* I haven't heard. Acosta himself is a killer?"

"Maybe not anymore, Abby, but they said that when he was lower in the cartel pecking order, he was a hit man, and he killed scores of cops, politicians, a few priests, and even, well…"

Ike fiddled with a pen. "Even what, Johnny?"

"…even a few lawyers."

Ike's phone rang. He checked the caller ID. "This is him." He looked at Johnny. "Sorry, buddy, but you gotta go—and remember, no one knows about the ride from Oklahoma, Lakota being here, nothing."

Johnny stood, gave a little salute, and backed out of the office.

Ike flipped his phone to speaker and set it on the desk. He tapped the Answer button. "This is Ike Thompson, Lakota. I'm here with Abby, and you're on speaker."

Silence.

Ike widened his eyes at Abby. "How was your trip?"

"You're both alone?" The reporter's voice sounded shaky.

The front door chimed as it shut behind Johnny. Val was at her desk. Ike rose and closed his office door. "Completely alone, Lakota." He sat back down.

"Bree's not there?"

"No, Lakota," Abby said. "Just Ike and me."

"Good, because I'm telling you upfront that getting Pharamundo to release the drug Bree's boy needs is a hopeless pursuit."

Ike shifted in his chair. "Then why…"

"Because when I thought of the love she has for her kid and her absolute refusal to give up hope, I couldn't say no to her."

"Yeah, well." Ike arched an eyebrow. "I kind of know what you're talking about, but why do you feel there is no chance of the drug being released?"

"Why? Money. Money and power. From everything I've learned, yeah, the curative drug exists. My contact inside Pharamundo says it's even passed internal evaluations, is ready to be released, and the company has even been producing the drug in secret labs under strict supervision, but all that information has been viciously quashed by the company."

Ike sighed. "That sounds like a lot to keep hidden."

"It is, but Pharamundo has the wherewithal and especially the financial incentive to do it. And the fact of the matter is, no organization on earth has the power to stop them. The U.S. government, you might think? Think again. Pharamundo owns the government regulators."

No power on earth? Ike remembered the blaze of energy, the intensity in Bree Wilson's eyes.

Abby angled the phone toward her. "I'm not doubting you, Lakota, but I don't see how something like this can be happening in this day and age."

"Oh no? Think of what happened during the opioid crisis. Big Pharma lobbied hard for laws to *not* regulate opioid production, distribution, and usage. And all that while record numbers of fatal overdoses were racking up across the nation. Now the same thing is happening with ALLD."

Ike crossed his arms. "But Bree talked about exposing this to the media."

Lakota laughed. "You would think that would do it, and maybe it would've twenty years ago, but not today. Today, the mainstream media is dominated by Big Pharma. Last year, Big Pharma spent over eight billion on advertising. Do you think the media is going to ruffle Big Pharma's feathers with that much money on the line? I tried to do it and look what happened."

"Lakota," Abby said, "Bree told us about the drug to treat ALLD being the company's big money maker."

"She's right. It's called Respir-ezy. And if Pharamundo releases the curative drug, just like that they destroy Respir-ezy's multi-billion-dollar annual profit. Poof!"

Abby balled her hands into fists. "And in the meantime, Bree's boy will die an unnecessary, excruciating death."

"And thousands of others."

* * *

Abby had some things she needed to take care of at the office, and Ike decided to head home. As he drove, he thought about how one of the true comforts in his life was knowing that Leaner was always waiting for him. As he pulled into the driveway, the garage door rising as the sun was setting, he anticipated the dog's welcome.

In the garage he climbed out of the car, and as soon as he turned the handle to enter the house, Leaner began to whimper happily, his nails clacking and slipping on the hardwood floors. Ike laughed and braced for the dog's boisterous greeting. "Ohhhh, all right, big guy." He got down on one knee to be at the dog's level. "Oh, yeah, you're a good boy, you are. Are you ready to go out?"

Leaner bounded for the sliding glass door to the backyard. Ike followed, opened the door, and the big dog charged into the yard. Ike decided to join him out there as the heat had finally eased a bit. But first, to keep the mosquitoes away, he tracked down his cigar cutter and grabbed one of his prized Cuban cigars from the humidor. He then eased into a deck chair on the patio, making a mental note to take care of the few weeds sprouting between the neatly laid pavers. He lit the cigar and puffed away, the fragrant smoke hanging in the still air, protecting him more effectively than any mosquito spray could. Leaner meanwhile was busy exploring the perimeter of the fence, looking for any entry points some upstart squirrel, gopher, or raccoon may have made since his last reconnaissance.

But soon the comfort of being in Leaner's company, the pleasure of the tobacco, and the calming surroundings wore off, as Ike's concerns kicked back in. Lakota Holt had hardly been positive in what he'd said. In fact, his coming sounded like a complete washout. And who knew how much time Ike and Abby might waste in this quagmire?

Leaner was back to check on him, and Ike, chomping down on the cigar, gave the dog a hug, the dog's wagging tail beating out a steady rhythm on the back of the deck chair. Ike laughed. God, he loved this dog. Oh, he loved Abby too, but he could never see Abby enjoying a smoke-filled hug as much as Leaner did. That was one thing dogs had over women—it was easier to be a guy around them. Don't shower for a few days? No problem for Leaner. He doesn't shower at all. Have chili for dinner and need to pass some gas? Leaner won't look sidelong at you for it. He'll probably join you cutting a few loose. Forgot to text back after three or four hours? Leaner doesn't even have a phone.

"Okay, okay." Ike released the hug. "I have to do some thinking, big guy." Leaner settled at his side. Ike hated that when he thought about cutting expenses, the first thing that came to mind, probably because it would be the easiest to do, was laying off Val. But that wasn't happening. He'd sell his car and house first. She was, and had been for years, a brick of support for him. She'd saved his butt so many times and perhaps even his life. But there *were* things he could cut back on. He could cancel his golf magazine subscriptions, give up cigars, eat out less, but the more he thought about it, the more he realized that those things would hardly make a dent. One thing was sure, though—paying for more stuff like Johnny's flight to Oklahoma was out. He took a puff and racked his brain for other big things to cut, but as his cigar grew shorter and the mosquitoes circled closer, he couldn't think of a single thing. He gazed at Leaner. "What do you think, boy?" A mosquito buzzed Ike's ear, and as he grabbed the chair's armrests to get up, he thought of how he'd been paying Mallory's apartment rent. Ah! *That* he could, and would, cut as soon as possible.

"Come on, Leaner, let's get inside before the mosquitoes massacre us." He resolved to write Mallory a letter and drop it off at the post office on his way to work in the morning.

Chapter Twelve

Despite the drizzle that glazed his bedroom window in the morning, Ike was feeling better about things. A good night's sleep always improved his perspective. And despite Lakota Holt's pessimism, he was glad that they were at least going to try to help Bree and her son. Before his father had been murdered in prison, he'd always told him, *Son, if you do the right thing, the universe will provide a way.* Ike hoped that was true now. After a quick shower, he put on some coffee and let Leaner out. He proofread the letter he'd written Mallory about no longer paying her rent, careful not to spill coffee on it. It was a simple letter—simple but unequivocal. And White Pines delivered local mail so quickly—if he got it in early enough, maybe she'd even get it today.

He addressed the envelope, sealed and stamped it, and set it next to his keys. He let Leaner in, toweled him off, being sure to wipe his wet paws. He refilled his bowls with nuggets and water, apologized for leaving, and assured him, rather dishonestly, that he'd be back soon. Leaner's limp tail was proof the dog wasn't buying it. Ike snatched up his keys and the letter.

As he drove to the post office, his windshield wipers swiping on the delay speed to clear the drizzle, he noticed flashes of light behind him. He checked his rearview mirror. It was the sun, still low in the sky, peeking through the swift gray clouds. He turned the corner and behold—high in the sky—a massive rainbow. He took it as a good omen, and his upbeat mood only grew as he dropped off Mallory's letter at the post office. But when he pulled into the office lot and saw

Johnny Lagattuta's BMW next to Abby's car, his optimism vanished. What now?

Val's car wasn't there yet, so it would be just the two of them. Alone. Ike tried desperately to get his positive mood back, but the effort was futile. Johnny was hanging around Abby way too much, and Abby, knowing how Ike felt about that, was letting him. Maybe encouraging him. Either that, or Ike's jealousy was getting the best of him. He slunk in the back and walked quietly to her office.

When he saw Johnny, passive, stretched out, and nearly asleep in a chair across from her desk, he was embarrassed for not trusting Abby. Johnny definitely wasn't a morning person, so for him to be there that early, something major must be up. When Ike knocked on the doorframe, Johnny strained to sit up.

Abby, sitting behind her desk, rose. "Ike, I'm so glad you're here. I wanted to discuss what Johnny just told me with both of you before Val arrives."

Val knew everything there was to know about what happened in the office, so whatever this was about, she need not be excluded, but whatever. "I'm listening."

Abby's voice was full of emotion. "Johnny says my father is on the verge of breaking the law, which means at the very least he'll be facing fines and additional conditions on his parole. At the worst, his parole will be revoked—and he'll be going back to jail."

"Hey, Johnny." Ike nodded to him. "Appreciate you coming in. So, what was the source of your information?"

The private investigator leaned forward, balancing his elbows on his knees. "A detective buddy keeping a close eye on Hank Norton and what's going down with the White Pine's development. He noticed Abby's father on the verge of crossing some legal lines that couldn't be uncrossed. He said if he keeps going, he's going to get busted along with Norton or maybe because of him."

Abby hugged herself. "It's the same thing that happened in New York, and the worst part is he doesn't think he's doing anything wrong. He sees it as normal, as what needs to be done to succeed in a tough business. Once, he even said to me, 'In big-time real estate, only criminals get things done.' "

"Well." Ike leaned against the doorframe. "We'll have to talk to him—"

"That does nothing, Ike. We already did that. *I've* talked to him a hundred times."

Johnny rubbed his eyes. "Maybe you could ask Ursula Rush to give him a good talking-to. A warning shot over the bow from the new State's Attorney oughtta put the fear of God in him."

Ike tilted his head at the private investigator. "I don't know about that, Johnny. Ursula'd put the fear of God in him *and* put him in jail. But maybe Josh Chin."

Abby threw up her hands. "No, neither of them. It's too risky. No one but us three should know."

Johnny turned to her. "You're not just gonna let him go down, are you?"

"Of course not. And now that I'm thinking about it, maybe the three of us are complicit with what we know? Maybe *we're* criminally liable?"

"Just knowing?" Johnny scratched his head. "Nah, I don't think so."

Ike leaned a hip into the doorframe. "Johnny's right. Three things would need to happen for that. One, we'd need to be aware a crime has been committed. Two, we'd need to assist the person who committed the crime. And three, we'd need to hinder their apprehension. So, we've only got one of three. We're in the clear—so far."

Abby widened her eyes at him. "But he's not."

The room fell silent.

Finally, Abby broke the quiet. "I don't know, maybe this sounds crazy, but what if I were to just turn him in? Before he gets in too deep, I mean?"

Ike walked over and rubbed her shoulders. "It won't come to that, Abby. We'll figure something out. We will."

* * *

That afternoon, Mallory stormed into the law firm, clutching a handful of papers and barreling towards Ike's office. "Really, Ike?"

He bounced up from his chair. "Not here, Mallory. Not now."

She brandished one of the papers. "You're not giving me time to get back on my feet? You're cutting me off? Not paying my rent?"

"That's right."

She held out another paper. "*And* you're divorcing me? Just because I made a mistake. Ike, my God, I went to our house and you *changed the locks*? You changed the locks on *our* house?"

"It's not your house anymore. You forfeited any right to call it yours." The words hung in the air. Who cares what she thinks? But then he remembered the pellet gun in her apartment—and the Glock he'd bought her. He swallowed hard.

Her eyes filled with tears. "Ike, please believe me, I get it that you're upset. You have every right to be. And I get it that I made a mistake, a big mistake. But I've changed. I'll do better. I'll be a better wife. Please give me one more chance and you'll see. Please, Ike."

"Mallory—"

"I failed you. I know I drove you to that slut."

He rolled his eyes.

"I'm your wife, baby. We took a vow, till death do us part, remember?" She reached for his face but he knocked her hand away. "Oh God, Ike, we lost our babies." The tears fell. "But we can try again. We can still have a family. I know we can."

Ike couldn't believe she was playing the miscarriages they'd had for sympathy. But they had lost three babies, and it had shattered both their hearts. He closed his eyes and felt the tears welling up behind them. "Mallory." The sound of a slap. He opened his eyes. Abby was holding her cheek.

Mallory shoved Abby to the floor. "Get out! Get out of my sight!"

Ike grabbed his estranged wife's arm. "It's over, Mallory! Don't you get it? I've nothing left inside for you. Our love is dead. Dead!"

She wrenched free and glowered over Abby. "Stay away from my *husband*! If you don't, I promise you, I swear on my dead children, you'll regret it."

Val came running, and together, she and Ike strong-armed Mallory out the front door.

Mallory rapped on the window, tore up the papers, and flung them in the air. "I'll never divorce you, Ike. Never!"

* * *

Ike and Val ran back to Abby as she was getting to her feet.

"Oh my God, Abby." He retrieved her glasses. "I'm so sorry."

"No, it's okay. It was my fault." She slipped the glasses on. "I shouldn't have butted in. I don't know, I heard her yelling and I thought maybe I could calm things down somehow. Obviously, I was wrong."

Val hugged her. "She's nasty, Abby. There's no reasoning with that one." She brushed Abby's cheek and headed back to her desk.

Ike put his arm around Abby and walked her to the recliner in the corner of his office. "Are you okay?"

She exhaled long and slow as she sank into the soft cushions. "I suppose, but honestly, all this nonsense with Mallory is getting old."

"Understood. But the nonsense is over, Abby. I'm making sure of that. It's a done deal." But again, he remembered the pellet gun in Mallory's apartment—and the Glock there too.

"She said she'd never divorce you. I heard her."

Chances were it *was* going to be difficult divorcing Mallory. Perhaps very difficult. He wasn't a divorce lawyer, but he knew how long divorces could take when one of the parties fought it. "I'll make it happen, Abby. I will." He went to his desk, opened the bottom drawer, and pulled out a bottle of scotch. He took a glass from a cabinet and poured two fingers' worth of the whiskey. He walked the drink over to her.

"No thanks. I'm okay."

He sat on the recliner's arm and downed the drink. What a mess. He felt like he and Mallory were some white trash couple like you'd see on the TV show *Cops*. But he'd deal with it. Like his father would always say, *You can't leave a place you've never been.* Then he thought of Bree's son wasting away, and that gave him perspective. He and Abby may have a rough road ahead, but nobody was dying. "Maybe, if you feel up to it, we can get started on Bree's situation again?"

She sat up. "But how can we? We haven't heard from Lakota at all."

Ike set the empty glass on the floor. "I know. Really, I was hoping—or maybe it was wishful thinking—that he was just getting settled in, but now I'm not so sure. He's got our email address, but he wouldn't give us the number of his burner phone. He just said he'd call us. Truly, he's seeming more and more like a ghost. Like he's just disappeared. I guess when there's a price on your head, you know how to vanish. Maybe he's moved to another place, but if he had, we'd likely have seen a credit card charge. We know his rental is a Corolla and have the address of his motel, but he said to never go there unless it was a life-or-death situation. So I'm holding that in reserve as the nuclear option."

"But there must be something we can do now."

"Right." He picked up the glass and stood. "We can start our own investigation."

She started to get up but then hesitated, her eyes lighting up. "And maybe do some social media posts to get the word out?"

"Good idea, and run some paid ads to see if we can find Pharamundo employees willing to talk. Which will be risky for sure, but running them we may be able to gather some information to help Lakota."

She scooted forward. "But why would Pharamundo employees talk to us?"

"I think the disgruntled ones might, the ones who've been fired and have axes to grind."

"You think they'd just talk to us?"

He extended his hand and helped her to her feet. "Well, we'd have to do something like offer confidential interviews for a cash payment. That should draw some interest. Because somebody out there must know the truth about what's happening."

Chapter Thirteen

A week went by, and still no phone communication from Lakota. Bree Wilson called to say she hadn't heard from him either. Fortunately, he'd sent a few emails, but they were all somewhat vague. Ike was sitting at his desk going through them, trying to discern a pattern that might hint at what he was up to, but with no luck. And not only no luck, Lakota had been so well-spoken over the phone, but his emails were short and choppy, almost as if he hadn't written them. The social media ads they were running were only drawing a few non-committal responses, mostly inquiring about the amount of the payment, but no one signed up for an interview. The one thing the ads were unmistakably doing though was racking up charges in a hurry. A knock on Ike's office door. Abby. She held an open laptop.

"I was going through Lakota's credit card charges and look what I found." She flipped the laptop around.

Ike pushed a file to the side. "A Polaroid camera *and a crossbow*. Are you kidding me? Maybe the camera makes sense but a crossbow?"

"And did you see the price of the crossbow?"

"Twelve hundred dollars. Oh man."

"Think he's getting paranoid?"

Ike scratched behind his ear. "Well, he is Native American. Maybe he's tired of eating McDonald's."

Abby frowned. "Nice racist joke."

"Sorry." But the money was flooding out, and they still hadn't received the email regarding the Goodwin/DeCarlo settlement from DeCarlo's lawyer, and Ike was beginning to wonder if they ever would. It was slowly but surely becoming clear to him—he never should've let them get involved with Bree Wilson. Once again being soft had gotten them entangled in a quagmire. "A twelve-hundred-dollar crossbow. No communication. Abby, I really think it's time we did some background checking on this guy."

"You think he's a fraud?"

Who knew? "Not a fraud necessarily, but he doesn't seem to be who we thought he was."

She tilted her head from side to side. "We do know that he's afraid for his life."

"No, we know that he *said* he was afraid for his life."

She sighed. "Well, that's true."

"And what about the crossbow?" He stared down at the carpeting. "I don't know, I'd just feel more comfortable knowing more about him."

"Yeah, me too, definitely."

"So let's get started." He flicked on his computer. "I'll check in the search engines, and you go through social media and see what you can find. Then let's meet back here to discuss what we've come up with."

"You got it." She left.

An hour later, she returned, laptop tucked under her arm. "Well, that was interesting. How did you do?"

"Not great. But you go first."

"Well, just to give you some idea, his Facebook profile photo has him thrusting his middle finger into the camera." She set the laptop on his desk and spun it to face him. "So Lakota is hardly the relaxed, thoughtful person we spoke with over the phone."

"I saw several other photos of him though." She smiled apologetically. "He really is handsome."

"Okay."

"So what did you come up with?"

He gathered up some papers. "Come on, let's sit in the conference room. We can spread out on one of the tables there."

They went to the spacious room and sat side by side at a long, glass-topped table, the air conditioning purring overhead.

Ike could feel her energy. She was probably still a little wound up from what happened with Mallory, but he could feel goodness, warmth, and love coming from her. It was the opposite vibe he'd been getting from his estranged wife for so long now. He put his arm around her. "You okay?"

She smiled and leaned into him.

"All right then." He spread out the papers. "Look at this." He slid a yellow-lined paper in front of her. "I called Lakota's last five employers."

"Why are so many things scratched out?"

"Because I had to keep coming up with more excuses for why I was inquiring about him. Believe me, nobody wanted to talk about him."

"I found something unsettling, too." She set the laptop on the table. "This isn't the first time he's been fired from a newspaper job."

"Really?"

She hit some keys, then scrolled. "Here it is. He's been canned five times and all for the same reason—fabricating the articles he wrote."

Ike slunk back in his chair. "Well, that complicates things. Or could it be that all those newspapers had a problem with him telling the truth?"

She shrugged her shoulder. "One newspaper, okay. Two, maybe. But five? I think we may have to come to terms with the possibility that he's not as ethical as we'd thought. And, uh, speaking of not all that ethical, Ike, can I, uh, talk to you about my father again?"

What now? "What's up?"

"Actually, I have a proposition I want to run by you."

* * *

The following day, Ike and Abby drove to Hank Norton's apartment building to pick up her father. They took him to a deep-shaft rock quarry on the far south side of Chicago. After parking the Lexus, they walked down a winding asphalt path for a couple of hundred yards to a viewing platform cantilevered over the side of the quarry. The land below bore the scars of the violence perpetrated against it, having been reduced to a sheer gray basin, at the bottom of which lay an acidic, green lake. The smell of diesel fumes mixed with the stale air, and the flash of vertigo Ike experienced made him feel like he was standing on the edge of a man-made Grand Canyon. Massive earthmovers by the lake appeared to be no bigger than children's toys. Workers, wearing yellow hardhats, shiny in the sun, walked alongside the machines, looking no larger than ants.

Herschel backed away from the railing. "What the hell? Why did you bring me here? This looks like a place where they dump mafia hits."

Abby touched his elbow. "Daddy, please."

"We needed to be away from prying ears, Herschel." Ike could see where the man was coming from, though.

THE PERFECT PROSECUTOR

"Look, Daddy, we've received reliable information that through your dealings with Hank Norton, you may have violated the terms of your parole."

Her father blew out a breath. "And you had to bring me to this godforsaken place to tell me that? I thought you were going to throw me over the side into the lake."

"Come on, Daddy, this is serious. The fact of the matter is you're a hairsbreadth away from going back to jail."

He stepped back from her. "And where, pray tell, Princess, did you get this damning information?"

"It doesn't matter."

He flexed his hands. "Well, how do we know it's reliable?"

Abby looked at Ike.

"It's from someone with close ties to the police investigating the downtown White Pines development, Herschel."

Her father wiped the sweat from his forehead. "Ah, yeah, well, wonderful, thank you, but I have to tell both of you that I really think this is *meshuggah*. You bring me out to this godforsaken place to scare me with this crap. It's absolutely *meshuggah*."

"It's not crazy, Daddy. I almost turned you in."

Her father locked on her eyes. "You what?"

"That's right. That's how serious this is. I almost turned you in—to keep you from getting into even more trouble." She held his stare.

A breeze wafted the diesel fumes around.

Herschel finally looked off. "I *need* to make money, Princess."

Abby crossed her arms. "Oh come on, enough with the Princess stuff already. I'm not five years old anymore, and you're not thirty."

The older man nodded slowly. "All right, all right, that's fine, but I do need to make money."

Again, she looked at Ike.

He reached for his wallet. "That's where I may be able to help."

Abby's father pivoted to Ike as if he'd just noticed him for the first time. "Oh, you think so, do you?"

"Yes, but not if you're going to be hostile about it, Herschel."

Abby stomped her foot. "Oh, please just hear him out."

Her father put his fingertips to his temples. "You bring me to where they dump dead bodies. You tell me you nearly turned me in. And now I should listen?"

Abby touched his shoulder. "Daddy, please."

He closed his eyes. He shook his head slowly. Finally, he clasped her hand. "Okay, okay."

Ike fingered through a stack of credit and business cards, finally settling on one. He held it out to the older man.

Herschel read from the card. "Department of Financial and Professional Regulation, Licensed Real Estate Managing Broker. Icarus Thompson." He caught Ike's eye. "What does this mean to me?"

Ike nodded. "It means I can hold your license so you can sell real estate. You'd be working for me earning a legitimate income."

Herschel peered out into the quarry, then back at Ike. "That may actually be doable. At least for a start."

Ike slipped the card back into his wallet. "Considering your background…" He paused to let the implication sink in. "…it's not guaranteed, but over 95% of those who disclose their conviction on their applications get approved."

Abby clutched her father's hand. "You'd have to go to real estate school to complete a program, and then you'd have to pass the state exam."

"I could do that."

"Of course you can, Daddy. And you'll do great. And most importantly, you won't have to worry about going back to—"

Up went his palm. "Don't even say it, Abby." He focused back on Ike. "But what do I do for money until I complete the coursework and pass the exam?"

Ike patted him on the back. "I can help you with that too."

As they returned to the car, Ike started thinking about Lakota's twelve-hundred-dollar crossbow, his own mortgages, and all his other debts piling up. Sure, why not, what the heck, he could support Herschel for a while—what was one more expense? As he turned the engine, he could feel a headache coming on.

* * *

Ike's headache intensified as the day progressed. And getting a text from Josh Chin asking him to meet for dinner, which almost certainly meant trouble, didn't make it any better. He popped three aspirins and drove to the restaurant to meet the prosecutor.

He parked between a Bentley and a Maserati in the restaurant's garage. Not a lot of places made the Lexus look tacky, but this one did. When he closed his door, the sound echoed off the concrete walls and off his throbbing head. When he'd faced great uncertainty before, he'd always reverted to the strategy he'd used in golf—hope for the best but expect the worst. He clung to that now.

Stepping into the restaurant, he felt as though he'd stepped into a photographer's darkroom. Dim, refracted light faintly illuminated crimson tables, creating a reddish ambiance. The tables were set with glossy black bowls on white saucers, each place setting accompanied by a pair of chopsticks. Heavily cushioned, black leather backrests invited guests to sit comfortably, while ornate bamboo screens separated each table from the next, providing privacy and adding an exotic touch. Gentle ambient flute music played from speakers unseen. This was the kind of place where people who did not want to draw attention dined. And people had big money. A petite Asian American woman in a simple black dress, no makeup save cherry-red lipstick, approached. Ike's mouth went suddenly dry as he uttered his friend's name. The woman bowed demurely and nodded for him to follow.

Josh was ensconced at a corner table at the far edge of the main dining area. He wore what looked to be a maroon—although the color could be influenced by the lighting—suit coat and a silver bow tie. "Thank you, Jing," he said to the hostess and pointedly waited for her to leave.

Okay, here we go. "Josh, how are you?"

"I'm good, Ike. How are you?"

"Yeah, good, too. Good too." He was glad the waiter showed up with ice water, and he took a healthy sip.

"I'm glad to hear that, and now I'm sure you're wondering why I asked you here on such short notice, so let's not waste any time."

Ike actually wished they could waste a little time to give his headache a chance to subside. "Absolutely."

THE PERFECT PROSECUTOR

"Now this is between us, Ike." Josh leaned over and his voice trailed off to barely a whisper. "Completely off-the-record, including this meeting."

"Of course, my friend."

Josh folded his hands on the table. "I'm hearing some disturbing things on the grapevine. The most concerning one being that Pharamundo's legal team may be on the verge of suing you."

Ike slid the weighty cloth napkin from under the chopsticks. "Suing me for what, Josh?"

"Aiding and abetting a whistleblower under the False Claims Act."

What the hell. "Josh, if anyone should be suing someone under the False Claims Act, I should be suing Pharamundo. What would be the basis for their suit?"

Josh looked off before returning his gaze to Ike. "Aiding and abetting a whistleblower. They're claiming you're promoting a whistleblower's false claims against them."

"Promoting a whistleblower's false claims? How so?"

The prosecutor widened his eyes. "All the Facebook, Google, and YouTube ads you're running."

Ike's temples throbbing, he suddenly saw little white flashes in his peripheral vision. "But, Josh, what whistleblower am I aiding?"

"It doesn't matter." The prosecutor's lips thinned into a tight line. "I've *seen* the ads, Ike. They're on the cusp of accusing Pharamundo of fraud. Did you really think that wouldn't draw a strong response?"

Ike took a few more drinks of water to buy time. "Well, I knew they were risky, but I felt we needed to do it. We need the information, Josh."

"And are you getting it?"

Ike stared at the chopsticks, the white flashes flickering.

Like a vision from a dream, a waitress in a shimmery gold top emerged from the shadows.

Josh held up a hand. "Give us a couple minutes."

The woman faded away as silently as she'd appeared.

"Look, Ike, I know you're trying to help the Wilson woman and her son. That's a good thing, and I commend you for it. But you don't know what you're getting into with Pharamundo."

Ike told himself to focus. "They couldn't just be saber-rattling?"

"Oh, to a degree maybe. But if they're not, are you willing to pay the consequences? Not only does Pharamundo have a battery of top-shelf legal talent, they have crack investigators—former FBI and NSA. And if that isn't enough, the company has ties to the cartels, and they've demonstrated they're not afraid of using them." He leaned back against the cushion. "Tying you up in court for years would mean nothing to them, Ike. Do you want to fight a legal and investigative juggernaut for two years? Five years? Are you in a financial position to?"

Ike gulped down what was left of his water, the ice cubes clacking against his teeth.

Chapter Fourteen

After a sleepless night, Ike struggled to shake off the lingering effects of Josh's warning and the resulting headache. But an even bigger headache loomed as they still hadn't heard from Lakota. And Josh was right—he and Abby were no match for Pharamundo. Ike was even on the edge of bailing on the whole thing, but before he did, he was determined to find out what the hell had happened to Lakota.

He dressed and headed to the office. He was relieved to see Abby's and Val's cars in the lot. He hurried in and stopped at Abby's door, but she was on the phone. When she noticed him, she held up a forefinger and when she hung up, she smiled big. "My father has already signed up for his real estate classes."

Her father again. Okay. "Well, what do you know? I guess you *can* teach an old dog new tricks."

Abby's face fell. "Are you calling my father a dog?"

"No, Abby, of course not. It's just an old saying."

"Oh, Ike, I was just joshing with you." She got up and hugged him. "And speaking of joshing, what did Josh have to say last night?"

Ike felt his rough whiskers against her smooth cheek—he'd been too preoccupied to shave. "Well, he didn't say anything good if that's what you mean, but I can explain in the car."

"Huh? In the car?"

"I'm sorry. I want you to come with me—we need to find out what's up with Lakota. We've got the name of the motel he's staying at." He walked off.

"Wait, wait, wait." She held up a hand. "You want to go to his motel? But that's what you were calling the nuclear option."

"Well, don't you think it's time? Buying the crossbow. No calls. Meaningless emails, and even they stopped. What are we supposed to do?"

"No, it's okay." She gave him a little smile. "I was just surprised."

"Sure." He felt for his keys in his pocket. "So are you ready?"

"Give me a few."

He checked in with Val, who was emailing past clients, soliciting business. He thanked her and said they'd be gone for a couple of hours.

They piled into the Lexus and drove to a far southwestern suburb, Ike explaining *most of* the risks Josh had warned him about at dinner the night before. But it was amazing—over the course of the drive just being in Abby's presence vanquished what was left of his headache.

She was taking in the surroundings. "Kind of a ratty neighborhood, don't you think? All the telephone poles leaning, the electrical wires looping across the street. It has a 1950s look."

"Lakota wanted anonymity." Ike slowed the Lexus. "The motel is just up ahead."

"Okay, so if his car is there, we just wait till he comes out? What's the plan?"

"Hold the wheel for a sec." He reached into the backseat, grabbed a box the size of a pack of cigarettes, and handed it to her. "We attach this to his car."

She read from the box. "Mini GPS tracker/locator." She looked at him. "Attaching this to his car—is that even legal?"

"Not without his consent, it isn't." He eased off the gas. The Cardinal Motel's sign stood out as a beacon of red in the drab neighborhood, crowned by a yellow neon arrow pointing to the building.

"And do we have that?"

"No."

She put both hands on the console and stared at him. "Wait a minute, Ike. What are you getting us into? This suddenly isn't feeling so right."

He took a long, careful look at the motel as they cruised by. "Things change, Abby. Drastic problems require drastic solutions. Attorneys *need* to know things."

"Attorneys also need to obey the law."

He pulled a U-turn, feeling the headache pinching at his temples again. "Come on—he's been missing for days."

"He hasn't contacted us for days, Ike. That's not necessarily missing."

"Yeah, okay."

She tapped the console. "So we break our promise to Lakota, *and* we break the law, all because we're attorneys who need to know things?"

"Look, Abby, I know this seems extreme." He gazed over at her. "I should've cleared this with you before we came out here, and now, hey, if you want, I can drive you back to the office and come back on my own."

She fell back in her seat.

Two vintage Coca-Cola vending machines stood at the entrance to the motel parking lot, opposite an ice maker with a rusty door. Faded yellow lines indicated parking spaces, each space with its own oil stain. Only three vehicles were in the lot: two minivans and a Jeep, all bunched in a corner. Cracked and crumbling white fascia boards topped the single-story horseshoe-shaped building, but the clean windows gave it a reasonably respectable look.

"Well, Lakota's rental Corolla obviously isn't here." Ike snorted out a laugh. "I wonder if he drove back to Oklahoma?"

Abby again turned to him. "I have to tell you, Ike, your tough talk, your 'look' to me earlier was uncalled for."

He frowned. He had no place taking anything out on her. "Yeah, you're right, Abby. My bad. The pressure's just been eating me up lately."

Her shoulders relaxed. "All right. Anyway, I don't think Lakota's on his way back to Oklahoma. He didn't seem like the cut-and-run type."

"Agreed. It's just we have so little information to go on." He pulled into a space far from the office.

"So what now?"

He reached into the back again, this time grabbing a thin metal strip.

"Tell me you're kidding."

"Actually." He checked behind them. "I'm not."

"You're going to break into Lakota's motel room?"

"If I can." He opened his door.

"Oh my God," she said, but she climbed out.

Ike scanned the lot. "I don't want to spend a lot of time in there."

"Oh, I'd say that's a good idea." She smirked. "Your first in quite a while actually."

She was right. It was a crazy risk but he was hellbent on doing it. It took a bit of jiggling—his heart beating wildly—but the jimmy finally did its job. He pushed the door open slowly, revealing a bright room with pastel walls and fuchsia carpeting. A couple of chairs stood next to a circular wooden table, a queen-size bed with a blue and pink flowery coverlet occupying the middle of the room. A chest of drawers with a portable TV on top stood in one corner. The room looked like it hadn't been slept in, or perhaps the maid had recently tidied it up. Abby wandered off as he opened the drawers in the chest. In the top drawer were a few pairs of boxer shorts and socks. The middle drawer contained two cotton golf shirts and a pair of dungarees. The bottom drawer was empty.

"Ike."

He joined her in the bathroom.

She pointed to the mirror, where a Polaroid photograph of a lakeside mansion was taped. "And this." She opened what looked to be a makeup case on the vanity.

"What the hell?" he said softly.

She read the company name aloud. "Superstar Face Paint Pro Palette."

Ike stuck his finger into one of the tins, held it up to his nose, and sniffed. "I don't get it. What could he possibly be doing with this?"

"Oh wow."

"What?"

"Think about it. Lakota is Native American. He buys a crossbow. Could this be…" She dabbed a finger into the red tin and smeared the face paint across one cheek and then the other. "…war paint?"

Ike snatched the photo off the mirror. "Come on, let's get out of here."

As they climbed into the Lexus, they caught a glimpse of a sleek gray BMW with deeply tinted windows pulling away from the motel entrance.

* * *

When they returned to the office, Val met them at the back door. "Johnny's in your office, Ike."

"Okay." Here we go again. "Tell him we'll be there in a minute."

Val took off, and Ike turned the deadbolt.

Abby squinted at him. "Why do you think he's here?"

"We'll soon find out." He hoped it wasn't about her father—or her.

Johnny was standing by a bookshelf, looking at photos of Ike and Mallory back when they were a happy couple.

"Hey, Johnny." Ike tossed his keys onto the desk.

"Ike." Then Johnny nodded to Abby.

She smiled. "Johnny."

Ike held the private investigator's eye. "So, what's up, my friend? You've been a real regular around here lately."

"Yeah, but I wish I didn't have to come in with this news."

Ike and Abby exchanged looks—and waited.

The private investigator motioned to the chairs. "Please, come on, both of you, have a seat."

Eyeing the private investigator steadily, Ike sat. Abby too.

"I was listening to my police scanner today, and I picked up a sketchy transmission from a patrol unit in Delavan, Wisconsin, which is just over the Illinois border, about a car crash. I couldn't make out much of the call, but it sounded like a pretty bad one." Johnny glanced from Ike to Abby. "But then..." He pursed his lips. "...the scanner came in clear, and they reported that a man named Lakota Holt was killed in the crash."

Ike and Abby sat silently.

Johnny shook his head. "I know, it's a shocker."

Ike slammed his hand on the desk. "Pharamundo got to him. That's all there is to it."

Abby put a hand to her mouth.

The private investigator spoke softly. "The cop on the scanner was calling it an accident."

Ike stood. "It was no accident, Johnny. No. No way. Plain as day, they murdered him."

Chapter Fifteen

Ike and Abby did what they could to find out about the crash, but for two weeks their calls to the Delavan Police Department were stonewalled. The cop who filed the accident report kept putting them off until finally saying, "Look, I'm busy with important things. Why don't you call my supervisor!" So Ike did, but the supervisor was unavailable. So Ike left a message, that wasn't returned. He left several more. Finally, threatening to sue and go to the media, he got a copy of the accident report.

The report was poorly done. Scribbled like a six-year-old wrote it. It said Lakota was alone in the vehicle and pronounced dead at the scene. The vehicle wasn't examined. No witnesses interviewed. Nearby homes weren't canvassed. It had only the most rudimentary diagram of the scene. Only one photo. In short, the officer doing the report did a lousy job. Either that, or Delavan's protocol for accident investigations was incredibly substandard. Probably both. Worse yet, the medical examiner officially designated the crash an accident and refused the request to perform an autopsy. When Ike and Abby pressed the district attorney to intervene, she said the police and medical examiner had conducted a satisfactory investigation and the matter was closed.

Seeing no way forward, Ike and Abby were resolved that if it ever came to a trial, they would explore every option, including pushing for the Cook County prosecutor to file charges there instead of in Walworth County, Wisconsin.

At that point, only a tip via email kept their hopes alive. It was anonymous, sent from a burner email address.

THE PERFECT PROSECUTOR

Check the car's brakes.

That afternoon, Abby came into Ike's office excited. She'd located the tow truck yard where Lakota's Corolla was being stored. She set a yellow sticky note with the details onto his desk.

Ike put a forefinger to his cheek and stared at the note. Finally, he looked up, and a quote from Cervantes, on a placard on his desk, caught his eye. *In order to attain the impossible, one must attempt the absurd.* It seemed appropriate for what they were facing.

He grabbed the note and picked up the phone.

It was a huge risk. He told the manager of the tow truck company yard that his brother had died in the crash and that he wanted to know what his brother had experienced in his final moments by examining the wreck. To show his appreciation for granting the favor, Ike offered the man five hundred dollars. After that, the manager was quick to oblige, and he set up a time to corral the guard dogs in the yard and leave the gate unlocked.

Thank goodness Ike's mechanic, Ken, was slow business-wise. He said he could accompany them. Ike informed him that the Corolla needed to be inspected due to an insurance company lawsuit as to the cause of the crash. There'd been a fatality, so millions of dollars were at stake, and the insurance company on the other side would dearly want to know what his inspection yielded, so could he keep this under wraps? He could. Ike handed the mechanic three crisp one-hundred-dollar bills. "Consider this a thank you for your time," he said, lowering his voice. "No need to mention this to anyone, all right?" Sure, the mechanic understood.

* * *

They set out for the tow truck yard on a sweltering morning, the cumulus clouds already mushrooming high in the sky. Ike drove himself, Abby, and Ken. He considered telling Bree Wilson about it but figured the fewer people responsible for what they were about to do, the better. It was a ninety-minute drive from White Pines to Delavan. Ike explained to Ken that he wanted just a general inspection of the Corolla. (He didn't mention checking the brakes, not yet anyway.) That explanation took about five minutes. The rest of the trip was pretty quiet. The rolling hills and lush countryside were beautiful, but in Ike's amped-up state of mind he couldn't appreciate the scenery.

The GPS locator said they were less than a mile away and instructed them to take a gravel road—which wound through a grove of runty, half-dead trees—until they arrived at the yard.

"Wow," Abby said in a scratchy voice. She cleared her throat. "This looks like redneck city."

A rust-pitted sign on the chain-link gate read KEE-SHAWN 24 HOUR TOWING & RECOVERY. A sign alongside it warned DO NOT ENTER. Added to those were several BEWARE OF DOG signs. Behind the rusted fence stood a sun-faded, two-story wooden structure. Large white numerals, "404," were painted on the building's exterior, the paint washed out by time. A stack of damaged eighteen-wheeler chassis sat next to, and in places leaned against, the building.

The plan was for Ken and Ike to enter the yard, and Ken would do the inspection. Then they'd get the hell out. Abby would stay in the car on the other side of the gate and honk if trouble arose.

The men walked cautiously to the fence. With all the beware of dog signs, Ike couldn't help but wish he'd brought along his Raging Judge Magnum revolver. Only a massive sidearm would be able to take down these potentially fearsome beasts. The gate, as promised, was unlocked and they entered. Then they heard it. A rumbling emerging from the 404 building, escalating into a snarling, culminating in ferocious barking as the dogs within sensed their presence. Soon, concussive *thumps* sounded through the humid air like low-energy shock waves, and the building shook, suggesting the dogs were slamming their chests into its rickety walls.

"Ken." Ike checked to make sure he had his phone. "I don't want to stay here any longer than we have to."

The mechanic, a sheen of sweat already forming on his forehead, slipped on a pair of rubber gloves. "Believe me, I'm with you on that."

The Corolla had plummeted down a gully and smashed into a tree, and in the process, the engine had been pushed substantially back into the car. From a distance, the Corolla looked like half a car. Ike's anger flared thinking that Pharamundo, no, that some individual within the company, might have done this to Lakota.

Ken made quick work of his inspection. Right off, he said, "I don't have to tell you that this car is totaled and would be a complete write-off for the insurance company. If anything, it's worth maybe five hundred bucks for scrap metal. Maybe." He leaned into the open driver's side window. "This was one hell of a wreck. Do you know what happened?"

"That's what I was hoping you might tell me."

The mechanic shrugged. "Well, obviously the guy lost control. Why is anybody's guess."

The thumping intensified from the 404 building. Ike checked his watch. The manager said they had a half hour. If those dogs got loose...

"It's too bad, Ike. I could've told you what I did just from photographs. It's a shame we had to come all the way out here." He cast a nervous glance at the building.

Ike crossed his arms, the cryptic message from the burner email *Check the car's brakes* preoccupying him. "But what about the inside?"

"Totally worthless. Nothing salvageable. Like I said, maybe five hundred bucks for scrap metal."

Ike had hoped Ken would've examined the brakes as a matter of course and time was running out. "Think you could get a look at the brakes?"

The mechanic, sweat stains forming at the armpits and neckline, again checked the quaking walls of the 404 building. "Uh, I'd have to crawl in from the passenger side to get any kind of look at them."

Ike bit his lip. "I'd appreciate it."

One last glance at the building, and the mechanic rounded the front of the car and struggled to squeeze through the passenger window.

The Lexus' horn started honking.

Ike couldn't see the car from where he stood. He grabbed his phone. "Yeah, Abby."

"Ike, a pack of dogs is out here. They're all over, jumping on the hood, super aggressive."

"I'll call when we're about to leave." He noticed the time and ended the call. Damn it—they were there longer than a half hour. He was ready to tell Ken to give it up, the guy cramped in the crumpled wreck in the 95-degree heat.

"Hey, Ike?"

Ike ran to the passenger window. "Yeah, Ken, what?"

The mechanic lay with his head on the car's floorboard. "Ike?"

"I'm here. I'm here. What?"

"I really think somebody may have remotely hacked this car's onboard computer."

Ike touched the car's windshield pillar and yanked his hand back—the metal was scorching. "Okay. Why do you say that?"

"Because the brake pedal is damaged, and it's not from the impact of the crash. The driver likely pushed down on the pedal with such force it even left an impression on the floorboard. And the parking brake is jammed and mangled, meaning the brakes were probably disabled in the hack, and the driver smashed the brakes with his feet but even so was unable to stop the car. And look here." He pointed to what was left of one of the seats. "There was so much smoke residue from the engine block that the residue is even on what's left of the seats in the interior. This engine was definitely massively overworked."

"What does that mean, Ken?"

A drop of sweat dripped from the tip of the mechanic's nose into his eyes. He blinked hard a few times. "Well, the hack likely boosted the accelerator, forcing the engine to work much harder than it was originally meant to. And so the car accelerates wildly while the poor guy has no brakes. From the damage the brakes show, he must've tried everything he could to stop it before he crashed."

Damn. Somebody did kill him. "Okay, Ken. Now, come on, let me help you out of there." Ike leaned in and guided the mechanic's head away from the sharp metal jutting from the dash.

"Thanks, yeah. I'm good now." The mechanic managed to get into a sitting position. From there he muscled himself out of the passenger window. He removed his gloves and stuffed them in his back pocket, rivulets of sweat flooding down his face. "Unbelievable. Somebody hacked the car to make it crash, which would actually mean that they—"

"Come on," Ike said loudly over the thumping. "We'll talk in the car."

The men crept past the 404 building, then upped it to a silent trot, Ike pulling out his phone and hitting Abby's speed dial button. "They still there?"

"I haven't seen them for a while. Hurry."

The men bolted for the car.

* * *

Ike dropped off the mechanic, and when he and Abby arrived at the office, Val was again waiting for them at the back door.

"I'm so sorry to keep bothering you." She sighed. "But we've been getting calls on a home for sale…being sold by your real estate company."

Abby squinted at the secretary. "What? We have no listings."

"All right. Okay," Ike said. "Let's stay calm here. I think I know what may have happened."

Val nodded. "Herschel took one of your FOR SALE signs from the basement."

"Exactly."

Abby rolled her eyes. "Oh God, this is getting ridiculous."

"Val, see if you can get him in here, will you?"

"You got it." She headed up front.

"Never a dull moment, huh, Abby?"

She closed her eyes and shook her head. "I'm speechless. The nerve of the man is endless."

He took her hand and walked with her to his office. "Don't worry. We'll straighten him out. In the meantime, we need to figure out what to do with what we just learned."

"Sure, but give me a couple of minutes here, okay? The man has me reeling."

He offered her a drink.

"I don't need it." She sat in one of the chairs by his desk, took off her glasses, and rubbed her eyes. "I just can't believe what he's doing."

Ike sat across from her. "Well, you have to admit, he is a self-starter."

"Yeah right," she said in a defeated tone. "He hasn't even taken his first real estate class yet."

After a few minutes, he caught her eye. "You good?"

"Yeah, okay."

"What's been going through my mind is that our visit to Lakota's wreck has painted us into a corner. I didn't think through how it would play out. See, we should've gone to Ursula first and asked her to open an investigation. As it is, when she does—if she does—the first thing she's going to want is verification that there's been no tampering with the evidence, which is basically what we just did."

"So what are our options?"

"Well." He put his hands behind his head. "We can pay Ursula a visit and fess up, but she's going to want to know how we got into the tow truck yard."

"And?"

"Well, Ken, the mechanic, I think I can keep out of it, but I don't know about the tow truck yard manager."

Abby tinkered with the placard on his desk. "What if we don't go to her? With what Lakota told us about how financially devastating having the drug released would be, we've already got a solid motive. Can't we do our own investigation?"

He scratched his chin. "Not if Ursula hasn't authorized it, but even if we did, our investigative resources pale compared to the State's Attorney's Office. Thing is, if we go to her, or if we don't go to her and she ends up opening an investigation on her own, she's going to demand to know how we got in there, and when she finds out, that could get ugly for us."

Abby pushed the placard away.

"Unless." He glanced at her.

"Unless what?"

The intercom on his desk buzzed. He jabbed a button. "Yeah, Val?"

"Herschel Blum is here."

Ike widened his eyes at Abby. "Send him back."

Abby sat up. "Ike, do most of the talking, okay? He just gets me too wound up."

"I got this."

Herschel charged into the room, all smiles that quickly faded. "Hey, why the long faces? Did somebody die?"

Ike wasn't playing games with him. He stood. "Herschel, the office has been getting calls on a home for sale—a home that *you're* selling."

Abby's father turned to the front, then turned back. "That's funny; Val didn't mention them to me."

Ike glanced at the ceiling, then at the older man. "Herschel, you're not *allowed* to sell real estate yet. You selling real estate at this point is *illegal*. You don't have your license yet."

"Oh, yeah, yeah. All that. I'll get it soon enough, but I figured while I was waiting, I could still stir up a little business." He winked. "You know, make us all a little something."

"And how were you planning on selling the home without being able to put it on the Multiple Listing Service?"

He threw up his hands. "Simple. I steer the listing to you, which I was going to do today. You're a broker so you can list it. Then maybe you kick a little something back to me. You know—win-win. Didn't Val tell you?"

"Herschel, Val would never tell me that."

Abby's father turned toward the front again. "Val!"

Ike touched the older man's shoulder. "You didn't tell Val that."

"Well…" Herschel shuffled his feet, avoiding Ike's gaze. "…I guess it's possible that it slipped my mind."

"Herschel, now listen very carefully to what I'm about to tell you because you need to extricate yourself from this mess. You need to immediately yank the FOR SALE sign from the property and tell the owner a conflict came up and you won't be able to sell the house."

"You want me to kick the business to the curb?"

Ike had to think about that. He could really use the listing and the commission money, not to mention the closing costs. But too many ethical lines had already been crossed, and his experience told him that would eventually catch up with him. "Herschel, believe me, I'm all for making money, but it's got to be done the right way."

The older man's chin dropped. "Okay, Ike, you're the boss. You got it. I'll get the sign and tell the guy." He nodded to Abby and started out of the office.

"Be patient," Ike called after him. "When you get your license, things will really open up for you."

When Herschel got to the front, he stopped and gave Val a hug.

Ike smiled. "Your father is definitely an original."

"Okay, sure. Anyway, thanks for talking to him."

"But will he listen? That's the question."

"We shall see." She nodded. "Now I was thinking about what you said about Ursula…"

"Right…" He had to think. "…yeah…Ursula…"

"You said that even if she opens an investigation, she's going to want to know how we got into the tow truck yard, and when she finds out, that could get ugly for us *unless*…"

"Right. That could get ugly for us unless, like I said, we go to her and flat-out tell her the truth."

Chapter Sixteen

In the morning, Ike made an appointment to talk to Ursula. He decided to speak with her alone to leave Abby out of it in case things went south. On the drive there, he wondered if he was doing something stupid. If upon hearing the truth, Ursula stuck it to him, he could be censured, suspended, or even disbarred. And considering how judges love to make a show of holding attorneys to higher standards, he could even wind up in jail.

It wasn't a good sign, either, that Ursula made him wait two hours to see her. Finally, the secretary nodded for him to enter.

He'd visited Ursula before, but not since she'd been elected State's Attorney. Her new office was three times the size of the old one and furnished with deeply polished cherry wood cabinets that contrasted pleasantly with a gleaming mahogany desk. Her desk chair and chairs in front featured bookkeeper-green accents.

Ike put out his hand. "Thank you for seeing me, Ursula. I know how busy you must be."

The State's Attorney had neatly styled reddish hair with just the tiniest hints of gray at the roots. She wore a yellow blazer over a purple top and a single strand of pearls. She stayed sitting at her desk. "Indeed, Mr. Thompson," she, originally from the deep south, said in her folksy drawl, but she didn't shake Ike's hand.

The implication was clear—she was holding a grudge. Most likely from his aggressive closing argument, questioning her integrity, in the arson case when they'd last faced off in court. Most likely adding to her irritation, she'd eventually charged Nick Hendrickson, the person Ike and Abby had pointed to as the arsonist, for the crime. Ike wondered if he should cut his losses, turn on his heel, and walk out? But then he thought of Lakota's crumpled car and of Bree's son wasting away, and he decided to roll the dice.

He laid everything out for her, including Bree's pursuit of the curative drug from Pharamundo. He told her Bree had reason to believe Pharamundo had the drug but refused to release it for economic reasons. Of how Pharamundo got Lakota Holt fired from his newspaper job and then of the "accident" causing his death. Wasn't it obvious that Pharamundo had a motive for murdering the young reporter because he got too close to ending their cash cow?

Ike owned up to bribing the tow truck yard manager. He admitted having a mechanic examine the wreck. He explained there was no other way to have it looked at because of the stonewalling by the Delavan Police. In other words, he'd done what he thought was right under the circumstances. He'd done what he'd done in the pursuit of justice. And his actions, while wrong, had likely uncovered that a murder had taken place and that a murderer was out there on the loose. Would she help him? Would she open an investigation?

"Well." Ursula folded her hands on the desk. "So, you did what you did in the pursuit of justice, did you?"

Ike had heard that scathing tone of voice from her before and knew better than to answer. That was just a preamble.

"You had difficulty gaining access to examine the vehicle. And so, *in the pursuit of justice*, you neglected requesting a judge's authorization to examine it, and instead, you, an officer of the court, committed a Class 2 felony by bribing the tow truck yard manager. Would that be an accurate assessment of the situation, Mr. Thompson?"

Once on a first-name basis, he now knew to stay silent.

"And now, correct me if I'm wrong, but you'd like me to say that I certainly don't like your methods, and I think it was wrong for you to break the law, but like you, I too am a believer in the pursuit of justice, and like you, I don't want another murderer out on the streets, so I'll, well, look the other way this time. Just this time, though, and don't do anything like this again, okay? Is that what you were expecting to hear, Mr. Thompson?"

Ike bit his lip.

"Because if it was, I'm afraid you'll be most disappointed with my response. As you said, so brilliantly in your compelling closing argument in the Hendrickson case, 'the wheels of justice turn slowly.' And the sad fact, Counselor, as I'm sure you're well aware, is that there are thousands of murderers out on the streets that need to be brought to justice. Does the urgency to do so invalidate our ethical responsibility as officers of the court? Does it mean we can break the law because we're trying to do the right thing? It does not. Sir, you chose speed over legality. Facility over integrity. Justice obtained outside of the rule of law is not justice. It's vigilantism. And vigilantism is a crime."

Ike just told himself to breathe.

Ursula crossed her arms. "Now what I *should do* is turn you over to the ARDC, and almost certainly they will suspend your law license and may well disbar you. Instead…" She narrowed her eyes at him. "…I'm going to recommend that, despite your inexcusably unethical actions, that the commission take into consideration that what you did ultimately may begin the process of bringing a murderer to justice. I will suggest, but offer no guarantees, that you be allowed to continue to practice law because of your knowledge regarding and perhaps beneficial involvement in this case. I will also recommend that you attend an attorney's professional ethics program and be fined ten thousand dollars. Do you have any questions?"

Ike stood. "No, State's Attorney. Thank you."

* * *

Back in the office, Ike asked Val if she was okay with him talking to her computer geek son, Tommy. The secretary said, sure, and actually thought that now might be a good time to get him because he was hanging out at a comic book store in nearby Bensenville. Ike asked if it would be okay if Abby and he swung by there. He explained about the remote computer hack of Lakota's car leading to the fatal crash and thought Tommy might be able to explain how it happened. Val texted her son and heard back right away.

"He said no problem but that he'd only be there another hour." She laughed. "But if I know my son, he'll be there till they close the place."

As Ike and Abby drove to the store, he explained what had gone down at Ursula's. He said she was bitter, even remembering specifics from his closing argument in the Hendrickson arson case, but considering what she could've done to him, he felt she'd been damn lenient. Even so, she hadn't committed to opening an investigation into Lakota's death. He knew she was overwhelmed with cases to be investigated, so who knew how long it would take her to move on it? Who knew how long it would take her to do anything? So, they'd at least come somewhat clean with her. Now it was a question of keeping their efforts rolling and their ads looking for disgruntled Pharamundo employees running. But their first priority had to be finding the person who sent the burner email about checking the brakes of Lakota's wreck.

Ike slowed as they neared the store. "The online map said the Comic Book Emporium was on the left side of the street."

"There, Ike. Next to the hot dog place."

He turned into the crowded strip mall lot.

Posters were plastered over every inch of the store's windows. Superheroes swooping, flying, saving the earth from asteroids, aliens, and who knew what else. The sign on the front door stood out from the posters. OLD AND NEW COMICS SOLD HERE. Ike wondered if that meant used and new comics, but he wasn't going to pursue the question because he wouldn't be buying either. And if the ARDC levies the ten grand fine, he wouldn't be buying anything at all for the foreseeable future. The transom window above the door held an air conditioner running hard and leaking sporadically in the heat, so they had to time their entry to stay dry.

Inside, a young couple sat at a card table near the window, staring at their phones, and a man stood near a wall of comics stacked up to the ceiling in a haphazard arrangement. Ike wondered how anyone could reach the top comic books. The man turned, and Ike realized it was Tommy. The teenager had sprouted up. He wore his shaggy brown hair to the top of his glasses, a long-sleeved white shirt, and blue jeans with a belt that had somehow missed one of the loops.

"Hey, Tommy."

"Oh, hey, Mr. Thompson."

Ike held his hand out to Abby. "Do you remember Ms. Blum?"

The boy blushed. "Sure, yeah, I think."

Abby smiled. "Hi, Tommy."

"Look, Tommy. I know you're having fun, so I'll ask you straight out. Could you help us find somebody online again like you did when you found that guy in the self-harm chat room?"

The teenager leaned into one hip. "Yeah, maybe. What's up?"

Ike explained about the remote hack of Lakota's car, the crash, and the mysterious email. "Could you find the guy who sent the email?"

"Well, it's pretty clear the guy's a hacker."

"Right."

As the teenager stared at the patchwork of posters on the window, the drone of the air conditioner seemed to grow louder. He tilted his head. "And if the guy was able to pull off a remote hack, he's a pretty phenomenal hacker because remote hacks are almost impossible to do. And phenomenal hackers are just about impossible to track down unless you're like the FBI or something. But for somebody like me, no."

"The local police wouldn't be able to?"

"No, not really. The only way guys like that would get caught would be if they made mistakes. But guys with that skill level generally don't do that."

Abby stepped up. "What about the burner email message?"

The teenager blushed again. "Uh, that really won't help. I mean, I can try to find the guy, but chances are it would take a really long time. I'd have to do a ginormous amount of research, study the guy and figure out how he thinks. Study his programs and code. Only after that, you'd try hunting down his IP address and looking for any mistakes he might've made. You'd have to hang out in hacker forums and hope some guys there might—it takes time to build trust—give you tips on how to find the guy."

"But you'll try?" Abby smiled.

The teenager attempted to hold back a smile of his own. "I'll see what I can do."

Chapter Seventeen

A week went by, and there'd been no effort on Ursula's part to open an investigation into Lakota's murder. Another week that Oliver sank closer to death. A police investigator hadn't gone to the tow truck yard to examine the crash. Absolutely no evidence was collected. The only things coming in were the hefty fees for the social media ads Ike and Abby were running. Then one day they hit on the idea of doing a press conference to bust things wide open.

Ike figured the only way to hook the media's attention was to provide graphic details about the crash, so instead of scheduling the press conference in a hotel ballroom, he contacted the tow truck yard manager again and persuaded him that holding the press conference in the yard would be free TV advertising. Ike even got him to build a makeshift podium from which he could speak.

Ike and Abby searched every possible media outlet they could think of and sent out a press release: "A shocking turn of events: how a car accident became a murder investigation." They gave the reporters one week's notice. They knew that they were playing with fire with Ursula, but they also felt they had to because she was doing nothing.

The day of the press conference arrived, and they trekked back out to Delavan.

The tow truck yard manager met them at the gate, a rottweiler lying in the dust thirty feet or so behind him. The man reminded Ike of photographs of the early twentieth-century lawyer Clarence Darrow. The man had the same broad forehead and piercing eyes. His hair was sparse and stringy and plastered to his forehead in the sweltering heat. He wore a mangy white dago-tee, sweated through, and the pronounced veins in his biceps showed he was no stranger to hard manual labor. Fortunately, the rottweiler seemed more interested in a fast-food wrapper than what was happening at the gate.

The manager called to someone who whistled, and the dog bounded away. He opened the gate and walked Ike and Abby to Lakota's wreck, where he'd stacked five wooden pallets as a makeshift podium. Ike climbed aboard to test its stability and noticed a news van kicking up dust as it barreled down the gravel road toward the yard. Satisfied the pallets would hold, he jumped down, and he and Abby made their way back to the Lexus and waited for the designated start time.

Abby swiveled around in her seat. "Some of them are coming really early, don't you think?"

"They have to set up with their lights and microphones and all. Testing everything to get their specs right."

"I suppose." She slid her hand behind his neck. "Are you nervous?"

"No, I'm good."

Her eyes shifted to the yard. "Oh look, the reporters with their microphones are taking turns being filmed in front of Lakota's wreck."

Eventually, ten or twelve reporters gathered around the pallets. No national networks showed, but there was one Chicago network affiliate. Ike had hoped for better attendance. The agreed-upon start time came and went as he held out for latecomers.

"Ike, they're staring at us."

They headed to the podium. Ike clambered up the pallets and did his best to look beyond the bright lights to survey the reporters. "Thank you all for coming. Especially in this heat." He rolled up his shirt sleeves and pointed to the Corolla. "As you can see, this car has been in a vicious crash. As the press release indicated, the local authorities first classified the crash as an accident, and it was only with the involvement of the Cook County, Illinois, State's Attorney that it became designated a murder. The victim, award-winning investigative reporter Lakota Holt, was alone in the car, which was not hit by another vehicle, nor was Lakota shot or stabbed, so you may be asking, how can this possibly be considered a murder?"

"Exactly," called a young reporter in a plaid shirt, holding a digital recorder high.

Ike widened his eyes at the reporter. "Well, it can because a hacker on the dark web remotely hacked the car's onboard computer while Lakota was driving, the hack boosting the car's accelerator and disabling its brakes, making it impossible to control the car. And all that in hopes of making the crash appear to be an accident.

"Lakota Holt was investigating a Fortune 500 pharmaceutical company, alleging that it was involved in massive fraudulent activity. It is the Cook County State's Attorney's speculation that a highly placed individual within the company hired the hacker to rig Lakota's car to stifle his investigation. The State's Attorney requests that anyone with information regarding this cowardly crime come forward. Thank you."

The reporters shouted questions, but one voice rose above the others. "Are any suspects in custody?"

"Not at this time."

Someone else shouted, "What's the name of the pharmaceutical company?"

"I'm not at liberty to disclose that at this time."

The young reporter in the plaid shirt again. "Why did the company want him dead?"

"As mentioned, the Cook County State's Attorney speculates it was to stop the investigation into the company's fraudulent activity." He pointed to a reporter dressed smartly in a purple blazer, her hair and makeup perfectly composed despite the heat.

The woman held up a pen. "Was *Mr. Holt* involved in any illegal activities? Did he have connections to the mob?"

A bead of sweat slipped down Ike's temple and collected in his ear. "Absolutely no to both questions. As I mentioned, Mr. Holt was an award-winning journalist with a stellar reputation." He pointed to someone else, but the woman in the blazer shouted another question.

"Did *Mr. Holt* frequent the dark web himself? Did he use bitcoin to make illegal payments or purchases there?"

Ike's heart rumbled in his chest. He ignored the questions and pointed to a woman in a green and white checked sleeveless dress.

"Is there any danger to the public that the hacker might strike again?"

"That's certainly a possibility and one of the reasons we're asking people to come forward with information. Thank you all very much." He jumped down from the pallets and, ignoring the questions from the reporters trailing him, hustled with Abby back to the Lexus.

* * *

Ike and Abby were barely rolling away from the tow truck yard when Ike's phone rang. He checked the caller ID on the dash. Ursula. He widened his eyes at Abby as his hand crept toward the Answer button. "This is Ike Thompson."

"Thompson, a staffer just notified me of your press conference. *Your* press conference. Your unauthorized press conference. And your speaking for me during your unauthorized press conference, casting aspersions against a Fortune 500 company. Thompson, *at the very least*, your actions have jeopardized my ability to do my job effectively and could damage this case and prejudice the jury. I promise you, there will be consequences." *click*

They rode along in silence for an hour.

Finally, Ike said, "Well."

Abby smoothed her hand over his shoulder. "We had to do something. Ursula has done absolutely nothing. Now at least people are hearing about it."

"I'm sure Pharamundo is hearing about it too."

"They knew about it from our ads, but yeah, they know about it big-time now. And we should be getting some interviews from those ads now too."

Ike merged onto the interstate. "But is this a good thing that we're doing, Abby? I don't know about you, but I hadn't even considered that turning the ignition could blow us up. Next time, I might think twice."

She checked her phone. "Ike, there's an email from a gobbledygook email address again. Another one of those burner disposable ones, I think. The subject heading says, 'You got it wrong.'"

"Well, open it."

She read the email aloud. "I'm no coward. They lied to me. I never meant to hurt anyone. Under the right conditions, I'll help."

"That's it?"

THE PERFECT PROSECUTOR

"Yes."

He reached for the dash display, tapped PHONE, then TOMMY. The phone started ringing. "Tommy, it's Mr. Thompson."

"Oh, hey."

"I think we may have a breakthrough with the hacker."

"Yeah, I'm sorry, Mr. Thompson, but that guy is buried deep. Pretty untouchable. I couldn't find any mistakes he'd made, and he must have a pretty good reputation in the hacker forums because nobody would help me find him."

"I appreciate your efforts, Tommy, I do, but what I'm trying to tell you is that the hacker contacted us."

"Yeah?" The teenager's voice came through the car's speakers a little crackly.

Ike leaned into the steering wheel. "And he said he didn't mean to hurt anybody."

"Ah, he's probably a gray-hat hacker, then."

"Gray hat, Tommy?"

"Yeah, gray-hat hackers are between white and black-hat hackers. White-hat hackers hack places but only to help them improve their security. Black-hat hackers are the bad guys, stealing data, ransomware, DDoS attacks, all that. Gray-hat hackers are somewhere in between. Not completely ethical but not completely…"

Ike looked at the dash. "That last didn't come through, Tommy. Gray-hat hackers are somewhere in between. Not completely ethical but not completely…"

"Uh, they're not all bad."

Ike glanced at Abby. "So the hacker might've been telling the truth about not wanting to hurt anyone?"

"Yeah, but at the same time, the guy's a hacker, right? They're generally not the most truthful."

Ike nodded. "I hear what you're saying."

"How did you hear from him?" The teenager sounded genuinely curious.

"Email, from one of those disposable email addresses. So, Tommy."

"I'm here."

Another glance at Abby. "How do we contact him back?"

"Uh, you return his email."

Abby spoke up. "That will work even with a disposable email address?"

"It should, yeah."

* * *

Ike and Abby waited till they got back to the office to return the hacker's email. They settled in at Ike's desk, and he opened his laptop. The hacker had said he'd help under the right conditions, so their reply was simple.

What are the right conditions?

They got no answer, so Abby returned to her office.

A half hour later, an email popped up. Ike called Abby back in.

Total immunity. Get me that and I'll tell you everything.

"Well." Abby shifted from one foot to the other. "At least he knows what he wants."

Ike raised his eyebrows. "So…"

"So…Ursula."

"Exactly." He searched her eyes. "I suppose now we have to let her know."

"Uh, I would say so, yes."

"Both of us on a conference call? Right now? Go for broke? Are you up for it?" He tapped his teeth together.

"Not really, but I suppose if we have to, we might as well get it over with." She sat and nodded at the desk phone.

"Or maybe we should engage the hacker first?" He lurched back in his chair. "I mean, what if after hearing us, Ursula shuts us down? Or who knows how she'll respond to the hacker? I say, let's at least contact him first and see what he has to say."

Abby shrugged. "I don't know, Ike. On this one I'd say it's your call."

He pulled the laptop close. "What do you think? Something simple?"

She leaned in. "Yes, just say the immunity may take a while but it's doable, and we'll get back to him when we know more."

He typed and hit the Send key. "Now, what the hell, let's bite the bullet and call Ursula."

She grabbed the edge of the desk.

"I'm just concerned that if we tell her too soon…" He rubbed his temples, the lines on his forehead deepening.

"You're overthinking it, Ike. You obviously want to call, so go for it."

"Right." He pressed Ursula's preset and put his phone on speaker. He was amazed that she picked up.

"State's Attorney, it's Ike Thompson."

"I can see that."

"You're on speakerphone." He glanced at Abby. "Attorney Blum is here with me."

Ike told her what happened with the hacker.

They waited for her reaction.

"Well," Ursula began. "Thank you. It seems you've made this easy for me. Not that you were ever officially *on* this case, but now you're officially *off* it. Any questions?"

Ike smirked. "No, State's Attorney."

The line went silent.

Ike laid his head on the desk. When he raised up, he said, "Forget her. Let's try to get in touch with the hacker again before he goes dark."

"Ike, might that not be a bit reckless? She's the State's Attorney for all of Cook County, after all."

"Well." His gaze shifted from the documents piled on his desk to the window, where saturated, rain-filled clouds were drifting by. "What about why we got involved with this in the first place? Bree and Oliver? I mean, at this point, hasn't this thing become bigger than Ursula?"

"Hey." She shrugged. "You know I'm all for helping Bree and Oliver. I'm just saying it would be a huge gamble going any further without Ursula involved."

"But isn't all of life a gamble, Abby? Crossing the street is a gamble. So, Ursula might burn us or she might not. My father always used to say, 'Don't worry about maybe problems.'"

Abby laughed softly. "Maybe problems, Ike?"

"So what do you think?" He abruptly stood, causing his chair to screech against the floor. He locked eyes with her. "Really, where do you think we should go with this? We need to decide now or the hacker may go cold."

She bit her lip and looked away, while her fingers drummed a quiet rhythm on the desk. Finally, she glanced at him, exhaled slowly, and nodded. "Contact him."

He sat and logged back in. "For now, I think we play it cool and stay away from asking who hired him."

"I agree." She smoothed her skirt with one hand while the other adjusted a small placard on the desk. "Don't scare him off."

Ike typed *What more can you tell us?* and angled the laptop so Abby could see.

She leaned closer. "That should be okay."

He hit Send. "Let's hope he's still around."

"Make sure to save these emails."

"They're saved automatically. I just have to make sure not to accidentally delete them. Oh, look, he replied." He clicked on the email.

What more can you tell ME?

"Abby, come sit by me so we can do this together." He waved her over.

She pulled up a chair alongside him.

"That's better." He typed. *The investigation is still in the early stages, but when the time comes, we should be able to get you the immunity. Now, why, may I ask, are you doing this?* He checked with Abby. She nodded and he hit Send.

The reply came quickly. *I told you they lied to me. They said the hack was a demonstration for an insurance company to show the vulnerability of the car's software. I've done the same demonstration before and never had any problems.*

Abby grabbed the laptop and typed. *But you had to trigger the hack when you were told because the car needed to be moving.* Ike tapped the Send key.

The reply took longer this time. *I figured that's when they would be recording the hack. The guy who hired me told me he'd installed a kill switch to power the car down in case of an emergency. I'm telling you the dude lied. He's a psychopath. He killed the guy.*

Abby caught Ike's eye. "Maybe ask who *he* was?"

"I think it's too soon." He pulled the laptop closer. *Thanks for doing the right thing.*

The reply came right back. *Yeah, well, I'm not doing anything until you guarantee me immunity. Don't bother writing back till you do.*

Ike widened his eyes at Abby.

Her forehead wrinkled. "I would have never expected this, especially from a hacker."

"Me neither. I guess some people still have a conscience. Even hackers."

Abby steepled her fingers before her face. "And Ursula…"

"Yeah, well, Ursula. We'll just have to deal with her when the time comes."

She laughed. "And then—if we're not in jail—we'll get jobs waiting tables or driving Ubers when we get disbarred."

"I don't know, Abby. I believe with this new information, we'll have a lot more leverage with her."

She rubbed her chin. "I hope so."

"So." Ike cleared his throat. He waited for her to look at him. "Speaking of waiting tables, want to grab dinner somewhere?"

She offered only a hint of a smile before saying, "Sure, okay."

He exhaled deeply and gazed into her eyes. "Are we good? I didn't pressure you into what we just did?"

She raised her eyebrows slightly. "Actually, you've been pressuring me into a bunch of stuff lately, but yeah, sure, we're good."

He pulled her close and kissed her. "And maybe afterward you could…uh…spend the night?"

"Oh." She closed her eyes and drew back a little. "I'd like to—"

"Then do it. I miss you staying with me. A lot."

She shook her head. "It's really just too much pressure with your wife—"

"Soon-to-be *ex*-wife."

"Yeah, well, that's all well and good, but honestly, until it's official, I can do without the stress." She stood and took a few steps away from him.

He swallowed. What could he say?

"And you know what?" She glanced out of the office before turning back. "After this crazy day, maybe I'm just burned out, I don't know, but for whatever reason, I'm just not feeling it tonight. I'll take a rain check on dinner."

Chapter Eighteen

Abby left, and Ike began his drive home. The evening brought with it a descending haze, thick and polluting. Thank goodness Leaner was waiting for him. Ike went into the backyard with the dog and sat on a deck chair, a worn, yellow tennis ball in his hand. Leaner loved to play fetch, but after a couple of retrievals, he sensed Ike's low mood and plopped down beside him.

"Yeah, buddy." Ike dropped the ball and stroked the dog's head. "Looks like I may have messed things up with Abby. She said she just wasn't feeling it, whatever that means."

A pair of squirrels chased each other up and down the oak tree in the corner of the yard. They normally would have been in mortal peril having entered Leaner's kingdom, but the dog chose to stay by his master's side.

This whole mess, Ike was thinking, started with altruism, and along with that, his losing sight of the most basic fact, namely, that being a sole proprietor meant being an attorney *and* a rainmaker. Okay, sure, it was good that they were trying to help Bree and her kid, but where had that gotten any of them? Lakota dead. False hope for Bree. Ike and Abby's careers on the line. And now Abby's just not feeling it. The haze hung heavy in the air, smothering the sun's last rays.

Abby was right after all. She was smart to stay away. He *was* still married. And God only knew what Mallory was capable of. No wonder Abby was warming up to Johnny.

"Hey, Leaner, what do you think? Is this all just a desperate mess leading to disaster or is there still hope somehow?" The dog nuzzled under his hand. "Yeah, buddy, thank goodness I've still got you. And who the heck knows, this might turn out okay after all, right?" The dog leaned into him. The smell of a neighbor's barbecue wafted into the yard. Ike hugged his dog, then stood. It was time to give him his dinner.

* * *

The social media ads asking for interviews finally paid off. A Pharamundo employee agreed to talk but only at a motel room way out in Dundee, Illinois. The man's email was clear —he demanded complete anonymity. Ike and Abby drove there in the morning. Pointedly, neither spoke of things cooling off between them and instead discussed what to ask the interviewee. They relied on GPS to get there, and as they got closer, they had to drive down a steep, tree-lined road with no guardrails. The motel was a two-story building with a sign that read MOTEL in boldface black letters against a beige background. The sign harmonized with the beige color of the motel room doors, each of which was accompanied by a black plastic chair. A low-slung, vintage, cobalt blue Cadillac with a vinyl roof and whitewalls sat alone in the parking lot.

Abby gathered up her notebook as Ike pulled into the lot. "This should be interesting."

"You've got the payment envelope?"

She held it up as Ike parked next to the Caddy. They walked the few steps to room 8, the intense heat and humidity enveloping them.

A barrel-chested man, possibly in his fifties, with a bushy beard and tinted glasses, opened the door before they knocked. Surprisingly, considering the heat, he wore overalls, a flannel shirt, the sleeves rolled up, and a camouflage hunting cap. By all rights he appeared to be a mountain man, and yet he smelled of fine cologne. His eyes, as best they could see them behind the glasses, surveyed the parking lot, and then he stepped aside for them to enter.

"Thank you for meeting with us, sir. I'm Ike Thompson, and this is my associate, Abby Blum."

The big man held their gaze in a heavy silence for a long time. Finally, he said, "Mac."

A plastic-framed painting of a fish, hooked on a line and leaping, hung askew over two neatly made twin beds with caramel-colored checkered bedspreads. A modest table and a black plastic chair sat adjacent to a pair of tan cushioned chairs. The room was way too warm and reeked of stale cigarette smoke and Lysol. Grabbing the drapery rods, the man yanked the curtains shut, the brass rings making a zinging sound. He pointed to the chairs.

Abby immediately sat in the plastic chair. The two men joined her in the other chairs.

Early on, Ike realized there would be no point in pressing the man. He could sense from his imposing presence that despite the rustic vibe of his clothing, he was a man of significant intelligence and experience. The man would give what information he would and that would be that.

Abby laid the payment envelope on the table. "You'll be wanting this, I'm sure."

The man slid it back. "Keep it. Now let's get this over with. For starters, before we go any further, this is a one-and-done deal. I'll have no further contact with either of you. Is that understood?"

Ike gave him a thumbs-up.

Abby balanced the notebook on her lap and rummaged for a pen in her pocket. "Could you start by telling us what your experience is like working for Pharamundo?"

"I *was* working for them. I took early retirement."

"Oh, my bad. Was." She jotted it down.

The man crossed his arms, forearms bulging. "There's no sense wasting time. Here's the deal. Pharamundo International has only one god—profit. And the company will do anything to satisfy its god's demands. Sure, on the surface, their PR campaign is lily-white, all about developing new medicines to cure diseases, benefit humanity, all that. But on the inside, the company's soul is black as night, and it has evolved to be that way because of one man—Thomas Acosta."

Ike scooted forward in his chair. "Why did you take early retirement?"

A beeper rang, trilling little chirps. The man snatched it from his belt and squelched it. "Because I had a terrible habit that made the company uncomfortable—I told the truth."

Abby raised her pen. "And that's why you're here today?"

"I'm here because I saw your press conference."

Abby shifted in her chair.

"And I can tell you firsthand that's not the first time Pharamundo has done something like that." He brushed the sweat from his forehead with his shirt sleeve. "Look, I already told you more than I should have. Let's just say that I approve of what you're doing." He stood and stepped toward the door.

Abby jumped up and blocked his path. "Thanks, Mac, but please, can you tell us anything else to help us?"

He glared at her. Finally, he said, "Look, you don't know me. You never saw me before. This conversation never happened. Do you understand what I'm saying?"

"Loud and clear, Mac. Loud and clear." She held the notepad and pen at the ready.

The man tugged on the bill of his cap. "Thomas Acosta is a killer. Yes, he's a billionaire, but what he thrives on is not just money but power, and not just power but domination. He feels no laws, social norms, or ethics apply to him. Family, friends, makes no difference. Others exist only to gratify his desires. Cross him and you'll pay. Cross him enough and he'll kill you.

"So his employees live in mortal terror, and the fear compels them to obey his commands, no matter how unethical. He gets away with it because of the company's legal firepower, deep pockets, and its carefully cultivated and maintained network of corrupt government bureaucrats." He checked his wristwatch, then stared at Abby and then at Ike. He sighed. "That said, there is one thing and one thing only that will put the fear of God into Thomas Acosta—a jury trial. Good luck to you both. Trust me, you're going to need it." He stepped toward the door, and this time Abby slipped out of the way.

"Mac!" Ike called.

The man stopped in the doorway but didn't turn.

"Can we give you an email address? Just in case."

"Just in case what?"

Ike looked down.

Abby grinned. "You know, just in case you ever get lonely and crave some truly delightful company."

THE PERFECT PROSECUTOR

The man turned and glared at her again until finally a faint smile emerged and spread to the corners of his mouth. "Just tell me it."

Abby raised the pen. "It's pretty complicated. I'll write it down for you."

"Just tell me."

Abby did, and the man was out the door.

* * *

On the drive back, Ike and Abby were silent for quite a while.

"A very different kind of guy, don't you think?" Abby said, breaking the quiet. "He dressed like a real hick but seemed sophisticated somehow."

Ike leaned his elbow on the center console. "Did you see his watch?"

"Yeah, it looked like one of those that sell for thousands."

"I'm not sure, but I thought I heard the trace of an accent too."

She adjusted the air conditioning vent upward. "Yeah, and overall, I got the feeling there was a lot more he wanted to tell us."

"Well, the more we learn about Pharamundo, I would think that might be a common occurrence with any interviewee." He upped the cruise control a few miles per hour.

They fell silent again as they rolled past billboard after billboard on the highway.

Eventually, Abby started scrolling through her phone. After a while, she said, "Oh, Ike, you have to hear this."

"What?"

"I searched for *Pharamundo International,* and one of the articles that came up says a drug researcher at the company has gone missing. Says she's a mid-level employee reported missing by her husband, who is also an employee of the company. The woman left no note, and as of now, the police have no reason to suspect foul play is involved. A Pharamundo spokesperson issued a statement: *Pharamundo International is deeply concerned about the disappearance of Elizabeth Castro, a valued member of the company's research team. Castro left work three days ago and has not been seen or heard from since. Pharamundo is working closely with and fully cooperating with law enforcement. The company's concerns are heightened by the fact that Castro has recently experienced mental health issues.*"

"That's weird."

"What?"

Ike pulled into a gas station. "That they would mention mental health issues. You'd have to wonder if that was a mistake or intentional."

"And what about violating HIPAA?"

He put the gear selector into Park. "That too."

"You know what else I think is unusual..." She shifted her knees toward him. "...is that we just got done talking to Mac and now we come across this story. Like they might be connected somehow."

"I suppose there could be a connection." He opened his door, climbed out, then ducked his head back in. "Want anything from the mini mart?"

"Thanks. No, I'm good."

As Ike gassed up the car, the pump nozzle icy in his hand despite the heat, gasoline vapors wrinkling his nose, he thought about the employee's disappearance. Abby might be right—it could be related to their interview with Mac. Oh, it was hardly likely, but plenty of unlikely scenarios had been unfolding lately. He tweaked in the last few spurts of fuel and settled the nozzle in its cradle. He climbed back in. "I certainly think it wouldn't hurt to find out more about this."

"I was just about to say the same thing."

Chapter Nineteen

The Pharamundo employee's disappearance became more widely publicized in the days that followed, her polished corporate headshot, arms confidently crossed, blue business suit, pearls, a warm smile, making its way across the Internet. Ike and Abby repeatedly requested an interview with the woman's husband, Jeffrey Castro, and after a week he finally consented. Oddly, he insisted on meeting in a decaying, abandoned parking lot in a dead shopping mall at midnight. Ike and Abby shored up their questions and met him the following night, Abby joking that they should ask him if he was a vampire.

The attorneys arrived first, estimated the center of the parking lot, and waited. Heat lightning flashed high in the sky but no rain fell. The Lexus' air conditioning blew cold, but outside it was still steaming, the car's thermometer reading 89. A shadowy, the actual color difficult to discern in the darkness, late-model Audi rolled into the lot and killed its headlights. It parked quite a ways from them, and a man in a light-colored tracksuit climbed out.

"Here we go." Ike jumped out and Abby joined him.

They headed over.

Closer, they could see that the man appeared to be in his mid-40s and had a gray, neatly trimmed goatee with a brown mustache. The man smiled distractedly but didn't offer his hand. "Jeff Castro. Yeah, thanks for coming," he rasped, his voice scratchy like a smoker's.

Abby returned the smile. "Thank *you* for agreeing to meet."

Castro checked over his shoulder and began walking. "I think we should keep moving."

Ike and Abby followed.

Eyes down, hands in his pockets, the man rambled along. "You're probably wondering why I took so long to agree to meet."

Ike was glad he'd worn his gym shoes—walking was unsteady on the chunky, broken-up asphalt. "We're just happy you're here."

"But see, I can tell you why—I finally realized Pharamundo was lying to me." He stopped and rubbed the back of his neck, still avoiding eye contact. "Yeah, they were flat-out lying. They're painting Elizabeth as some sort of gofer, some mid-level researcher. Hell, she's the head of New Drug Development. And now, as if that wasn't bad enough—they're making her out to be some kind of mental defective. My wife's a doctor! She's brilliant! A genius even! Oh, she can be kind of wild, it's true, but that goes with being a genius, doesn't it? And what does blowing off a little steam hurt? The way I see it, for all she's done for Pharamundo, and really the world, she deserves to live any way she wants. What Pharamundo has a problem with is her getting too close to what she knows about Acosta."

Abby held up a hand. "Thomas Acosta, Pharamundo's CEO?"

"Right." He resumed walking. Thunder rumbled in the distance. "He's having them put out press releases like they're concerned she's disappeared, but I'm telling you, something bad is happening, something terrible. Acosta is a vicious person."

Ike swatted at a mosquito buzzing his ear. Sweat was forming on his chest, the back of his legs, his forehead. "Why do you say that, Jeff?"

Castro stopped again and glared at Ike. "Because I know him. I've worked at the damn company for twenty-six years, and I've seen what he's capable of. Hell, I've seen what he's *done*. For the last six months, I've been terrified for Elizabeth and for our son too."

"How old is your boy?"

"He's six." A flash of lightning revealed that the man's eyes were bloodshot.

Ike followed up quickly, "And why would you be worried about *him*?"

"I'm not going there."

"Jeff." Abby took a step ahead and turned to catch his eye. "You say your wife was too close to what Acosta was doing, but LinkedIn shows her job title as a clinical researcher, which would be quite far down the food chain from the CEO."

Castro cackled. Branching lightning spider-webbed across the roof of the sky. He waited out the accompanying thunder. "Pharamundo did that LinkedIn post, not Elizabeth. I *told you*, she's a medical doctor. The head of New Drug Development. She's brilliant. The LinkedIn post is a smokescreen to keep competitors from wooing her away—and learning Acosta's filthy secrets."

Abby adjusted her glasses. "Jeff, do you know who Mac is? He worked at Pharamundo and recently took early retirement."

Castro kicked a chunk of asphalt and almost lost his footing. "No idea. But I can tell you he's nobody important in the company."

THE PERFECT PROSECUTOR

* * *

Back in Ursula's waiting room the next day, Ike and Abby decided to take their shot. Bree's Oliver was going downhill in a hurry, and with the new information gained from Jeff Castro, come hell or high water, they had to bring Ursula into the loop. It was hard not to take personally her making them wait so long, but if they got in at all, it would be sandwiched between her appointments, as a steady stream of lawyers, elected officials, and supplicants traipsed in and out. After two hours, the secretary motioned for them to go in.

Ursula, sitting at her desk, was laser-focused on a laptop screen. Finally, she peered over her glasses, which she always wore perched halfway down the bridge of her nose. "Don't tell me anything I don't want to hear."

Abby stepped forward. "State's Attorney, we have additional evidence in the Lakota Holt murder investigation that we feel may prove incredibly important."

Ursula drilled Abby with a look. "Why, that is remarkable, Ms. Blum, because for the life of me, I am trying to figure out how two attorneys warned from working on this case have somehow come across additional evidence for it. Maybe I'm not seeing something your razor-sharp legal minds are. Please enlighten me as to how that is possible."

"State's Attorney." Abby spoke calmly. "The information basically fell into our laps, and we felt we had a duty to report it."

Ursula crossed her arms. "Right! Evidence fell out of the sky, and now you're just doing your job reporting it. Oh happy day!"

"State's Attorney…" Ike took out his phone and searched for a video. "…a killer—"

Ursula slammed the laptop shut. "No, Thompson. Your courtroom melodrama may work on juries, but it doesn't work here."

Ike's gaze dropped.

"All right, this charade is over." Ursula nodded toward the door.

Ike and Abby had barely made it there when Ursula shouted, "Hold on!" She let out a deep sigh before waving them back in. "What information are you talking about?"

Chapter Twenty

For two weeks, Ike and Abby were stuck in a holding pattern, constrained not only by Ursula's warnings but by the lack of information their searching into Lakota's murder was yielding. They realized Ursula would need more evidence to bring charges, and that she'd have to name a suspect—or suspects as this could actually turn out to be a contract killing. Still, they were grateful she'd heard them out. Even so, as far as they knew, the case lay dead in the water.

At the end of the two weeks, Ike even broached to Abby the possibility of telling Bree there was nothing more they could do to help her. Only a phone message left on the office answering machine after hours sparked hope. Jeff Castro was coming into the office the next day.

* * *

Ike and Abby both arrived at the office early the next morning so as not to miss Jeff Castro if he came early. They discussed what his visit could possibly be about, how they might react to it, and what they'd ask him. Around quarter to ten, Castro breezed in. Ike stood and watched him. The man almost seemed a different person from the shadowy figure they'd encountered in the middle of the night in the shopping mall parking lot. His gray blazer was sharp. He wore an open-collar white shirt. His glimmering wristwatch, blue with multiple dials, messaged that he had money. The only flaws in his otherwise dapper appearance were his bloodshot eyes and jittery demeanor. He checked in with Val at the front desk, and now Ike hurried out to greet him. The men shook hands, and Ike led him to Abby's office and shut the door behind them. Abby, sitting behind her desk, smiled, and the two men sat across from her.

Castro immediately bounced up as if there'd been a spring on his chair. "Look, I didn't exactly come clean with you guys the last time."

"It's okay," Abby said, waving him down. "Just relax."

The man checked behind himself before sitting.

"Abby's right, Jeff. You're among friends."

She gazed at him. "You're here about Elizabeth, aren't you?"

Castro closed his eyes. "Remember I told you that Pharamundo was only paying lip service about wanting to find her?" He opened his eyes. "Well, they still haven't done a thing. All they *have* done is threaten me—relentlessly—if I don't fall in line with what they're ordering me to do. Oh, they don't come right out and command you. They're too sophisticated with their legal team watching over everything, being sure to maintain plausible deniability. But I know what they're doing, and I know that all the threats are ultimately coming down from Thomas Acosta."

Ike leaned an elbow on the armrest. "Abby and I were wondering if the police had informed you of any leads?"

"No, nothing yet. But at least the police are *trying*. I believe that much, anyway. But Pharamundo…" He shook his head.

Abby rested her chin on her hands. "Pharamundo what, Jeff?"

He stared at her and then at Ike. "I think they killed her."

Silence.

"I'm telling you, you don't know what Acosta's like." He put his fingertips to his temples. "If you don't obey his every command, he'll destroy you. So why does anyone work there? Because Pharamundo pays well. That's their hook into you. And after a while, that hook sinks so deep, before you know it, you're thinking, breathing, and dreaming about the company 24/7—and doing things you never would've imagined."

Ike and Abby sat silently.

"I'm ashamed of what I've done working for them. But what I've done was done out of fear for what Acosta would do to my family." His chin dropped to his chest. "And now look what he's done to Elizabeth."

Ike put a hand on the man's shoulder. "What else do you want to tell us, Jeff?"

Castro flashed him a sidelong glance. "Plenty, believe me. But the reality of the situation is that I'm going to need immunity first."

Ike squeezed his shoulder. "We don't have the authority to grant that, Jeff. A prosecutor would have to file a motion with the court requesting it."

"I figured as much." He stood.

"Jeff, relax." Ike patted the man's empty seat. "We can't grant immunity, but there's a workaround for the time being. Do you have a dollar on you?"

Castro gave Ike a dull stare.

Ike stood. "If you give us a dollar to retain us as your law firm, you'll have attorney-client privilege, and whatever you tell us will be just between us. Then ultimately, if any of this ends up in court, we'll go to the prosecutor and try to get you immunity."

A muscle twitched in Castro's cheek. "You're sure about that?"

Ike met his eyes. "A hundred percent sure."

"I mean, are you sure about anything I tell you is just between us? Anything at all?" His voice faded to a hoarse whisper.

Ike nodded. "Anything, Jeff."

Castro looked around the office for a while. He crossed his arms over his chest. Finally, he reached for his wallet, plucked out a dollar bill, and laid the bill on the table.

Ike stashed it in his pocket. "Thank you for the money. I'm pleased to inform you that you have retained us to be your lawyers."

"That's it? It's that easy?"

"Yep."

Castro looked hard at Abby and then at Ike. He bit his lip. "I got the go-ahead from Thomas Acosta to have a hacker rig Lakota Holt's car."

* * *

For three straight afternoons Ike and Abby interviewed Jeff Castro. Legally speaking, he'd essentially confessed to committing murder. But prosecutors often followed the "fry the bigger fish" strategy, letting the small fries off the hook in order to catch the whopper. In other words, if Ursula felt there was a strong chance Thomas Acosta could be convicted, Castro had a shot of being granted immunity. Additionally, as head of Pharamundo's IT department, Castro had access to droves of sensitive data, including emails and text conversations with Acosta. He'd even taped, illegally, some of their phone conversations.

THE PERFECT PROSECUTOR

When Castro would leave for the day, Abby and Ike would discuss what had gone down. They agreed that his willingness to testify against Acosta was likely motivated by him seeking revenge for what he believed was the CEO's role in his wife's alleged death. Ike wasn't thrilled about having to pay even more bills, but he called Johnny Lagattuta and asked him to investigate Elizabeth Castro's disappearance since there wasn't much of a revenge motive for her death without her being dead.

Beyond that, Ike and Abby had doubts as to the timing of Castro's coming forward. They also doubted that Thomas Acosta would have been so lax as to have made incriminating texts, emails, and phone calls. However, the fact that Castro was the head of IT and his wife was the head of New Drug Development were strong indicators that the couple *did* indeed have exceptional access to classified information—and to Acosta. As far as Ike and Abby were concerned, Castro was the smoking gun. What they told Ursula would have to be done in a vague way that didn't violate Castro's attorney-client privilege but at the same time conveyed the urgency and importance of the matter. It would be a high-stakes balancing act, but at least now they felt like they had a real chance of getting her to move.

* * *

Done with the exhaustive interviewing of Jeff Castro and fully prepared to present the fruit of which to Ursula, Ike and Abby nevertheless drove to her office in somber silence since that place had become associated with rejection and humiliation. So, summoning as much courage as they could and armed with their briefcases and laptops as their weapons, they smiled at her secretary and like penitents took their places in the waiting room. In their final discussions before getting in to see her, Ike argued for not mentioning their doubts about the reliability of Castro's information, while Abby thought it incumbent upon them to do so. But in the interest of presenting a unified front, finally she relented. After an hour, the secretary gestured for them to head in.

Ursula wasn't wasting any time. "You have two minutes."

Abby pulled out a chair across from her desk.

"Don't sit." Ursula glared at her.

That did it! Ike was done being pushed around. Ursula had been badgering them for far too long. Let her do her worst. He didn't care anymore. "Look, Ursula, I've had it with your bullying. Did we mess up? Yes. Did we break the rules? Yes. So go ahead and do what you have to do…" He grabbed his phone from his pocket and pulled up the video he'd prepared beforehand. "…but we're attempting to obtain justice for a young reporter heartlessly murdered and…" He hit Play and handed her the phone. "…for a young boy losing his life so that a greedy pharmaceutical company can keep reaping its exorbitant, monopolistic profits."

As she watched the video, the color slowly drained from the State's Attorney's face. Her eyes widened and her breath caught as her office filled with the soft, rhythmic beeping of monitors emanating from the phone's speaker. When the video ended, she blinked once, twice, and set the phone down gently on her desk. She drew a slow breath before meeting Ike's eyes. "All right," she said, her voice a little shaky. She took another breath. "What do you have?"

Chapter Twenty-one

Five weeks later a grand jury indicted Thomas Acosta for first-degree murder. Ike and Abby dashed to the courthouse, where Ursula, in a light gray business suit accessorized with an emerald dragonfly pin, stood on a podium before a bank of microphones. She was flanked by Peter Harkin and other Assistant State's Attorneys. She blinked a few times into the bright lights and adjusted her glasses before reading from a statement.

"Good afternoon. Today, we are announcing charges of first-degree murder against Thomas Acosta, the CEO of Pharamundo International, in connection with the death of investigative journalist Lakota Holt.

"On July 3rd of this year at approximately 10 a.m., Thomas Acosta murdered Lakota Holt by hiring someone to cause his brakes to fail in Walworth County, Wisconsin. Mr. Holt, driving alone, was killed in the horrific automobile crash originally believed to be an accident. Subsequent investigations, however, revealed that the car's online computer system had been remotely hacked forcing the car to crash." She stared out at the reporters. "Clear-cut evidence has been discovered that Mr. Acosta had a strong motive for killing Mr. Holt, who'd been investigating Mr. Acosta's company, Pharamundo International, for fraudulent activity. We have additional evidence that Mr. Acosta, through an intermediary, hired a hacker to rig Mr. Holt's car, causing the fatal crash.

"I'd like to thank the Cook County Sheriff's Office and various police departments for their joint investigative efforts into this heinous, heartless crime. I also extend my deepest sympathies to Mr. Holt's family and friends, who've suffered an immeasurable loss. I would ask that you would respect their privacy and allow them to grieve. Thank you."

A hubbub ensued, with questions shouted melding chaotically until one voice rose above the others.

"Has Acosta been arrested?"

Ursula leaned on the podium. "Yes, he's been arrested and booked and is being held in Cook County Jail awaiting a bail hearing."

An African American reporter waved his hand back and forth. "Will you be asking for a hundred-million-dollar bail?"

Ursula half-smirked as if she'd been anticipating the question. "The nature of the crime and the seriousness of the charges will be thoroughly evaluated, and a bail amount will be requested accordingly."

A reporter in khakis and an aqua-colored shirt, sleeves rolled up, his press pass dangling from his neck, called out, "Will the hacker and the go-between be testifying against Acosta?"

"That information will be revealed at trial."

The African American reporter again. "Is Acosta going to be able to buy his way out of this one like he did his last trial?"

Ursula smirked. "We have strong evidence and will be pursuing justice in this case as we do for every case we handle. Thank you all for coming."

* * *

Ike and Abby had been discussing for a while that if an indictment were handed down against Thomas Acosta, they might request joining the prosecution team for the trial. Ursula, after seeing the video of Oliver, had seemed newly open to their at least limited participation. Nevertheless, her receptivity had a veneer of iciness. So, Ike and Abby carefully crafted an email to her, stating that while they were sure she was the perfect prosecutor for the trial, they nevertheless had a wealth of information and strategies they believed would significantly benefit her chances of winning. Yet the information was too sensitive to be discussed in any other way than in person. Would she be willing to meet them at a restaurant of her choosing?

To their surprise she accepted. They drove out to the restaurant.

The Captain's Table was a sensible choice, as the privacy was exceptional, thanks to the royal blue-upholstered booths and velvet backdrop partitions between tables. A circular fish tank dominated the center of the restaurant, which had a vacation resort vibe. Ike and Abby arrived a half hour early. And waited an hour past the agreed meet time. Which was okay with them. Because this meeting would be critical. This meeting would be everything.

The hostess escorted Ursula to the table.

The State's Attorney didn't apologize for being late. She sat, removed the lemon slice from a glass of water, and took a sip. "So? Here I am." She glanced at Ike and Abby, and then her eyes scanned the place as if looking for a suspect.

A meeting between a prosecutor and defense lawyers could be seen as crossing the line of propriety. Such meetings took place occasionally, but it was a risky scenario with the potential for serious repercussions for both sides. Ike appreciated her offering the olive branch by coming.

"So let's relax," he said. He waved to get a waiter's attention, and they ordered drinks.

Ursula was silent until the waiter left. "Look, I'm thoroughly relaxed, and as you might expect, I don't have a lot of time, so you might as well say what you have to say."

"Sure." Ike looked at Abby and then at the State's Attorney. "We want to be on your prosecution team for the Acosta trial."

"I figured as much," she said barely audibly.

The drinks arrived.

Ike straightened his shoulders. "We'd give you everything we've got."

"We would," Abby added.

"Yes, wonderful, but as you both know, or should if you don't, your best intentions aren't going to be enough. Switching from defense to prosecution necessarily creates major problems." She scoped the place again. "First and foremost, the defense mindset is etched into your brains. It's hard to overcome. You're used to defending, to finding flaws in the prosecution's case. To seeing the trial from the defendant's perspective. Prosecutors, on the other hand, look at cases through the lens of the victim and the public. You're used to developing a personal relationship with your clients. Prosecutors have to maintain a more distanced and less attached approach. They have to be more neutral. Additionally, you'll feel like you're betraying your ideals. Like you're sleeping with the enemy. I'm telling you both flat out. It's a bad idea."

A waiter approached and took their orders.

Ike was hoping the food would soften Ursula up, so he made small talk until the food arrived. Then, certainly, he was hungry, and perhaps they all were because they ate in silence for quite a while. Finally, he slid his napkin under the edge of his plate.

"Ursula, I heard what you were saying, but let me tell you what I do know. I know how you work, and we would be able to fit seamlessly into your system. We understand defense strategies and we'll share everything we know, and with the legions of high-priced defense attorneys Pharamundo commands, our input could prove the difference. Lastly, we're team players…" Abby nodded. "…and we'll be fully under your authority. We'll do the grunt work. Whatever you need."

"Thompson—"

He held up a hand. "One last thing, if I may. Ursula, we care. We care about the injustice done Lakota Holt, and we care about Oliver Wilson and the thousands like him dying needlessly."

"You care." Ursula sipped her wine. "Will you still care when Pharamundo's lawyers tear you to shreds because you're not suited for being prosecutors? Okay, you mean well. That's commendable. But trust me—on this one, forget your heart and use your head and walk away."

* * *

No decision was made at the restaurant. However, Ike and Abby remained determined to contribute in any way they could. They sensed that Ursula, by stopping short of categorically turning them down, had tacitly allowed them to stay involved in the case in an unofficial capacity. So they familiarized themselves with the case details by combing through public records, building a timeline of events, and identifying potential witnesses they could connect with later. Undoubtedly Pharamundo was a formidable adversary, yet with Ursula leading the prosecution, they believed the team could be strong. Ursula had the position, the experience, an expert command of Illinois law, and with her southern drawl juries ate her up. She was the perfect foil for Pharamundo's legal team with their Ivy League, well-heeled pretentiousness.

And now, with the charges finally announced, Pharamundo wasted no time going on the offensive. Their legal team launched a barrage of motions: dismissals for insufficient evidence, changes of venue, suppression of evidence, and countless discovery disputes. A particularly frivolous motion earned them a rebuke, but one strategic move proved more troubling. Specifically, a demand to exercise their client's constitutional right for a speedy trial, cloaked in the guise of the CEO's fervent desire to clear his name. It was almost certainly a tactical maneuver aimed at overwhelming Ursula, given her already tremendous caseload.

Chapter Twenty-two

Everything moved at a lightning pace now. Deemed to be a low flight risk since the company's headquarters was located in Chicago, Acosta's bail was set at fifty million dollars, a mere pittance for the billionaire. Ike supposed the low bail wasn't surprising considering it came from Judge Chantel Morton, an African American who already in her young career as a jurist had drawn negative publicity from conservative groups for her liberal rulings and had developed a reputation as a defendant's judge. Acosta *did* have to surrender his passport, obey a "no contact" order to stay away from all witnesses, and wear an electronic monitoring device, but despite those things, Ike and Abby would've been much happier with a more conservative judge.

Morton, not yet forty, a beautiful woman with steady blue eyes, flowing brown hair, and a bit of a high forehead, had made quite a name for herself for her ruthless efficiency, and it was thought that one day she would be a likely choice to be elected to the Illinois Supreme Court. The prosecution filed a motion for Morton to recuse herself, but she resolutely denied it. Appealing was an option, but the appeals court was deeply liberal as well and sure not to reverse Morton's decision. Amazingly, State's Attorney Rush was able to push through motions to get immunity for Jeff Castro and Elizabeth Castro, who, despite her disappearance, was on the witness list, as well as for the hacker who remotely hacked Lakota's car. But there'd be no anonymity for the hacker, as granting him anonymity would almost certainly be grounds for an appeal on the Sixth Amendment that a defendant had the right to face the witnesses against him. Two things were rapidly becoming abundantly clear though—Pharamundo wanted this trial over in a hurry, and Judge Morton was more than happy to oblige.

The motion for a speedy trial being granted was only the first shocker. The next was that Ursula pulled out of the prosecution team. Citing an overwhelming caseload, she assigned the trial to one of her Assistant State's Attorneys Peter Harkin. The third shocker was that Ike and Abby were officially admitted onto the team as contracted special prosecutors for this one case only. And with Harkin coming so late into the mix it was looking like Ike and Abby would *de facto* be doing the actual litigating.

Funny, Ike thought, Harkin dressed as sharply—designer suits, crisp shirts, silk ties—as the male attorneys for Pharamundo. And Pharamundo's female attorneys—stylish business skirt suits, chic heels—were high-class fashionable as well. He and Abby had gone up against Harkin in court before and knew him to be professional, but the rumor in the attorneys' lounge was that he was a little too cocky for his thirty-five years and had his sights set on a political career. Ike was uncertain about taking on the role of lead prosecutor, the memory of his major mistakes in the Hendrickson arson trial still fresh in his mind.

On the defense side, Cyrus Black, dubbed "The Monster" in legal circles, at six feet nine inches tall, towered over his team of attorneys, which included one African American male and four females, two African American and two white. Black, a Yale Law School grad, had argued extensively before the United States Supreme Court. He was formerly the U.S. Attorney for the Northern District of Illinois and currently is the managing partner of Black Law. His hourly rate unknown, his firm was paid, often in seven figures, on a case-by-case basis.

Jury selection finished, witness lists turned in, discovery cleared, the day for opening statements had arrived.

* * *

The Circuit Court of Cook County Third Municipal District building was an imposing structure. Sheer, monolithic walls rose above a massive, sloping concrete sidewalk that led upward to the revolving door entrance. Squad cars and paddy wagons lined the street between the courthouse and the multi-story garage. Ike, with Abby as his audience, had been preparing an opening statement for the last three nights just in case he was called upon, and when he received the call from Harkin in the morning, he knew that the moment had come. Now, as he and Abby climbed the long sidewalk to the courthouse, he wasn't sure if the tingle in his stomach told him he was ready—or about to flop.

In the hallway, Black, impossible to miss because of his size and stately stature, held court with who looked to be Pharamundo executives. The picture of calm confidence, the man either didn't notice or ignored Ike and Abby as they passed by.

The gallery, with its rows of heavy wooden benches, was filled with Lakota Holt's family and friends as well as curiosity seekers and the ever-present legal junkies. The media was well represented, despite the lack of press the case had generated so far, perhaps because they'd lost one of their own. The room hummed with whispers, the rustle of papers, and a tenseness born of the uncertainty as to what was about to unfold. Ike pushed through the courtroom swinging gate and felt funny heading to the prosecution table instead of to the defense table. This was a first for him, and although he knew he was joining the prosecution for the right reasons, it still felt awkward—and maybe even like a big mistake.

Harkin, already at the table, rose and was friendly enough. Despite the young Assistant State's Attorney's reputation, Ike wasn't disappointed to have the bright young lawyer on their side.

Black and Thomas Acosta, along with the defense attorney's entourage, made their way to the defense table. No acknowledgments were made by either side. Was a morality tale shaping up? Brilliant, Ivy League, superstar defense attorneys versus a motley crew of Midwestern prosecutors cobbled together at the last minute? Maybe Ike even felt a little like Illinois lawyer Abraham Lincoln taking on the east coast establishment legal powers that be. And although Ike had hardly been friendly, the Monster's snub rankled.

Abby caught his eye. "Are you ready?"

"Ready as I can be." He forced a smile. "I gotta be honest though. I'd rather have Ursula at the helm. Like I said before, *she'd* be the perfect prosecutor for this trial."

Abby flashed him a wink. "Well, I guess you'll just have to take over that role now."

The bailiff called, "All rise."

Judge Morton swept in from a side door and took her place on the bench. "Good afternoon. This court is now in session, and we convene this day for the case of the State of Illinois vs. Thomas Acosta. Ladies and gentlemen of the jury, you have been sworn to impartially and fairly weigh the evidence presented in this case and render a verdict according to the law, as instructed by the court." She looked to the prosecution table. "Is the prosecution ready to proceed with the presentation of their case?"

Ike stood. "It is, Your Honor."

"Then you may proceed."

Ike brought a cheat sheet of five bullet points of his opening statement to the attorney lectern. He hoped not to look at it, but these five points had to be made, and he'd mentally check them off one by one as he made them. "Good morning, ladies and gentlemen of the jury. My name is Ike Thompson, and I am one of the prosecutors for this case. Today we will be trying a case for the ultimate crime—murder. Not an accident. And not just any murder, but the brutal murder of the weak by the strong. Murder of the powerless by the powerful."

He made eye contact with each and every juror. "Ladies and gentlemen, I've seen a photo shoot in a luxury real estate magazine that featured Thomas Acosta's elegant corner office on a high floor in Willis Tower in downtown Chicago. It's among the priciest real estate in the world. Acosta's desk is white onyx with solid gold inlays. Priceless oil paintings by renowned artists Frida Kahlo and Diego Rivera adorn the walls. Breathtaking views look out on the Chicago Loop and Lake Michigan. The office is a vision of whiteness, cleanliness, of would-be godliness, if you will." He shifted to where he and Acosta would be in the jury's line of sight. "And yet from that inner sanctum of white, the blackness of Thomas Acosta's soul was revealed. In a reprehensible act, he ordered the fatal remote hacking of investigative journalist Lakota Holt's car's onboard computer, murdering the promising 28-year-old reporter. Why? Because Mr. Holt had been investigating Acosta's pharmaceutical company's fraudulent activities. To complete his barbarity, Mr. Acosta attempted to mask the cold-blooded murder by attempting to make it look like an accident." Ike walked back to the lectern, peeking at his notes.

"We all know them, don't we? People who insist on getting their way regardless of what happens to those around them. People who aren't afraid to pressure others to get what they want. People skilled at manipulation. People that are cruel. In a word, bullies. And that sums up Thomas Acosta—he is a bully. A millionaire at nineteen, he made the Forbes list of billionaires by the time he was twenty-five. And make no mistake, he got there by using his company's monopoly power to ruthlessly crush competitors, so as to keep the prices of his drugs exorbitantly high. He got there by being more concerned with profits than people." Ike glanced at his notes. Two down, three to go.

"The victim, Lakota Holt, on the other hand, just barely scraped by economically. In fact, he had a hard time hanging on to jobs because he cared more about the truth than his employers' need to coddle the powers that be, powers like drug giant Pharamundo International. The loving son of Keokuk and Hope Holt, Lakota had seven brothers and sisters." He turned to acknowledge the family members in the front row.

"And yet, despite his meager resources, Lakota made it a point to help those in need. One of those people was Bree Wilson, whom you will hear from later. Bree's only child, eight-year-old Oliver, is dying from ALLD, Acute Lung Liquefaction Disease, a fatal illness becoming more and more widespread across the country. Moved by their suffering, Lakota's heart went out to Bree and young Oliver, and he attempted to find out if Pharamundo already had the drug they'd been working on for years to cure ALLD. And *that's* what Thomas Acosta couldn't tolerate—because if the curative drug for ALLD was found to exist, Pharamundo would lose billions in profits. *That's* why Thomas Acosta pressed a button on his iPhone that sent the murderous text authorizing the fatal hack of Lakota's car.

"Ladies and gentlemen, the evidence will show how Thomas Acosta committed murder for hire. Bree Wilson will testify as to her relationship with Mr. Holt. She will say that Mr. Holt had made close contact with a high-level executive in Pharamundo who knew that, despite the company's adamant denials, the curative drug for ALLD existed. You'll hear from the policeman who filled out the crash report. And from the automobile mechanic who examined Mr. Holt's decimated vehicle and discovered that the car had been remotely hacked causing the fatal crash. You'll hear from the hacker who did the hacking. And lastly, you'll hear from Jeffrey Castro, the head of Information Technology at Pharamundo and the man who acted as the final conduit in Thomas Acosta's monstrous scheme." Ike glanced at Abby, who gave him a little nod. He checked his notes. Only one left. He slipped the notes into his suit coat pocket.

"Have any of you…" He scanned the jury. "…been bullied? Maybe when you were a kid on the playground at school somebody teased you or made fun of your appearance or worse? Or as an adult, you were bullied at your job or intimidated by powerful companies like Pharamundo?" He kept eyeing the jury. "If you were, then you know what it's like to wish you had a big brother to stop the bully from tormenting you, don't you?

"Lakota Holt was bullied. He was bullied by Pharamundo. The company got him fired from his newspaper job. Then they threatened his life, and ultimately, when Lakota wouldn't be intimidated, Thomas Acosta, the company's

CEO, took matters into his own hands." Ike bit his lip and nodded. "Yes, if only Lakota had a big brother powerful enough to stop the great big bully that Thomas Acosta had become. If only he had." More nodding. "But do you know what, ladies and gentlemen? *You* are Lakota Holt's big brother now. You have the power to stop this ruthless killer. Like all bullies, Thomas Acosta thought he was untouchable. He believed he could silence anyone who dared to challenge him. Now it's time to prove him wrong by finding him guilty of first-degree murder. Thank you."

It was hard to know what Harkin thought of Ike's opening statement, but when Ike returned to the prosecution table, Abby squeezed his hand. All he knew was that he'd hit all five of his points and so with the lack of extensive prep was satisfied. Now the judge was talking.

"Will the defense be making an opening statement?"

Cyrus Black slowly unfolded from his chair, his rise seemingly endless as he stretched to his full height. His presence commanded the attention of the courtroom, given his imposing physical size and perhaps his imposing intellect, as if he were a force that could not be ignored. Even Ike couldn't help but be drawn in by the man's formidable bearing and the sense of calm it inspired in the tense courtroom.

"Thank you, Your Honor, yes, it will."

Morton flicked the hair from her shoulder. "Please begin."

The defense attorney bowed his head slightly. "Ladies and gentlemen of the jury, my name is Cyrus Black and I represent Mr. Thomas Acosta, the defendant in this case, who is seated at the defense table." Black turned and nodded to him. "Ladies and gentlemen, let me start Mr. Acosta's defense by asking you a question. Do you think success is a crime?" He ambled to the attorney lectern, bringing no notes. "Perhaps I should introduce myself first. I'm originally from Australia, Brisbane, to be precise. Oh, I'm quite American by now since my parents moved to New York City when I was thirteen. But there is a saying Down Under about cutting down the tall poppy. It even has its own name—The Tall Poppy Syndrome. And the Tall Poppy Syndrome is about successful people being unfairly criticized for no other reason than…being successful. Successful people are the tall poppy, so to speak. So when people feel that someone has become too successful, they heap criticism on them. They cut them down to size. They cut down the tall poppy." He pursed his lips but soon his eyes lit up. "So let me tell you, it was refreshing coming to America and realizing that there is no such saying here. That *most* Americans…" He glanced at the prosecution table. "… admire the hard work that goes into being successful."

He made his way to the jury box and tapped the railing. "Yes, America is the land of opportunity, but even here a few anti-success sayings exist. Like, lightning strikes the tallest trees. Or the nail that sticks up gets hammered down. So while *most* Americans applaud and admire hard-earned success, a few will always be envious. And there will even be some who go a step further and assign evil motives and unethical tactics to successful people, no matter the evidence to the contrary. Ladies and gentlemen of the jury, in this trial what the prosecution will attempt to convey is that Thomas Acosta is a tall poppy."

Black returned to the attorney lectern and planted both hands on it. "Is Mr. Acosta a successful businessman? You bet he is. But he probably got there by employing unethical business practices? He probably cheated? No, Thomas

Acosta rose by tirelessly devoting himself to improving people's health and well-being. He rose by bringing others along with him, by committing his finances so that his company researched, developed, and produced some of the world's most innovative drugs to manage and cure a broad range of diseases. He rose by fighting to ensure that Pharamundo's drugs were affordable and accessible to all, regardless of income, despite rising costs and increasing healthcare complexities."

He tilted his head. "And that's not all Mr. Acosta has done with his hard-earned money. Many prestigious organizations have recognized his exceptional generosity. He's been awarded the Carnegie Medal of Philanthropy, the Skoll Award for Social Entrepreneurship, the Muhammad Yunus Award for Social Business and Poverty Alleviation, and the Clinton Global Citizen Award. Through the years, he has given away over five hundred million dollars, and he has committed to the Bill and Melinda Gates program for pledging at least fifty percent of his wealth to charity." Black held his arms out to the jury.

"Ladies and gentlemen of the jury, it's easy to get drawn into the strong emotional pull of The Tall Poppy Syndrome. But I ask you now, please do not hold Mr. Acosta's success against him. Ladies and gentlemen, emotion has many wonderful real-world attributes, but one area it has no place in is in a court of law. The arguments you will hear from the prosecution will appeal solely to your emotions. Some shamelessly so. But this trial must be decided on facts.

"Oh, but the prosecution will claim to have factual evidence, but I assure you under closer inspection what they call evidence is only wishful thinking, conjecture, and smoke and mirrors. In contrast, we will present actual facts that clearly establish that Thomas Acosta is an innocent man. First, we

THE PERFECT PROSECUTOR

will call Eric Hanson, an automotive expert, and he will testify that Mr. Holt's vehicle could not possibly have been remotely hacked. Then Officer Vincent O'Malley, a Chicago Police officer, will testify that Bree Wilson's random attack of Mr. Acosta was just that—random. Next, Dr. Amanda Lee, Pharamundo's chief pharmaceutical representative, will testify that Pharamundo International goes far above and beyond the established protocols for creating new products. Then, Ellen Price, from the Department of Health and Human Services and lead negotiator for the government agency, will testify that Pharamundo is in full compliance with all of the requirements of its contract to develop the drug to cure ALLD. Finally, MIT grad and certified in Information Technology, Data Science, and Data Analytics, Prajit Kumar, will testify that the technical testimony by the prosecution is flawed and utterly untrustworthy."

Black waited a few moments, then leaned heavily on the lectern.

"Ladies and gentlemen, my request of you during this trial is simple—listen carefully to what *the facts* are and only what the facts are. Because when you do, you will clearly see that Thomas Acosta is not guilty. Thank you."

Chapter Twenty-three

After opening statements concluded, Judge Morton was wasting no time. "Is the State ready to call its first witness?"

Harkin turned to Ike, who rose. "We are, Your Honor."

"Then please proceed."

A chill ran through Ike as he realized that for the first time in his life he was about to question a witness as a prosecutor. "Your Honor, the State calls Gerald Hopper."

Crew-cutted, a tall cop in a dark blue uniform took the stand.

Ike made his way to the attorney lectern and ran through the foundational questions establishing the man's credentials before asking, "Officer, did you respond to the crash on 22E318 Blackbird Ridge Road in Delavan, Wisconsin, in Walworth County on July 3rd at approximately 10 a.m.?"

"I did."

Ike widened his eyes at the cop. "And did you find a body in the crashed vehicle?"

"Yes."

He leaned forward. "And was the person in the crashed vehicle alive or deceased?"

The officer shifted in his seat. "The occupant was deceased."

"Were you able to determine the deceased man's name?"

The officer's gaze flickered briefly to the gallery before returning to Ike. "His name was, uh, Lakota Holt."

Ike kept trying to hold the man's eye. "And how did you know that, Officer?"

The cop raised a hand. "Because his wallet had credit and photo ID cards."

"And were you able to determine that the victim matched the photo IDs?"

The officer's posture stiffened slightly as he replied, "I was."

Ike stepped toward the witness. "Officer, did you take a photo of the crash scene?"

"Yes."

Ike nodded to Abby, who pressed a button on her laptop, and the police photo of Lakota's mangled Toyota Corolla, a hunk of twisted metal and shattered glass wedged into a tree at the bottom of a gully, came onto the video screen on the wall across from the jury box. "Your Honor, I would like to submit this photo as State's Exhibit 1."

Morton looked to the defense table. "Any objection?"

Black spoke up, his voice deep and resonant. "No, Your Honor."

Morton glanced at the video screen. "The photo is admitted into evidence as State's Exhibit 1."

Ike hesitated as long as he could to let the dramatic photo burn into the jurors' minds. "I have no further questions, Your Honor."

"Very well." The judge turned her attention to the defense table. "Your witness."

Black was up, notes in hand. "Thank you, Your Honor." He tucked the notes under his arm, buttoned his suit coat, and walked to the lectern. "Good morning, Officer."

"Morning."

"Officer, on July 3rd at 10:00 a.m. you filed an *accident* report at the scene, did you not?"

"Yes."

"And in that *accident* report, you wrote that…" The attorney spread his notes on the lectern. "… based on your observations at the scene and the facts gathered at the time, you determined that the cause of the *accident* was an error on the driver's part, didn't you?"

"At the time—"

"Sir," Black said with an edge in his voice, his eyes never leaving the cop's. "I asked, if based on your observations at the scene and the facts gathered at the time, you determined that the cause of the accident was an error on the driver's part. That question requires a yes or no answer."

"Yes."

"Officer." Black's tone lightened. "How many of these accidents would you say you've worked over the course of your career?"

"Oh." The cop looked off. "I would say close to a hundred."

"You would say close to a hundred." Black waited for the cop to look back at him. "Officer, you've undergone accident reconstruction training, haven't you?"

"I have."

Black nodded. "And that training includes analyzing and interpreting evidence at the scene of the accident, such as skid marks, vehicle debris, and impact marks, to help draw conclusions as to the cause of the accident, doesn't it?"

"It does."

"Very good." Another nod from Black. "Officer, on that stretch of Blackbird Ridge Road where the accident occurred, there have been other accidents, haven't there?"

"Yes."

Black's eyes widened. "In fact, there have been other accidents there that caused fatalities, haven't there?"

THE PERFECT PROSECUTOR

"Unfortunately, yes, there have been."

"So there have been other fatal accidents there," Black announced with an air of final certainty before looking back to the witness. He seemed to give the cop an approving look. "Officer, when you filed that *accident* report on July 3rd at 10:00 a.m., you had no idea you'd be testifying in a murder trial, did you?"

The cop rubbed the back of his neck. "No, I didn't."

"No further questions, Your Honor."

Ike looked at Abby, and the concern in her eyes was apparent.

Morton waited for Black to return to the defense table. "Will the prosecution be redirecting?"

Now Ike looked at Harkin, who turned away. He stood. "Yes, Your Honor."

"Proceed, please."

Ike held his chin for a bit as he stood at the prosecution table. "Officer Hopper, are you aware of police officers being trained in cyber remote hacking of a vehicle?"

The cop leaned back in his chair. "I've heard of it."

Ike tilted his head. "Have you personally had any training in understanding the basics of automotive electronic systems and how they're vulnerable to hacking?"

The cop shook his head. "No."

"Any training in learning the different types of hacking techniques used to remotely control a vehicle?"

The cop sent Ike a sarcastic glance. "Unh-uh."

Ike nodded slowly and then stopped. "Officer, have you had *any training whatsoever* in cyber remote hacking of a vehicle?"

The cop waved his hand dismissively. "I have not."

"No further questions, Your Honor." Ike sat.

Morton looked to the defense table. "Mr. Black, re-cross?"

"No, Your Honor."

The judge leaned toward the clerk and said something, then straightened up. "The prosecution may call its next witness."

Ike didn't even bother to look at Harkin. He stood. "Your Honor, the State calls Bree Wilson."

The young mother was practically through the swinging gate before Ike finished speaking. The clerk swore her in, and she took the stand.

"Good morning, Ms. Wilson."

"Good morning."

Bree sat up straight and made steady eye contact—two great traits for a witness. In his prep with her, she'd been well-spoken, sincere, and utterly credible. And a true believer in the righteousness of her quest. "Ms. Wilson, please tell the jury the circumstances under which you came to know Lakota Holt."

"Okay." She folded her hands on her lap. "For several years now I have searched for a drug to cure Acute Lung Liquefaction Disease, ALLD, from which my eight-year-old son, Oliver, is dying. During my searches, I came across an article in a medical journal saying that Pharamundo International was actively developing just such a drug. I made several inquiries to Pharamundo to learn what stage of development the drug was in, but I received no replies."

Ike crossed his arms. "So what did you do then?"

She kept up the good eye contact. "I then, in another medical journal, happened to read an article by the investigative journalist Lakota Holt, and I admired his willingness to write truthfully about controversial topics, so I emailed him at his newspaper to see if he'd be willing to help me."

Ike tilted his head. "And did you receive a response from Mr. Holt?"

"Yes. To my surprise, he wrote back. Turns out he also was aware Pharamundo was working on a drug to cure ALLD and, furthermore, that the company had a contract with the government and that he believed Pharamundo might be slow-walking—"

"Objection, Your Honor." Black was on his feet. "Hearsay and it assumes a fact not in evidence."

"Sustained," Morton announced firmly. "The jury will disregard the witness' previous statement."

Ike ventured toward the witness stand. "Ms. Wilson, what did your personal searches lead you to believe about Pharamundo and what it might be doing with the drug?"

The witness waited as if she was afraid of being interrupted again. "Essentially the same thing," she said. "That Pharamundo was indeed slow-walking the drug's development or even that the drug already existed and the company was keeping it secret."

Ike stopped. "And why do you think the company would be doing that?"

Bree glanced at Acosta before returning her gaze to Ike. "Money. Pharamundo currently has a tremendously financially successful drug to treat ALLD on the market. It's called Respir-ezy. Bringing out the new drug would interfere with that. If it brought out the new drug, the company would essentially be competing with itself. Additionally, the company had been working on the new drug for years and displayed no progress updates, information regarding clinical trials, or the potential side-effects of the drug. It had conveyed no information about the drug whatsoever."

"Respir-ezy is Pharamundo's brand name for the drug you mentioned. Do you know the drug's generic name?"

"Supravil."

Ike did his best to sound curious. "Okay, Supravil, or Respir-ezy, same thing, is wildly successful, but if Pharamundo already has developed the new drug, why not bring it out as well?"

Bree spoke resolutely. "Because the new drug would *cure* ALLD, not just *manage it* like Respir-ezy. If the curative drug is released, it will end Respir-ezy's massive profit run and ultimately bring in fewer profits itself because the new drug will cure ALLD."

Ike crossed his arms. "So, how did Mr. Holt go about finding out if the curative drug existed?"

"Objection," Black bellowed from the defense table. "Foundation. Counsel has not yet laid a foundation of factual basis that serves to explain how Ms. Wilson would know about the responsive actions of Mr. Holt."

Morton looked at the defense attorney. "Yes, that's sustained."

Ike sighed silently. "Ms. Wilson, did you have a conversation with Mr. Holt about the existence of a curative drug for ALLD?"

"Many times. He told me—"

Again, the Monster was up. "Your Honor. Hearsay."

Morton gave Ike a look and a touch of a smirk. "Sustained."

Ike took a few quick breaths. There had to be a way to get this out. "Ms. Wilson, did Mr. Holt tell you that he had

THE PERFECT PROSECUTOR

made contact with an executive at Pharamundo and relay to you the executive's belief that a curative drug existed?"

"Yes to both questions."

Ike breathed easier. "Ms. Wilson, please describe your relationship with Mr. Holt."

Her face brightened. "It was warm and caring. Lakota took a liking to my son, Oliver, and that motivated him to keep digging to find out if the curative drug existed."

"Objection." Black again. "Assumes facts not in evidence."

Morton looked at the defense attorney. "How so?"

"Your Honor, there is no evidence that such a curative drug as yet exists. The existence of a curative drug at this point is pure conjecture."

"All right, that is sustained." Morton checked her notes, then turned to the jury. "The jury will disregard the notion that a curative drug exists."

Ike felt it was a petty objection, but the judge had to sustain it. He could've come back and asked about the *alleged* curative drug, but that would have made him look petty as well. "I have no further questions, Your Honor." He returned to the prosecution table.

In the meantime, as was her reputation, Morton kept things rolling. "Defense, your witness."

"Thank you, Your Honor." Black, notes in hand, was up quickly and headed to the attorney lectern. "Good morning, Ms. Wilson."

"Good morning."

"Ms. Wilson, let me begin by saying that I'm genuinely saddened that your son is so gravely ill."

"Thank you."

"And I truly hope you find the best medical care for him."

Bree offered a small, appreciative smile.

Black returned the smile. "Ms. Wilson, is Oliver currently on Pharamundo's drug Respir-ezy to deal with his ALLD symptoms?"

"He is."

A quick nod. "And, ma'am, how long has he been on the drug?"

"Since he was five."

Black, all serious now, caught her eye. "So, three years, would that be right?"

"Yes."

Ike jotted on Abby's notepad. *He's slick.* Black was a real pro. Starting Bree out with softball questions because she's a sympathetic witness, calling Oliver by name.

The defense attorney's eyes softened. "And Respir-ezy has helped with his symptoms, hasn't it?"

"At first, yes, it helped a lot, but through the years, it lost much of its effectiveness."

"I understand, but isn't it also the case that during those years, your son's ALLD has progressed?"

"Well, yes, of course."

The big attorney hunched his shoulders. "So the drug has helped slow the disease's progression, hasn't it?"

"Yes, it has."

"It has. Very good." Black folded his hands on the lectern. "Ms. Wilson, what sort of customer service have you received from Pharamundo?"

Bree looked at him. "I'm sorry? What sort of customer service?"

THE PERFECT PROSECUTOR

"Yes. What sort of customer service have you received in your dealings with Pharamundo?"

"Oh, okay." A hint of a frown creased her face. "I would say it's been good."

"You'd say it's been good. Thank you." Black's thin smile didn't quite reach his eyes. "And at one point, Pharamundo has actually *helped* you afford Respir-ezy, hasn't it?"

She swallowed. "It has."

"In fact, when you lost your job, Pharamundo supplied the drug at no cost to you for eleven straight months, didn't it?"

She pressed her lips together, her "Yes" slipping out as if against her will.

The big attorney was camped out at the lectern now, taking his time going over his notes. Finally, he began. "Ms. Wilson, earlier you testified that Pharamundo, despite having a government contract to produce the drug, did not release progress updates or information regarding clinical trials or potential side effects of its curative drug in development for ALLD, didn't you?"

Bree's left eye twitched. She looked at Ike before looking back at Black. "I did."

Black abandoned his notes and moved to the witness stand. "Ma'am, do you have firsthand knowledge of Pharamundo's contract with the government for the development of the new drug?"

"No, I just assumed—"

"I didn't ask what you assumed." He leaned toward her, the edge back in his voice. "I asked if you had firsthand knowledge of Pharamundo's contract with the government for the development of the new drug?"

Bree's jaw tightened. "No, I didn't."

"And, in fact…" Black's eyes narrowed. "…you don't have any firsthand knowledge about progress updates either, do you?"

She exhaled. "No."

"And you don't have any firsthand knowledge of how the drug's clinical trials are conducted, do you?"

A frown. "No."

"And how clinical trial side effects for the drug are processed, reviewed, and reported?"

She shook her head. "No."

Ike knew he needed to object, but he couldn't take his eyes off the Monster.

"And as you sit here today, ma'am…" The defense attorney raised up to his full height. "…you most certainly do not have any firsthand knowledge that a curative drug for ALLD exists, do you?"

Ike was up. "Objection! Argumentative!"

"Overruled," the judge said curtly, barely glancing at Ike. She turned to the witness. "Please answer the question, Ms. Wilson."

Bree stared at the floor. "I do not."

"No further questions, Your Honor," Black said flatly, and he returned to the defense table.

The judge tapped a pen on the bench, seemingly waiting for the tension to subside. Finally, she addressed the witness. "Thank you for your testimony, Ms. Wilson. You may step down."

After Bree left the stand, the judge looked to the prosecution table. "Okay then. State, whenever you're ready, you may call your next witness."

Abby had interviewed their medical expert three times. She stood. "Your Honor, the State calls Brian O'Connor."

The medical doctor was sworn in and took the stand. Abby ran through the questions establishing his credentials as the head of the immunology department at Elburn Community Hospital, then settled her notes on the attorney lectern. "Dr. O'Connor, please explain to the jury what ALLD is."

The physician, in a blue suit, pale blue shirt, and a subtly patterned red tie, had deep, black eyes and a prominent forehead sparsely covered by wispy gray hair. "Of course. ALLD, or Acute Lung Liquefaction Disease, is an autoimmune disease that damages the body's immune system by attacking the body's healthy cells in the lungs. The immune system overreacts to something that is a non-threat, an allergy, and works to destroy it."

"And what are the symptoms of ALLD?"

He sat up a little. "At first, they're mild and often mistaken for the common cold: coughing, congestion, runny nose. But as the disease progresses, it gets increasingly difficult to breathe. Fluid builds up in the lungs, and the patient eventually drowns in their own bodily fluids."

A few of the jurors squirmed.

"Fluid builds up in the lungs, and the patient eventually drowns in their own bodily fluids." Abby's brow furrowed. "Doctor, what causes ALLD?"

"A genetic abnormality."

She tilted her head at him. "And what causes genetic abnormalities?"

The physician waved a hand. "Oh, they can be caused by many things. They can be passed from generation to generation—chromosome abnormalities. Environmental factors such as exposure to radiation or the chemicals in tainted groundwater can cause them. Basically, they can be caused by anything that causes mutations in a person's genetic makeup."

Abby pushed her glasses up onto the bridge of her nose. "But as was mentioned previously, Doctor, there are drugs to treat ALLD, aren't there?"

"Treat, yes. Cure, no. In ALLD, the body's immune system is so out of control that the drugs used to treat it may provide temporary relief, but ultimately, they are as ineffective as trying to stop a locomotive with cardboard. The immune system overpowers all attempts to treat the disease and eventually takes the victim's life. The drugs that treat the disease can keep the immune system partially at bay, but it's never enough to be completely stable."

Abby walked to the witness stand. "Doctor, is there any hope of curing ALLD in the near future?"

"Many attempts have been made…" His hands rested in his lap. "…but so far they have all failed."

"But is there no hope for a cure?"

The physician smiled. "There's always hope for a cure."

Abby turned to the judge. "No further questions, Your Honor." She straightened her notes from the lectern.

"Okay." Morton addressed the defense table. "Mr. Black, cross?"

"Yes, Your Honor."

The hulking man rose and passed by Abby on his way to the attorney lectern. "Thank you for your testimony, Doctor."

The physician nodded.

"Sir, where exactly is Elburn Community Hospital?"

"It's in an unincorporated area near Elburn, Illinois."

"Elburn, Illinois," Black said as if he'd just invented the words. "Very good. Tell me, Doctor, is Elburn Community

Hospital, near Elburn, Illinois, a member of the Illinois Health and Hospital Association?"

The physician guided two strands of gray hair off his forehead. "Actually, I don't believe it is."

Black raised his eyebrows. "You don't *believe* it is?"

"No, actually, I'm quite sure it isn't."

Black wandered off a few paces from the lectern. "Doctor, is the hospital a member of the American Medical Association?"

The physician shook his head.

Morton leaned toward the witness. "You have to speak your answer, please."

He shook his head, managing only a feeble "No."

Abby pushed her shoulder into Ike's and jotted on her legal pad. *Argumentative?*

Ike would've liked her to make the objection, but it would look insubstantial. He wrote: *Let's see where this goes first.*

Black tilted his head at O'Connor. "How about the American College of Allergy, Asthma, and Immunology?"

O'Connor blanched. "No."

"Well okay, then. Let's move on to something else." Black returned to the lectern. "Doctor, in your earlier testimony, you stated that you're the head of the immunology department at Elburn Community Hospital, didn't you?"

"That's right." The color slowly crept back into the physician's face.

"Sir, how long have you held that position?"

"Well, let me see, it'll be coming up on eight months," O'Connor said, but then, his voice growing more confident, he added, "But I've been working in the field of immunology for over twenty years."

Ike did a mental eye roll. O'Connor was justifying himself and in so doing appeared weak.

Black walked to the defense table, retrieved a folder, and approached the judge. "Your Honor, I would like to offer as evidence a copy of Dr. O'Connor's previous testimony from a civil lawsuit." He gave her a copy.

Morton looked to the prosecution table. "Is there any objection?"

"No objection, Your Honor," Ike said. He knew what it was and what was coming.

"So noted." Morton added the transcript to the pile of documents in front of her. "The transcript is admitted into evidence as Defense Exhibit 1."

Black went to the prosecution and handed Ike a copy, then he returned to the witness stand, gave a copy to O'Connor, and remained there. "Now, in a minute, Doctor, I'm going to ask for your help, but before I do, I believe that prosecutor Blum asked you…" He read from the folder. " 'Doctor, is there no hope for a cure?' And you replied, and this was your sworn testimony, 'There is always hope for a cure.' That's accurate, isn't it?"

Looking away, the physician answered, "Yes."

"Thank you. Now, this is where I'm going to need your help." The defense attorney turned a page in the folder. "Please read the testimony that you gave under oath, starting on line thirty-four. Do you have it?"

O'Connor began reading aloud. " 'I am sorry, but all the research and data on ALLD points to the conclusion that there is no possible cure at our current level of medical technology, and any claims of a cure are certainly a false hope.' "

Black decisively moved away from the witness stand. "No further questions, Your Honor."

"Hmm. All right then." Again, Morton checked with the prosecution table. "Redirect?"

Ike conferred with Abby and Harkin. "No, Your Honor."

Morton excused the witness and checked the wall clock. "Well, I think we're close enough to lunchtime to take a break. Please be back here at one-thirty, and in the meantime, let me remind the jurors that you are not to discuss this case with anyone or among yourselves outside of the courtroom. It's crucial that you stay free from outside influences to ensure that you consider only the evidence presented at trial when coming to your verdict. See you at one-thirty."

Chapter Twenty-four

Peter Harkin checked his cell phone messages even before he left the prosecution table to go to lunch. Perhaps he was only attending the trial to be the eyes and ears of Ursula Rush. Perhaps he was there to take the fall for her if they lost the case. But one helpful thing was that by looking at his phone, he'd reminded Ike to check in with Val at the office. So Ike sat on one of the gallery benches and gave her a call. She reported that nothing earthshaking was happening, but she did have a few things to share. Seemed Abby's father was staying out of trouble, and Johnny Lagattuta finally called—and sent a bill—saying he hadn't uncovered any leads on finding Elizabeth Castro, but he was quite sure she wasn't dead.

Ike and Abby agreed there'd been nothing earthshaking so far in the trial either. They'd anticipated Black would portray Acosta as a maligned successful businessman. Now, the next witness would be Ike's mechanic, Ken O'Day, who'd examined Lakota's wreck at the tow truck yard. Ken should prove to be a solid witness, and Ike had no worries about him being on the stand. But then again, facing cross-examination from Cyrus Black, even good witnesses could be made to look bad.

1:30 rolled around quickly, and Ken looked every bit a mechanic as he was sworn in and took the stand. He wore olive-green cotton pants, a long-sleeved denim shirt over a white T-shirt, and he had a tiny piece of toilet paper stuck to his chin from what appeared to be a shaving mishap.

Ike slipped a laser pointer into his pocket and approached the witness stand. He ran through the foundational questions and found himself needing to focus on calling the mechanic Mr. O'Day, as he was so used to calling him Ken. "Mr. O'Day, do you have any special designations as a mechanic?"

"Yes, I'm an ASE Master Mechanic."

"And what does ASE stand for?"

"Automotive service excellence."

"Automotive service excellence. Very good. Mr. O'Day, after examining Lakota Holt's heavily damaged Corolla, what was your professional opinion as to what caused the car to crash?"

With a confident nod, the mechanic said, "I believe the car's onboard computer was remotely hacked."

Ike turned to the jury. "You believe the car's onboard computer was remotely hacked. Would you please explain to the jury what remotely hacking a car's onboard computer entails?"

Another nod. "A car being remotely hacked means that someone took control of the car's onboard computer from a location outside the car allowing them to input commands to the car that override the driver's actions. This would result in the vehicle operating under conditions that it was never designed to handle."

Ike took a step back. "And how does that pertain to the crash of Mr. Holt's car?"

"Well, the hacker instructed the car's computer to boost the accelerator and disable the brakes, making it impossible for the driver to control the car. The car would be wildly out of control. Essentially, a runaway vehicle."

"And what does boosting the car's accelerator refer to?" The mechanic's testimony was coming off well: decisive, positive, credible.

"That's when a boost in power causes the engine to race at maximum speed, as if the driver had pressed the gas pedal to the floor."

"Okay." Ike tilted his head. "And what led you to believe that these were the reasons for the crash?"

The mechanic leaned back, a self-assured smile forming on his lips. "Well, because of the car's damage."

"Your Honor, I would like to submit the following photograph…" Ike nodded to Abby, who pressed a button on a laptop. A photo of Lakota's badly damaged Corolla sitting in the tow truck yard came on the giant video screen. "…as State's Exhibit 2."

Morton checked with the defense table, and there was no objection, so she admitted the photo into evidence.

"Now if you would, Mr. O'Day…" Ike handed him the laser pointer. "…please walk us through what you found."

The mechanic shifted to the edge of his chair. The laser's red beam jumped around on the screen until it settled on an area of one of the car's badly damaged seats. "If you look closely, right here you can see smoke residue even on the interior seat fabric, and that residue is from the engine block being extremely overworked. And I mean extremely overworked."

"Please elaborate."

"Sure." The laser danced on the ceiling until the mechanic realized what was happening. "A car's engine being extremely overworked means that someone forced it to perform way beyond its intended capacity."

Ike waited.

"Well, overworking an engine results in damage to the engine's internal components. Things like warped cylinders or even a cracked engine block." He resettled the pointer on the sooty fabric. "And it can also cause smoke residue from the engine to be expelled into the car's interior, as we can see here."

As we can see here? The mechanic's testimony was knocking it out of the park. "And were there any other signs that this was a remote hack?"

The mechanic steadied the laser on the car's badly damaged brakes. "Just look at the brake pedal and the parking brake. Both damaged, the parking brake mangled like a pretzel. And the brake pedal even left an impression on the floorboard. It's clear that the driver was doing absolutely everything he could think of to stop the car."

Ike gestured for Abby to shut down the image on the screen. "Thank you, Mr. O'Day. I have no further questions, Your Honor."

Morton handed a document to the clerk and then focused on the prosecution table. "Will the defense be cross-examining?"

The male African American attorney stood. "It will, Your Honor."

"The witness is yours."

The attorney, shoulders back, excellent posture, strode to the lectern. Impeccably clean-shaven with close-cropped hair, he projected a military bearing. In an IBM-blue suit, slightly bluer than the Monster's, white shirt and neatly tied red necktie, he smiled at the mechanic. "Good afternoon."

"Afternoon."

"Before I get started." He placed his hand over his heart. "I have to say that I've done a fair amount of work on my own car and know how difficult that can be. I admire your being a master mechanic."

"Appreciate it."

"Mr. O'Day, let me begin by asking if you knew what Mr. Holt's driving habits were like?"

"I did not."

"So…" The attorney shrugged slightly. "…as far as you know, he could've been a pokey driver or even a lead foot?"

"I suppose that's true."

The attorney rubbed his chin and tilted his head a touch. "And so, if Mr. Holt happened to be a lead foot and drove that car hard, it's possible that *that* could've caused the smoke residue that seeped onto the car's interior fabric after the crash, isn't it?"

"Well, I doubt—"

"Mr. O'Day, I just asked if it was possible."

The mechanic rolled his neck. "Well, it would take an awful lot of driving under those conditions, but I suppose it's possible."

"So it's possible." The attorney left the lectern and stepped closer. "Some rent-a-car companies are notorious for running cars down and not providing the scheduled maintenance, aren't they?"

The mechanic looked to Ike, who broke eye contact.

"Mr. O'Day?"

"Yeah, yeah, a few are."

The attorney crossed his arms. "Smoke residue can also be caused by excess torque from an improperly tuned engine, can it not?"

Ike's jaw tightened. He did not like where this was headed, but there was nothing to object to. *Hang in there, Ken.*

The mechanic touched the blood-dotted scrap of toilet paper on his cheek and looked off. "Again, unlikely, but yeah, it can."

The attorney waited until the witness looked at him. "You know, some of those rentals get driven awfully hard. Are you aware of the condition of Mr. Holt's car, specifically the brakes, before the accident occurred?"

A smirk played on the mechanic's lips. "No, I am not."

"Do you know if the car had any previous collisions that damaged the brakes or accelerator?"

O'Day answered, "Can't say that I do." He added a sarcastic smile.

The attorney returned to the lectern. "A couple of months ago, one Monday morning, I received a letter in the mail that my car needed to come in for a manufacturer's recall. Just the sort of letter you want to get on a Monday morning." A few chuckles from the gallery. "The recall was about a defect in the brake master cylinder. They said the defect could result in a loss of brake fluid pressure, rendering the brakes ineffective and causing them to fail. So I dutifully took my car in and had it taken care of. Do you know, sir, if Mr. Holt's car had any manufacturing defects or was involved in any recalls?"

"I don't know the car's history."

The attorney turned to Morton. "No further questions, Your Honor."

* * *

Next up was the hacker who hacked the Corolla's onboard computer. Especially considering the nature of his profession, Raj Sharma clearly appeared not to be thrilled about testifying in open court, but immunity and outrage over his efforts being used to murder someone evidently supplied the impetus he needed. Before the trial, Ike hammered home that the immunity granted him applied only to his involvement in the Holt murder. If he spoke of anything illegal beyond that, he'd be liable to prosecution. Raj was older than Abby and Ike had imagined he'd be. Most hackers are teenagers, right? Sharma instead was maybe fifty, hair prematurely going gray, dark-skinned, dark beard, and he always, at every opportunity anyway, seemed to be smoking thin cigarettes rolled in crinkled brown paper. Intelligent and articulate with only a hint of an accent, Ike thought he'd play decently for the jury. Now they would find out. Morton asked for their next witness, and Sharma was sworn in.

Ike took notes to the lectern with him. He made eye contact. "Good afternoon. Would you please state your name and occupation for the court?"

The hacker's lips curved into a subtle, confident smile. "My name is Raj Sharma, and I am an Internet security consultant."

Ike settled his notes on the lectern. "Mr. Sharma, what are an Internet security consultant's job duties?"

Another faint smile. "For the most part, they probe companies' websites to find their security vulnerabilities."

"Okay." Ike nodded. "And, sir, what do you do when you find such vulnerabilities?"

Sharma rested an elbow on the armrest. "I report them to the system's owner so they can be patched before they're exploited."

Ike drew his head back. "So in a sense then, you're a hacker?"

Sharma laughed. "More than in a sense."

"Really?" He glanced at his notes without seeing. "But, Mr. Sharma, you said that you report security vulnerabilities *before* they can be exploited."

"That's accurate. I'm a white-hat hacker. I hack only for good purposes."

Ike scratched the back of his head. "And yet you admitted in your sworn statement that you hacked Lakota Holt's Corolla, which caused the fatal crash. How can that be hacking for good purposes?"

The hacker's levity dried up. "That happened because I was lied to."

Ike drew back again. "And how were you lied to, sir, and by whom?"

Sharma crossed his arms over his chest. "According to *what I was told*, the hack was done for an insurance company to assess the security of the Corolla's onboard computer. I'd done a similar hack, and it had been carried out under secure conditions and was professionally supervised to minimize the chance of any injury. I had no reason to believe this demonstration would be any different."

Ike pointed at him. "But you contracted for this job anonymously on the dark web. If everything you did was so aboveboard, why the need to do it secretly?"

Sharma relaxed his arms. "Because sometimes companies don't want their security vulnerabilities to be made public. By working anonymously, they're able to protect their identity and keep their vulnerabilities secret."

"And they want to remain anonymous even from you?"

The hacker stroked his beard. "That's right."

Ike referred to his notes. "Which website on the dark web were you contacted on and by whom?"

Sharma looked off into the distance. "The hacker message board was called XSS. I don't know if it's still up. The guy who contacted me? All I know was his screen name—Z92."

Ike pivoted to the prosecution table. "I have no further questions, Your Honor."

Judge Morton spoke with the clerk and pointed to something on the clerk's desk. She then asked if the defense would cross-examine. They would.

Black took his time getting to the attorney lectern. "Good afternoon, Mr. Sharma."

"Good afternoon."

The big attorney took hold of the lectern. "Sir, you were given immunity from prosecution in exchange for your testimony against my client, weren't you?"

"Yes."

Black pursed his lips. "And it's true that you agreed to cooperate with the prosecution to limit your own criminal exposure, isn't it?"

The hacker held up both palms. "I haven't done anything wrong. I'm just here to tell the truth."

Black looked away and then back. "Sir, you may claim that you're just here to tell the truth, but claiming you did nothing wrong is in and of itself disingenuous. The reality is that the prosecution has offered to lessen your exposure by your cooperating at trial because you *have* committed a crime."

Ike stood. He needed to protect his witness. "Objection, Your Honor. Argumentative."

Sharma's head jerked from the judge to Ike and back again.

With a nod to Ike, Morton said, "The objection is sustained."

Black started pacing. "Sir, while I was listening to your earlier testimony, I couldn't help but think about how dangerous the Internet can be. Identity theft, stalking, cyberbullying, predators, phishing scams. And that is just on the regular Internet. The dark web is even more dangerous, isn't it?"

"It can be if you don't know what you're doing."

Black widened his eyes at the hacker. "And yet, the dark web is where you make your living, isn't it?"

Sharma blew out an exhalation. "For the most part, yes, it is."

Black held out his hand. "And yet, sir, in your testimony you claimed, 'I hack only for good purposes,' did you not?"

"Yes, that's what I said."

The defense attorney scoffed. "And so in your desire to hack for good in this case, things just went wrong because someone lied to you, isn't that what you testified?"

"Yes."

Black silently returned to the attorney lectern and settled himself. "Mr. Sharma, does a lot of lying take place on the dark web?"

The hacker leaned to the side of the witness chair. "It does."

"It does, and yet you trusted that this totally anonymous Z92 was telling the truth, didn't you?"

"I'd had similar dealings with other insurance companies —"

Black pointed at him. "That wasn't my question, sir. I asked if in a place where lying is rampant, you trusted that the totally anonymous Z92 told you the truth."

The hacker gripped the arms of the witness chair. "I got to the point where I trusted him, yes."

Black tilted his head. "Or perhaps trusted *her*? For certainly, there's no indication of gender in Z92, is there?"

"That's correct. It could've been a female."

Black narrowed his eyes at the hacker. "And you didn't *know* that Z92 was representing an insurance company, did you?"

"Like I said before, I've dealt with insurance companies before—"

"Again, sir, that wasn't my question. I asked if you didn't know that Z92 was an insurance company."

"No, I didn't technically *know*."

"So not only did you not know that Z92 wasn't an insurance company, you had *no idea* who Z92 was, isn't that right?"

Sharma's gaze fell to the floor. "They sounded like an insurance company."

"They sounded like an insurance company." Black glanced at the defense table. "So, sir…" He turned back to the hacker. "…on a dark web message board where other hackers congregate and are known to lie rampantly, you didn't *know* that the person contacting you was an insurance company. In fact, you didn't know who they were at all, and on top of all that, isn't it true that you had no way of finding out who they were?"

Sharma scowled. "It's an anonymous message board, okay? Yeah, I had no way of finding out who they were."

"So you had absolutely no knowledge that Z92 was a Pharamundo employee or operative, did you?"

The hacker sent the attorney a flat stare. "No."

Black paused, then slowly approached the witness stand. He placed both hands on the edge, leaning in. "And so you have absolutely no knowledge that Z92 is Thomas Acosta, do you?"

Sharma looked at Black's hands and then up at the big attorney. "That is correct."

"I have no further questions, Your Honor."

Judge Morton informed the court that her schedule necessitated recessing court until tomorrow morning at 9:00 a.m. She apologized for the inconvenience and once again warned the jurors of their responsibility not to discuss the case.

Chapter Twenty-five

After Morton recessed court, Harkin chatted with Ike and Abby at the prosecution table for a few minutes but then disappeared. It was clear that he had no real interest in litigating the case himself.

The sudden free time surprised Ike and Abby and left them pondering their next move. Ike suggested it would be easier to discuss things at his place.

Abby gave him a sidelong look. "Do you really think that's a good idea?"

"Well, we have to discuss the case, don't we? It would be best to do it somewhere we're comfortable, right?" He tilted his head. "And you're comfortable at my place, aren't you?"

Abby shut her laptop. "When your wife isn't there."

Ike's throat tightened. "Abby, I've had the locks changed. Mallory's been served divorce papers. And if all else fails…" He grinned. "…I have several guns in the house."

"Yeah, that's funny, Ike. Ha ha. Yeah, you're a real cowboy." She looked at him long and hard. "All right, I'll come —*to discuss the case*." Finally her countenance softened as she added, "And I do miss Leaner anyway."

So, she was still miffed, but at least she was coming over —and that was one more reason to be grateful for Leaner. He stopped for Chinese carryout, and when he arrived home, Abby's car was in the driveway with the engine idling.

At the house, Leaner was happy to see Ike but even more excited to see Abby again. The dog seemed drawn to her feminine nature. After dinner, Ike let the dog out into the backyard and suggested they join him there. But Abby said the humidity would frizz her hair, so they settled in on the sofa and from there watched Leaner patrol the backyard.

Ike sat on his hands. He wanted to touch her so badly, but with how iffy things had been between them, he was hardly feeling confident that she wanted to be touched. And they did have to discuss the case. "Are you still thinking Jeff Castro is likely to perjure himself on the stand tomorrow?"

She took off her glasses and set them on the cocktail table. She rubbed her eyes. "Probably. But really, with him basically being all we've got, how can we not go with him? Okay, Bree's testimony may have helped establish motive, but Black basically destroyed all our other witnesses."

Ike stretched his legs out, looking for a more comfortable position. He plopped his hands onto his thighs. "Agreed."

She held his eye. "And so if we let Castro testify, are we suborning perjury?"

He raised his eyebrows. "Good question. Let me see if I can remember the definition. Suborning perjury is actively or knowingly encouraging, inducing, or causing another to commit perjury. Actually, I don't think we've met that bar. We're close though. Very close. Our escape hatch would be *knowingly*. Because we don't *know* that he's lying. We're just suspicious."

"What about our obligations to deal with witnesses we suspect are lying?"

"Well, there are ways of dealing with that, too. For starters, we don't call him. But then what? Like you said, he's basically all we've got. The fact of the matter is if we keep him off the stand, odds-on Acosta walks. Maybe the justice system wasn't designed to work this way, but what we decide about him testifying or not may well determine the outcome of this case. I imagine there's plenty of lawyers out there who'd say it's better to let a guilty person walk rather than degrade the integrity of the judicial system. But, Abby, like deciding what to do about your father's indiscretions, everything in the law is gray." She looked so pretty to him. He'd done all he could not to touch her but felt himself caving. He leaned just a touch into her. "Think maybe you could stay over? We can head into court together in the morning."

She reached for her glasses. "Oh, I don't know."

Leaner started scratching at the sliding glass door.

"See." Ike nodded toward the door. "Even Leaner wants you to stay."

"Yeah, right." She gave him a very unhappy look. "And if Mallory shows up again?"

"I told you, I've got guns."

She rolled her eyes. Eventually, though, her gaze fell on the dog, which was still scratching away. She turned to Ike. "Do you really think he wants me to stay?"

He took her glasses, pulled her close, and kissed her.

* * *

Ike woke before Abby and made coffee. He returned to the bedroom, where she was completely under the bedspread. "Are you in there somewhere?"

"Who wants to know?"

He smiled.

"I can see you smiling out there." She pulled the covers down to her neck. "This bedspread is so sheer I can see right through it. It's pretty too, Ike. Lavender and lace. You have good taste and you're definitely in touch with your feminine side."

"Yeah, yeah." He knew she was giving him the business, as it was obvious that Mallory had chosen the frilly bedspread. "Now come on. We've got to discuss Jeff Castro's upcoming testimony. I made coffee."

She slid her legs over the edge of the bed. "Coffee will indeed get me to move."

At the kitchen table, Leaner once again leaned into her leg. She grinned. "I don't know why I like that he does this so much but I do. You know what I think would really help our case would be if we could unleash Leaner on the Monster."

Ike deadpanned, "I think we're going to have to unleash you on the Monster."

They drove to the courthouse together. Jeff Castro was their last witness, and having their last witness testify in the middle of the trial felt strange since, as defense attorneys, their last witness had always signified the end of the trial.

The courthouse was buzzing as usual. Peter Harkin just barely made it to the prosecution table before the bailiff announced Judge Morton's entrance.

Ike had to work hard not to challenge Harkin about his lack of commitment to the case. He forced himself to nod to the young prosecutor. Meanwhile, Judge Morton was organizing papers on the bench. She handed a document to the clerk, who marked it and returned it. Finally, she focused on the jury.

"Welcome back. I'm glad to see everyone made it. We have a full day of testimony in store, so unless there are any questions…" She raised her eyebrows and waited. "…let's get started." She turned her attention to the prosecution table. "The State may call its next witness."

"Here we go," Ike whispered to Abby as he stood. "Thank you, Your Honor. The State calls Jeffrey Castro."

Castro, in a sleek black suit, white shirt, and yellow necktie, goatee expertly trimmed, walked unhurriedly down the aisle and through the gate. Sworn in, he took the stand and sat rigidly.

So much for legal ethics, Ike thought, as he grabbed a notepad and walked to the attorney lectern. "Good morning. Would you please state your name and occupation?"

"Jeffrey Castro. I'm head of the Information Technology department at Pharamundo International."

"And how long have you worked at Pharamundo in that capacity?"

"Seventeen years. And I've been with the company twenty-six years."

"Okay, very good." Ike jotted something down. "And during all that time, have you seen employees come and go?"

"Of course." Castro glanced at the defense table but seemed to stop short of making eye contact with Acosta. "And with CEO Acosta's reputation for vindictively firing people, that's an awful lot of people."

Up popped Black. "Objection, Your Honor, the witness' statement is pure conjecture as to the mindset and motive of Mr. Acosta."

"Sustained." Morton turned to the witness. "Mr. Castro, please limit your answers to what you have observed, not speculation about motives."

Ike didn't let the objection throw him. "Mr. Castro, does your position as the head of IT call for a lot of contact with CEO Acosta?"

"Not usually." He adjusted the band on his wristwatch. "In fact, I've had very little contact with him until the last six months. In a corporation the size of Pharamundo, the IT head usually reports to the COO or CFO, not the CEO."

"In these last six months, what sort of contact have you had with Mr. Acosta?"

Castro sent another glance Acosta's way. "He's reached out to me and asked a lot of questions about the dark web."

"And is that unusual?"

The IT head settled back in the chair. "Not entirely, I suppose. CEOs have an interest in protecting their company from online attacks and avoiding data breaches. Certainly, some CEOs have a more hands-on approach to security than others."

"What sort of things did Mr. Acosta ask you?" Ike clipped a pen to the edge of the notepad.

"Mostly he wanted to know how to navigate anonymously on the dark web."

Ike widened his eyes. "Really? He wanted to know how to navigate anonymously on the dark web. What sort of things did he want to know how to do?"

"Like I said, how to operate there without being detected."

Ike took a few steps toward the witness stand. "Okay. And how did you answer him?"

Castro looked at the defense table again and this time seemed to hold Acosta's eye. "I explained to him how to set up a VPN. How to use burner email addresses. And how to use a proxy server. But he wasn't satisfied with those things. He wanted to know more."

Ike looked at the jury. "A VPN. Burner email addresses. And a proxy server. Can you explain to the jury what those terms mean?"

"Sure, a VPN is a service that encrypts your Internet traffic and routes it through a server in a remote location."

Ike held up a hand. "And that makes your computer anonymous?"

"*More* anonymous. Complete anonymity, if possible, is much more of a challenge."

Ike steepled his fingers. "And burner email addresses?"

"Those are disposable email addresses used for temporary communication and not associated with the user's identity." Another glance at the defense table. "They can't be traced."

"And a proxy server?" This was going as well as it could. Ike could even feel some of his old mojo returning.

"It's a server that acts as an intermediary between your computer and the Internet. It can help protect your privacy by masking your IP address. This means that malicious websites and other servers cannot see your real IP address, preventing them from tracking your online activity."

Ike returned to the attorney lectern. It was time to put the hammer down. "But you said CEO Acosta wasn't satisfied with those things. He wanted to know more. What else did he want to know?"

Castro smoothed his hands over his pant legs. "He wanted to know how to create fake online identities that could be used to purchase illegal services."

Ike looked at Castro, then at the jury, then back at Castro. "On the dark web?"

"Yes."

Ike flexed his hands. "And did you show him?"

The muscles in Castro's jaw tightened. "He was my boss. I felt I had to."

Ike nodded quickly. "Now let me backtrack for a minute. You said Mr. Acosta wanted to know how fake online identities could be used to purchase illegal services on the dark web. Please tell the jury what sort of illegal services are available for purchase there."

Castro widened his eyes. "Anything and everything you can think of."

"For instance?"

"Drugs, weapons, money laundering, sex trafficking, stolen credit cards, identity theft, cyberstalking, child pornography, anything," the IT head rattled off.

Ike tilted his head at him. "Murder for hire?"

Castro bit his lip. "Even that."

Ike nodded to Abby, and she pressed a button on her laptop and an image came on the video screen.

Ike caught Morton's eye. "Your Honor, I respectfully request that the following series of texts between Thomas Acosta and Jeffrey Castro be entered into evidence as State's Exhibit 3."

The judge studied the images on the screen, then turned to the defense table. "Do you have any objections to this, Counselor?"

Black glanced down at an open laptop before responding, "No, Your Honor."

"So noted. The text messages are admitted into evidence."

Ike took a few steps toward the video screen. "What we are looking at is a series of encrypted, disappearing text messages between yourself and Mr. Acosta, isn't that right, Mr. Castro?"

"Objection. Leading." Black didn't even look up from the laptop.

"Sustained."

Ike was so accustomed to cross-examining prosecution witnesses he'd slipped and asked a leading question. "Mr. Castro, what are we looking at on the screen?"

Castro pulled glasses from his suit coat breast pocket and slipped them on. He did not jump at answering the question, as he was most probably following Ike's pretrial suggestion to appear thoughtful. "These are encrypted, disappearing text messages between Thomas Acosta and myself."

"Now, as you just testified, sir, these text messages are encrypted *and* disappearing, but if the messages are disappearing…" Ike held his arms out wide. "…how is it that we're seeing them now?"

With his thumb and forefinger, Castro clutched his goatee. "The text messaging service Thomas Acosta and I used did indeed have disappearing messages, but before disappearing, the messages remained on the screen for fifteen seconds, and while they were there, I took screenshots of them, which I saved to my phone."

"And why did you do that, sir?"

Castro sent a sharp look at Acosta. "I did it because I didn't like where his questions were headed."

Ike pointed to the video screen, then turned back to Castro. "But, sir, with cutting-edge technology couldn't screenshots of the texts be faked?"

The IT head waved a hand. "They could, sure, but there are validation tools that can confirm metadata and detect tampering, and these images on the screen have been run through a battery of such tools by an independent validation agency."

THE PERFECT PROSECUTOR

Ike returned to the prosecution table, picked up some papers, and walked them over to the bench. "Your Honor, I'd like to offer this report from Independence Metadata Validation Inc. as State's Exhibit 4." He gave her a copy and then gave one to Black.

Morton held a hand out to the defense table. "Any objection?"

Black tossed the report to the side. "No, Your Honor."

Morton examined the report. "So noted, admitted as State's Exhibit 4."

Ike made his way back to the lectern and checked his notepad. "Mr. Castro, is there anything else that can be done to verify the authenticity of these texts?"

"There is. If I can have a laser pointer?"

Abby hustled one to him.

"If you look at the top of every text, you'll see…" He steadied the laser. "…where it says 'Thomas Aco…' and under that is a check mark with the word *verified*. That check mark and the word *verified* signify that the text is authentically from that sender."

Ike looked from the screen back to the witness. "Mr. Castro, please read the first text message from Thomas Acosta to you aloud."

The IT head cleared his throat. "At some of these forums, Jeff, you can even find people who will kill people, can't you?"

Ike pointed to the screen. "And your reply?"

"My reply was…" He sighed. "…actually, yes, you can."

"And in some of these text messages…" Ike approached the witness stand. "…does Mr. Acosta ask if there are ways to make murder look like an accident?"

Castro nodded. "He does. Several times. Look at number seven and number twelve."

Ike turned to the screen. "In text message number seven, Mr. Acosta asks, 'What are some of the ways of doing it?' Mr. Castro, what did Mr. Acosta mean by that?"

That got Black up in a hurry. "Objection, Your Honor. The question calls for speculation and asks the witness to draw conclusions about the defendant's state of mind."

"I'll rephrase, Your Honor." Ike told himself to breathe —no matter what happened, he couldn't let Black rattle him. "Mr. Castro, based on the context of your conversation with Mr. Acosta, what did you understand him to mean by the question, 'What are some of the ways of doing it?'"

"Well." Castro threw his hands up. "Hell, he wanted to know what the various ways were to make killing somebody look like an accident."

Ike didn't like the display of emotion, and he gave Castro what he hoped was a calming look. "I understand you're upset, Mr. Castro, but I need to know how you answered Mr. Acosta's question."

Castro's eyes glommed on to Ike's. He took two deep breaths, pushed his glasses up the bridge of his nose, and finally returned his focus to the screen. "I answered, poisoning, making it look like suicide, falls, heart attacks—but the most effective way of disguising murder is tampering with equipment."

Ike nodded quickly. "And please read Mr. Acosta's text in number twelve."

The IT head looked warily at Acosta before clearing his throat again and turning back to the screen. "And tampering with equipment. That could be a car, Jeff, right?"

"And your reply?"

THE PERFECT PROSECUTOR

Castro bowed his head. "See, at first I just thought he was curious about the dark web, about the perverse things that happen there. I didn't know he'd end up where he did. I figured he was just a strange guy asking strange questions."

"Please read your reply to his question, 'And tampering with equipment. That could be a car, Jeff, right?'"

Castro exhaled sharply, checked the screen, then eased out, "Absolutely could be a car, yeah."

"Further down…" Ike motioned to Abby, who scrolled on her laptop, bringing up new images on the screen. "…we see several text messages between you and Mr. Acosta specifically discussing the notion of tampering with a car to make a crash look like an accident, isn't that right?"

Black was up again. "Objection, Your Honor. Counsel is leading the witness. Counsel is instructing the witness what to say."

"Sustained."

Damn. Again he'd screwed up with a leading question. "I'll rephrase. Mr. Castro, please read out loud messages twenty-seven and thirty-one."

Castro did so in a clear voice.

Ike felt back in control. "Sir, are messages twenty-seven and thirty-one Mr. Acosta's questions about making a tampered car look like an accident?"

"Yeah, yes, they both are."

Ike held the witness' eye. "Did Mr. Acosta ask you if you knew where to find a hacker who would do such tampering?"

Castro nodded slowly. "He did."

Ike walked all the way over to the video screen and pointed at the screen. "And finally, what did Mr. Acosta say in message seventy-three?"

Castro sat silently.

"Mr. Castro?"

Still no response.

"Sir?"

Castro looked to the left, then to the right, then down. "He said, 'pull the string.'"

Ike paused, allowing the weight of the fatal words to settle on the courtroom. The silence stretched on. Then, clasping his hands together, he asked, "And, sir, what did you understand the words 'pull the string' to mean?"

Castro swallowed. He frowned. "That I was to engage a hacker to tamper with Lakota Holt's car."

Ike walked back to the prosecution table. "And what did you do?"

Hands to his temples, head down, Castro muttered, "I didn't know the guy would die. I swear to God I didn't know he would die."

Ike hurried to the witness stand. "And so, sir, what did you do?"

Castro muttered something indistinct.

Morton interceded, "Mr. Castro, you'll need to speak up."

In a scratchy, low voice, he rasped, "I pulled the string."

Ike was right there. "You engaged a hacker to tamper with Mr. Holt's car?"

"Yes, yes." Chin to his chest, shaking his head.

All right. Ike was more than satisfied with the IT head's testimony. Now he had to play the bad cop to draw the sting from Castro's testimony before Black would. "You did so even though you knew there was a good chance Mr. Holt would die, that his death was indeed the object?"

Castro's head was still down. "It's the worst thing I've ever done."

Ike touched the edge of the witness stand. "Why did you do it?"

"Why?" Castro lurched up. "Because I'd seen what Acosta had done to other employees who'd defied him." He shuddered and cast a furtive glance at the defense table. "He threatened me, you understand? Said I'd be *unfortunate* if I didn't engage the guy."

Ike crossed his arms and waited and waited and waited, the courtroom falling tomb-like quiet. "So why come clean now?"

Castro took several deep, ragged breaths as if garnering the strength to speak. "Because when I heard about the crash and the reporter's death, I knew I wouldn't be able to live with myself if I didn't come forward. Someone had to speak up." His eyes searched Ike's for sympathy. "Someone had to stop Acosta."

"I have no further questions, Your Honor."

Chapter Twenty-six

The judge turned her attention to the defense table. "Mr. Black, cross?"

The big man, notes under his arm, rose. "Thank you, Your Honor, yes."

"Proceed."

"Good morning, Mr. Castro."

"Good morning."

The defense attorney, a flicker of challenge in his eye, headed for the attorney lectern. "Mr. Castro, like several other prosecution witnesses, you've been granted immunity from prosecution by the government in exchange for your testimony against Mr. Acosta, haven't you?"

"Yes."

"And, sir, do you understand that while you may feel comfortable testifying because of the immunity, it does not guarantee that you can say whatever you want, and that if your testimony is discovered to be inconsistent, or misleading, or false, you may be charged with perjury and prosecuted?"

"I understand."

Black nodded. "Very well. Mr. Castro, have you ever spent more time on the Internet than you intended?"

"Yes."

"Asked more questions than you'd meant to?"

"Yes."

"I know I have. In fact, several prestigious organizations like the…" Black read from his notes. "…Social Science Research Center, the Internet Society, the Berkman Klein Center for Internet, and countless others have shown that we all do. And not only that, but while we're online, we become unaware of time passing, captivated by the Internet's sophisticated algorithms designed to grip our attention and not let go. Would you agree with that assessment, sir?"

Castro's eyes roamed into the gallery. "I would."

Black arranged his notes on the lectern. "Mr. Castro, it's difficult to know a person's mental and emotional state through texting, isn't it?"

"At times, I would say it is."

The defense attorney looked up from the notes. "Hard to know if the person is up or down emotionally?"

Castro just barely shrugged his shoulders. "At times."

"Impossible to know if they've been drinking or are under the effect of an illegal or prescription drug?"

The IT head held up a forefinger. "*That* may be a little more apparent."

"Okay, I can see that." Black jotted something on his notes. "But it would be impossible, sir, to know for certain what they were thinking, wouldn't it?"

"Of course."

"Accordingly…" Now Black held up a forefinger. "…it's impossible to know their intentions as well, right?"

Castro waved a hand lazily in the air. "I suppose you could say that. Unless of course, they tell you."

"And in his texts to you did Mr. Acosta tell you his intentions?"

The IT head looked off again. "No, he didn't."

Ike ran a hand through his hair. He felt like Black was setting Castro up for the kill.

"Very good. Thank you." The defense attorney waited for Castro to look at him, then narrowed his eyes. "Mr. Castro, have you yourself ever purchased illegal goods or illegal services on the dark web?"

Ike was up. "Objection, Your Honor. Relevance."

The judge focused on Black.

"Your Honor, the question is probative in that it shows the level of Mr. Castro's personal involvement and experience on the dark web."

Morton turned to the witness. "Objection overruled. Please answer the question, Mr. Castro."

Castro's eyes flitted to the prosecution table.

Ike bit his lip. *Can't help you, buddy.*

Black stepped to the side of the lectern, positioning himself to block Castro's view of the prosecution table. "Let me remind you, sir, that you are under oath."

The IT head's shoulders slumped. "I purchased three grams of marijuana—one time."

"On the dark web?"

"Yes, but that was before—"

"I didn't ask you when, Mr. Castro. Now let's move on." He rolled up his notes and held them in his hand. "Sir, did you know Lakota Holt?"

"No."

"Not at all?"

"No."

Black pointed toward him with the notes. "But you knew of him, didn't you?"

"I knew of him, yes."

"And your wife knew Lakota Holt personally, didn't she?"

"Objection." Ike stood. "Relevance."

Black didn't miss a beat. "Your Honor, this will establish the witness' state of mind at the time of his interaction with Mr. Acosta."

Morton raised a pen she held. "I'll allow it. Overruled. Please answer the question, Mr. Castro."

Castro rubbed his goatee. "Yes."

Black moved back to the lectern. "In fact, your wife had quite a close relationship with Mr. Holt, didn't she?"

The IT head glared at the attorney. "What are you insinuating?"

"I'm not insinuating anything, sir. I simply asked if your wife had a close relationship with Mr. Holt. Did she?"

"I don't know what my wife's relationship with him was like."

"Really?" The big man put a hand to his chin. "I think by all standards it can be said that Mr. Holt was a handsome man, and yet, you don't know what your wife's relationship with him was like?"

Abby bounced up. "Objection, Your Honor. Counsel is arguing with the witness. He's trying to tell the witness how to answer."

Black turned to the judge. "Your Honor, this is a question the jury is going to want answered."

"No, it isn't." Morton nodded to Abby. "Objection is sustained."

Black, while already on his way back to the defense table, sneered, "I have no further questions for this witness, Your Honor."

Morton excused Castro, and the judge's forehead furrowed as she checked her watch. "All right. It looks like we have time for one more witness before we break for lunch. Prosecution, please call your next witness."

Ike glanced at Harkin before turning back to Morton. "The State rests, Your Honor."

"Oh…all right." The judge checked the wall clock. "So now the defense can call its first witness."

"Thank you, Your Honor." Black perused a document at the defense table while still seated. "The defense calls Eric Hanson."

A stocky man, about five-foot-eight, took the stand. He wore a stylish green linen suit with a mauve dress shirt. He was nicely tanned, and his lips pressed into a thin line.

Black rose. "Sir, please state your name and occupation for the court."

"Eric Hanson. I'm the president of Modern Mechanic Automotive Institute."

"And what is Modern Mechanic Automotive Institute?"

Hanson spoke in a measured tone. "It's a chain of three hundred auto repair shops across the Midwest."

"And, sir, are you a mechanic yourself?"

The man's expression softened. "Yes, I'm a Certified Master Mechanic and also a Certified Master Automotive Technician."

Black raised an eyebrow. "A Certified Master Automotive Technician, what's that?"

"A Master Technician is a highly trained and certified professional who has advanced knowledge and expertise in diagnosing, repairing, and maintaining a wide range of automotive systems and components."

"And how long have you been a master mechanic and master technician?"

"For thirty-two years."

"Thirty-two years, wow." Black moved to the attorney lectern. "And in all that time, sir, have you seen several badly damaged cars after accidents?"

"Yes. Hundreds."

Black gripped the lectern and paused for a few long seconds. "Have you also seen accidents that were the result of remote computer hacking?"

A confident nod. "I have."

Black pursed his lips. "How many would you say you've seen over the course of your thirty-two-year automotive career?"

"Only two or three."

"Hold on." Black pushed off the lectern. "Only two or three in all those years?"

"Only two or three *bona fide* ones, yes, that's right," the man said in a clear, even tone.

"Bona fide ones? Please explain."

"Surely, most claims of remote hacking upon further investigation turn out to be unfounded." He hunched his shoulders. "Simply put, remote computer hacking is exceedingly rare."

"Most claims of remote hacking upon further investigation turn out to be unfounded," Black repeated slowly. "Simply put, remote computer hacking is exceedingly rare." A smile slowly spread on the defense attorney's face. "Mr. Hanson, did you investigate Mr. Holt's vehicle after the accident?"

"I did."

"And what is your professional opinion as to whether the tragic accident under consideration in this trial could have been caused by remote computer hacking?"

Hanson glanced at the judge and then at Black. "I think it was impossible."

A buzz rose in the gallery.

Morton waved the sound down. "Ladies and gentlemen, please maintain a respectful silence."

"You think it was impossible." Black tilted his head at the witness. "Then, sir, considering your vaunted credentials as a master mechanic and master technician and your extensive experience working on cars, what *do* you think caused the accident?"

"I don't know, but nothing I've seen indicates it was caused by remote hacking."

Another buzz in the gallery.

Ike twisted the college ring on his finger, the old nervous habit returning. This testimony was throwing a lot of shade on their theory of the case.

Black took his time. "Mr. Hanson, the prosecution's mechanic testified that he believed the driver of the vehicle pressed down so hard on the brake pedal that it left an impression on the floorboard. He added that the parking brake was mangled like a pretzel. And that both the damaged brake pedal and the mangled parking brake were the result of the driver's desperate attempts to stop the car. Would you agree with that assessment?"

Hanson was shaking his head even before Black finished. "Absolutely not. It's *extremely* unlikely that the braking components would be damaged by the driver's actions to stop the car, no matter how desperate he was. The Corolla's brake pedal is made of high-quality steel and just about indestructible. The rubber cover may have been scuffed or even torn off, but the pedal itself would not be damaged. And as far as the brake pedal making an impression on the floorboard? The hydraulics wouldn't allow it. The parking brake, on the other hand, could be damaged by the driver using excessive force, but if it was, it would be jammed in a locked position against the floorboard, and it would not be *mangled like a pretzel*. No, those damages were not caused by the driver's actions."

"Thank you. Your Honor, I have no further questions."

As the witness left the stand, Morton jotted a few notes. "Mr. Thompson, cross?"

It was the first time she'd called him by name. It seemed he was clearly the lead prosecutor in her eyes now. He stood. "Yes, Your Honor." He grabbed a yellow legal pad and brought it to the attorney lectern. "Good morning, Mr. Hanson."

"Good morning."

"Sir, you testified that you've been a master mechanic and master technician for thirty-two years, isn't that right?"

"Yes."

Ike leaned an elbow on the lectern. "But being the president of a large automotive repair chain, certainly you don't spend all your time working on cars, do you?"

Hanson didn't hesitate. "I still work on them occasionally, but yes, I do mostly administrative work these days."

Ike widened his eyes at the man. "Sir, when was the last time you *did* work full-time as a mechanic?"

"It's been a few years, I would say."

Ike glanced at the legal pad. "Oh, but, Mr. Hanson, on your tax returns, you show that you haven't worked as a mechanic for over twenty years, isn't that right?"

"Well, technically—"

"Sir, it was a simple question. You haven't worked as a mechanic for over twenty years, isn't that right?"

Hanson's nostrils flared. "Yes, that's right."

"And the work you *have* done for the last twenty years has been administrative, hasn't it?"

Hanson shifted in his seat, fingers drumming lightly on the armrest. "Like I *said*, I still work on cars, but yes, I spend most of my working time overseeing the operation of the company."

"Working in the office?"

"Right."

"And you don't leave the office to examine car wrecks as they come in, do you?"

Hanson shifted in his seat. "Well, no, not regularly anyway."

Ike leaned forward. It was time to take a gamble. He fixed the witness with a hard stare and picked the number fifteen. "In fact, sir, it's been at least fifteen years since you've personally examined a wrecked vehicle, hasn't it?"

Up came Black. "Objection, Your Honor. The question is leading, suggestive, and assumes facts not in evidence."

Ike was ready. "Your Honor. I'll rephrase. Mr. Hanson, could you tell us when was the last time you personally examined a wrecked vehicle?"

The witness smirked. "I'd say five years."

"You'd *say* five years." Ike nodded. "Mr. Hanson, your company, Modern Mechanic Automotive Institute, has received millions of dollars from car manufacturers who have a vested interest in downplaying the risks of remote hacking, hasn't it?"

Hanson stiffened. "As with most automotive repair chains, Modern Mechanic Automotive Institute has received funding from various sources, including car manufacturers.

But that doesn't mean we parrot their views on remote hacking or anything else."

Ike snorted in a breath. "Let's be clear, Mr. Hanson. You just testified—under oath, sir—that the money you've received from car manufacturers hasn't impacted your company's direction or policies. Yet, as part of receiving that funding, you've actually been bound by terms that prohibit you from making public statements detrimental to their reputation or financial interests, isn't that right?"

Hanson looked long and hard at Black before turning back to Ike. "Well, the agreements we sign are standard in the industry and are meant to—"

"It was a yes or no question, sir."

Hanson exhaled slowly, a faint whistle escaping through his clenched teeth. "Yes, we've signed NDAs."

Ike gestured to the jury. "For their benefit, sir, please explain what NDAs are."

The business owner's face fell. "NDAs, or Non-Disclosure Agreements, are legally binding contracts that prohibit parties from disclosing specified information."

Ike was ready and waiting. "And those NDAs prohibit you from disclosing information about *remote hacking* that could be detrimental to the car manufacturers' interests, don't they?"

Hanson shook his head dismissively. "Actually, the agreements are quite complex. They're designed to protect proprietary information while still allowing us to contribute to public safety discussions—"

"Again, sir, it was a yes or no question. Do the NDAs you've signed and are legally bound by prevent you from disclosing information about remote hacking that could be detrimental to the interests of the car manufacturers *who fund your organization*?"

A look away from Ike and a quick shrug. "In some cases, yes, they do."

Ike abandoned the lectern and took deliberate steps toward the witness stand, buttoning his suit coat with a fast, precise gesture as he closed the distance between them. "So, *sir*, despite your earlier testimony about remote hacking when questioned by the defense attorney, there may be relevant information you're not sharing with this court due to the conditions and restrictions of the NDAs your company has signed with the car manufacturers, isn't that right? And I remind you, sir, that you are under oath."

Hanson's jaw tightened before muttering, "Yes, that's possible."

Ike caught Morton's eye. "No further questions, Your Honor."

Chapter Twenty-seven

Court broke for lunch, and despite it being relatively late in the season, the weather was still freaky hot. Ike and Abby, feeling a desperate need for fresh air, braved the thunderstorm risk and went out for a walk. The gusting wind provided at least a little relief from the heat as it propelled the massive, black-bellied cumulus clouds roiling overhead. They made their way to a quiet residential neighborhood.

Abby looked over at him. "So, what do you think? Seems to me Black keeps hammering on motive and means."

Ike loosened his tie. "Yeah, that's my take too. He keeps focusing on the notion that the car's computer wasn't hacked. So there goes the means for committing the murder. And if Black can get the jury to believe the curative drug doesn't exist, the motive we've postulated for killing Lakota is out the window too."

"And we have no one to establish that the drug exists. Unless Elizabeth Castro was to somehow show up."

"Maybe…" Ike watched a couple of kids throwing a Frisbee. "…but that's a big if."

Abby plucked a dandelion and twirled it between her fingers. "So, maybe our chances aren't looking so good right now, but if you consider the miracle that this case even got to trial, then who knows."

"That's the spirit," he said with a wry grin.

The wind swirled and Abby pulled her hair behind her ears. "And really, when I first heard about Pharamundo being connected to the cartels, I was skeptical, and I was even more skeptical of Jeff Castro's assertion that Pharamundo killed his wife. But do you know what? Now I'm not so sure."

"Well, whether they killed her or not, we still have to face the fact that she's missing and have to go forward without her."

"And speaking of the Castros, I actually thought Jeff did pretty well on the stand except…" She tossed the dandelion. "…when he got pigeonholed into admitting he bought marijuana on the dark web. I can't help but think that took him down a couple of notches credibility-wise in the eyes of the jury."

"Eh, I don't think it was too bad. To me, the question seemed vindictive on Black's part. Castro did what we needed him to do, and he was sufficiently contrite about being complicit in Lakota's murder."

"Ike, between you and me." She lowered her voice, glancing around cautiously. "For his sake, I *hope* he perjured himself. It's dreadful to think he did what he may have."

"I hear you. But trust me, this won't be the first time you'll have to do triage with your conscience."

She widened her eyes. "Triage with my conscience. Hmm."

"Abby, the law is an exercise in risk management."

She gently tugged on his elbow. "So how are we standing in the risk management department for this trial?"

He waved a hand. "Well, we've taken on more than I would've liked, but with a jury involved, you're never out of the ballgame as long as you can win them over."

"And will we be able to?"

"We have to."

They turned the corner and headed back to court.

THE PERFECT PROSECUTOR

Ike cinched his tie back up. "Right now, we need to be thinking about what Black is going to throw at us next. Unless they switch the order, it should be Pharamundo's medical expert, a highbrow big shot doctor in the field of immunology."

She stopped him and straightened his tie. "Ah, I think you'll tear him to shreds on cross. Just channel your inner Ursula."

He sighed, only a hint of a smile playing on his lips. "Right."

* * *

Back in court, Morton motioned to the defense table. "You may call your next witness."

One of Pharamundo's female lawyers stood. "The defense calls Lucas Ford."

A man, immaculately clean-shaven, gray yet vital, in a sleek olive-green suit, white shirt, and tan necktie, took the stand and was sworn in.

Despite the female lawyer calling the witness, Black rose for the questioning. "Good afternoon. Please state your name and occupation."

"Lucas Ford and I am a physician and a clinical immunologist." The doctor's voice was steady.

"Sir," Black said on his way to the attorney lectern, "please tell the court, what exactly is a clinical immunologist?"

A brief nod. "Clinical immunologists diagnose and treat diseases related to the immune system."

"And where, sir, do you work and what is your position there?"

The physician leaned back in the chair, one arm set casually over the armrest. "I'm based at Northwestern Memorial Hospital in Chicago, but I have an office and privileges at the University of Chicago Medical Center as well."

Black raised an eyebrow. "Are you a member of any professional associations?"

The physician didn't hesitate. "Yes."

"The American Medical Association?"

"Yes."

"The American College of Allergy, Asthma, and Immunology?"

"Yes."

"And, sir..." Black left the lectern and headed for the witness stand. "...what is your position at the American College of Allergy, Asthma, and Immunology?"

"I'm the president."

"The president." Black glanced at the jury and then back at the doctor. "Doctor, what experience do you have with ALLD? Do you treat or study ALLD patients on a regular basis?"

Ike mulled a compound question objection but passed, thinking it would come off as trifling, especially so early in Black's questioning.

"Yes," the physician replied in an easygoing manner. "I've been researching and treating ALLD patients for several years now."

The big defense attorney crossed his arms. "Doctor, this trial has shown that Pharamundo has a curative drug in development for ALLD. What do you know about that, and how long might it be until the drug is released?"

The physician took longer to answer this time. "Well, in my opinion, while it seems Pharamundo has made great progress in developing the drug, such a drug is nevertheless most likely several years away from release. Even a properly managed course of drug treatment isn't always effective, so the search for a full cure is inevitably a tediously long process. Pharamundo is developing the drug to target the root cause of the disease in order to eradicate it, but that is an even more difficult undertaking given how little we know about the genetic abnormality that causes ALLD."

Black ambled back to the defense table. "No further questions, Your Honor."

Ike thought the judge had a 'good luck with cross-examining this one' look in her eye as she called his name.

Ike stood. "Yes, Your Honor, thank you." He grabbed his notes and beelined to the witness stand. "Afternoon, doctor."

"Afternoon."

Ike narrowed his eyes at the physician. "Doctor, are you being paid in any way by the defendant, Pharamundo International, or their legal team to testify in this trial?"

The witness glanced at Black. "I am being compensated, yes."

"And in what form and what amount is that compensation?"

Black was up. "Objection. Your Honor, Counsel is attempting to prejudice the jury."

Morton motioned to the attorneys to join her. "Both sides, please approach."

Ike and Abby, Harkin staying behind, and Black met at the bench.

The judge cupped her hand over the bench microphone and nodded to Black. "Tell me what's going on."

Black leaned in, the bench only just above his midsection. "Your Honor, Dr. Ford is an eminent physician and his time is incredibly valuable, and for someone of his vaunted professional stature, five hundred dollars an hour in compensation is reasonable and customary. The prosecution is attempting to prejudice the jury by implying that the doctor's testimony is somehow influenced by what may be perceived as excessive compensation."

Ike stepped up. "Your Honor, the jury needs to know that the doctor is not here simply because of goodwill, and knowing the amount of his compensation is essential for a fair trial. I am entitled to show the bias of the witness to the jury."

Morton gazed at the jury. "Well…" She turned back to the attorneys. "…the jury already knows the doctor is being compensated for his testimony. I do not see the amount of his compensation as being essential to the jury's understanding as to the motivations of his testimony. The objection is sustained."

Ike knew that Morton had the discretion to limit his cross-examination, but that did not mean that her ruling was right. Hell, the jury has a right to know how much Ford had been paid for his credentials and his opinions as a gun for hire. But he had to move on. He squared his notes with a crisp tap against the bench and returned to the witness stand.

"Doctor Ford, ALLD is an autoimmune disease, is it not?"

"Yes."

Ike took a deep breath. "And from what I understand, it causes inflammation in the lungs and ultimately liquefies them. So, a curative drug would ideally target both autoimmunity and inflammation. Sir, considering that there are already several effective drugs for treating autoimmunity and several effective drugs for treating inflammation on the market, why haven't Pharamundo's researchers been able to develop a curative drug when it seems so simple to combine existing drugs into a single, effective treatment?"

The physician shifted and glanced at the judge before returning his attention to Ike. "Well, ALLD may be treated with existing drugs, yes, but a simple combination of existing drugs is not the answer. To find a definitive cure, a company must work on understanding the genetic abnormality responsible for ALLD because such a full understanding is required to properly cure it, much like for any autoimmune disease with a genetic component. This is why it's taken so much time and why the research is still ongoing. No, solving this particular problem is not simple or straightforward. The human immune system is one of the greatest mysteries of medicine."

Ike swiped at a drop of sweat sliding down his temple. "Doctor, pharmaceutical companies have been sued for slow-walking or withholding curative drugs for the purpose of maintaining the sales of their other drugs, haven't they?"

The physician stroked his smooth chin for a few moments. "Such suits have been filed, yes, but I would say that it's natural to be skeptical of a company like Pharamundo, which has such vast financial resources, that fails to deliver a drug as promptly as anticipated."

Ike's eyes were glued to the floor as he returned to the prosecution table. "No further questions, Your Honor."

Meanwhile, Morton was already asking for the defense's next witness. Attorney Black was ready.

"Your Honor, the defense calls Vincent O'Malley."

Ike leaned over and jotted on Abby's legal pad. *I blew it.*

She tapped him with her elbow and whispered, "You did fine. Now stay up."

A burly Chicago cop in a navy-blue uniform, light blue shirt, navy tie, shiny silver badge over the breast pocket, settled in on the stand. Clean-shaven, ruddy-complected, the cop had a friendly countenance.

Black's countenance was noticeably less friendly, as documents in hand, he strode to the lectern. "Please state your name and occupation."

"Vincent O'Malley. I'm a police officer in the Chicago Police Department, First District." The cop's voice was a tad shaky, and he cleared his throat.

Black was all business. "Officer, part of your beat includes the heart of downtown Chicago, the area known as the Loop, doesn't it?"

"Yes."

"Your Honor, the defense presents this document as Defense Exhibit 2." Black took a copy of the police report to Morton and the witness, while the African American attorney dropped off a copy at the prosecution table. Black refocused on the witness. "Officer, your police report on May 26th of this year states that at approximately four-thirty in the afternoon you were called to 233 South Wacker Drive at the base of Willis Tower. Tell us what you encountered there."

The cop sat up. "I was called to 233 South Wacker Drive to respond to a battery in progress. When I arrived, a private security guard from Willis Tower was attempting to restrain a woman grabbing Thomas Acosta."

"Thomas Acosta, the CEO of Pharamundo International?"

"That's correct."

"Then what happened?"

THE PERFECT PROSECUTOR

The police officer's jaw tightened. "I announced that I was a police officer, and at that point the security guard backed off, and I attempted to pry the woman off Acosta."

"To *pry* her off?"

The cop smiled. "She was pretty determined."

Black perused his documents. "Officer, your report states that the woman was yelling and screaming. Did you know what she was yelling and screaming about?"

"Not at that point. I was just focused on getting her off Acosta."

Black turned to Morton with a confident nod. "No further questions, Your Honor."

Morton widened her eyes at Ike. "Your witness, Counsel."

"Thank you, Your Honor." Ike brought notes to the attorney lectern. "Good afternoon, Officer."

"Good afternoon."

"Officer, you're a pretty big guy. How much would you say you weigh?"

"Oh, about 235." He shrugged and a grin played on his lips. "Maybe closer to 250."

Ike glanced at Bree in the gallery. "And I happen to know that Bree Wilson, the person you struggled with that day in the incident with Thomas Acosta, weighs 103. And yet, as you just testified, you had to pry her off."

The cop folded his hands on his lap. "I was surprised myself how strong she was."

"And at the time, again as you testified previously, Officer, you heard Ms. Wilson yelling and screaming, isn't that right?"

"Yes."

Ike leaned on the lectern. "Then it would seem to make sense that Ms. Wilson had a powerful reason for such behavior, wouldn't it?"

Shaking his head, Black was up. "Objection, Your Honor. Counsel's question calls for speculation as to the state of mind of Ms. Wilson."

Morton rubbed her ear. "Sustained."

Ike winced—Black's objections were starting to get to him. He had to force his attention back to the cop. "Officer, to the best of your recollection, describe Ms. Wilson's emotional state at the time the incident occurred."

"Well." He tilted his head slightly to the right. "As I said, she was grabbing on to Acosta, so I would say she was upset, very upset actually."

Ike held the cop's eye. "Would you say that she was mentally unstable?"

Black bounced up. "Objection, Your Honor. Again, the question calls for speculation as to the state of mind of Ms. Wilson."

Morton held up a forefinger. "No, I'll allow it but only as to the observations of the witness as to the conduct of Ms. Wilson, not as to the thought process or reasoning abilities of Ms. Wilson." She turned to the cop. "Please answer the question, Officer."

The cop stifled a yawn. "I wouldn't say so, no. She was just very upset."

Ike checked his notes. "Officer, have you followed how the media has reported on the incident?"

Black was up yet again. "Objection, Your Honor. Relevance."

Ike held up a hand to Morton. "State of mind, Your Honor."

"I'll allow it. Overruled." The judge gave Black a look before turning to the witness. "Please answer the question, Officer."

The cop crossed his arms over his broad chest. "I wouldn't say *followed*, but I did see a couple of things about it."

"Did you see the following media reporting on the incident?" Ike read from the news report. " 'It appears that the woman was mentally unstable and had no prior connection with the CEO, and it is believed the attack was entirely random.' "

"No."

"Again, the article says it appeared that the woman had no prior connection with the CEO. Officer, did *you* know who Thomas Acosta was before the incident?"

"No, I did not."

"You had no idea who he was?"

"No."

Again, Ike consulted his notes. "And yet you testified, 'when I got there, a security guard from Willis Tower was attempting to restrain a woman who was grabbing Thomas Acosta,' didn't you?"

"Yes."

"But if you didn't know who Thomas Acosta was, how could you have said 'a woman who was grabbing Thomas Acosta?' "

The cop threw up his hands. "I would think I must've heard her use his name."

Ike could feel an objection coming as if it was fluttering in the air. He hurried his next question. "Officer, do people who randomly attack others tend to know their names?"

"No, not if it's random. They would have no way of knowing."

"And yet Bree Wilson knew Thomas Acosta's name. Hmm." Ike's mouth turned down. "One last question, Officer. The media article described the incident as an attack. Would you agree with that assessment?"

The cop tapped his thighs. "No. I wouldn't. I've been called to plenty of attacks, and this wasn't one. An attack involves the intention to hurt somebody. I don't think the woman was trying to hurt Acosta. She was just hanging onto him and yelling about something."

Ike whirled to face the bench. "No further questions, Your Honor."

"Very well, then." Morton leaned toward the witness stand. "Thank you, Officer, you may step down." The judge checked something on her desk, then the wall clock. "I would say we have time for one more. The defense may call its next witness."

Black stood. "Thank you, Your Honor. The defense calls Amanda Lee."

A trim, attractive Asian American woman, sporting a striking blue muslin dress with a pink sash, took the stand. Black asked his foundational questions and then set his notes on the attorney lectern. "Ms. Lee, as a physician working for Pharamundo International what is your primary function?"

The woman had perfect posture. "As the chief pharmaceutical representative for the company, I work with other healthcare professionals to spread awareness of our products. I also work with patients to help ensure the best outcome for their healthcare and to help them make informed decisions, especially decisions regarding using Pharamundo drugs."

"Doctor, would you say you have extensive experience regarding the process for developing and launching Pharamundo's drugs?"

She smiled demurely. "I'm quite knowledgeable about Pharamundo's drugs, yes."

"Thank you." Black turned a page of his notes. "Doctor, please explain the process for launching new drugs at Pharamundo."

A quick nod. "Launching a new drug at Pharamundo involves a series of steps ranging from early research and development to production, testing, and marketing. These steps are highly regulated and monitored and must meet strict safety, quality, and environmental standards. To ensure a successful launch, Pharamundo has a team of dedicated professionals who review data, monitor results, and make sure all the necessary materials and resources are in place. Once all testing and regulatory hurdles have been successfully passed, we can bring the new drug to market."

Black turned another page. "Doctor, is it Pharamundo's policy to only release fully developed drugs?"

"Absolutely. We only release drugs once they've been fully developed and approved for release, as specified in our contract with the government. I will add that although our policy prioritizes the safety of our products and patients, we, like any pharmaceutical company, are not immune to delays or unexpected difficulties in the development process, which unfortunately can contribute to delays in a drug's release."

Ike wrote on Abby's legal pad. *She's a human tape recorder.*

Abby jotted. *I'll have some good questions for her.*

Black's voice deepened. "Doctor, are there any circumstances where Pharamundo might *not* release a fully developed drug?"

Another pert nod from the physician. "In fact, there are several. The drug may still have unforeseen side effects, making its release onto the market potentially risky. The drug may not be as effective as first thought, its benefits not outweighing the potential side effects. The company may be engaged in negotiations with the government regarding pricing or reimbursement for the drug or may be disputing the terms of the contract. Or the company may just be trying to obtain regulatory approval before releasing the drug."

"Thank you, Doctor." The defense attorney turned from the witness to the bench. "No further questions, Your Honor."

Morton looked at Ike. "Prosecution, cross?"

Abby stood. "Yes, thank you, Your Honor, and good afternoon, Doctor Lee."

"Good afternoon."

"Doctor, to the best of your knowledge…" Abby spoke on her way to the lectern. "…has Pharamundo ever held back a drug from release for financial reasons?"

The physician tracked Abby with her eyes. "Absolutely not. The public's welfare is always foremost in the company's mind. Furthermore, the company's transparency regarding their drug development policies, as well as the strict oversight of regulatory agencies, is a testament to Pharamundo's commitment to patient safety over profits."

"Patient safety over profits." Abby let the words linger in the silent courtroom. "Patient safety over profits. Doctor, were you involved in the decision-making process regarding whether to release the curative drug for ALLD?"

The physician's brow furrowed. "As of now there is no curative drug, so no such process has occurred. However, once the drug exists and is deemed ready to be released, the decision to release it will be made by upper management, specifically the upper management of the New Drug Development division. I will, however, be made aware of the circumstances surrounding such decisions once they've been made."

"So you're not directly involved in making such decisions yourself, isn't that right?"

The doctor's face fell. "Yes, that's right."

Abby took a few steps toward the witness stand. "So in fact, you don't know if upper management may have made the decision to withhold the curative drug for ALLD for financial reasons, isn't *that* right?"

"Pharamundo's mission statement—"

"That wasn't my question, Doctor." Abby stepped closer. "So you're unable to confirm or deny whether upper management made the decision to withhold the curative drug for ALLD based on financial reasons, isn't that right?"

She shifted in the chair and seemed to look at someone in the gallery. "Yes, that would technically be correct."

"So, as the company's chief pharmaceutical representative, you have no idea whether the drug was held back for financial reasons despite the risk of death to thousands of people who needed the drug to survive, isn't that right?"

That got Black up in a hurry. "Objection! Asked and answered. The doctor just said she didn't know. It also assumes facts not in evidence. There has been no established proof or testimony regarding the existence of a curative drug for ALLD, and therefore any questions related to its release are speculative."

Morton's eyes narrowed, her voice with a sudden edge in it cutting through the courtroom. "Objection is sustained." She fixed Abby with a stare. "Counsel, your line of questioning is bordering on misconduct. From now on you are to adhere strictly to the established facts of this case. Am I clear?" She paused, allowing her words to sink in before addressing the jury. "The jury will disregard Counsel's last question entirely. It has no bearing on the facts of this case."

Abby bit her lip. "Understood, Your Honor. I have no further questions."

The judge rolled her neck. "Well, that's certainly enough for one day." She recessed court and strenuously reminded the jurors of the late start at 1:30 p.m. the next day.

Chapter Twenty-eight

When Ike and Abby returned from the courthouse, Leaner was eagerly awaiting them. They greeted the dog with as much affection as they could muster, but their minds were preoccupied with the trial. Ike let Leaner out and filled his bowls with nuggets and fresh water. Then he microwaved a couple of TV dinners. The trays were hot, and forgetting to use oven mitts, he rushed them to the kitchen table. He opened a bottle of white wine and poured two glasses.

Abby sat and held her wine glass without lifting it. "Honestly, Ike, after getting read the riot act by Morton for my last question to Dr. Lee, I don't know what to think. I don't know where we can go in the trial either." She peeled back the plastic film on the tray and stared. "I hate to admit it, but I'd say our chances are looking about as good as these fish sticks and tater tots."

"Okay, so Morton was a little upset, but that's mostly your exhaustion talking, Abby. I mean, come on. There's still a lot of trial left." He nodded at her tray. "Besides, those tater tots really aren't bad."

She listlessly speared one with a fork. "So we really should discuss the trial now, right?"

He sipped his wine. "Or if you're too tired, we can get up early and go over it in the morning."

"But will discussing it really make any difference? The fact of the matter is Morton is running me down and Black is running the table. Let's face it—Acosta is going to walk. And the end result will be Ursula will have egg on her face, and we'll have her eternal wrath to deal with."

And Oliver will die and Bree will be heartbroken. But Ike wasn't going there. Abby had bucked his spirits up so many times, it was time to return the favor. Holding up a fish stick, he took a bite. "These are pretty good too."

She laughed. "Silly man, you are."

Leaner scratched at the sliding glass door, and Ike let him in.

The dog headed straight for Abby and promptly leaned against her leg.

Looking down, Abby said, "Okay, now I must admit that *this* is giving me real comfort."

"He loves you too."

She took a bite of the tater tot. "Hmm." She finished it. "You know what? They're really not bad."

* * *

They did what prep they could in the morning and headed to court. Everyone anticipating this being the final day of testimony, not only was the gallery packed, but an overflow crowd spilled into the hallway. Ike and Abby knifed their way through the throng. Harkin, as usual, scampered in just as the bailiff called the court to order.

Judge Morton looked refreshed, her hair pulled back neatly. "Welcome back, everyone. We have a lot of testimony ahead, so let's get straight to it. The defense may call its next witness."

Black rose and headed for the attorney lectern. "Thank you, Your Honor. The defense calls Ellen Price."

A slender African American woman, wearing a forest green business suit over a camel-colored houndstooth top, took the stand.

Black ran through her credentials as a federal employee in the Department of Health and Human Services before he got to the heart of his questioning. "Ms. Price, could you please explain to the jury the actions taken by the Department of Health and Human Services in regard to the government's contractual agreements with pharmaceutical companies?"

The woman smiled. "Of course. The department oversees agencies including the FDA, which regulates pharmaceutical products, and CMS, which negotiates and administers contracts with pharmaceutical companies for drugs covered by programs like Medicare and Medicaid."

"So, FDA would be the Food and Drug Administration, and CMS is Centers for Medicare & Medicaid Services?"

"I'm sorry. Yes, that's right."

Black tapped the lectern lightly with a pen. "So in essence what you're talking about is the government overseeing the process to protect the lives and health of the public?"

The woman leaned forward. "Precisely. Protecting the public is Health and Human Services' purpose."

The defense attorney stroked his chin. "Ms. Price, how familiar are you with the government process of negotiating and finalizing a contract with a pharmaceutical company?"

"Very familiar."

Ike knew this little game of theater had been extensively choreographed.

Black nodded. "Ma'am, what was your role in the contract process between Pharamundo and the drug in development to cure ALLD?"

The woman needlessly straightened the lapels of her suit. "I was the lead negotiator for the government side and responsible for ensuring that the pharmaceutical company fulfilled its contractual obligations and stayed in compliance with all government regulations."

Black raised an eyebrow. "So you know as much as there is to know from the government side about the contract between the government and Pharamundo regarding the drug in development to cure ALLD?"

Ike stood. "Objection, Your Honor. Defense counsel is testifying."

Morton exhaled deeply. "Sustained."

"I'll move on." Black gave Ike an angry sidelong glance before turning back to the witness. "Ms. Price, to the best of your knowledge, at this stage of its drug in development to cure ALLD, has Pharamundo fulfilled its contractual obligations and stayed in compliance with all the government regulations?"

"Absolutely."

The defense attorney turned to the judge. "No further questions, Your Honor."

Morton looked toward Ike. "Mr. Thompson, cross?"

Ike knew Price's testimony was accurate and that he had nothing to impeach her about, but he wasn't letting her off the stand with just Black's softball questions. "Yes, Your Honor, thank you."

He brought a yellow legal pad to the attorney lectern and set it there. "Good afternoon, Ms. Price."

"Good afternoon."

"Ms. Price, you referred to your role negotiating the contract between the government and Pharamundo regarding the drug in development to cure ALLD. During those negotiations, the government was not prevented from seeking competitive bids from other companies for the contract, were they?"

She shifted in her chair. "Our negotiating team decided that based on our requirements, Pharamundo was the only company capable of providing the drug."

"That wasn't my question, Ms. Price."

She crossed her arms. "No, the government was not prevented from seeking competitive bids."

"Thank you." Ike rested an elbow on the lectern. "So, ma'am, please help me understand. ALLD is killing thousands of people nationwide, and with all the pharmaceutical companies working on developing curative drugs, you decided that *only Pharamundo* could develop such a drug?"

She waved a hand back and forth as if scolding a child. "The department made the decision to entrust Pharamundo with exclusive rights to develop a cure for ALLD based on their track record of research and development. With the company's impressive record of successful drugs released in recent years, yes, the department felt that they alone would be best equipped to develop an effective treatment in a timely manner."

Ike suppressed a smirk, straightened up, and lifted the legal pad. "Ms. Price, isn't it true that several government watchdog organizations have determined that the use of no-bid contracts is an effort to avoid congressional oversight?"

"Oh, I'm aware of the stories," she said with a tired shrug. "But I assure you that sealed, no-bid contracts *are* open to scrutiny. Government agencies are required to report and publicly disclose their use, which guarantees such scrutiny."

Ike realized this was going nowhere good. Sealed no-bid contracts sound bad, but they have real uses, and this employee was well versed in them. Time to cut and run. He tucked the legal pad under his arm. "I have no further questions, Your Honor."

Morton conferred with the clerk for a few minutes, then turned to the defense table. "Mr. Black, you may call your next witness."

The defense attorney organized some notes. "Certainly. Your Honor, the defense calls Prajit Kumar."

A svelte man in a purple long-sleeved shirt, paisley necktie, and a neatly wrapped black turban made his way through the gate and took the stand. He had an untrimmed black beard shading gray, and deep intelligence shone from his dark eyes.

Notes in hand, Black approached the lectern. "Good afternoon. Would you please state your name, where you work, and what your position is?"

"Prajit Kumar. I work at Hope Institute for Cancer Research, and I am the Director of Information Technology there."

Black took a long look at the man. "Mr. Kumar, what qualifies you to be the Director of Information Technology at such a prestigious organization?"

"I have a doctorate in Computer Science and Molecular Biology from MIT and ten years' experience in the field," he said in a low, confident voice. "I'm certified in Information Technology, Data Science, and Data Analytics. I also sit on the board of a Fortune 500 company and several medical non-profits."

"Sir, have you examined the testimony provided by Jeffrey Castro, the head of Information Technology at Pharamundo International?"

"I have."

"In Mr. Castro's testimony, he claims to have taken screenshots of his text correspondence with CEO Thomas Acosta. Are you familiar with those screenshots?" Black pointed to his team, and the screenshots appeared on the video screen.

"I'm very familiar with them, yes."

"In fact, sir, have you created some images of your own to compare to them?"

"I have."

Black again pointed to his team, and a new set of images came on the screen. They seemed nearly identical to Jeff Castro's images that Ike had earlier entered into evidence. "Your Honor, I request that the images on the screen be entered into evidence as Defense Exhibit 3."

Morton looked at Ike. "Any objection, Counsel?"

"No, Your Honor."

"Said images are admitted into evidence as Defense Exhibit 3."

Black again. "The images on the right side of the screen are yours, is that correct, Mr. Kumar?"

"Yes, that is correct."

"And for the benefit of the court and the jury, I'd like to take a moment to bring to your attention the images on the left, which have been admitted into evidence as State's Exhibit 3 by the prosecution. These images represent a collection of text exchanges alleged to have taken place between Jeffrey Castro and Thomas Acosta."

"Duly noted." Morton rested her chin on her fist.

"Now," Black said, his voice slowly rising, "Mr. Castro not only insisted that the images he presented were authentic, but he testified that an additional safeguard of the images' authenticity existed." He checked his notes. "He testified, 'If you look at the top of every image, you will see where it says "Thomas Aco…" and under that is a check mark with the word *verified*. That check mark signifies that the text is authentically from the sender.' And yet, Mr. Kumar, on the right side of the screen, your images have the exact same shortened wording, check mark, and the word *verified*. How can that be?"

The man smiled. "If you'll notice carefully in my images, the user's surname is also truncated, cut off at the 'o' letter in 'Aco.' And my images are actual images whose metadata has also been validated."

"Please continue, sir."

"Well, why was the surname truncated at the letter 'o'? Because all of these images have been generated by a user named Thomas Acorn."

The gallery murmured.

Black left the notes at the lectern and stepped closer to the witness stand. "So the texts submitted by Mr. Castro could have been sent by anyone with the first name Thomas and a surname beginning with Aco?"

"Exactly."

Black crossed his arms. "And so the texts cited by Mr. Castro as being from Thomas Acosta might not have been from him at all?"

Kumar nodded. "That is indeed accurate."

The murmuring grew.

Morton waved the sound down. "Let me remind the gallery that if you cannot remain quiet during the proceedings, I will have you removed from the courtroom."

As the buzz waned, Black gathered his notes from the lectern and returned to the defense table. "No further questions, Your Honor."

Morton tapped her fingers on the bench. "Mr. Thompson?"

Ike wanted to ask Abby and Harkin for their opinion on questioning the witness, but he was concerned that the jury would notice his uncertainty. So he decided to cross the witness himself, as their case was looking shakier and shakier, and there seemed to be little left to lose. "Yes, Your Honor. Thank you. Good afternoon, Mr. Kumar."

"Good afternoon."

"Sir, you're aware that, and as you testified, there are validation tools that can check if an image's metadata is real or fake and whether the metadata in an image has been tampered with, are you not?"

"Yes, I am aware."

Ike gritted his teeth. "And, sir, is it not possible that while your images are indeed authentic, that Mr. Castro's images are authentic as well?"

"Well, you need to consider that some validation tools are—"

Ike held up both palms. "Mr. Kumar, I asked if Mr. Castro's images might be authentic as well?"

The witness eyed Ike carefully. "Well, if that is the condition of your question, then, yes, Mr. Castro's images *could be* authentic."

Ike felt that going any further could only cause problems. "I have no further questions, Your Honor."

As he sat at the prosecution table, feeling good about his brief cross, he heard Black ask for and Morton grant a redirect. He sighed.

Black stood but didn't leave the defense table. "Mr. Kumar, can you elaborate to the jury about the metadata validation tools used to evaluate and authenticate digital images?"

"Yes. They're quite simple actually. More than anything, such tools depend on the accuracy and truthfulness of the information they analyze, and while they can provide valuable supplemental evidence, they are not definitive and can only give a rudimentary glimpse as to the authenticity of an image. In other words, while such tools are important, at this stage of their development, they should never be taken as entirely trustworthy."

"No further questions, Your Honor."

Morton caught Ike's eye. "Recross?"

Ike thought about it. He glanced at Abby. Her eyes were hardly hopeful. "No, Your Honor."

Morton again conversed with the clerk for a while, and then her focus turned to the defense table. "Mr. Black, you may call your next witness."

Suddenly, Black and Acosta were having words. Ike couldn't quite make out what they were saying, but there was no doubt that they were arguing. What the hell?

"Mr. Black?" Morton leaned back in her chair and waited.

As if the spell finally broke, the big attorney rose. "Your Honor, may I have a few moments to consult with my client?"

"You may."

Ah, this was just theater for the jury, Ike thought. Black was winning big, so for sure he wasn't putting Acosta on the stand. Ike turned to Abby and Harkin. "All that pretrial posturing to the media about Acosta's burning desire to take the stand to clear his name is out the window now. Black'll never let him up there. This little act of Acosta pretending he wants to is all for show."

The defense attorney and his client continued to argue, Black even grabbing Acosta's shoulder at one point as if to keep him down. Finally, Acosta shook him off and boldly crossed his arms over his chest. Black sat and fell back in his chair.

The courtroom grew quiet, and Ike whispered, "I'm telling you, it's all for show."

"Whatever it was," Abby whispered back, "it looks like they've come to some sort of resolution."

Harkin was on the edge of his seat and fingering his phone.

Black closed his eyes for a few seconds, then when he opened them, he looked at Morton. "Your Honor, the defense calls Thomas Acosta."

"Oh my God." Ike leaned toward Abby and Harkin and said above the gallery's buzzing, "I can't believe it. This is our chance."

All eyes were on the defendant as he walked to the witness stand. The man radiated a vigor, an intensity, that seemingly set him apart from the ordinary humans gathered there. As he was sworn in, Ike felt a tangible sense of the weight and importance in the air, aware of the significance of his testimony.

Shoulders slumped, a notebook held loosely in hand, Black dragged himself to the lectern. He plunked the notebook down and without looking up from it said, "Please state your name, occupation, and professional responsibilities."

Acosta settled on the stand. "My name is Thomas Acosta, and I'm the CEO of Pharamundo International. My responsibilities include overseeing the overall strategic direction and operations of the company, as well as ensuring that the company remains financially sound and compliant with all relevant laws and regulations. I also work closely with our research and development team to ensure that we continue to innovate and bring new products to market that improve and save patients' lives."

Black kept his eyes on the jury as he asked his next question. "Sir, are you familiar with the regulatory bodies governing the pharmaceutical industry and the process by which new drugs are approved for use on the market?"

"I am."

"Then…" Black finally looked at him. "…please elaborate on your knowledge of Pharamundo's decision to enter a sealed, no-bid contract with the federal government for its drug in development to cure ALLD."

The CEO's gaze held a keen glint, assessing the room before he spoke. "Of course. We were fortunate to be awarded a sole source contract with the government for our ALLD drug in development. While such arrangements are atypical, in this case the government determined that a national security element was involved and that Pharamundo's research was the most promising path to quickly finding a cure."

Black took a step back from the lectern. "You say *quickly*, sir, and yet the curative drug for ALLD has been in development for years."

Acosta held up a hand. "Yes. But dealing with the government in such a process inevitably creates delays. And because of the difficulty developing such a niche drug, there have been delays from Pharamundo's side as well. However, I can also say with 100% conviction that such delays were only in the interest of the safety and well-being of our customers."

THE PERFECT PROSECUTOR

Black nodded to him. "Sir, what is the name of the drug in development for ALLD?"

"It does not have a name."

"Why not?"

Acosta turned to the jury. "Because the drug in development for ALLD does not as yet exist."

Theatrically up went Black's eyebrows. "You can say that unequivocally—a drug in development for ALLD does not as yet exist?"

"Yes. Unequivocally."

Black stepped back to the lectern and opened the notebook. "Sir, do you know who Lakota Holt was?"

"I do now."

The attorney turned a page. "When did you first become aware of who he was?"

"When my personal assistant informed me that State's Attorney Rush announced the charges against me."

Black was making steady eye contact now. "So you'd never heard of Mr. Holt until those charges were announced?"

"That is correct."

The big man leaned on the lectern, engulfing the notebook. "Sir, earlier in the trial, Jeffrey Castro, the head of IT at Pharamundo International, testified that you and he, in secret encrypted texts, discussed how to engage a hacker on the dark web to tamper with an automobile. Did such texting between you and Mr. Castro take place?"

"No."

The defense attorney straightened up. "Never?"

"Never."

Black nodded. "But you have texted with Mr. Castro?"

"Yes, but never about those things."

"What *did* you text about?"

Acosta's hand drifted to the gold cuff link on his left sleeve, giving it a slight twist. "Well, among other things, the need to upgrade the company's network infrastructure to support the growth of the business, the need to develop a new IT training program that prioritizes inclusion for gender identity and sexual orientation, and the need to continue our community outreach programs with a focus on better meeting the needs of underserved and marginalized populations."

Black closed the notebook. "I have no further questions, Your Honor."

"All right." Morton folded her hands on the bench. "Mr. Thompson, your witness."

"Thank you, Your Honor." Gritting his teeth, Ike gathered up a legal pad and slowly made his way to the lectern. *This is it—everything hinges on the next few minutes.* "Mr. Acosta, good afternoon."

"Afternoon."

Ike set the pad on the lectern. "Sir, is it fair to say that it's Pharamundo's policy to seek out sealed, no-bid contracts with the government regarding the development of its drugs?"

Acosta waved a hand. "No, it isn't. In fact, in this particular instance, the no-bid sealed contract was proposed by the government, *not* by us."

A kink in Ike's back twitched. Why in the hell had he asked an open-ended question on cross? *Focus.* "Sir, you said there is no name for Pharamundo's drug in development for ALLD, isn't that right?"

"Yes."

"And so a drug in development for years is only named on the day it is released to the public, is that correct?"

Acosta frowned. "Of course not. Developmental drugs are named in advance, but the drug for ALLD has not reached the naming stage yet."

Ike pushed away from the lectern, only to lean back against it. "Sir, is it your habit as CEO to be aware of major news stories critical of Pharamundo?"

"Of course."

Ike pulled a sheet from the legal pad. "Of course. And, sir, you just testified to defense counsel that you'd never heard of Lakota Holt until State's Attorney Rush announced the charges against you, isn't that right?"

The CEO rested his forearms on the armrests. "It is."

Ike checked the sheet. "And yet, two months before Mr. Holt's death, he published a series in the major national periodical *New York Magazine* casting aspersions about Pharamundo's business practices. Were you aware of the series, sir?"

"I was not."

"You were not." Ike pretended to jot something down. "Mr. Acosta, as CEO, are cybercrimes, ransomware, and corporate espionage a concern for you?"

"They are a concern for all CEOs."

Ike gave him a quick nod. "So, accordingly, you guard your business against all varieties of cyber threats?"

"I do my best."

Ike wandered from the lectern but kept his eyes on the witness. "You protect your sensitive information from bad actors?"

"We attempt to, yes."

He stopped. "Sir, in the course of guarding your business against cyber threats and protecting your sensitive information, do you ever communicate via encrypted text messaging?"

"Yes."

Ike ambled toward the witness. "Can you tell us examples of how you've used encrypted text messages for business purposes?"

Acosta shrugged. "Well, I've used it for discussing strategic negotiations, for complying with government regulatory agencies, and for having secure communication with key shareholders."

Ike stepped right up to the witness stand. "Have you used it for discussing cyber threats as well?"

Acosta held Ike's eye, unflinching. "I have. Addressing security concerns in a digital environment is paramount."

"Right." Ike twisted the ring on his finger. "Would it be safe to say, sir, that as the head of Information Technology at Pharamundo, Jeffrey Castro plays a foundational role in addressing the company's cyber security concerns?"

The CEO hesitated, subtly raising an eyebrow. "It would."

"Mr. Castro would in effect be *the head* of digital security, would he not?"

The CEO's fingers subtly drummed an erratic pattern on the armrest. He inhaled sharply, then forced his hand flat. "That's right. What's your point?"

Ah, at last some irritation. Ike ignored his question. "Mr. Acosta, you've communicated with *Jeffrey Castro* via encrypted text messaging, haven't you?"

Acosta's face tinted red. "I don't recall every specific mode of communication I've used to communicate with employees."

Ike jostled himself. "What? You don't recall if you've *ever* communicated with your company's *head of security* via encrypted text messaging?"

Black was up. "Objection, Counsel is arguing with the witness and is misstating what the witness' answer was."

"Sustained." Morton pointed at Ike. "Counsel, please rephrase your question and ensure that it accurately reflects the witness' previous answer."

"I'll move on, Your Honor." Ike inched closer to the witness stand, noting Acosta's face growing redder. Ike felt if he kept going, he could break him. In his most insulting tone, he asked, "*Sir*, do you or your staff possess *any* record of your communications with Mr. Castro in *any* form? This includes, but is not limited to, encrypted text messages, emails, faxes, or any other documented means of communication."

Acosta forced a smile, but the smile faltered at the edges, as something much darker flickered in his eyes. "Of course such records exist, but when you say encrypted text messaging, there are several such apps. I have communicated extensively over the years with Mr. Castro, and so yes, it's *possible* that some of my communications with him may have been via encrypted messaging."

Ike pulled his head back. "Quite honestly, *sir*, I'm shocked that your memory has suddenly failed you so spectacularly."

"Objection!" Black jumped up and in the process bumped the prosecution table. "Objection, Your Honor! Counsel is badgering the witness!"

Morton banged the gavel as the buzz in the gallery grew. "Mr. Thompson, I will not tolerate further questioning in this manner. This is a court of law, not a playground. Please behave accordingly."

Ike scowled at Acosta before turning to the judge. "No further questions, Your Honor."

Morton took a deep breath and exhaled it slowly. "Well, now that we have that out of the way, I suppose it's time to get back to conducting this trial. Yes. Okay. All right, Mr. Black, you may call your next witness."

"The defense rests, Your Honor."

Just then, the judge was handed a note from one of the bailiffs. Morton read the note, then carefully surveyed the courtroom. She read the note again. She looked off into the distance. Finally, she placed her hands on the bench and leaned forward. "Members of the jury, Counsels, and family members, I know this has been a difficult trial and trying time for all involved, so I regret to inform you that due to an unforeseen circumstance, I have to recess court until tomorrow morning at nine a.m."

Jurors slumped. A few groaned.

"I understand that this delay may be inconvenient for many of you, but I assure you that the trial will resume tomorrow morning with no further delay. I apologize for this disruption and I thank you for your patience and understanding. See you tomorrow morning at nine a.m. sharp. Court is recessed until then." Morton stood, gathered up her bench book and notes, and with not so much as a glance at anyone, her robes swirling, exited the courtroom.

The gallery bustled. Harkin flittered off.

Abby turned to Ike. "What do you think this means?"

Ike rubbed the back of his neck. "I really don't know."

"I mean, she practically ran off the bench."

"Yeah. It's very unlike her to delay things too."

Abby stood. "I guess it's just one more unusual thing about this trial. Maybe the stress finally got to her too."

Ike rose to join her. "Could well be."

"And speaking of stress, your cross really put Acosta under the gun. Nicely done!"

Ike sighed. "You know, I don't know what got into me. At one point, I felt like I was going to throttle the guy."

"Well." She touched his elbow. "You did great."

"Thanks but I lost my cool. My outburst and Morton's rebuke will go against us big-time."

"Ike, really—"

"When I asked him if he messaged anyone with encrypted text and he stonewalled me, I pictured Oliver lying in his sick bed, a chalky blob, just barely breathing—dying, while Acosta was amassing billions. I just lost it."

"Hey." She gave his elbow a little tug. "You still made some killer points with the jury. They saw Acosta bail on that question, and he came off as a weasel. No, you did serious damage to his credibility."

He forced a smile. She was trying to build him up, and he knew enough to shut up. Still, he felt bad.

Abby crossed her arms. "So what are we going to do now?"

The gallery had nearly filed out.

"Keep preparing the closing argument." He tilted his head at her. "And the more I think about it, Abby, the more I think you should give it."

"No, no, oh no. You've been practicing delivering it."

"There's still time for you to rehearse."

"Look, Ike, buddy, how can I put this nicely?" She got up in his face. "Even *if* you screwed up crossing Acosta, now you need to man up. You need to man up because this thing is not over."

Chapter Twenty-nine

Ike psyched himself up as he and Abby drove together to the courthouse in the morning. Abby was right about his needing to man up, and he'd rehearsed the closing argument so many times yesterday, with Abby as his audience, that he no longer needed to refer to his notes. He'd give it his all, but even so, he couldn't shake the feeling that his meltdown yesterday crossing Acosta and Morton's rebuke had cost their chances big-time. That *he'd* cost their chances big-time. He chuckled cynically to himself. It was looking like Ursula had been right—he was totally unsuited to being a prosecutor.

Abby stroked his temple. "You got this, buddy."

"Thanks."

A line of cars sat waiting to get into the courthouse grounds. Cops, attorneys, reporters, defendants, criminals of all sorts, and who knows who else were scurrying around, the sun burning down mercilessly on them all. Squad cars lined the street in front of the courthouse. Ike was lucky to find a spot in the garage, and he and Abby hustled up the long, sloping concrete walkway to the courthouse.

Abby squeezed his shoulder before the reporters spotted them and shouted questions.

They made their way through the revolving doors at the end of the walkway, and as they approached their courtroom, Ike noticed some black-haired men, relatively short in stature, wearing ill-fitting but expensive suits. One man in particular stood out. Hair slicked back in a ponytail, he had a thick black mustache, pockmarked skin, and an emotionless stare. They brushed by him and into the packed courtroom.

THE PERFECT PROSECUTOR

Ike was surprised to see Harkin at the prosecution table already. At the defense table, Pharamundo's team—Black, arms crossed, comfortably leaning back in his chair—wasn't even conferring. Their actions, or lack of action, conveyed, *Let's get this not-guilty verdict over with already. We've got planes to catch.*

The bailiff closed the door to the hallway. "All rise. Court is in session."

Morton entered, this time pointedly scanning the courtroom on her way to the bench. She sat. "You may be seated."

Ike did some surreptitious deep breathing.

The judge examined a few documents, then smiled weakly. "Good morning, everyone. Thank you all for your patience yesterday. I am ready to resume the trial. Bailiff, please bring in the jury."

The jury was seated.

"Members of the jury, welcome back. I want to thank you for your understanding in the aftermath of yesterday's unexpected recess. I know this has been a taxing, deeply emotional trial, and I appreciate your commitment to see it through to completion. Today, we will hear the closing arguments from both sides. But before we begin, I have a few instructions for you.

"First, please remember that the evidence presented during the trial is the only evidence you are to consider when deliberating on this case. Second, you need to be aware of the fact that closing arguments are not evidence. They are statements by the attorneys meant to help you better understand and interpret the evidence that has been presented during the trial. Now if that's clear, let's get started." Her focus shifted to Ike. "Mr. Thompson, will the prosecution be making a closing argument?"

Ike glanced at Abby before rising. "Thank you, Your Honor, it will." He fastened the top button on his suit coat as he approached the jury box. "Ladies and gentlemen of the jury, let me begin by saying that with all of the commotion accompanying this trial, all the conflicting claims, the sideshows, that I believe we must not lose sight of the fact that ultimately this trial is about the heartless murder of young journalist Lakota Holt. A man who cared deeply about people. A man who cared deeply about telling the truth.

"Today, we live in a world dazzled by wealth and power, don't we? Magazines are devoted to billionaires and their exploits. Sayings glorify success at any cost. 'Might makes right.' Or the Golden Rule is 'he with the gold makes the rules.' And I'm sure we've all heard the saying, 'Money talks.' " He settled near the middle of the jury box and crossed his arms. "But I would say, 'Money talks, but does it tell the truth?' Because the truth in this case is of how a single mom named Bree Wilson fought to save her dying son by confronting one of the richest, most powerful, greediest, most unethical men in the world. Of how a compassionate physician named Brian O'Connor testified that the curative drug her son so desperately needed likely existed. And how a mechanic testified that the computer in Lakota Holt's car had been rigged, giving him no chance to control the hurtling vehicle.

"Then you heard from Raj Sharma, the white-hat hacker for good, of his inadvertent participation in the murderous scheme by rigging Lakota Holt's car to crash. Next, the head of Pharamundo's information technology department testified that Thomas Acosta fully intended to and did indeed murder Mr. Holt. Acosta murdered him coldly, cowardly, with the push of a button from his luxury high-rise office."

THE PERFECT PROSECUTOR

Ike drifted back to the prosecution table. He'd memorized the closing argument, but negative thoughts were intruding—his gaffe from yesterday—and, his heart beating wildly, he was thinking of everything at stake—justice for Lakota and hope for Oliver. He examined his notes, then whirled and thrust an arm at Black and his associates. Then he pivoted to the jury. "Ladies and gentlemen, I'm sure you didn't recognize any of Pharamundo's multi-million-dollar defense team before this trial began. And why would you? These aren't the kind of people you'd bump into on your street. No, they're too busy jetting across the country, even the globe, shielding Pharamundo's executives from an endless barrage of criminal charges." He turned back to the defense table and pointed directly at the Monster. "They're hired guns, supported by the company's deep pockets. Hired guns that are relentless in their pursuit of victory, using every trick in the book to silence any opposition. They spare no expense in hiring the most expensive expert witnesses and employing the most underhanded and unscrupulous tactics to snuff out those charges."

Ike made his way back to the jury box. He stood stock-still and made eye contact with every juror. "And yet, ladies and gentlemen, there is one thing that all of Pharamundo's wealth and power cannot snuff out—the truth. The truth that Thomas Acosta murdered Lakota Holt.

"Ladies and gentlemen, this is indeed a case of David and Goliath. A case in which David stood no chance against the unimaginable power, wealth, and evil of Goliath." Ike planted his hands on the jury box railing. "Nevertheless, there is something different about this case from that ancient tale. There is something different because *you* are involved. Because *you* are the thing that even mighty Pharamundo cannot defeat. *You* are the heroic David, whose sling of a guilty verdict can take down the giant. And so I ask you, ladies and gentlemen, to use that sling and launch that stone. I ask you to bring justice to Lakota Holt. I ask you to find Thomas Acosta guilty of murder in the first degree as charged."

As he returned to the prosecution table, Ike was wondering what the look on Abby's face meant.

She lifted up her phone. "Johnny just texted. He's bringing Elizabeth Castro in to the courthouse."

* * *

As he sat, Ike narrowed his eyes at his associate. "Don't kid around, Abby."

"I'm not. Johnny said they should be here within the hour."

Ike put a forefinger to his temple and closed his eyes.

Meanwhile, Morton was moving things along. "Mr. Black, is the defense going to be making a closing argument?"

"It is, Your Honor."

"Please proceed."

The courtroom went suddenly quiet as Black slowly rose his immense frame from the defense table. "Thank you, Your Honor." He sauntered to the jury box, his presence commanding attention. "Ladies and gentlemen of the jury, indeed, we are gathered here today because a young man tragically lost his life. But, ladies and gentlemen, let us not compound that tragedy with another by convicting someone for a crime he did not commit. For in today's day and age anything goes, does it not? Black is white. White is black. The world often spins reality to its opposite as fast as the earth itself spins. And only the boldest, the most outrageous claims seem to captivate most people's attention and thereby often become the most believed. In this case, Thomas Acosta, a man who has dedicated his life to helping others heal, a giver extraordinaire, has been portrayed as evil, as a money grubber, and as the ultimate slander—a murderer. The prosecution has foisted these falsehoods on you over and over in hopes that you will eventually come to believe them.

"The prosecution also said they had powerful evidence and yet what evidence have they presented? A doctor who testified that ALLD is curable? Thomas Acosta believes it's curable too. That's why his company is working so hard to develop the cure. A mechanic who examined the car involved in Lakota Holt's accident after it had been sitting in the tow truck yard for days, possibly having been altered multiple times? A self-admitted hacker who operates in the bleak underworld of the dark web and only testified under the protection of immunity? And yet another prosecution witness hiding behind the grant of immunity? Ladies and gentlemen, when the prosecution needs to resort to granting witnesses immunity, it's a sign that their case is intolerably weak. It's a sign that they are devoid of evidence. It's a sign of prosecutorial desperation.

"So in this case, the prosecution has asserted that the motive for the alleged murder of Lakota Holt was that the curative drug for ALLD was already in existence, and yet, the chief pharmaceutical rep for the company, a medical doctor, has testified, under oath, that the drug does not as yet exist. Thomas Acosta has testified the same. And on top of that, a United States government official has certified that Pharamundo has dotted all the 'i's and crossed all the 't's in its handling of the contract it holds with the government to develop the drug. Next, the defense's technology expert has proven how effortlessly the images of the supposed incriminating texts between Mr. Acosta and Mr. Castro can be faked. Ladies and gentlemen, with such a simple and comprehensive refutation of such *evidence,* the credibility of Mr. Castro's entire testimony is cast into doubt.

"Moving along, there is an ongoing debate in the legal world as to whether the defendant should take the witness stand in his own defense. Clearly, the preponderance of evidence in that debate favors the defendant *not* testifying. The reasons for such thinking are several. There's the fear of the defendant contradicting other defense witnesses' testimony. And an even greater fear that the defendant would be exposed to damaging questions under cross-examination. And yet, Mr. Acosta *insisted* on taking the stand in his defense. Ladies and gentlemen…" Black bit his lip and shook his head slowly. "…he insisted because he had nothing to hide. He insisted because he wanted to tell the truth. He insisted… because he'd done nothing wrong.

"Ladies and gentlemen of the jury, the prosecution has played you. They have played on your resentment toward big pharmaceutical companies and great individual wealth. They have tugged on your heartstrings by shrouding their entire argument in the heavy emotion of the terrible suffering of a young mother fighting for the life of her dying son. They have attempted to neutralize your reason by appealing exclusively to your emotion. But, ladies and gentlemen, this isn't a movie or a social media network. It is a court of law, and in courts of law, defendants are tried according to the law and by facts *only.*"

The defense attorney folded his hands over his stomach. "Ladies and gentlemen, the prosecution had the burden of proving Thomas Acosta guilty beyond a reasonable doubt. They have failed to do so. They have failed miserably. And so I ask you to assert *your* reason when you evaluate the facts in evidence. In so doing, you will reach the inescapable conclusion that Thomas Acosta is innocent of any wrongdoing. Therefore I ask you to follow the law and the facts and your reason to find him not guilty."

Black's closing argument was what Ike had expected. It was Johnny's text that was blowing his mind.

Abby clutched her phone. "He just texted again. He's pulling into the parking garage across the street."

As Black sat, Morton turned to the jury. "Members of the jury, thank you for your close attention during closing arguments. This has been a complex case, and I appreciate your dedication in following the evidence presented. We will now take a break for lunch. Please be back in the courtroom at 1:15 p.m. as the trial will resume promptly at 1:30. When you return, I will provide you with final instructions on the law before you begin your deliberations. The instructions will be crucial in guiding your discussions and reaching a verdict. In the meantime, please refrain from discussing the case amongst yourselves or with anyone else."

Harkin bolted the prosecution table without a word. Abby showed Ike Johnny's text. "So what do we do?"

"Go meet them."

Abby stood. "Let's do it."

They followed the people clogging the courtroom aisle, eventually making it into the hallway. They then ran to the escalator, which was also crowded.

"Do you think we'll even recognize her?" Abby held the moving stairway's handrail.

"Well, we saw her corporate headshot. And remember, she'll be with Johnny. But come on, this is taking too long."

He grabbed her hand, and they weaved through the escalator riders. At the bottom, they ran for the revolving door exit, only to find it jammed with people too. As they drifted along with the others, they caught glimpses of the people ascending and descending the lengthy, inclined concrete walkway to the courthouse, a low fence separating those coming from those going. Ike, taller, had the better vantage point. "Nothing yet. But there's a lot of people out there."

As the line thinned, they finally exited the courthouse's cool interior into the sweltering heat, joining the crowd plodding along outside.

Abby caught hold of his arm. "Come on. We'll be able to see better from here." She led him up onto a concrete bench beside the walkway.

"Yeah, this is definitely better, but I still don't see them." He shielded his eyes from the sun. "Wait! There they are! They're at the crosswalk in the street and headed this way. Elizabeth's in a cream-colored pantsuit, and Johnny's in a blue sport coat. They just got to the base of the walkway. See them?"

"Yeah, yeah."

"Now we'll have to get to the fence to grab their attention as they go by. Hey, wait a minute! What the hell!" The man with the brutal face and ponytail wearing the ill-fitting suit who'd been standing outside the courtroom before the trial began jumped the fence separating the walkway. "Oh, this is not good."

Ike leapt from the bench and attempted to hurdle the fence but caught the top of it and fell hard onto the concrete, people cursing him for bumping into them. He pulled himself up by the fence and ran after the man. Just as he got within range, the man whipped out a pistol and fired, sending Elizabeth Castro crumpling to the concrete. Nearby cops drew their guns, but the man seized a black lady, pressed his pistol to her head, and began shouting something in Spanish. Ike edged forward. The man kept on down the walkway and got off two more shots. Then a young cop calmly walked up behind the man and point-blank shot him in the back of the head. The man toppled onto the walkway, taking the black lady down with him. Cops converged, one kicking the man's pistol away and another helping the lady stand, her face splattered with the man's blood.

Ike ran to Johnny, who was kneeling, cradling Elizabeth Castro in his arms.

"Johnny, are you hit?"

"No, but she's…" The private investigator shook his head. "…in trouble."

Ike shouted for a doctor as onlookers gathered. Abby pushed through the rabble.

Streams of blood spurted rhythmically from a wound in Castro's chest, turning her top crimson. Eyes bulging, she wheezed and gasped for air.

Abby knelt and took her hand. "Hang in there, Elizabeth. Help is on the way."

A voice boomed. "I'm an Emergency Medical Technician. Everyone, give me room!" Abby and Johnny backed off, and the EMT, a broad-shouldered blonde woman, crouched beside Castro but then looked up. "I need an article of clothing!"

Ike ripped off his suit coat and gave it to her.

The EMT pressed the coat to the chest wound and stroked Castro's cheek with her free hand. A siren murmured in the distance. "Stay with me now," the EMT demanded. "The ambulance is here. No, no, no! Stay with me!" She slapped Castro's face, now a ghastly white, as the executive began to convulse. "Stay with me damn it!" But soon the convulsions morphed into weak twitches, and Elizabeth Castro's breaths grew shallower and shallower until they finally ceased altogether.

The EMT hung her head.

* * *

Ike and Abby didn't get home until seven that evening. As always, they were greeted affectionately by Leaner, but they had little warmth to return. The shock of witnessing Elizabeth Castro's murder had wiped them out. Judge Morton recessed the trial until tomorrow morning, but the police had questioned them for hours. Abby collapsed onto the sofa in the living room while Ike let Leaner out, then grabbed a couple of beers from the fridge and joined Abby on the sofa.

He popped his beer can.

She rolled hers over her forehead. "Some day, huh?"

He took a swig. "Yeah, some day."

"I still can't believe everything that happened."

"You and me both."

She opened the beer. "Poor Elizabeth Castro. What a way to die, especially after she'd decided to do the right thing and testify. I feel bad for her husband too and especially bad for their little boy."

"For sure. And what about Bree and Oliver Wilson? Elizabeth Castro's testimony could've been the game changer, turning things around for us—and them."

"Oh God, yes." She blew out a breath. "I think I must've blocked them out because they were too painful to think of."

He leaned back on the sofa.

She eased alongside him. "So what happens now? I mean, without Elizabeth Castro's testimony?"

"Hard to say." He put his arm around her. "But if I know Judge Morton, she's going to push for the trial to be closed out tomorrow."

"Just send it straight to the jury deliberating?"

"I think so."

She glanced up at him. "But there must be other possibilities."

He nodded. "Well, she could declare a mistrial. But remember, she's a defendant's judge. No, I think it will go straight to jury deliberations. She probably won't say as much, but she's more than likely thinking we never really had Elizabeth Castro's testimony anyway. That, and I'm sure she wasn't pleased that we got Elizabeth to trial so late, especially after closing arguments. She'll think we were gaming the system and showing up the court."

Abby stared off into the distance. "So the jury deliberates and…"

Ike sighed. "Yeah."

Chapter Thirty

In the morning, Ike and Abby woke to rumbles of thunder. The bedroom was so dark. Leaner was crying to go out. Ike obliged him, and they started getting ready, including Ike retrieving and loading their pistols. He let Leaner in, wiping his muddy paws with a towel, filled his bowls, and they set off in the rain. At a drive-through, they stopped for coffee. Back out on the street, Abby's phone pinged. An unfamiliar series of digits flashed on the screen—a number so random it could only be a burner. No caller ID, no subject line. She opened it.

"Ike, you better pull over."

"Why?"

"Just pull over."

He slid the Lexus onto a gravel shoulder.

She read the text aloud. "I didn't expect him to go that far. I knew Elizabeth Castro. She was a good woman. Yesterday, I received a certified mail package from her. It held a flash drive with her video testimony for the Thomas Acosta trial. She sent it in case she was murdered before she could testify. I'll bring it in, and I'm willing to testify as well. Mac."

Ike laid his head on the steering wheel. "Unreal."

Abby placed the phone on her thigh. "Will Elizabeth's, or Mac's testimony for that matter, be allowed in this late in the trial? Will Morton let it in?"

"We'll have to convince her. But this could be just the break we need. Oh man." He ran his hands through his hair. "For now, I would say just text him back. And tell him to get to a secure location." He pulled back onto the road. "Now we have to make it to court on time. We don't want to irritate Morton by being late."

Abby sent the text as the rain came down harder. "Ike, he texted right back. He said he's already in a safe place."

"Ask him how long it would take him to get to the Rolling Meadows Courthouse from where he's at."

She texted and waited. "Okay, here it is. An hour, he says. Maybe a little more."

"Okay, tell him to sit tight. Tell him we'll contact him when the time comes and that we will come get him." He turned onto the courthouse grounds. "Oh, look at this. TV antenna trucks everywhere. What a zoo. Elizabeth Castro's murder has generated a media frenzy."

Abby texted as Ike pulled into the parking garage. He wound around the ramps until he finally found a spot and killed the engine. Abby held up the phone. "He wrote back saying, 'copy that.' But what does that mean?"

"He must be former military. I think it means he received and understood your message."

"Oh God, this is so wild."

"Yeah, it's wild, but it's also a stroke of luck. Elizabeth Castro's video testimony should be damaging, but even if it's not, the sympathy the jury will feel for her testifying from beyond the grave will be substantial. If this plays out the way I'm thinking it might, it actually puts a guilty verdict back within reach. Close reach. That's *if* Morton lets it in." He grabbed his umbrella and opened the door.

The courtroom was buzzing. Overflow in the hallway. A huge contingent of media—five times larger than yesterday's, laptops open, earbuds tucked in—rustled in the gallery. The benches jammed. As it turned out, Judge Morton was the one who was late. The bailiff called the court into session. Once things settled down, Ike stood and asked if he could approach the bench. Abby, Harkin, and Black joined him there as Morton clicked off her microphone.

In hushed tones, Ike explained about the substitute witness for Elizabeth Castro and his possession of her video testimony. Before he finished speaking, Black talked over him.

"Your Honor, I vehemently object to the prosecution's attempt to introduce new evidence at this late stage in the trial. Allowing evidence after closing arguments violates fundamental fairness principles. Elizabeth Castro's video testimony, being hearsay and without proper authentication, is highly dubious as evidence, and it violates my client's right to confront the witnesses against him as there is no opportunity to cross-examine Ms. Castro. Additionally, the substitute witness is not on the witness list, and as I understand it, the witness has no knowledge of the facts at issue and anything he would say would be inadmissible hearsay."

Morton nodded thoughtfully. "Mr. Black, I understand your concerns, but while it is true that evidence presented so late in a trial is most unusual, it is not without precedent in certain circumstances, such as when a witness is only recently located and then dies. I also believe it is important to hear the testimony of the substitute witness in question. Therefore, I will watch the video testimony in my chambers and then decide. And both counsels need to be present while I do so. My decision regarding admissibility will be based on the contents of the video and the testimony provided by the substitute witness."

The defense attorney pushed into the bench. "Your Honor, the jury will be prejudiced by a last-minute witness testifying. Their testimony will have an outsized influence on the jury's decision-making ability."

THE PERFECT PROSECUTOR

The judge took a deep breath and let it out slowly. "Mr. Black, the court has a responsibility to hear what this new testimony might be to prevent a possible miscarriage of justice, and then, *as I said*, I will determine if it is in the interests of the jury making a fair decision to hear it. And rest assured that should the substitute witness be allowed to testify, you will have the opportunity to cross-examine him. Now, please let's move on."

Black glanced at the defense table, then back at Morton. "Your Honor, the defense feels compelled to demand a mistrial because we will not have time to effectively prepare for this new evidence."

Morton's lips thinned to a tight line as she gripped the edge of the bench. She closed her eyes, and when she opened them, she released her grip and straightened her robe before speaking. "Mr. Black, I assure you I understand the defense's concerns, very clearly, but the jury has been impaneled after a fair and thorough selection process, and it would be a waste of judicial and trial resources to restart the trial at this late stage. The defense has had ample time to prepare for trial, and the sudden death of one witness and the substitution of another bearing their testimony should not constitute an undue burden on you nor derail this trial." She turned to Ike. "Mr. Thompson, how soon can you have the witness appear in my chambers?"

"Two hours, Your Honor."

"Then I am going to dismiss the jury for now, but I will have them remain on the premises and be available to return as needed. I will expect all of you in my chambers in two hours sharp."

* * *

When Ike and Abby left the courthouse, a thunderstorm was raging. Holding their umbrellas up against the wind-driven rain, they hurried down the long, sloping walkway, getting soaked to the skin, a gust flipping Ike's umbrella inside out with a loud *thwack*. In the parking garage, they shook off the rain as best they could and climbed into the Lexus.

Abby pulled the hair off her forehead, took a facial tissue from her purse, and dried her glasses. "I gotta tell you, Ike, this is all feeling pretty crazy."

"Yeah, what a storm. You saw what happened to my umbrella."

She fixed him with a flat stare. "I meant going to get Mac without the police accompanying us."

Ike blew out a long exhalation. "Abby, there's no time for the police. We've got our guns—"

"Oh, yeah, okay, we've got guns—and that's a good thing—but I really think this situation calls for something more, don't you?"

He shrugged. "It does, but there's no time. We've just got to take our chances. You know how to use the Ruger."

She crossed her arms. "Okay, yes, you took me target shooting at the range a few times, but I am not ready to shoot a human being."

He started the car. "You may find you're able to if they're about to shoot you."

"Oh, come on. Don't make it like we're going to a gunfight at the OK Corral."

"We're not. We'll be okay." He did his best to give her a reassuring look. "Now any more texts from Mac?"

"We'll be okay," she mumbled, switching her phone's text notifications back on. Thunder reverberated through the parking garage. "No."

"All right, text him, ask his street address, and tell him to be ready because we're on the way."

Abby turned away, then turned back and sent him another blank stare. Finally, she blurted, "Fine."

Ike navigated through the parking garage, winding his way until he reached the exit. As he approached the garage's threshold, he paused, his attention caught by the spectacle before him. The relentless rain was pouring off the garage roof in sheets, creating a mesmerizing waterfall-like display.

Abby huffed, "Okay, I sent it."

Ike crashed through the translucent watery curtain out onto the storm-swept street. Before too long he thought a van was following them. He pulled to the side of the road. The van cruised past.

Abby again set her phone onto her thigh. "Why did you pull over?"

"I thought someone was following us. Besides, until we hear from Mac, we don't know which direction we're headed. I just started for the highway."

The windshield wipers slapped haplessly at the bucketing rain. A little moat appeared in the drainage ditch on the side of the road. Lightning flashed from the heavy black clouds massing above the treetops.

Abby leaned against her door. "Oh, Ike, should we really be doing this? I mean, I think we need to rethink this. I'm not the most courageous person, but I'm not a coward, and this is beginning to seem like a crazy-bad idea."

"We have to do it."

She pushed off the door. "*Why* do we have to? I mean, these cartel guys are killers. Look at what happened to Elizabeth Castro. Broad daylight. And with cops all over the place

—the Mexican guy had to know he was going to get killed, but he shot her anyway."

He reached over and squeezed her shoulder. "It'll be all right."

She grabbed his hand. "What I'm trying to say is I'm scared."

He exhaled deeply. "Well, for the record, so am I. But the fact of the matter is if we don't get Mac right now and get him to Morton's chamber on time, chances are Acosta is going to walk."

Her chin fell to her chest. "All right," she sighed. "So much for sanity." Thunder cracked, and her phone pinged. She wiped away a tear and checked the screen. "He's in someplace called Calumet City. He gave an address."

"Damn it." The Lexus fishtailing, Ike floored it up onto the road and headed for the highway. "That's almost an hour away. It's way down southeast near the Indiana border. We might not make it back in time. Put the address in a mapping app and text Mac and tell him we'll be there soon."

Rain jumping off the hood, lightning flashing, the Lexus hydroplaned along the curving highway entrance ramp. Again, Ike thought someone was following them, but the rain made it impossible to know for sure. He drove on. With the poor visibility and how fast he was driving had there been a wreck in front of them they would've joined it, but there was no other way. Finally, hoping his luck would hold out just a little longer as they neared Calumet City, he asked Abby if she had the safety off on her Ruger.

"I'm not going to shoot anybody, Ike."

"Right." He glanced at her. "But please take the safety off just in case."

"No."

THE PERFECT PROSECUTOR

The app announced they'd reached their destination.

Abby squeegeed the condensation from her window with her hand. "It's just the office of a trailer park." Her phone pinged. "Mac again." She read the text aloud. "Proceed to C26 and wait. Leave the engine running."

Ike turned into the trailer park and splashed along the winding asphalt drive, the double-wide trailers marked alphanumerically with reflective aluminum address numbers. He made it through the "A"s and "B"s, and when he got to the "C"s, he took hold of his Glock.

Abby got another text and read it aloud. "Affirmative, I've made visual contact. Two vehicles are pulling up behind you. A green Chevy Malibu and a black Ford pickup."

Ike put the car in Park, swiveled around and couldn't see anything but water streaming down the rear window. "What the hell! I don't see anything at all." Gradually, a glimmer appeared and slowly solidified into a pair of headlights.

Abby read another text aloud. "Three men will leave trailer 26C. I'll be the one wearing a brown camouflage cap, and I'll get into the back of your vehicle, so make sure the door locks are open. Once inside, I'll instruct you what to do next." Abby stared at Ike as the Malibu pulled up alongside the pickup. "This is crazy. He's *telling* us what to do. And it doesn't even sound like Mac. Affirmative? Visual contact?"

Ike shrugged. "I don't know what to tell you."

"Oh, this is so not good, Ike."

Lightning flashed down behind 26C, thunder exploding simultaneously, and a door from the trailer swung open. Three burly, bearded men in overalls and hunting caps descended carefully—a step at a time—the trailer's wooden front stairs.

Ike turned to Abby. "Now for the last time, Abby, take the safety off your gun."

"I told you I'm not shooting anybody!" She set the pistol onto the floor. Then she wiped the foggy windshield with her sleeve. "And which one has the brown cap? All the caps are dark. How are we supposed to see? Oh God, here comes one of them."

The rear passenger door wrenched open, and a man piled in, his head lowered, raindrops spilling from the bill of his cap. He yanked a fake beard from his face and looked up.

Ike held his Glock on the man. "Who the hell are you?"

"You won't be needing that, Mr. Thompson. I'm a member of an executive protection service hired to facilitate yours and attorney Blum's safe passage to the Rolling Meadows courthouse. Please just follow my instructions. Begin by following the pickup truck." He dug a phone out of his pants' pocket and hit a speed dial key. "I have secured the attorneys, and we are in transit to the courthouse. ETA…" He checked his watch. "…approximately fifty-three minutes."

Ike set his pistol back into the console. "I don't understand. What's happening?"

"Please just follow the pickup truck, sir. There's very little time to spare. I'll explain as we go."

Ike slammed the gear shifter into Drive, and the Lexus' front wheels spun as he hit the gas. "I have to tell you, whoever the hell you are, that the lack of information we've received is totally unacceptable. We need to know what's happening."

"Sir, ma'am, my team's mission is to deliver you safely to Judge Morton's chambers in a timely manner. That's all I know."

Ike grumbled, "Your team? The burly guys with the beards?"

"Yes."

"Why three of you?" Ike scoped him in the rearview mirror.

"It's a diversionary tactic, sir." The man brushed the wetness from his pant legs. "And the pickup in front and the Malibu behind will guarantee we're not being followed."

Ike snorted. "So Abby and I are just decoys? Sitting ducks in case someone attempts to kill Mac?"

The man focused back on his phone. "We don't look at it that way, sir. We call it providing team protection to keep everyone involved safe. I assure you that your secure passage is my highest priority."

Abby slid her pistol to the side with her foot. "Well, which vehicle is Mac in?"

"Ma'am, he is in neither. I've just been informed that he has arrived safely and is sitting in Judge Morton's chambers."

Chapter Thirty-one

The bodyguard escorted Ike and Abby to the courthouse, discreetly leading them to Morton's chambers, where bookshelves lined the walls and the air was fragrant with the smell of old books. A desk flanked by the U.S. and Illinois flags was the centerpiece of the room, with two kidney bean-colored leather chairs in front of it. Around a conference table with a pull-chain lamp on it sat Morton, Black, and Mac, who had switched out his overalls for an Armani suit. His beard, fake or otherwise, was gone, too, and an open laptop sat in front of him.

The judge gestured to Ike and Abby. "Mr. Thompson, Ms. Blum, you already know Mr. Black. And this is Mr. Acosta," she said, indicating the man in the Armani suit. "But for clarity's sake, this is Miguel Acosta, Thomas Acosta's brother. Please join us."

Ike and Abby didn't move.

Morton waited…and waited. "Counselors?"

Finally, Ike pulled a chair out for Abby, and they sat.

Morton took charge. "Now before we get started, I would remind all of you that the jury is waiting, and for you specifically, Mr. Acosta, that when the time comes, while I insist on an accurate version of what your testimony may consist of, please cut out any extraneous or repetitive details that are not significant to *this case only*." She turned to Ike and Abby. "Mr. Acosta has provided us with a flash drive containing Elizabeth Castro's video testimony."

Black was shaking his head. "Your Honor, again, I must object to the late introduction of both the video and this new witness. The video itself is hearsay, and the credibility of this new witness has not been evaluated."

Morton turned decisively to the defense attorney. "Mr. Black, believe me, I am well aware of your concerns about the admissibility of this new evidence. Nevertheless, I have decided to admit the video conditionally, subject to the testimony of the individual who provided it. We will evaluate that testimony later. For now, let's view the video."

A gentle whirring emanated as a screen descended from the ceiling. Morton nodded to Acosta, who pressed a button on the laptop.

Abby leaned over and whispered in Ike's ear, "Can you believe this is happening?"

The screen glowed to life, displaying a vastly different image of Elizabeth Castro, in stark contrast to her perfectly put-together corporate headshot, than Ike and Abby were expecting. Looking gaunt in a baby-blue warm-up suit, bags under her eyes, a strand of hair falling across her forehead before she secured it in a ponytail, the executive leaned forward, staring blankly at the camera. "My name is Elizabeth Castro," she said in a hoarse whisper. She took a deep breath and spoke louder. "I am currently employed as the head of New Drug Development at Pharamundo International Corporation, and I swear under penalty of perjury that the contents of this video testimony are true and accurate."

Harkin slipped into the room and took a seat at the far end of the table.

"I have avoided testifying in open court," Castro continued, "because of Thomas Acosta's ongoing threats against my life, and because of those threats, I have been in hiding and on the move. Mr. Acosta has already attempted to kill me, and I am absolutely convinced that he killed Lakota

Holt, too, and that he killed him for the same reason he is certain to kill me…" She checked over her shoulder. "…and that is because I knew, and Lakota had discovered, that the drug to cure ALLD exists. I have followed the trial as best I can, and I know that defense attorney Cyrus Black's inferences that the curative drug does not exist are disingenuous, and Thomas Acosta's testifying that it does not exist is a flat-out lie. The curative drug for ALLD exists and is called Curedex-N.

"Curedex-N has been ready for market for eighteen months. I have avoided making a public statement about this because I feared repercussions from Thomas Acosta." She looked to the side and adjusted the webcam before reaching for something off-screen. She returned with a black handheld digital voice recorder. She appeared to adjust a wheel on it, held it up to the screen, and hit a button. A few seconds of silence were followed by a scratchy male voice. "Listen, you pathetic excuse for a human being. You think you can beat me? You think you're going to be a good little girl and tell the world about Curedex-N and walk away unscathed? Not a chance. I'm Thomas Acosta, and you, you've become nothing but a liability, and you know what happens to liabilities at Pharamundo. I've got eyes everywhere, Lizzie. I'm gonna find you and when I do, your screams won't matter. I warned you. You should have just kept your mouth shut."

Miguel Acosta pressed a key on the laptop. "That's it."

Ike looked at Black, whose intense stare remained fixed on the blank screen.

Finally, as if snapped out of a trance, the defense attorney turned to Morton. "Your Honor, I maintain my objection."

Morton seemed ready for it. "Your objection is noted, Counsel, but overruled for now. These issues go to the weight of the evidence rather than its admissibility. We'll also hear from the new witness in due course."

Black's face flushed. He pushed out a short breath, staring at the judge for several moments. "In that case, Your Honor, I request a recess to consult with my client regarding this development."

"Granted." Morton flexed a hand. "We'll reconvene here in one hour."

* * *

When the attorneys left the judge's chambers, Harkin went his separate way, as usual. Ike and Abby, meanwhile, found an empty conference room and sat at a table there.

Abby blew the hair off her forehead. "Thomas Acosta's brother! My head is spinning."

"Yeah, crazy, Abby. I'd heard Acosta had a brother but that was the extent of it." He grabbed his phone and put the man's name into a search engine. Miguel Acosta's photo, the man looking much slimmer and younger, was at the top right. Ike read the summary of the post aloud. "Miguel Acosta defied the odds by rising from humble beginnings to become one of Mexico's first billionaires. Through strategic real estate investments, he revitalized blighted neighborhoods, offering hope and stability to low-income communities. His visionary approach transformed lives and inspired others to prioritize social impact alongside financial success. He resides in Mexico City with his wife and children."

Abby smirked. "Well, that would explain his bodyguard detail that facilitated such an elaborate, and certainly expensive, ruse getting him safely to the courthouse."

"Right. But anyway, *if* Morton admits his testimony, and that's a big if, it would be brother against brother. Sibling testimony is often thought to be biased, but I believe Miguel's credibility with the jury will be enhanced because he's standing in for Elizabeth Castro, which makes him a target himself."

"So you think this could really help us out?"

He tapped his fingertips together. "I do. And Elizabeth Castro testifying that the curative drug exists solidifies CEO Acosta's motive for murdering Lakota."

"Good." Abby brightened. "And for sure, Pharamundo is going to be in legal trouble for breaking its contract with the government to release the drug as soon as it was ready, and now they'll *have to* release it ASAP, which will cause them to take a disastrous financial hit." She smiled. "And save Oliver Wilson's and thousands more lives."

Ike cracked his neck. "I don't know, Abby, you may be getting a little ahead of yourself. First, the video was only admitted conditionally. I'm sure we'll have a battle about that, and Miguel's testimony has not been admitted at all."

"You don't think Morton will allow Elizabeth's video?"

"Oh, she may allow it under the dying declaration hearsay exception. Especially with the recorded death threat from Thomas Acosta, and well, yeah…" He bowed his head slightly. "…with her death. But even that's no guarantee."

Abby leaned back. "And what about Miguel Acosta testifying? Think she'll allow that?"

He waved a hand. "That depends on what he has to testify. If he corroborates Elizabeth's testimony, testifies to her state of mind, or more importantly, to the relationship Elizabeth had with Thomas Acosta, she may let it in. But Morton keeping their testimony out isn't the only way the existence of Curedex-N could be blocked."

She narrowed her eyes at him. "Ike, there's no way they'd kill Miguel Acosta at this stage."

He rubbed his chin. "I suppose that's true, as I'm sure security is going to be heightened to the max from here on out. But even if she allows both testimonies, there are other ways of keeping the Curedex-N reveal suppressed." His phone pinged. He checked it. "That's Morton. Black is back. Come on."

They headed to the judge's chambers, joining Black, Acosta, Harkin, and the judge at the table there.

Morton, as usual, wasted no time. She motioned to the defense attorney. "Mr. Black."

The big man crossed his arms. "Thank you, Your Honor. My defense team and I have thoroughly discussed with our client the deceased witness' video testimony, the substitute witness' potential testimony, and their impact on his case. After careful consideration, we have concluded that a plea deal is the best course of action. I have explained the terms and implications of this plea to my client, and he understands them fully. Your Honor, with Mr. Thomas Acosta's informed consent and on his behalf, he is willing to enter a plea of guilty to a reduced charge of reckless homicide. In return, we would request a sentence of two to five years in prison. This way, we can bring closure to this case and achieve a fair resolution for my client while also addressing the tragedy that befell the victim in this unfortunate incident. My client understands the seriousness of his actions but also believes this plea is in everyone's best interest."

The judge addressed the prosecutors. "Mr. Thompson, Ms. Blum, Mr. Harkin, any objections?"

Ike straightened his shoulders. "Your Honor, we need to address this new development. May we have a brief recess to confer outside?"

"You may." A touch of exasperation creeping into the judge's voice.

The prosecutors made for the door, Harkin texting as they went.

In the hallway—brown tile floor, beige walls, and not the best globe lighting overhead—Ike nodded to Harkin. "Who were you just texting?"

"The State's Attorney. I'm sure she'll want to know about the plea offer."

Ike gritted his teeth. Harkin had been a thorn in their side from day one. "Well, she can know about it, Harkin, but we are the prosecutors for this case, and *we're* going to make the decision as to whether taking the plea bargain or going to trial is in the State's best interest."

"Right." Harkin smirked. "You can tell that to Ursula because she's on her way here."

Abby put her hands on her hips. "Not cool, Harkin."

"Hey, the State's Attorney is the chief prosecuting attorney for the county. What she says goes."

Ike sighed. Now what? He turned to Abby. "What are you thinking?"

She frowned deeply, clearly reluctant to discuss things in front of Harkin. Ike gave her a subtle nod, tilting his head down the hallway. Understanding the cue, she fell into step beside him. Once they were out of Harkin's earshot, Ike stopped. "So what do you think?"

Her hands balled into fists. "I think what's two to five years for what Acosta did? Reckless homicide? That's something you'd charge a teenager for one of his buddies getting killed while drag racing."

"Yeah. I'm of the same mind, Abby."

"*And* we have Elizabeth Castro's testimony and whatever Miguel Acosta might bring to trial as a witness."

Ike glanced at Harkin down the hall, then back at Abby. "Actually, we *don't* have Elizabeth Castro's testimony—or Miguel Acosta's, for that matter. Not yet anyway. And even if we have Miguel's, who knows if he'll be a help or a hindrance?"

"Ah, I'd say you never know, Ike. He might bring something to the table. And he said he'd testify *for* us. Why would he say that if he didn't have anything to add?"

He widened his eyes at her. "But even if he testifies, he'll have to face Black's cross."

She swallowed.

"Yeah, being crossed by Black will be no picnic, Abby."

She touched his arm. "But aren't we losing sight of something? If we don't go to trial, word getting out about Curedex-N may be delayed for years. Personally, I think that's why Thomas Acosta is willing to plead—he continues to make billions for as long as they keep word of the drug from getting out. And really, he's just a cartel gang member in a thousand-dollar suit, so he won't mind going to Club Fed —with its gym, swimming pool, and whatever other luxury accommodations it has—for whatever scant time he actually ends up serving. Whereas, if it goes to trial and he gets convicted, he's looking at life."

"Exactly. That's what I meant before by saying that Elizabeth Castro's, and Miguel's for that matter, testimony not being admitted wasn't the only way Curedex-N might remain suppressed. You're right—if we accept the offer, it could take years for word of Curedex-N to get out to the public."

Abby raised her eyebrows. "Years Oliver Wilson doesn't have."

He rubbed the back of his neck. "Exactly."

The sound of heels clicking.

Ursula was homing in on them, bringing Harkin along with her.

Ike glanced at Abby. "Okay, here we go."

The State's Attorney's complexion was heart-attack red. "Thompson, Blum, you two know that I have been patient regarding your involvement in this case. In fact, I've been beyond patient—I've bent over backwards. Now Harkin tells me you're reluctant to accept Thomas Acosta's plea offer, but as State's Attorney, I insist that we accept it in order to finally put this matter to rest."

Ike held out both palms to her. "State's Attorney, we appreciate your forbearance in this case. But we're talking about murder. Thomas Acosta murdered Lakota Holt as plainly as if he'd put a gun to his head and pulled the trigger. True, Pharamundo's army of lawyers has put on a solid defense, but it's clear now that Elizabeth Castro's video testimony and Miguel Acosta's testimony as a substitute witness are just the breakthrough we need to convict for first-degree murder—that's why Black made the offer. And, State's Attorney, justice calls for that verdict rather than the slap on the wrist the reckless homicide charge and the two-to-five-year prison term would be, which, by the way, will convey to the public that we have not done our job and that once again, Big Pharma has gotten off the hook. It will also indelibly tarnish the reputation of the State's Attorney's Office."

"That's a moving little speech, Thompson." Ursula scowled. "And *so many thanks* for your concerns about the reputation of the State's Attorney's Office, but the State *will* accept the plea offer. It's my call. End of story. We're not going to trial. Now prepare the paperwork to accept the plea agreement."

She huffed off, waving for Harkin to follow.

Ike and Abby stood silently.

Abby again put her hands on her hips. "She's been busting our chops from day one. What do we care what she thinks?"

"We'll care the next time we come up against her in court."

She pivoted to him. "Ike, again, let's not forget what we cared about when we took this case."

He shut his eyes, drew in a deep breath and pictured Oliver's sick room. The brand-new baseball glove, unused. Hockey stick, golf clubs—all new, all untouched. Posters of his heroes on the walls. And he lay there unaware of all of it, tubes piercing his paper-thin skin, tubes and machines somehow keeping his failing body alive. Ike opened his eyes, his voice quavering as he fought back the lump in his throat. "Come on." He grasped Abby by the hand, and they walked together down the hallway to the judge's chamber.

They hesitated at the door. Ike squeezed Abby's hand firmly, and she nodded. He reached for the doorknob.

The judge, Black, and Miguel Acosta's attention locked on them as they strode into the room.

Ike thrust his chin out. "We're taking it to trial."

Black's body stiffened, the color draining from his face.

"All right." Morton exhaled. "You're sure about that?"

Was she warning them off? He didn't care. "Absolutely sure, Judge."

Morton leaned forward, her eyes lingering on Ike for a moment before shifting to Black. "Very well. Then in the light of the State's decision, Mr. Black, do you have anything to say?"

The defense attorney straightened his tie. "Yes, Judge. We request the rest of the day to further review the new evidence being introduced."

"That's granted." She looked all around. "Anybody else?" No one spoke up. "All right then, I will dismiss the jury for the day, and the trial will resume tomorrow at 9 a.m."

Chapter Thirty-two

Ike and Abby knew that by rejecting Ursula's explicit order to accept the plea offer, they weren't just pushing boundaries —they were obliterating them. Now every moment they pursued the trial felt like a plunge into the abyss without a lifeline. One misstep could cost them everything. It was professional Russian roulette, but the stakes were too high to back down now.

Later that afternoon, Judge Morton admitted Elizabeth Castro's video testimony into evidence under the dying declaration exception to the hearsay rule. Following negotiations between the prosecution and the defense, the prosecution agreed to a stipulation proposed by the defense that only a transcript of her testimony would be presented to the jury, as displaying the video could potentially prejudice their decision.

Meanwhile, Miguel Acosta provided a summary of his anticipated testimony to Judge Morton and both the prosecution and the defense. Based on the summary, the judge deemed his testimony relevant and granted him permission to testify. She also arranged for him to be placed in protective custody, but before that, she allowed Ike and Abby to interview him. Unsurprisingly, Peter Harkin did not attend.

Ike and Abby challenged Miguel about why he, as Mac, lied to them about having been a former employee at Pharamundo. He explained that his paramount concern at the time was to remain anonymous for fear of his brother. When they asked why Elizabeth had chosen him to send the flash drive to, he said it was because they'd become friends due to their mutual interest in new drug development. That was it? A mutual interest in new drug development? Yes. When Ike asked him aggressive questions Cyrus Black might hit him with on cross-examination, Miguel brushed the questions aside, insisting he'd been cross-examined in many high-profile trials and would be able to handle whatever Black threw at him. After they were done questioning him, sheriff's deputies whisked him off.

Ike and Abby were left alone in the interview room.

Abby scratched her cheek. "That wasn't what I expected. I mean, how are we to anticipate what he might say on the stand?"

Ike tapped his fingers on the table. "I agree. He's got to have reasons for not being more forthcoming. Maybe he's afraid of implicating his brother. Or maybe it's because he's got a wife and kids to think of."

"Or how about, he wants to stay loyal to both Elizabeth's memory *and* his brother, but that seems unlikely as it was pretty apparent he despises his brother."

"I don't know." Ike thought of his brother, Evan. "You'd be surprised how deep sibling loyalty can run."

"I suppose." She adjusted her watchband. "Or maybe he just doesn't trust us."

Ike nodded.

Neither spoke for a while.

Abby sat back, the sound of the chair scraping across the floor breaking the heavy silence. "Well, the big question is, what are we going to do tomorrow in court? You know, the old saying that lawyers should never ask questions they don't know the answer to."

"Well, we do know, like you said, that he volunteered to testify *for* us."

She hunched her shoulders. "Right, but couldn't he blow things up too?"

"He could."

"So what do you think?"

Ike massaged his temples. "Well, I think we roll the dice with him. See where things go tomorrow when he's on the stand and make adjustments on the fly."

Her forehead furrowed. "Oh, that sounds so risky."

"Abby, the law is an exercise in risk management."

A muscle in her cheek flexed. "Seems I've heard that somewhere before."

* * *

With night falling, Ike and Abby finally left the courthouse. They drove straight to Ike's, and as they turned onto his block, Abby said, "It's going to be so good to get home."

Ike liked it that she'd called his place home. "Yeah, how 'bout it?" He pushed the clicker and pulled into the garage. When they opened the door to the house, the sound of Leaner's nails slipping and sliding on the hardwood floors and his joyful whimpering lifted their spirits.

After they greeted the dog, Ike let him out.

Abby then joined Ike at the sliding glass door, put her arm around his waist, and leaned her head on his shoulder.

He put his arm around her. "Did you expect practicing criminal law would be this fun?"

"Oh my."

"You have to admit." He hugged her. "It's not boring."

"Tell me about it." She gazed up at him. "So much was happening today, I just now realized we haven't eaten a thing."

He nodded. "So what do you think—microwave a frozen pizza? At least it's fast."

"That's fine. There's lettuce in the fridge, so maybe a salad too. I feel like I have to eat at least a little something healthy."

He gave her another hug. "Good idea. Let me check on Leaner's food first, and while I do, can you get the mail?"

"Sure." She slid from under his arm and walked off.

The dog's feeding station was two stainless steel bowls on an elevated bamboo stand alongside the kitchen island. Ike grimaced. Both the water and food bowls were untouched. It was Leaner's way of protesting, a canine hunger strike, being left alone for so long. Oh well, now that they were back, hopefully, he'd make up for it. After letting him in, Ike caught a glimpse of Abby at the front door. She was sorting through a handful of letters like a dealer shuffling a deck of cards. Drawing closer, he noticed her reach for a package on the stoop. The way the package was oddly bulging and the hastily applied duct tape quickened his pulse.

"Abby, don't touch it!"

She recoiled. "Ike, what the hell!"

He pulled her back.

A neighbor was walking up the sidewalk to the house.

Ike thrust out both palms. "Jerry, stay back!"

The man, in shorts and flip-flops, jerked to a halt.

Ike wiped the sweat from his brow. "Sorry, Jerry, but I don't like the looks of this package."

"Actually, that's why I was coming over." The man scratched his knee. "A plumbing supply company emailed to say the pipes to fix my kitchen sink had been delivered, but the photo showed the package on your stoop."

Ike bent low to check the address. Oh God. He carried the package out to his neighbor. "Sorry, buddy."

"No problem." A concerned look. "Hey, take it easy, okay?"

Ike forced a smile.

Abby walked out to him. "You thought it was…"

He rolled his eyes. "Yeah."

"So the adventure continues, huh?" She laughed kindly and slid her arm through his. "Come on, Bomb Squad Specialist, let's eat."

He glanced back at his neighbor crossing the street as they walked. "I don't know, Abby; it just looked dangerous to me."

"Hey, don't worry about it. We're both keyed up." She shut the door behind them and firmly twisted the dead bolt. "Pizza, you say?"

"Yeah. Do me a favor and grab one out of the freezer. I'll be right back."

She went to the kitchen, slipped out a pizza from a stack of them in the freezer, and when she turned, Ike was back holding a shotgun. With an apologetic look on his face, he leaned the gun into the corner but said nothing and neither did she. They silently ate their dinner.

When they were done, they discussed Elizabeth Castro's video testimony, their interview with Miguel Acosta, and what to expect tomorrow.

After that, thinking it might help them unwind, they watched TV on the sofa in the living room. An hour slid by without the intended effect, and facing such a huge day tomorrow, they agreed getting to bed early was their wisest option. When Ike's phone rang they both jumped.

He checked the caller ID, laughed, and put the phone to his ear. "Hi, Mom."

"Honey, I just saw on the news about your witness being murdered on the courthouse steps. Are you and Abby okay?"

"We're fine, Mom."

"But they made the trial sound so dangerous. Mexican cartels might've been involved."

"That's what the media does, Mother." He gave Abby a quick eye roll. "The more they can scare you, the more viewers they get and the more money they make. So thank you for the call, but we're fine."

"But, honey, we're dealing with the cartels down here, too, and they're absolutely brutal."

He glanced up at the ceiling. "Mom, Chicago is 1700 miles from Phoenix. We're fine."

She hesitated. "All right…"

"We're fine," he said resolutely.

Finally. "Okay, Icarus. Please just be safe."

He gave Abby a little smile. "Now Abby and I are going to get to sleep so we can get up early and be ready for what should be the last day of the trial tomorrow."

"Oh, I can't wait for this one to be over."

"Mom."

"All right, all right, just be safe, son."

"We will. We are."

"Okay, then. Love to Abby. Good night."

"Love you too. Good night."

Abby leaned into him. "I think more like your mother than you."

"Oh, don't say that." He laughed. "That's a scary thought."

THE PERFECT PROSECUTOR

They went to the bedroom, Ike toting the shotgun, Leaner right behind. He carefully laid the gun on the floor and set the alarm on his phone. As Abby went off to the bathroom, he walked to the closet, opened a gun locker, and hefted his massive Raging Judge Magnum revolver. Leaner settled into his usual spot, the carpeting worn there, at the foot of the bed. Ike changed, lowered the thermostat, pulled the bedspread down, and just as Abby returned placed the Raging Judge under his pillow.

"Oh, Ike, come on, that's overkill."

"Maybe, but it's just for tonight and it certainly can't hurt." He grabbed the shotgun and leaned it against the nightstand. "And this won't either."

She sat on the edge of the bed, palms on her thighs. "Honestly, all these guns are making me nervous."

"Don't think about them. Just get some sleep. We both need sleep."

She pointed to the shotgun. "What if that falls, leaning like that?"

"It's fine."

"What if Leaner bumps it?"

"Leaner hardly ever gets up from his spot, and even if he bumps it, the safety is on. Now come on. Sleep. We need sleep."

"Still…" She fell back into the bed and pulled the covers over her head. "…if it tips in the middle of the night, it'll scare the life out of us."

He shut off the nightstand lamp. "Abby, now come on. It's bad enough I'm seeing bombs in plumbing supply packages." He joined her, pulled the covers off her face, and took her in his arms.

"I'm not the one putting a gun under my pillow."

He held her tighter. "Maybe you should."

"Not funny, Ike. Not funny at all."

He stroked her cheek. "Come on, we'll be okay."

Her body tensed. "You know, you keep saying that, and the more you do, the more I think we're not going to be. Really, we should've at least gone to a hotel."

"We'll be okay." He kissed her but she didn't return it.

"Okay, yeah, we'll be okay." She turned away.

He could hardly blame her for being concerned. He was hardly calm about the situation himself, but he had years of dealing with this sort of thing under his belt. "Abby, I love you." He caressed her shoulders and eventually she turned back to him.

"I didn't want to make it sound like I was blaming you. I'm not." She frowned but kissed him. "I'm just not used to this. Not at all."

"I get it, Abby. I do."

Her body finally relaxed. She closed her eyes and after a while began to breathe rhythmically and soon she was out. The warmth of her body and the love he felt for her had always produced a narcotic effect that put him to sleep more effectively than any sleeping pill, but tonight as he drifted off, he experienced that chaotic intersection between wakefulness and sleep, thoughts and images caroming wildly about his fatigued brain. Perhaps he slept for a while. Perhaps not. Either way, he was aware of the passage of time and accepted that the hellish state would likely continue until morning. But then he felt Abby shifting, and when she jerked upright, he woke. "What is it, Abby?"

"Leaner's growling."

He sat up in the pitch-black bedroom. He heard nothing. He cupped his ears. "Okay, now I hear it." The dog was somewhere out in the house, emitting a low-pitched rumble. Ike slowly swung his legs over the side of the bed, his feet searching for slippers. Once found, he reached for the shotgun. Gripping the weapon firmly, he snatched his phone from the nightstand and flicked on its flashlight.

"But they'll see you!"

Right. He must still be half asleep. He killed the flashlight and, his heart racing, felt along the wall with his free hand until he made it out of the bedroom. Down the hallway he followed the sound. It was a wary, determined growl. A waiting-for-something-to-happen growl. In the front room a faint light filtered through the sliding glass doors. Leaner was posted there like a sentry, hackles bristling down his back.

The dog was fixated on something in the backyard. Ike pushed the safety off the shotgun. "What is it, boy?" he asked softly, searching the yard, but there was nothing to see in the darkness. Slowly, and as quietly as he could, he racked the slide of the shotgun, chambering a round. Leaner didn't acknowledge his presence—his growling rolling on, the hackles raising even higher. After several minutes, Ike still couldn't see a thing and realized it was time to make a decisive move. But before he did, it occurred to him that these might be his last few moments on earth. And all he could think of was that he'd never see Abby's face again. He gritted his teeth, nestled the butt of the shotgun in his shoulder, and flipped on the backyard spotlight.

In the corner of the yard, a family of raccoons hightailed it up the oak tree. Leaner leapt, front paws slamming against the door, and barked furiously. Ike knew enough not to touch him in such an excited state. Eventually the dog dropped onto all fours and began whimpering as it paced back and forth alongside the door. Ike unchambered the round and put the safety back on the shotgun.

There would be very little sleeping this night.

Chapter Thirty-three

Ike woke to the sound of his phone alarm, finding himself in the chair next to his bed, the shotgun resting on his lap. Leaner was back in his customary spot at the foot of the bed, and Abby was buried somewhere under the covers. He fumbled for his phone on the nightstand and after two or three attempts managed to squelch the alarm. From beneath the covers came a muffled voice.

"Are we still alive?"

Ike laughed. "Uh, that would be a yes."

"Good. Do me a favor then and let me know when you get back from the trial. I'll be right here waiting for you."

He yawned so deeply his jaw hurt. "Believe me, Abby, I'd like to crawl in there with you."

She tugged the covers off enough to peek at him. "Then do it." She ducked back under.

He got it. It was hard to get up and go to work when you felt like you might be killed, but if you wanted to be a criminal trial attorney, the risk had to be faced and the fear overcome. "Hey, just sayin', weren't you the one who wanted to practice criminal law?"

"That wasn't me." A little headshake. "You're confusing me with someone else."

"All right, but now I need the real Abby Blum, my co-counsel, to get up and get fired up. Come on, let's give this thing our best shot."

With a smirk, she crawled out of bed.

They shuffled around silently getting ready. Ike took care of Leaner's needs. Now all they had to do was get to the trial in one piece. They arrived at the courthouse grounds without incident. They arrived to a media extravaganza—reporters and cameramen everywhere, surrounded by a nearly military level police presence. It seemed that after Elizabeth Castro's death was splashed all over the national media, the powers that be in Illinois were insisting on zero tolerance for any more untoward publicity. Ike and Abby battled their way up the long, sloping walkway hounded by reporters shouting rapid-fire questions. Inside the jumble that was the courtroom, they settled at the prosecution table. No Harkin, which wasn't unusual as he usually showed up at the last minute. Black and his team were arrayed comfortably at the defense table. The bailiff called the court into session, and Morton glided in and took her place on the bench.

Ike nudged Abby. "Still no Harkin."

She nodded. "That can only be a good thing."

Just then, State's Attorney Rush, Harkin at her side, pushed through the swinging gate and beelined to the bench. Ike and Abby looked at each other and decided to join them.

Ike held out his arms. "Your Honor, what's going on?"

Morton put out her palm to quiet him. She focused on Ursula. "This *is* most unusual, State's Attorney. You know full well this should've been taken care of before and by a formal motion."

"Your Honor, it is only the urgency of the situation that necessitates me doing this here and now."

Morton pinched the bridge of her nose. "All right. Let me get Mr. Black up here." She motioned to him. "And then you may proceed but please be brief. As you can see, we have a trial waiting to happen."

The defense attorney joined them.

THE PERFECT PROSECUTOR

Ursula gripped the bench. "Your Honor, Mr. Thompson and Ms. Blum have made a mess prosecuting this case from the start. They did not properly oversee the investigation into Lakota Holt's death, nor did they sufficiently protect the State's witness Elizabeth Castro and are more than likely indirectly responsible for her death. They have brazenly ignored directives from my office. They are essentially rogue and I am removing them as prosecutors from this trial."

Morton raised an eyebrow. "Essentially rogue?" She hunched her shoulders slightly. "Well, as you know, State's Attorney, we are quite far along in the trial."

"I understand, Your Honor."

"I assume you have another team in place to take over?"

A quick nod to Harkin. "Yes, Your Honor."

The judge settled back in her chair and surveyed the courtroom. She looked at her clerk and then back at Ursula. She leaned forward. "State's Attorney," she began, her voice measured, "while I do understand that you have absolute authority to make all prosecutorial decisions, I am deeply concerned about the timing of this proposed change. We are at a critical juncture in this trial and replacing the prosecution team now could severely disrupt the proceedings and potentially prejudice the case. As I'm sure you will agree, the integrity of the trial is paramount and that prosecutors Thompson and Blum's familiarity with the case cannot be dismissed lightly."

Ursula clenched her jaw. "Your Honor, I—"

Morton raised a hand listlessly while gazing directly at the State's Attorney. "I'm not fighting you. It's your decision."

"Your Honor." Ursula exhaled sharply.

"It's your decision," Morton repeated with a slight tilt of her head.

Ursula hesitated. Her lower lip trembling, she sighed and then nodded curtly. "Very well, Your Honor. I will allow them to continue, but I will be closely monitoring their performance." She turned on her heel and was gone, Harkin trailing her.

Ike, Abby, and Black returned to their respective tables.

The judge sat up. "All right, then. Now we have a trial to finish." She called the lawyers back to the bench.

Black arrived first and stood directly in front of the judge. Ike and Abby had to sidle in next to his massive frame.

Morton offered a knowing look all around. "Just so we're clear, Counsels, the video of Elizabeth Castro's testimony is not admitted into evidence but its transcript is. Now are there any questions before we get started?"

No one spoke up.

"Thank you, Counsels, please return to your tables." She turned to her right. "Bailiff, please bring in the jury."

The jury was seated.

Morton addressed the jurors. "Members of the jury, the prosecution and defense have agreed that instead of viewing a video of Elizabeth Castro's testimony, you will hear a transcript of that testimony read aloud. You should consider this transcript as you would any other evidence in this case." She tapped her gavel lightly on the bench. "Now the prosecution may call its next witness."

Ike leaned a shoulder into Abby. "Here we go." He stood. "Your Honor, the State calls Miguel Acosta."

A female sheriff's deputy brought him out, the man looking dignified in a tan suit, no tie, with a white silk handkerchief in the breast pocket. He was sworn in and took the stand.

Ike, notes and copies of Elizabeth Castro's transcript testimony in hand, breathed in deeply through his nose on the way to the attorney lectern. "Good morning."

"Good morning."

"Would you please state your name and occupation for the record?"

"Miguel Acosta, and I am the CEO of Acosta Worldwide Properties."

"Thank you, Mr. Acosta. Now, sir, could you clarify your relationship with the defendant, Thomas Acosta, who stands accused of murder?" Ike looked to the defense table.

"Thomas is my brother."

"Thomas is your brother. Thank you." Ike settled his documents on the lectern. "Mr. Acosta, I must say that I would think that this must be a challenging situation for you, and I appreciate your willingness to cooperate with these proceedings."

"Of course."

Ike nodded to him. "Very good. Now, Mr. Acosta, are you familiar with this case?"

"I am."

His hands feeling a little shaky, Ike rested them on the lectern. "Please introduce yourself to the jury and provide some background information about yourself."

The man nodded briefly. "Well, I'm forty-five years old, married with three children—two boys and a girl. As mentioned, I'm the chief executive officer of an international real estate corporation headquartered in Mexico City."

Ike looked over his notes. "Sir, you've received awards for your humanitarian efforts. Among them the International

Property Awards, the Global Real Estate Awards, and the Forbes Real Estate Business Awards. Would you expand on the humanitarian focus of your business that has led to these distinctions?"

Miguel lowered his gaze. "Well, while it's true that I've been blessed and am grateful for the awards, I believe the best award is helping people. But I know I'm not here to talk about that."

Miguel was even more of a dream witness than Ike had anticipated. Sincere and humble, and he brought the focus of his testimony back to the trial. "Mr. Acosta, what is the nature of your relationship with your brother? Are you two close?"

"Are we close? Never." He folded his hands on his lap. "But before I get started, let me state for the record that I love my brother and bear him no ill will. Okay, Thomas and I grew up in a little town in the state of Michoacán in southwestern Mexico. Our parents were poor and broke their backs working sixteen-hour days picking avocados in the scorching heat to give us a leg up in life. But, even as a young child, Thomas wasn't satisfied with what our parents provided. So, when the success of the avocado industry attracted the attention of the drug cartels, it was a natural for Thomas to get involved with them."

Up came Black. "Objection, Your Honor. This testimony is highly prejudicial and irrelevant to the current case. The witness' personal opinions and descriptions of events unrelated to the case at hand are not admissible."

Ike was ready. "Your Honor, the witness' testimony provides firsthand knowledge and insight into the behavior of the accused, making it essential for a fair and accurate determination of the facts in this case."

THE PERFECT PROSECUTOR

Morton wasted no time. "I agree. Objection overruled."

Ike needed that. "Mr. Acosta, can you tell the court about your brother's involvement with the drug cartels?"

The man sighed deeply. "It changed him. The money, the power, the violence—it all thrilled him. It was like pouring gasoline on a fire. He embraced their ruthlessness. He started selling drugs, and when I threatened to turn him in, he beat me up."

"Sir, what was your parents' relationship with Thomas like?"

Miguel looked down at his hands. "At first they tried to discipline him, but that went nowhere. Then they pleaded with him, but the deeper he became enmeshed with the cartels, the less he listened. So, very early on, it became clear that his allegiance was to the cartels and not to family. Soon, my parents were terrified of him."

"And what's your relationship with your brother like today?" The words were delivered with a practiced softness. He wanted to keep a nice even tone to things before he dropped his bombshell question.

Miguel chuckled. "It's nonexistent. When we were young I tried to guide him—he's my little brother after all—in the right direction, but after he got into the cartels, there was no talking to him. He was a big man there. He had money. He had power. He had women. He didn't need me. He didn't need anyone."

Ike glanced at Abby—*here goes*—then looked back to the witness. "To your knowledge, Mr. Acosta, has Thomas ever murdered or ordered someone murdered?"

Black sprang up. "Objection! Prejudicial and the question calls for evidence that has not been presented."

Morton let out a barely audible sigh. "The objection is sustained. Mr. Thompson, please ensure that your questions remain relevant to the case and within the parameters of admissible evidence." She turned to the jury. "The jury is instructed to disregard the prosecutor's last question and any implications it may have raised."

Morton's irked tone in delivering the rebuke had been damaging, but Ike had plenty more arrows left in his quiver. And just what were the parameters of admissible evidence in this trial anyway? He'd probably find out as he went along. "Mr. Acosta, tell us about your relationship with Elizabeth Castro."

"Elizabeth and I shared a mutual interest in new drugs under development."

Ike tamped down his notes on the lectern and groaned inwardly. He knew that answer was coming, but it still sounded so implausible. "Okay, and, sir…" His eyes flicked up from his notes. "…did she in fact contact you with information regarding a new drug?"

Miguel picked a bit of lint off his pant leg. "She did."

"And when was that?"

"Approximately a year and a half ago."

Ike fought not to look at the defense table—he could feel an objection was in the works. "So that would be eighteen months ago," he hurried out. "And what information did she communicate to you?"

"She told me that Curedex-N existed."

Again, hurry. "Curedex-N, Pharamundo's drug to cure ALLD?"

Black was up. "Objection, Your Honor. Counsel's question assumes a fact not in evidence. There has been no verifiable evidence presented regarding the existence of such a curative drug."

Ike struggled for a breath. Black was trying to cut the heart out of Elizabeth Castro's testimony in one fell swoop. If he couldn't discuss the drug, he had nothing to say. He looked at Abby, who shrugged. Finally, it came to him. "Your Honor, the defense has stipulated to the admissibility of Elizabeth Castro's testimony, which expressly identifies that the drug exists."

Morton lightly rested her head on two fingers. "I… agree. Objection is overruled. Mr. Acosta, please answer the question."

The witness didn't hesitate. "Yes, Curedex-N is Pharamundo's curative drug for ALLD."

It took a while for Ike to catch his breath. Black's objection about wanting to disallow discussion of Curedex-N brought home in a hurry why the defense attorney was called the Monster. *Okay, they're waiting, Thompson.* "Mr. Acosta, when Ms. Castro contacted you eighteen months ago regarding the existence of Curedex-N, did she mention any concerns she had about revealing the drug's existence?"

"She mentioned that she had a great fear of retaliation by Thomas."

Ike glared at the defendant. "Thomas Acosta, CEO of Pharamundo International?"

"Yes."

Ike made a show of paging through the documents on the lectern. "Sir, has Elizabeth Castro contacted you more recently?"

"She has."

Ike headed for the witness stand. "And when was that?"

"Two days ago."

He stopped long enough to ask, "And *how* did she contact you, sir?"

"She sent me a flash drive as certified mail."

"She sent you a flash drive as certified mail." Ike continued on to the witness stand. "And what was on that flash drive?"

The witness looked at the defense table before returning his gaze to Ike. "Her video testimony for this trial."

Ike placed his hands on the witness stand and leaned in. "Did she send you anything else, sir?"

Miguel looked at Ike for a long time before answering. "Yes, there was a note that said if something were to happen to her before she could testify, I was to deliver the flash drive to the prosecutors in this case."

Ike was feeling his sea legs back under him. "The note said you were to deliver the flash drive to the prosecutors in the event that *something should happen to her before she could testify.*" He abruptly returned to the attorney lectern, grabbed the copy of the transcript of Elizabeth's testimony and walked back to the witness. "Would you please read this sworn testimony of Elizabeth Castro for the jury?"

Miguel's hands trembled as he took the transcript. He read slowly and carefully the dead witness' testimony which clearly contradicted Thomas Acosta's testimony that Curedex-N did not exist. It also revealed that greed was the reason he withheld the drug, and it spoke of his threats, which forced her into hiding. Ike took in the jury's rapt expressions.

He was in no hurry. He wanted the raw power of Elizabeth Castro's testimony to impact the jury. He wanted it to floor them. Finally, it was time to move on. Now, concerned that there might be more to Miguel's relationship with Elizabeth Castro than he'd let on in their interview, Ike needed to do what he could to draw the sting out of what could be an awkward situation further along in the trial. But draw the sting from what? "Mr. Acosta, did you know Elizabeth Castro *before* she contacted you eighteen months ago?"

"Yes."

"And why was that, sir?"

"I'd reached out to Elizabeth because I had heard that Pharamundo was working on a curative drug for ALLD, and I knew she was the head of New Drug Development."

Miguel maintained eye contact throughout, which was awesome. "And, sir, why is it that *you* were interested in the curative drug for ALLD?"

The witness crossed his arms, nearly hugging himself, and rocked for a while. Finally, his voice cracking, he said, "My interest was because my youngest son was dying from ALLD."

Someone in the gallery cried, "Oh!" and a buzz of hushed conversations spread across the courtroom. Ike glanced at the jury. Their gazes were fixed on Miguel. Now so was his.

Morton admonished the gallery.

Who knew why Miguel had kept this to himself, but Ike had a hunch where his testimony might end up. "So, eighteen months ago, when Elizabeth Castro informed you that Curedex-N existed and that she was terrified of what Thomas Acosta might do to her for revealing its existence, did she do anything else?"

"Yes."

Ike hesitated for as long as he could as the tension built in the courtroom. "And what was that?"

"She sent me a supply of Curedex-N."

A hubbub rose in the gallery.

Ike spoke loudly over the noise. "She sent you a supply of Curedex-N—and did you give it to your son?"

The gallery fell silent.

Miguel's chin sunk to his chest. "I did."

Ike let the anticipation build. Then he finally asked the question everyone in the courtroom was thinking. "And what happened?"

Miguel took a deep breath and blew it out slowly. "My son…" A tear streaked down his cheek. "…was cured."

The gallery exploded, Morton adding to the ruckus by banging the gavel and calling for quiet. Miguel used his pocket handkerchief to wipe his eyes.

Finally, the commotion died down.

Ike stood there for a while, marveling at the moment like everyone else, before slowly, deliberately enunciating, "No—further—questions, Your Honor."

Back at the prosecution table, Abby jotted on a legal pad and slid it toward him. *Well done. See, you were the perfect prosecutor, after all.*

He nodded, but on the inside, a storm of adrenaline, pride, and uncertainty raged.

Abby turned and smiled at Bree Wilson and Lakota's family.

Morton asked if Black would cross-examine.

"Oh, yes, Your Honor." The big man, clutching notes, hastily passed the attorney lectern on his way directly to the witness stand.

Ike glanced at Abby. She gave him a quick, knowing look, slipped the cap off her pen, and readied the legal pad.

Black nodded. "Good morning, Mr. Acosta."

"Morning."

THE PERFECT PROSECUTOR

The huge attorney made the beefy CEO look small. "Mr. Acosta, earlier, you testified that you love your brother, didn't you?"

"I did."

"That you bear him no ill will?"

"That's right."

Black held Miguel's eye. "So, sir, your brother joined a gang, sold drugs, terrified your parents, beat you, and yet you bear him no ill will, isn't that right?"

Abby was up. "Objection. Asked and answered."

"Sustained," Morton said, her expression tinged with a hint of a scowl. "The witness has already answered that question. Move on to your next question."

Black nodded perfunctorily. "Sir, have you ever felt the desire to get even with your brother for such harsh treatment?"

Miguel rubbed his chin. "I'm sure I may have thought about it at one time or another."

"Did you think about it when you heard Elizabeth Castro had been murdered? Is that one of those times, sir?"

Miguel narrowed an eye at the defense attorney. "When I heard that Elizabeth had been murdered, all I felt was deep sadness."

"Mr. Acosta, I understand how saddened you must have been to hear about the tragic loss of your friend. However, at this point, I would like to focus on something specific you mentioned a few moments ago." He took a step back and crossed his arms. "Sir, you testified that Elizabeth Castro informed you of the existence of the alleged curative drug for ALLD eighteen months ago, isn't that right?"

"Yes."

Black drew his head back. "And yet you sat on that knowledge all this time?"

Miguel sighed. "Well, I—"

"I wasn't asking for an explanation."

Miguel's eyes fell. "Yes, I knew about the drug and didn't say anything."

"The alleged drug." Black hunched his shoulders. "For eighteen months?"

"That's right."

The defense attorney glanced at his notes. "Sir, regarding Elizabeth Castro's video testimony, do you know if it was made under coercion?"

Abby whispered to Ike, "He's going to use the exclusion of the video against us."

"I do not," Miguel said flatly.

"So, for all you know, she may have had a gun pointed at her head while her testimony was being recorded, isn't that right?" Black again caught Miguel's eye.

The witness dabbed his forehead with the handkerchief. He looked around for a while before answering. "I don't know if it was or not. I suppose it was possible."

"Right. You suppose it was possible." The Monster scowled. "Sir, reading the transcript of Elizabeth Castro's testimony doesn't convey any visual or auditory cues that might have been present in the video, such as facial expressions, tone of voice, or body language, isn't that correct?"

"Yes, but I saw—"

"And, in fact, sir, for all we *know* from the transcript, her entire statement might be fabricated, isn't *that* correct?"

Ike had to defend him. He jumped up. "Objection, Your Honor. Defense counsel's question is purely speculative and outside the scope of proper questioning. The prosecution cannot make unsubstantiated claims about the witness' knowledge or intentions."

Morton focused on Black.

The defense attorney stretched his neck from side to side. "Your Honor," he sighed. "The question is not purely speculative. I am simply pointing out that the witness cannot confirm or deny certain aspects of the video testimony based on the information provided in the transcript. It is important to establish the limitations of the evidence being presented to the jury."

Morton leaned back in her chair. "That is accurate, Mr. Black. The objection is overruled." She turned to Miguel. "Please answer the question."

"Okay, anything is possible, I suppose," Miguel said, glaring at the defense attorney. "So yes, her statement could've been fabricated."

Black returned the glare. He paused, his gaze sweeping across the jury before settling on his notes. The courtroom fell silent as he began, "Mr. Acosta, before Elizabeth Castro supposedly gave you the alleged curative drug, to the best of your knowledge, she believed that the drug existed, didn't she?"

"Yes, of course she did."

"Yes, of course she did," Black echoed, stepping closer and leaning in on the witness. "So, sir, do you also happen to know if Ms. Castro believed in Santa Claus?"

A few titters in the gallery. Ike looked sidelong at the jury. Most of them were smiling, unsure whether they should laugh or not.

Miguel again glared at the big attorney now hovering over him. "No, actually, I don't."

"Did she believe in leprechauns?"

A ripple of giggles spread across the courtroom.

Now Miguel scowled. "I don't think she did."

"The tooth fairy?"

People were flat-out laughing now.

Morton, fighting back a smile, raised a palm. "All right, all right, that'll be enough of that." She turned to Miguel. "I assume, sir, your answer to that last question is no as well?" Which caused the courtroom to erupt.

Miguel waited for the laughter to cease. "Yes, that's right."

"Thank you, Your Honor." Black backed off a few feet. "Mr. Acosta, switching gears, would you say that your net worth is in excess of five billion dollars?"

Ike stood. He was kicking himself for not objecting earlier, but now he had to do something, anything, to stop the bloodshed. "Objection. Relevance."

Morton turned her attention to Black.

The defense attorney bit his lip. "Your Honor, the witness' net worth is relevant because it goes to his motive for testifying. Additionally, the witness' excessive wealth could imply that he may have had a closer relationship with the murdered witness or more of a stake in the outcome of the trial than was previously known."

Morton leaned marginally toward the witness. "The objection is overruled. Please answer, Mr. Acosta."

Miguel tilted his head. "I would say in excess of five billion, yes."

"So you've got a lot of money?"

"Relatively speaking, yes."

"Relatively speaking." Black smiled. "Sir, have you ever given any of that *relatively speaking lot of money* to Elizabeth Castro?"

Miguel squared his shoulders. "I have."

"Hmm." Black widened his eyes at the jury before returning his focus to Miguel. "For as long as you've known her, sir, how much money would you say you've given her?"

"That's hard to say."

Black shrugged. "How about a ballpark estimate? More than ten thousand dollars?"

"Yes."

"More than one hundred thousand?"

"Yes."

"A million dollars?"

Miguel stared at his brother as he answered, "I'd say I've given her a little over a million."

Abby whispered to Ike, "Wonder what that stare was all about?"

The defense attorney put a forefinger to his cheek. "And did Ms. Castro pay that money back?"

Miguel blinked a few times. "Well, actually, it wasn't a loan. It was a gift."

"A gift." Black turned to the jury, his eyebrows arching. "Okay, then." He took another step back. "Mr. Acosta, have you met Elizabeth Castro in person?"

Ike bit the inside of his cheek. He felt like Miguel was drifting in open water—with a shark circling.

"I have."

"And when was it you first met her?"

The witness shifted in his chair. "We met five years ago at the World Economic Forum in Davos, Switzerland."

"Uh-huh." Black nodded with a glum grin. "Just bumped into each other there?"

Miguel glanced at Ike, then the judge, before answering. "It was an arranged meeting. We'd been corresponding for quite some time and discovered we both had an interest in the forum's initiatives to provide access-priced, life-saving medicines to low-income countries."

Black stepped back to the witness stand. He was silent for an uncomfortable length of time and in the process all eyes were drawn to him. Finally, his gaze locking on Miguel with unwavering intensity, he said, "Mr. Acosta, were you and Elizabeth Castro lovers?"

Miguel didn't flinch. "Yes."

The defense attorney started back to the defense table but stopped halfway and pivoted to the witness. "Sir, were you aware that Elizabeth Castro had a close relationship with Lakota Holt?"

Abby stood. "Your Honor, prejudicial."

Morton turned her attention to the young lawyer. "I assume you're making an objection, Ms. Blum?"

Abby swallowed. "I am, Your Honor. I object on the grounds of defense Counsel's question being more prejudicial than probative."

Ike tried to subtly stretch out the kink in his neck. Morton knew damn well Abby was making an objection and just picked on her because she was new.

Morton shook her head. "No, the objection is overruled. Please answer the question, Mr. Acosta."

"I had heard Elizabeth knew Lakota."

"That wasn't my question, sir." Black walked boldly back to the witness stand. "My question was, were you aware that Elizabeth Castro had developed *a close relationship* with Lakota Holt?"

Miguel looked at Ike again, then at the judge before answering. "I had heard something to that effect, yes."

THE PERFECT PROSECUTOR

Black stood motionless, his imposing presence seeming to fill the room. He locked eyes with Miguel yet again, letting the uncomfortable silence drag on. Finally, with chilling calm, he spoke. "Mr. Acosta, did you arrange to have Lakota Holt and Elizabeth Castro murdered?"

Ike and Abby jumped up in tandem, Ike crying, "Objection! This is highly prejudicial and inflammatory!"

Morton gave Black a look. "I couldn't agree more. Objection is sustained."

Black welcomed the scolding with a ghost of a smile. "I have no further questions, Your Honor."

Shoulders noticeably slumping, Morton addressed the prosecution table. "Will the State be redirecting?"

Ike raised a forefinger. "Can we have a moment, Your Honor?"

"You may."

He turned to Abby. "What do you think?"

A grit determination rose in her eyes. "God, Ike, we have to. We have to do what we can to rehabilitate him."

"Absolutely."

She grabbed her legal pad. "I got this." She stood. "Yes, Your Honor, thank you."

Morton motioned toward the stand. "The witness is yours."

Abby walked briskly to the attorney lectern and set up the legal pad. "Mr. Acosta, opposing counsel questioned the plausibility of you still loving your brother after he beat you up. My question for you, sir, is, is that not the true meaning of love—to love someone even after they've hurt you?"

Black was up shaking his head. "Your Honor, Counsel is testifying."

Morton didn't hesitate. "Sustained." Then to Abby: "Please stay within the scope of the cross, Counsel."

Ike bristled. The judge's decision to sustain the objection was questionable, and her scolding of Abby again was un-called-for. Morton's bias as a defendant's judge was coming to the fore—and at the worst possible time.

Abby scratched behind her ear and checked her notes. "Mr. Acosta." She made solid eye contact. "Opposing counsel said the reading of Elizabeth Castro's testimony left out much of the meaning that viewing the video would have supplied. Sir, when you spoke to Elizabeth on the phone, did she speak of her fear of Thomas Acosta?"

"She did regularly."

Abby planted her hands on the lectern. "And, sir, what would you say her emotional state was during those conversations?"

Black was up again. "Objection. Calls for speculation."

The judge waited on Abby.

She focused on the judge. "Your Honor, the question does not call for speculation. The witness can answer based on his knowledge and experience."

Morton offered Abby a subtle nod and held her gaze for a brief moment. "Objection is overruled. Mr. Acosta, you may answer."

"Elizabeth was distraught. At times, she wept uncontrollably."

Abby made her way to the witness stand. "Sir, opposing counsel showed off his comedic talent by asking you if Elizabeth Castro believed in Santa Claus, leprechauns, or the tooth fairy, but I noticed you didn't laugh. Why not?"

Miguel set his jaw. "Because he was making fun of a woman who lost her life. A woman I loved. And that to me was no laughing matter."

"I have no further questions, Your Honor."

Ike patted Abby's hand when she returned to the prosecution table. She'd rehabilitated Miguel as much as humanly possible. He whispered, "You did great." But something was in the air. Ike was no mystic, but he could feel it. He had no idea what, but it felt like a sea change, a paradigm shift. His attention was drawn to Black. The defense attorney's face was flushing as he engaged in another heated discussion with his client.

Morton straightened some papers on the bench. "Mr. Black, recross?"

The defense attorney and his client were still going at it. Morton gave him a few moments. She gave him a few more. Finally, she frowned and said, "*Mr. Black*, will you be re-cross-examining the witness?"

No way, Ike thought. He won't dare. This trial is over.

Black stood. He glared at his client one last time before looking up. "Yes, Your Honor."

Ike slunk back in his chair.

Morton did a double take. "Oh, I see." She took a deep breath. She looked around. She checked her watch. "Very well, but at the same time, we've gone longer than anticipated and are quite near the lunch break. Accordingly, I would ask that if at all possible, you keep your recross brief."

Black nodded quickly. "Should not be a problem, Your Honor."

"You may proceed, then."

Thomas Acosta yanked on Black's sleeve, forcing the big man down to him. Black's jaw clenched. The veins in his throat bulged. His nostrils flared. More arguing ensued. Finally, Black shook free. "Pardon me, Your Honor, but may I have a moment to confer with my client?"

Morton sighed out a breath. "You may but please be brief given the time constraint."

Black and Acosta again locked horns. Ike half-thought they'd come to blows. Finally, Black's face thoroughly flushed, he rose to his full height.

"Your Honor, after consulting with my client, we believe it would be in our best interest to have a lengthier recross. We request that it take place after the lunch break to ensure a thorough examination of the witness."

Morton bit her lip and sat silently for a while. Finally, she made a tired wave toward the prosecution table. "Mr. Thompson, any objection?"

This was madness. Abby's redirect had been so brief, what could Black possibly have to ask to ensure *a thorough examination* of the witness? Ike scowled. "Your Honor, the defense has had ample time to formulate a recross. The projected delay is unnecessary."

Black cast one last nasty look at his client. He hesitated. Finally, his eyes settled on Morton. "Your Honor, the information that may be revealed during the recross is extremely consequential and will undoubtedly transform the jury's perception of this case."

Morton drew her head back slightly. Then she checked her watch again. "Okay, I'll allow it. We will recess for lunch and resume with the recross. However, from here on out, I expect both parties to be mindful of the time and proceed with focused intent. I'll expect you all back in an hour and a half. Court is recessed until then."

Chapter Thirty-four

Needing a break from the courtroom's intensity, Ike and Abby left the courthouse. For once it was a little cooler out, and they rolled down the windows in the Lexus and started driving with no set direction.

Ike adjusted his rearview mirror. A shiny gray BMW had been hanging behind him for quite a while. He opened the console and fingered his Glock. Finally, he swerved onto a side street and the beamer rolled on. He told himself to get a grip. They still had to, as Abby pointed out, finish the trial strong. "I can't imagine why Black is going to recross Miguel Acosta and what information *may be revealed* during it, as he so ominously said." He glanced at her.

She tilted her head. "I think I know why."

"Okay."

"Because I challenged him about his comedic talent."

Huh, she was probably right. A lawyer recently out of law school—and you can bet Black knew that—tossing the esteemed Monster's questioning back in his face would more than likely not be taken lightly. "Anyway, we'll soon see what he has up his sleeve and how his recross will *undoubtedly transform the jury's perception of this case*." He rested his hand on her shoulder as they drove in silence. The fresh air seemed to revive them until he turned into a cul-de-sac, and the smell of skunk filled the car. They shut the windows as fast as they could and drove back to the courthouse.

* * *

As soon as they pulled into the courthouse parking lot, it was clear something was amiss. Across the street, people rushed up and down the long walkway to the courthouse, a chaotic energy radiating. Ike parked, and they fought their way through the reporters to the prosecution table and waited along with everyone else for the judge's arrival. Whispers filled the gallery. A few reporters packed up their laptops and scrambled into the hall, while others huddled together, phones and digital recorders at the ready. What in the world was going on?

Finally, the bailiff called, "All rise!" Judge Morton entered and took her place on the bench. Once everyone was seated, she requested that the jury be brought in. The jurors filed in, exchanging concerned glances as they took their seats.

Morton struck the gavel, which she'd never done to start a session, and the sound cast a stunned stillness over the courtroom. "Ladies and gentlemen, I regret to inform you that the defendant, Thomas Acosta, has removed his electronic monitoring device and his whereabouts are currently unknown." She paused, allowing the buzz in the courtroom to settle, then gazed thoughtfully ahead, taking a measured breath. "I have issued a warrant for his arrest, and law enforcement is actively attempting to apprehend him.

"Now, I must instruct the jury to disregard any rumors you may hear about Mr. Acosta's flight and to focus solely on the evidence that has been presented thus far here in court. And while Mr. Acosta's absence may raise questions and create a sense of unease, it is important to remember that his flight does not automatically imply guilt or innocence in regard to the charges he is facing in this trial. Once again, it is the evidence presented here in court and your careful consideration of it that will ultimately determine the outcome of this trial. I would also remind you to avoid any contact with the media about the case and to maintain your oath of secrecy until the trial has officially concluded. We will keep you informed and update you as the situation develops. Thank you for your cooperation. Court is adjourned until further notice."

Amidst frantic conversation and even a few shouts, Black and his team huffed out along with the gallery, pouring into the hallway. Ultimately, only Bree Wilson and Lakota's family remained, waiting for Ike and Abby at the gate.

The dark circles under Bree's eyes had become embedded, like a sad clown's makeup. Her gaze settled on the prosecutors, a mixture of defeat and desperation in her eyes. "So what does this mean?"

Lakota's family waited for an answer to the question as well.

Ike stepped up to the gate, which felt like a protective wall separating the legal and non-legal worlds. "It means we're going to have to do a few things differently, and unfortunately, the trial will be delayed, as the judge most likely is not going to continue without Thomas Acosta present. For now, though, there is still the hope that he will be arrested and returned to trial."

Lakota's mother, worry-worn, deep lines etched into her cheeks, began to cry. "So is he going to get away with it?"

Ike knew that was a real possibility. Although it was his practice not to lie to clients if he could at all help it, looking into the woman's contorted, tear-streaked face, he couldn't seem to get the truth out.

"No." Abby came to his aid. "I'm sure they're doing everything they can to get him back. Believe me, justice will be served."

The woman wiped her eyes with the back of her hand. "But how can it be if he's not even here?"

Now Abby went mute.

Ike clenched his fists. "They'll get him back. Right now, the Sheriff's Office, and I'm sure the Chicago and Illinois State Police too are searching for him. And if he's known to have fled across state lines—"

"Oh God." Bree closed her eyes.

"—the U.S. Marshals will get involved."

Abby slipped through the gate and hugged both women.

Chapter Thirty-five

Ike and Abby took Bree and Lakota's family out to eat to empathize and address their many questions. Why did Acosta flee? How did he manage to? Did Cyrus Black know about it beforehand? What can they do to help find him? Will his fleeing stop Curedex-N from being released? How will they stay informed? In the middle of the meal, Ike got a call from Josh Chin. Ike told him what he and Abby were doing, and Josh conveyed that while meeting with Bree and Lakota's family was appropriate, taking them out to eat might not be the best idea because it could be perceived as showing favoritism or potentially influencing witnesses and thereby possibly jeopardizing the case. Ike couldn't help but think of Ursula's rebuke that as defense attorneys they didn't know how to go about being prosecutors. But it was too late now for self-recrimination. Josh ended by saying that although they were of course going to be notified if anything happened, if he heard anything outside the official channels, he would pass the information along.

Driving home from the restaurant, Abby fell asleep with her head against the window. Ike felt a pinch in his gut, reminding him that his ulcer was still there. Darkness had just about fully reclaimed the sky as they pulled into the driveway.

They were happy to see Leaner. As usual, the affectionate dog couldn't help but make them feel at least a little better. Ike let him out and checked his bowls. After a quick dinner, they grabbed a couple of beers from the fridge and collapsed on the sofa, Leaner at their feet. Before they knew it, they were nodding off.

Ike kissed Abby's cheek. "Come on, time for bed."

His phone rang. He jerked forward and checked the caller ID. "Yeah, Josh."

"Ike, listen," the prosecutor said with a sigh. "Some information just came in. It wasn't conclusive enough for the Sheriff's Office to contact you, so please don't call them with questions."

Ike tilted the phone away from his ear so Abby could hear, and she leaned forward to listen in.

"Okay, Josh. What have you heard?"

The line fell quiet, broken only by occasional scratches of static. "Well…" More staticky silence. "… the latest GPS tracking before Thomas Acosta's electronic monitoring device was cut off had him in the vicinity of the Schaumburg Illinois Regional Airport."

Ike held his breath.

"Ike, a private jet registered to the Acosta family flew off twenty minutes after that."

"An Acosta family jet, not Pharamundo?" Ike thought of Miguel.

"Yes, Acosta family. And this brings the U.S. Marshals into it. They're coordinating with the FAA and all the relevant agencies to track private flights arriving at regional airports in the U.S., but…the jet had more than enough fuel capacity to make it to Mexico, and they won't be able to stop it."

Abby rolled her eyes.

Ike gritted his teeth. "So that's it? He's gone and there's nothing we can do about it?"

"All is not lost, Ike. With him skipping out, Ursula has egg on her face, and she's on fire to get him back. And you know what Ursula on fire can be like. Now, I'm sorry, but I have to go."

"Yeah, okay, sure. Thanks, Josh." Ike hung up. He shook his head and blew out a breath. "What's that famous line, 'the best laid plans of mice and men…' "

Abby frowned. " '…often go awry.' Yeah, it's true enough, but you know, we can't give up hope. Not now. No, not now. Not after everything we've been through. Not after everything Bree and Lakota's family have been through. But right now, I am running on empty, Ike, and just really need to sleep."

He caressed her shoulder. "That's right. That's right."

They headed to the bedroom, Leaner not far behind.

Abby pulled out her phone to set an alarm. "How's the battery on yours?"

He checked. "Uh, it's kinda low." He opened a drawer in the nightstand, took out a charger, and plugged it into the wall jack.

They changed into their pajamas. Abby climbed into bed and buried herself under the covers. Ike got Leaner's leash and secured him to the bedpost so that he could sleep in his customary spot at the foot of the bed but not wander the house.

"Nothing personal, buddy." He stroked the dog's snout. "Just don't want you patrolling for raccoons in the middle of the night." He went to the closet and returned with a shotgun, leaning it up against the nightstand.

Abby peeked from under the covers. "Again with the shotgun?" She lifted his pillow and nodded at the massive

Raging Judge revolver. "And I thought this was only for the one night?"

"Abby, we can't be too safe." He climbed into bed, leaned over, and shut off the nightstand lamp.

"Whatever." She sighed. "I'm hardly going to argue with you at this point."

He went to hug her, but she turned away and yanked the bedspread back over her head.

"Good night, Abby."

"Yeah, good night."

And she was out. Ike, eventually soothed by the sound of her rhythmic breathing, soon followed. And he slept. At least for a while, but soon he was again caught up in that tormented world between waking and sleeping. Regret for his missteps in the trial. Sorrow for Bree, Oliver. Lakota's mother's tear-stained face. Hatred for the powerful evil that was Thomas Acosta and Pharamundo. Soon, the half-awake, half-asleep misery evolved into a new torment as he dreamed he was walking down an ancient street lined by architectural ruins like he was in ancient Rome or Athens. But there was no pleasure in observing the classical structures, only a vague unease. He walked faster, hoping to leave his disquiet behind, but to no avail. His heart raced. Walk faster, he told himself. Faster. Then the ground under his feet began to shake, just a slight trembling at first, but the shaking intensified and intensified and…

Abby pushed his shoulder. "Wake up. Leaner is growling and tugging at his leash."

Ike sat up. The dog was indeed straining at the end of the leash, jostling the bed. Ike tried to make sense of the situation, but his mind was still half in the dream. "Leaner, stop. Don't worry about the raccoons."

THE PERFECT PROSECUTOR

"No." Abby grabbed his arm. "It can't be about the raccoons—he's not out there to see them."

Ike's mind flashed to the shotgun. He grabbed for it, but the desperate attempt sent the gun clattering to the floor. A heartbeat of silence ticked by. Then the click of a switch. Light flooded the room. Thomas Acosta, pistol raised, fired, the muzzle flash a little torch, the report deafening, and Ike went down in the corner. Leaner lunged at the man, snarling and snapping. Acosta leveled his pistol at the dog, cocked the gun's hammer, and took a step closer. A tremendous shot rang out, and Acosta was knocked back as if he'd been hit in the chest with a sledgehammer. He dropped the pistol and staggered back, walking stiff-legged until he collapsed.

Abby ripped off the bedspread, still clutching the Raging Judge, a wispy, white puff easing from the end of the barrel. She held the massive pistol on Acosta's fallen body, but soon her hands shook, her strength overcome by the weight of the gun. She laid the pistol on the pillow, grabbed Ike's phone from the nightstand, and dialed 9-1-1.

* * *

Ike sensed light but refused to open his eyes. *No, not yet.* Instead, he homed in on the contrasting smells of medicine and freshly laundered linens while simultaneously attuning his hearing to the sounds of approaching footsteps and the intermittent squeaking of a wheel. And in one fell swoop, all those sensations were snuffed out by the searing pain that pulsed in his shoulder. The pain jolted his mind further awake, radiating like a wildfire to his elbow and then down into his fingertips. He shifted and the pain screamed. *Don't move. Oh God, don't move.* After finally settling, with his good arm he ever so gently reached across his chest. His fingers dabbed along a soft cotton fabric until they reached a stiff, crusty area, like the bark of a tree. The more he felt, the more his mind recalled the violence he'd endured the night before—a light flashing on…a gunshot…his shoulder knocked back…Leaner barking…another shot.

He opened his eyes.

"Well, hello there. Welcome back." Abby sat cross-legged on a cot next to his hospital bed.

Sunlight filtered through the half-closed curtains, casting a soft glow on the pastel-colored walls, where a crucifix hung alongside an unplugged TV. A tray table with a plastic pitcher on it sat on the other side of the bed. Okay, little by little, it was all coming back to him. "You spent the night here?"

Abby smiled. "I wasn't about to leave you here with all these pretty nurses fawning over you."

He chuckled. It hurt like hell.

"In case you haven't figured it out yet, you were shot there…" She pointed. "…in your shoulder. There was no damage to major blood vessels, nerves, or your shoulder cavity, so the doctor said you won't need surgery. You just need medication to manage the pain and then physical therapy."

"What about playing golf?"

She shrugged. "I didn't ask." She stood and took his hand, and he winced.

"Oh God, I'm so sorry. I'll get the nurse to increase your pain medication."

"No, it'll be okay. I'm okay." He held on to her hand.

"Are you sure? She said you could have more if you needed it."

"I'm fine. Really."

She softly caressed his hand. "Okay, then, oh, there's one more thing—Ursula arranged with the Sheriff's Office to station a guard outside your door."

So Ursula turned out to have a heart after all? But were they still at imminent risk? "Thomas Acosta?"

She gave his hand a gentle squeeze. "He's dead, Ike."

"You shot him?"

She nodded. "I'd ducked under the bedspread and could see him from there. After he shot you, he was going to shoot Leaner."

"And Leaner?"

"He's fine. Your neighbor Jerry's checking on him. Also, I called your mother and Val."

He nodded. "That was good."

"And Mallory."

His eyes locked on hers.

"Kidding."

He laughed and winced.

"Oh God, I'm so sorry. No more jokes. And I'm getting the nurse for more pain meds." She went to pull away but he hung on to her.

"I'll be all right, Abby. Just be with me."

She leaned over the hospital bed railing and kissed him tenderly. "Always, Ike. Always."

A nurse knocked and cruised into the room. "Ah, it's good to see you up." The perky redhead went to the other side of the bed and put her touchless thermometer on his forehead. "How's the pain?"

Abby answered for him. "It's really bad. He needs more medication."

The nurse held his wrist. "And how does our patient feel about that?"

"Maybe later. I'm okay for now."

"Ike."

"Abby, I'm fine."

The nurse let go of his wrist. "Your pulse is high, but I'd be surprised if it wasn't. No temperature. I'll check back in a bit." She left and, good to her word, returned in less than a minute. "Uh." She lifted the room card attached to the bed railing. "It says that you can have visitors, but only immediate family and close friends, and only for a short time." She adjusted the IV drip absentmindedly before looking at Ike. "But a woman is out in the hall and she's pressing the deputy to let her in. And well…she's crying."

Abby narrowed her eyes at the nurse. "What's her name?"

The nurse turned on her heel and was out the door. She ducked her head back in. "Bree Wilson."

Ike and Abby looked at each other.

The nurse widened her eyes. "No good, huh? I'll tell the deputy to have her leave."

"No, no," Ike said with a little self-waking headshake. "Nurse, please just give us a few seconds here." He gazed at Abby. "Are you ready for whatever this might be?"

Abby breathed in deeply. "I think so. But are you?"

"Yes." He caught the nurse's eye. "Okay, then. Please let her in."

The nurse left.

Bree rushed into the room, tears tracing her cheeks, and braced herself on the tray table next to the bed. "I'm so happy you're going to be okay, Ike, and I'm so sorry to bother you so soon after what happened, but I just couldn't help myself. And I'm sorry I'm crying so…" She shook her head, tears dappling the tray table. "…but I can't seem to stop."

Abby went to her and touched her shoulder. "Oh, honey, what's wrong?"

Bree reached into her pocket, pulled out a piece of paper, and unfolded it bit by bit. She took a step back and held the newspaper page so that Ike and Abby both could see. Two huge words sat alone on the page: *Curedex-N exists!* Bree clasped the paper to her breast. Her phone rang. "Oh." She struggled to get it out of her pocket and pressed a button to silence it. "Miguel Acosta took out a full-page ad in every print and digital newspaper in the country he could with the same two words." Her phone rang again. She turned off the ringer. "My phone's been ringing off the hook since this happened." She placed the paper on the tray table, wiped her tears, and took a long, deep breath. "CBS, ABC, and all the major news outlets are reporting that the ad has forced Pharamundo to release Curedex-N *immediately*!" She hugged Abby, then moved to do the same to Ike.

Abby sent him a frantic look but he shook his head.

Bree embraced him. "My boy's going to live, Ike! He's going to live!"

Ike smiled at Abby, her eyes misting, while Bree kept hugging him. And in that moment, he felt no pain whatsoever. None. All he felt was a warm feeling welling up deep inside him.

The End

Acknowledgments

It takes an awful lot to put a book like this together, and the people who helped along the way seem endless. I'll do my best to thank everyone, but if I've left someone out, please know I apologize and truly appreciate your help.

Thanks to Tom M.—my source code, catalyst, and creative spark. And a brilliant legal mind.

Robert M. Dreger was a rock throughout the writing, editing—everything. He gave so much time helping, even with his already very busy schedule. He's the world's most creative attorney and provided invaluable legal feedback and superb stylistic advice.

To the ingenious S.W. Pelzer—this book is immensely better thanks to his clear-eyed, extensive, and sometimes rough-around-the-edges (but always brilliantly helpful) advice. S.W. knows the world, and he shared his vision with me. Thank you, S.W.

Angela Norton provided so much insight and feedback. She knows the nuts and bolts of the legal world and grounded the book with her wisdom and expertise.

Jonathan S. offered seminal and key advice that steered the book in the right direction.

Karen G. gave ongoing common-sense advice and indispensable, supportive friendship throughout.

And to the wonderful beta readers: Val A., Rick W., Deb H., Venla H., and Eeyore.

To the superb formatter Mike Dworski—thanks, Mike.

To my editor Lisa Lee—thanks for another great job, Lisa.

THE PERFECT PROSECUTOR

And to my newsletter followers—thank you for your help, support, and patience. You guys are the best!

Also by Gregg Bell

The Perfect Lawyer (Ike Thompson Legal Thriller #1)

The Find

Man of God

Saving Baby

Bloody Sunrise

I Love You I Kill You

Betrayed Heroes

The Test

A Woman Unhinged

Jamie's Gamble

Oops-A-Navy

Dupes-A-Navy

Yippee Ki Yay-A-Navy

About the Author

Born in Chicago, Illinois, Gregg Bell spent his formative years playing 16" softball, hanging out, and trying not to get into too much trouble until college when he absconded for the University of Florida. There, he took creative writing classes and spent his free time bodysurfing at St. Augustine's gorgeous beach. After his sojourn in the sun, he was drawn back north and graduated from the University of Notre Dame. Through jobs ranging from laying asphalt to working in corporate America, the one constant in his life was writing. It still is. A lifelong Midwesterner, he lives in suburban Chicago and, like everyone else who lives there, complains about it being too hot in the summer and too cold in the winter.

Website: https://greggbell.net/

Get Gregg's free legal short story ebook "The Perfect Client" by signing up for his newsletter by going to his website or by pasting the following into an online browser:

https://greggbell.eo.page/kgvvq

The Perfect Prosecutor

© 2025 by Gregg Bell

Published by: Thriveco, Inc.
207 North Walnut Street, Itasca, IL 60143
All Rights Reserved

ISBN: 9798305012712

Without limiting the rights under the copyright reserved above, no part of this publication may be reproduced, stored in or introduced into a retrieval system, or transmitted, in any form, or by any means (electronic, mechanical, photocopying, recording, or otherwise), without the prior written permission of both the copyright owner and the above publisher of this book.

This is a work of fiction. Names, characters, places, and incidents either are the products of the author's imagination or are used fictitiously, and any resemblance to actual persons, living or dead, events, or locales is entirely coincidental.

Printed in Great Britain
by Amazon